BENEATH A RADIANT MOON

An Immigrant Saga of Love, Family, and Survival
Across Continents

PJ JONAS

ISBN KDP: 9798247059271

ISBN Ingrams: 978-1-953100-70-2

Cover design by dreams2media

First Trade Paperback Printing by Scarsdale Publishing September 2024

10 9 8 7 6 5 4 3 2

Editor: Vee Cowart

www.scarsdalepublishing.com

Acknowledgments

I would like to thank my family and friends for their support and encouragement, and whose input was invaluable: Karen Bowers, Laura Bowers, Linda Castorena, Mary Conover, and Marilyn Miller; to my critique partners, Pamela Mortenson (and friend), Jennifer Rand, and Melinda Gers.

Thanks also go to my local writing support group, Red Sands Writers Circle. The members were my alpha readers who provided weekly support and motivation which kept me writing through the early days while learning how to write fiction. Special thanks to: Justin Tate, Mike MacNeill, and Leslie Bratspis.

I also thank Sharona Wilhelm, the owner of Scarsdale Publishing, for believing in *Beneath a Radiant Moon* and taking it on for publication. Sharona's insightful hands-on review along with editors, Vee Cowart, whose expert skills and eagle eyes identified some critical issues, which helped to make my book the best it could be in the final stages; and Blake Madder who worked with me on the earlier stages. And I thank Rebecca Poole of Dreams2Media for the gorgeous book cover.

beneath a radiant moon

PL JONAS

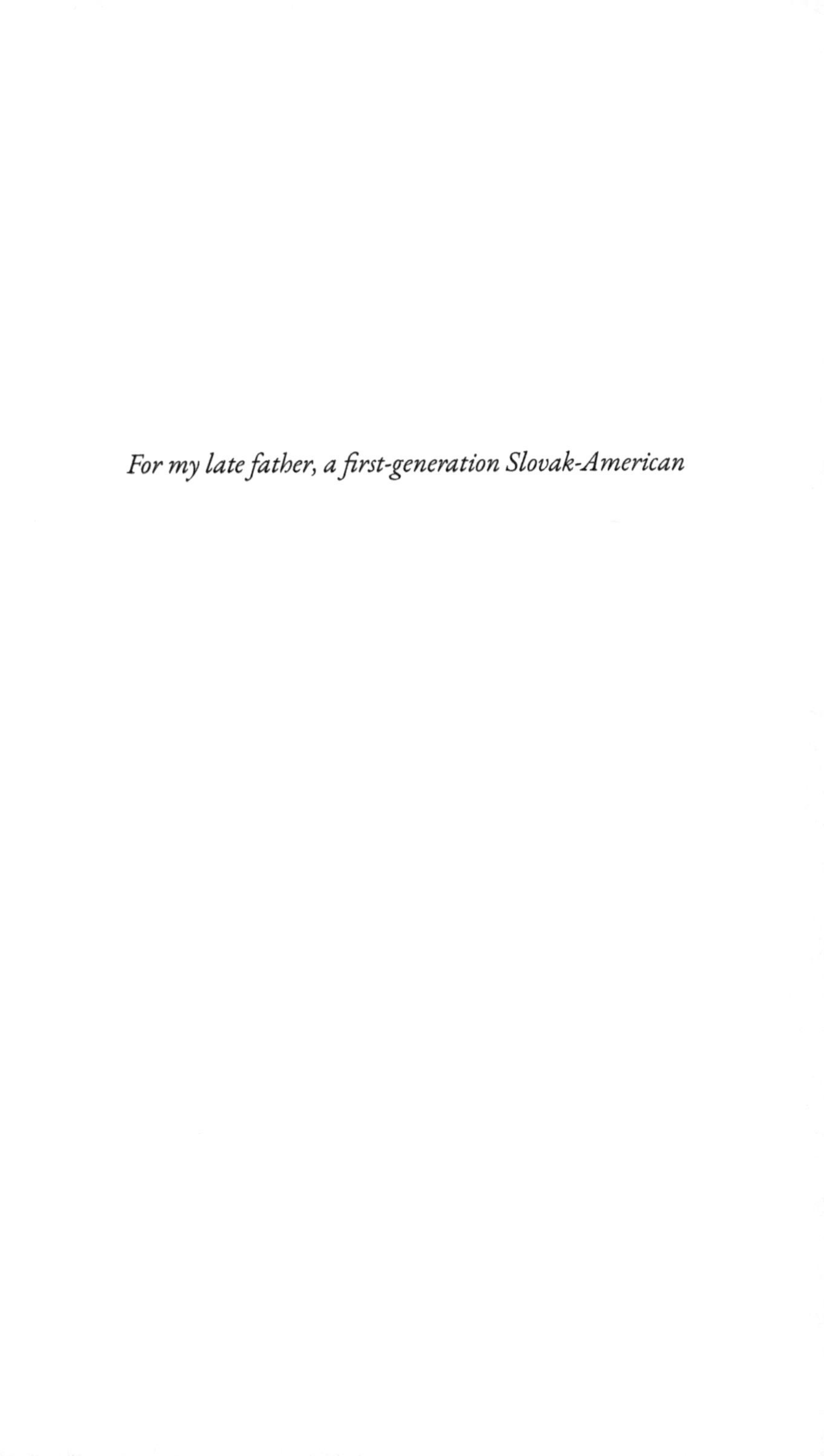

For my late father, a first-generation Slovak-American

Part I

HUNGARY

Chapter One

October 1907
A Village in Southern Hungary

MORNING SUNLIGHT FILTERED THROUGH THE SMALL windows of the mud-brick cottage. The aromas of pork and garlic from the *klobasa* sausage, and the sweetbread *kolac* filled with prunes, nuts, and poppy seeds drifted through the modest space. I ignored the rumble of my stomach as I set my beautiful boy, Little Jan, on the floor to play. I would wait until the feast. Today was my sister's wedding day. She was starting a new life with Tomas, as I had five years ago with Janos.

I hurried past my mother-in-law, Maria, and stepped out the door into the chilled morning air. From the barn, our cow mooed, begging to be milked.

"I'm coming, dear Frieda," I called, though I went first to the chicken coop.

The hens clucked and cooed on their nests. I reached beneath them for eggs, dropped them into my basket, and continued to the barn at the edge of our narrow strip of land.

The familiar scent of damp hay and dung greeted me in the thatched-roof barn. I set the basket on a bale and patted Frieda's flank. She flicked her tail and mooed again.

"*Dobrý deň*, Frieda," I greeted her, and settled onto the stool. "This is a special day, please be generous with your milk."

I pressed against her warm flank and allowed the rhythmic milking to steady my thoughts.

Milk splashed over the rim. I groaned, having filled the pail without my realizing it. I patted Freida's side, and she mooed again.

"You have more for me, then?" I laughed and swapped in an empty pail, then distracted myself by humming while I worked.

Maria appeared in the doorway. "Are you about done with Frieda? I'll take the eggs. You need to get going."

"Almost finished," I said without pausing.

She collected the egg basket and left. Maria and I had struggled at first when I married Janos Lacko, but over time, we found an understanding, and when Little Jan was born, Maria helped me as tradition demanded.

At last, I finished with Frieda, then carried the pails inside, where Maria prepared butter and cheese. The extra milk would serve the wedding feast.

Seven of us shared the cottage, my in-laws and their younger sons in the main room with its big wood table, and Janos, Little Jan, and me in the small second room. Like other homes in our Slovak community, embroidered linens and brightly painted ceramics decorated the space.

"Mira, it's getting late." Maria frowned.

I smiled and nodded.

"I'm done. Let me change, and I'll be on my way."

I set the klobasa and kolac in a basket on the big table. In my room, I shed my apron and changed from my everyday dress into my *kroje*. I relished the smooth white blouse with large, puffed sleeves extending to my elbows and embroidered neckline, the red pleated skirt that fell below my knees, and my good black boots. And last, I tied on the special white apron with vertical rows of heavy embroidery and changed my plain scarf to one that matched my hazel-green eyes.

I smoothed my skirt, fluffed the sleeves, and stepped into the main room. "You will watch the baby and bring him later, yes?" I smiled at Maria.

"Of course, dear. Aneta will be eager for you. This is a big day for her and Tomas."

Little Jan ran to me, reddish curls bouncing, his aqua-blue eyes shining, just like his father's. He was almost four and growing up fast. "Mama, take me with you."

Maria scooped him up. "Not now, Little Jan. We'll meet her later. My, you're getting too heavy for me already."

I kissed his cheek. "See you tonight."

"*Ďakujem*," I thanked her. "See you and everyone else later tonight." With the basket of sausages and kolac over one arm, I waved to them on my way out the door.

Bright sunlight peeked from behind incoming clouds, carrying the scent of rain. Blessed rain fell often on the Great Plain, and I hoped it would pass before the wedding party made their way into town.

I strolled down the dirt road, passing neighbors in their gardens. They waved; I smiled and waved back. Cottages lined both sides of the road, each with narrow plots stretching behind, chicken coops, vegetable gardens, fields, and barns squeezed onto every bit of land.

My thoughts swirled with happiness for Aneta and her betrothed, Tomas Hornak. Our families had arranged their marriage long ago. I prayed she would find the same joy I had with Janos and our son. Life was hard, but love made us content.

Soon, I reached my parents' cottage. Aneta burst through the door and rushed down the steps. She reached me, seized my hands, and kissed both cheeks. When she drew back, her smile shone through tears.

"I'm nervous, Mira. Come in and help me." She tugged me inside and picked up her sewing.

"Dobrý den, *Mamička*." I greeted our mother with a smile, gave her my basket, and kissed her cheek.

"Thank you, Mira. And you look wonderful too."

Papa often said Mama was the prettiest girl in the village. She always blushed and called him blind. Her oval face, deep-set eyes, and dimples gave her beauty a kind warmth. She wore her kroje—red apron, black pleated skirt, and a green bodice embroidered with touches of gold thread—an outfit she had cherished for years.

"Is that a new headscarf?" I asked.

"Yes, I found some forgotten linen," she said, clearly pleased.

I turned to Aneta, petite, pretty, and outgoing, very different from me, yet my best friend.

"I'm glad you're here." She held up the embroidered bodice. "Just a few stitches left."

"Beautiful work, Aneta. Mine never looks this perfect."

"That isn't true. Look at this border you did." She traced the threads with her fingers. "This is the most beautiful dress I've ever worn, thanks to you and Mamička."

Mama placed a bucket of water by her and smiled. "My two daughters, one married, one soon to be. I am so proud. Mira, help your sister dress while I finish the food."

"Yes, Mamička."

I laid out the wedding garments while Aneta hand bathed. Months of work had gone into the bodice, blouse, embroidered skirt, and layered petticoats.

Aneta dropped her everyday clothing in a heap on the straw-covered floor.

"Aneta," Mama raised her voice in dismay. "Pick up your clothes and hang them. Remember, you will be a wife now, and you can't be lazy anymore."

"Sorry, Mamička." Aneta picked up her clothes and hung them on the hook inside the wood cupboard near the bed.

When she finished dressing, she sat in front of me to plait her thick, dark hair.

"Did you hear about the American agent?" she asked. "He's interviewing the young men."

"There's been talk." I worked the braid. "Anna Sterba told me she saw Andras speaking with the agent. Sara is very set against him leaving Hungary."

Aneta waved a hand. "Sara worries about everything. Andras will do whatever he wants. Tomas is excited. He says he'll make much money." She squirmed as I braided. "He'll return home in no time."

"Many go hoping for riches," I blurted. I hoped Tomas wouldn't leave my sister so soon after marrying her. "Some return empty-handed, others never return at all. We have enough here."

"But Tomas is different," she insisted.

"Yes, very different." I gently placed the headdress made of periwinkle paper flowers, bright beads, and bits of tinsel over her braids. "You look beautiful." I handed her the small mirror sitting on the table.

She looked at herself in the mirror, then twirled with delight. Mama stepped up beside me and slipped an arm around me, and together we laughed.

"Come, Aneta, it's time for the ritual," Mama said at last.

Aneta sat as Mama clipped three curls from her neck, placed them in a metal bowl, lit a long piece of straw from the brick oven, and set the hair on fire. My nose twitched at the acrid smell. Once the hair had cooled and reduced to ashes, Mama and Aneta took the bowl outside to the little courtyard. This ritual was between mother and daughter, so I stood back and watched from the doorway.

With great solemnity, they let the ashes catch on the wind and float away. Mama cupped her face and kissed her cheeks.

Joy—and sadness—filled me, remembering the day she had performed the same ritual with me. Soon, Aneta would join Tomas's family, and our parents would be alone. How would they manage without her?

Chapter Two

My pulse quickened when Janos filled the doorway, blue eyes bright, his wavy reddish hair with gold streaks gleaming. He looked handsome in his kroje, embroidered vest over a full-sleeved white shirt. The ribbons at his waist flapped in the draft, and his trousers were tucked into polished leather boots. Zdenko and Ivan shouldered past him toward the food with boyish whoops. Maria and Anton followed with Little Jan, who barreled into my arms where I sat on a bench against the wall. He gave me a kiss. I settled him beside me and motioned Janos to join us. He weaved through the crowd and sat on my other side.

"They are so happy," I said. He winked at me as if we shared the same thought. I laughed and shook my head. He kissed me on the cheek, then rose, and joined his father, who was in conversation with a neighbor.

Aneta sat next to me and chattered, but I only had eyes for my husband.

The rest of our guests arrived, and shortly after, music and boisterous voices announced Tomas's procession of family and friends was nearing our cottage. Aneta and I peeked out the window as Tomas arrived at the head of the entourage, dressed in a kroje similar to Janos's, but more embellished and with a new hat.

He marched up to the front door and said in a loud voice, "Aneta, I am here to ask for your hand in marriage. Please come out."

Inside, I gathered with other young women around Aneta as we played out the wedding tradition to send an impostor Aneta. We placed a veil on a family friend, and she went outside.

"This is not Aneta," Tomas cried with a laugh. "Send the real one."

To further the joke, we sent out a male cousin with a veil, which drew roars of laughter. At last, Aneta, properly veiled, went outside with the rest of us following.

Tomas bowed before our parents. "*Pan* Vargas and *Pani* Vargas, I respectfully request the hand of this beautiful Aneta in marriage."

"Of course, my son," Papa said, and Mama nodded.

Cheers rose, and the procession wound through town to the Slovak Lutheran Church.

The vows were spoken, rings exchanged, and I lifted Aneta's veil to reveal her face as a newly married woman.

Back at my parents' cottage, oil lamps glowed, and heat rose with the scent of food and tobacco smoke.

Papa, having had quite a bit of wine, pulled out his accordion and joined his friends in a sprightly tune. One played viola, and two others, from the Carpathian Mountains where Papa was from, played the Slovak *fujaras* releasing deep rich tones. And a cousin from a neighboring village joined in with a horn.

Everyone danced except Tomas and Aneta, who were expected to sit solemnly so that evil spirits wouldn't grow jealous. But Aneta's feet wouldn't keep still.

"Come, Tomas," she laughed, tugging at him.

"Sit," Mama warned.

"Katarina"—Papa tossed his hands in the air —"it's no use."

Aneta pulled Tomas up and into the circle, skirts flying, laughter spilling louder than the music. She hooked her arm in his, and they swung around to the quick beat of the music, beaming at each other. It was impossible to control Aneta. I smiled, secretly wishing I could be that free. Janos and I tended to follow the rules.

A stranger pushed through the crowd to where Tomas's parents sat in the corner of the room. Tomas pulled Aneta to the edge of where others were dancing and nodded in the direction where I sat with Mama and Little Jan. Aneta skirted the dancers, headed toward us as Tomas joined the stranger and Janos. Voices sharpened. Even Janos scowled. Aneta reached us and sat on the bench.

"Who is he?" I asked.

"Tomas's cousin," Aneta replied. "We didn't know if he would come tonight. He lives far west of here. He's involved with the Slovak National Party and is very politically connected. Tomas admires him."

"This is an outrage!" Tomas shouted.

The music stopped.

"It was a massacre," the cousin said loud enough to be heard by all. "Two days ago, in Černová, the *Gendarmerie* gunned down Slovaks during a peaceful demonstration."

Gasps rippled through the room. I jumped to my feet.

"Mama?" Little Jan said.

"Stay here," I ordered, and hurried to Janos's side. He took my hand and gently squeezed, just as Papa reached him.

"What happened?" Papa demanded.

"The people wanted their Slovak priest to lead the ceremony for a new church that was to be consecrated," the cousin said. "But the church officials appointed two Magyar priests instead."

"Why?" Janos asked.

"Because the Slovak priest was active in some pro-Slovak activities during the election campaign last year and was in jail." His mouth turned down in a fierce frown. "We all know pro-Slovak sympathy isn't taken lightly by the Magyars."

"What happened at the demonstration?" Papa asked.

"The Magyar priests led a procession through the village with a Gendarmerie escort—no doubt, for protection. Slovak parishioners attempted to prevent the procession and the consecration. It was peaceful until someone threw rocks at the Gendarmeries. They fired into the crowd without warning," he exclaimed.

"How many were killed? Were there injuries?" Papa asked.

"Fifteen people were killed, and many others injured, all Slovaks." The cousin dropped onto one of the benches against the wall.

Guests crowded around him and asked more questions.

"I thought the Slovaks were Catholics in Černová?" Janos's voice cut into the din.

"It doesn't matter whether they're Catholics or Lutherans like us," Tomas said. "This is a direct affront against all Slovaks."

The room erupted.

"This is one reason why so many of us leave this country, and I, for one, can hardly wait," Tomas blurted.

"Let us hear the whole story before making accusations," Janos said.

His fingers tightened slightly around mine.

Arguments split men and women into corners. My chest tightened. Was this oppression deliberate, another step in Magyarization? Ever since the Austro-Hungarian Empire had been established, the Slovaks and other minorities had been forced to become like the Magyars. They banned the speaking of Slovak in public and closed our secondary schools, all in the name of Magyarization.

"This is why men are leaving for America," Tomas said loud enough to be heard over the din. "We cannot be sure we will live to provide for our families." He looked at Janos. "Right?"

"Janos?" my father's neighbor said. "Are you leaving as well?"

The question hung in the air. I turned toward Janos, waiting for him to laugh off the question.

Instead, he nodded, his expression somber. "Yes. I met with the agent yesterday—Zdenko too. We decided to take jobs in America. More money, a better life."

"What?" I blurted. "You took a job in America?"

He frowned at me, then returned his attention to the men.

I opened my mouth to demand an answer, but Papa raised his accordion high. "Enough! This is a wedding." He struck up a bright tune. One by one, instruments followed until talk turned gay again. Aneta sang along, her voice steady again.

Slowly, people began eating and drinking again. A low murmur hummed through the room, but not all talk was of the wedding and the newly married couple. The news had cast a shadow that I suspected would last long after the festivities ended. I could only stare at my husband. What had just happened?

The musicians began a slow tune, and Janos took my hand and pulled me out to dance. I wanted to protest, but this was Aneta's wedding celebration, and many eyes were on Janos and me. My hands on his shoulders and his arms around my waist, we stepped side to side in rhythm to the music, turning in circles around the small space. He held me close as if nothing between us had changed. The words echoed in my head, refusing to make sense, *"We decided to take jobs in America."*

At midnight, the women circled Aneta, removed her head-dress, and tied the embroidered kerchief at her nape in the married woman's fashion. She sat with Tomas's hand in hers, humming as others danced.

Laughter and wine ran late. I slipped outside for air. I thought of my own wedding, of how Janos's uncles had come to ask my parents for my hand in marriage, and of how he had found me in the garden the day before. With his callused and warm hand, he took mine and asked if I wished to marry him. Of course I did. Love in an arranged marriage is a gift, and we have been blessed to love each other.

It's all I'd ever wanted, a husband, children, and a home of our own—though having our own home would take years, if at all. How would Little Jan and I live without him?

Chapter Three

February 1908

I LADLED HOT POTATO SOUP INTO BOWLS AND stared at the meager midday meal, the largest meal of the day. The big wedding feast was already a faded memory. Even the joy of the Vianoce eve celebration of *Štedrý večer* seemed long ago. Our stores from the fall harvest were dwindling fast, and we rationed what we could. At least we always had potatoes.

Janos and Anton came in from the rain, with Ivan and Zdenko close behind. They hung their slickers on wall hooks near the door and sat. I set out soup, eggs, bread, and butter before taking my place beside Janos.

Maria brought Little Jan from the other room and settled him next to me. Living with Janos's family often left me feeling like just another pair of hands. Maria had grown up in a house full of men and learned silence, not comfort.

Anton said a short grace.

"The tickets came from the American agent," Janos announced.

Spoons stilled. I dropped mine into my bowl.

"We leave in April," he added.

"Tickets!" Zdenko leaped to his feet. "I can't wait."

"Sit down," Anton barked. "Eat, or I'll fetch the switch."

Zdenko dropped into his seat, arms crossed. Nearing fifteen, he still acted childish.

"Are you sure he should go?" Maria asked.

She must question whether he's mature enough to go. I did. But maybe, away from Anton's control, Zdenko would thrive in America. That was the only good thing I had been able to glean from the men leaving.

Anton snapped, "Why ask now?"

"Papa and I agreed," Janos said flatly. "Zdenko will be more useful earning money than here. Better America than drafted into the military."

Maria sighed. "I suppose I must trust you."

"We'll help with plowing before we leave," Janos added.

Anton nodded.

"How long will you be gone?" I asked.

Janos flicked the nails of his free hand, a sign of his irritation.

I pushed on. "How will you get there?" My voice grew louder. "I don't understand what will happen. You told me nothing." I bit my lip, surprised by my outburst.

Janos stopped eating. "Mira, you knew it would be in the spring. I accepted the job. That is it." He tore off a hunk of bread from the loaf on the table.

I studied his face, leaner now than when we wed. We never had enough to eat, and it showed most on him.

"We go by train to Fiume," he said through his bread. "From there, the steamship to New York. Then another train to St. Louis. Vamos's uncle has a room. You remember Vamos?"

"Of course. His wife, Anna, is in my sewing circle. She's sad all the time."

Janos slammed his hand down. Dishes rattled. "Do not tell me these things," he whispered harshly. "Do you think this is easy for me?"

I reached for his hand. He pulled away.

Tears pricked my eyes. "I don't want you to leave. I thought you were happy—at least a little—with me and Little Jan."

Anton and Zdenko kept their heads down. Little Jan began to cry, and Maria ushered him and Ivan to our room.

Janos rose and paced. "How happy can we be, struggling to put the little we can on the table, and working, working, working with nothing to show for it? We'll send money so you and the rest of the family won't starve. We can save money for our dream of building our own home and owning a piece of land." He dropped onto the bench next to me. His expression relaxed into a forced smile, and he said in a softer voice, "I'll be home by *St. Mikuláš Day*. I promise."

"You promise?" I whispered.

He grasped my hand and squeezed gently. "Of course, my little Mira." He turned to his father. "Papa, forgive our outburst."

Anton shrugged. "We're all making sacrifices. Mira, we understand what you are feeling. We must work together."

I nodded and dropped my head in shame. The door of the other room opened, and Maria and the children returned. An awkward silence pervaded the space.

"I'm sorry for my anger," I whispered. "I know I'm not the only one sacrificing."

"I want cheese, Mama," Little Jan said sweetly.

I forced a smile. "There is none now, my love."

When the men went back to work, I sought Maria. "Wouldn't you rather they stay?"

She frowned. "Anton and Janos are our husbands. We

support their decisions. You spoke your piece. Nothing changed. What's done is done."

Her loyalty crushed me. Perhaps silence was easier for her. For me, every day with Janos felt like sand slipping away.

Later, in our room, Janos watched as I undid my hair and slipped into my nightdress. I checked that Little Jan slept on his cot, then closed the drapery around the bed and slid beneath the covers. His warmth eased me. We didn't speak— our closeness always spoke for us. I clung to him, inhaled his musky scent, and let the rhythm of his body burn into my memory. How I would miss these moments. I seared them into my heart to carry through the long months, maybe years, apart.

Chapter Four

April 1908

Two months later, we waved farewell to Janos, Zdenko, and Tomas as they started the long walk to the train depot. Anger smoldered in me, and with each step Janos took, the ache of abandonment deepened. The others drifted back to their chores, leaving me with Little Jan as I clung to the gate, knuckles white, until the men disappeared from view.

How could he leave us? Tears blurred my vision.

"Mama, is Papa coming back soon?" Little Jan asked.

I jolted from despair, wiped my cheeks, and forced a smile. "Not soon, dearest. Papa will be gone a while, but he'll return for St. Mikuláš Day."

Little Jan cried for days. Then less often. At last, he stopped.

However, I couldn't forget. At first, I thought the stress of Janos leaving had caused a delay in my monthly cycle, since it had happened once before. But the days stretched on, and my body betrayed me with signs I remembered too well, the queasy turn of my stomach at the smell of frying eggs, and the ache in my breasts.

Nearly two weeks after the men had left, Maria looked at me sharply one evening as I bent to lift the churn. "You're pale, Mira. Tired?"

"I'm fine," I replied too quickly, keeping my eyes on the butter as I scraped it into a jar.

She lingered a moment, then turned away, muttering about needing more salt.

I set the churn down and pressed a hand against my belly, still flat beneath my apron. Dread and wonder tangled together in my mind. I hated how pregnancy bent and weakened me, yet the thought of carrying another piece of Janos tightened my throat. There was no denying it; another child was coming. I released a breath. Would a new baby bring Janos home?

THE MORE TIME PASSED, THE MORE MARIA GREW resigned. Anton showed no emotion at all. Ivan, barely eleven, grew quieter. He idolized his brother.

Without Janos and Zdenko, Ivan labored in their place, before and after school. Maria and I worked the fields when needed, on top of chores. We slept little, but the work was done.

I grew weary. Should I tell my in-laws about the baby? No. Janos should know first.

Often, I helped at my parents' cottage now that Aneta had moved back with them. With no sons to rely on, Papa always hired an extra pair of hands during planting and harvest seasons. I doubted Anton would do the same, even when money came from America. His pride would not allow it.

May 1908

THE MEN WERE DUE TO ARRIVE IN NEW YORK ON April 23rd, two weeks after leaving. Aneta and I began checking the post each morning.

"Dobrý ráno," I greeted her at my parents' cottage.

She smiled. "Ready?"

We linked our fingers together and swung our arms between us like we did when we were young girls. She was in her usual cheerful mood, smiling and chatting away while I listened. Being with Aneta always lifted my spirits. Sometimes it seemed I was more affected by Janos's absence than Aneta was about Tomas.

We strolled through the village, passing Hungarian houses and shops I admired, built of stone with wood roofs and floors and whitewashed walls. The more affluent residents painted their homes in bright blue or pinkish tones that I wished we could do with our mud-brick cottage.

At the village center, we reached the Notary Office building, bustling with villagers. As we passed through, I recognized a few and greeted them with a nod and polite smile. The Notary was not a favorite among us Slovaks, though one himself. He had assimilated as a Magyar and became a government official and the postmaster. He waved us to the back, where he stood at the post counter. Greeting us in Magyar, he tilted his head back and looked at us through his glasses, which sat halfway down his bulbous nose.

"Ah, the wives of Janos Lacko and Tomas Hornak," his voice dripped with condescension as he flourished two envelopes in the air, which all could see. "Finally, your poor families have written."

Villagers turned to stare. I shrank back, mortified. Aneta, bold as always, stepped up with a smile.

"Thank you, sir." She held out her palm.

"Your letter, Mrs. Hornak, from your husband Tomas, uh, Mr. Hornak, and one for his parents." He smirked as he placed them in her hand. Then, louder, "And your letters, Mrs. Lacko. One from your husband, and one from young Zdenko."

Heat burned my cheeks, but I forced composure and took them.

"Enjoy your news. Sounds like they are settling in." He pushed up his billowy white sleeves and turned from the counter, puffing his chest out like a preening peacock.

We hurried into the street before speaking.

"I cannot stand him," I hissed in Slovak.

"Mira," Aneta warned in Magyar, "someone might hear."

I waved her off, though I knew she was right. Speaking Slovak in public could get us arrested, though that was more likely to occur in the northern regions.

"He is horrid," she whispered. "And reading our letters—*imagine.*"

We hurried home to read in private. I left Aneta at our parents' cottage, then reached home fifteen minutes later.

"Letters!" I shouted with excitement.

Maria looked up from cutting potatoes and wiped her hands on her apron. I handed her Zdenko's. With a sigh of relief, she clutched the letter to her breast.

Little Jan leaped into my arms. "Look, my love, Papa has written to us."

"Papa?" he asked, tugging at my letter.

I laughed softly. "Let me read it first."

It was the first letter Janos had written to me. My hands trembled as I unfolded the paper.

Dearest Mira,

Please forgive my taking a long time to write. We

are in St. Louis, Missouri. Zdenko was sick on the ship. They kept him a week at Ellis Island hospital, but gratefully he recovered. Tomas and I boarded nearby. It was costly, but worth it. I was surprised by the crowds of thousands arriving from several ships, including ours. Sad some were sent back.

We stay now with my friend Vamos at his Uncle Zsabo's place. He and his wife are kind, and their home nice with plumbing, running water like rain, and even an indoor privy with a chain you pull to wash waste down a drain. A mystery!

The streets are not paved with gold, but there are electric trolleys like Fiume. I work as a pipe fitter at a plant. Zdenko and Tomas are in production. Tomas already complains. We are learning English. Few here speak Slovak, though some Magyars live nearby.

I will wire money soon. I miss you. Kiss our boy for me. Write soon.

Your Jani

I hugged the letter to my chest.

"When is Papa coming home?" Little Jan asked.

"Not yet, love. We must wait for St. Mikuláš Day."

He frowned, then returned to his blocks on the floor.

Janos sounded almost cheerful in his letter, but I knew him well and felt he didn't want me worrying. They were in another country. How could I not worry? Yet, the distance between us narrowed just a little. I retrieved some paper and sat at the tiny table in our room and considered carefully what to say. I had planned to tell him about the baby but suddenly wondered if that would worry him. I hesitated. Would he feel a mixture of joy and sadness as I did? I must tell him and pray he would be happy about it.

Dearest Jani,

I am so happy for your letter. Sorry to hear of Zdenko's illness, but I too am grateful he is well. Life here is the same, except for one thing, I am with child—your farewell gift. I know another mouth to feed was not in your plans, but I am happy to carry another part of you. The baby is due in September. You will meet our son or daughter when you return. Please be glad, my love. I miss you. I promise to use the money wisely.

With all my heart,

Your Mira, Little Jan, and our newest little one

Chapter Five

July 1908

JANOS AND ZDENKO HAD WIRED MONEY IN EARLY summer. At first, most of the funds paid our back taxes. We breathed a sigh of relief at getting the Notary to stop his constant demands for payment. Fortune smiled at us, for we also expected a decent harvest of rye, hay, and corn for our stores. We also could buy another sheep for butter, cheese, and wool.

Janos wrote that they were using Americanized first names to make it easier at work and for the English-speaking folk. That made sense, since Janos was John in other languages. He chose John, but Zdenko chose Denny, which surprised everyone.

One overcast, but beautiful day, I was churning butter in the courtyard while Little Jan chased a stray chicken. He was growing so fast. I tried not to think about how much Janos was missing, but everything reminded me of him. I hated seeing his empty seat at the table every meal. I missed him most at night when I lay awake alone in our bed.

Maria came around the side of the house with a basket full of eggs and stopped next to me.

"Mama, Baba, watch me catch the chickee." Little Jan laughed and skipped.

"It's amazing how much Little Jan looks like Janos did when he was this age." Maria sighed, her face flushed.

"I see Janos in Little Jan more and more every day." I frowned. "Are you feeling well today?"

"Moving a little slow, I suppose. It's nothing. My head does hurt a bit."

"I'm almost done. Go on into the house to rest, and I'll be in shortly to make a compress of chamomile for your forehead." The butter was thick and ready to be scooped from the churn.

"You are a good daughter, Mira." She rubbed her brow and started toward the house.

I stared after her in surprise. She rarely paid me a compliment. She disappeared inside the house. I put the churned butter into a blue and red ceramic jar and wiped the inside of the churn with a cloth. When I lifted the churn, a twinge twisted my belly. I stopped short, and the pain quickly passed. I was about six months along and had started to show. With Little Jan, I hadn't begun to show until later due to my broad hips. I hoped for a daughter.

The next morning, just before I usually rose, Anton tapped on the door to my room.

"Mira, she won't get up," he said through the door.

"What? Oh dear, give me a minute. We'll be right out." I jumped out of bed, rushed to get Little Jan up and dressed, then went into the main room.

Little Jan ran over to her bed. "What's wrong with Baba? Why is she still in bed?" He pushed on the covers to wake her.

"Is she sick?" Ivan sat on the side of his bed, rubbing the sleep from his eyes, his dark brown hair sticking out all over. "She never stays in bed this long."

"Maybe." I turned to Little Jan. "Go outside with your *dedko*, while I get our morning meal ready."

Anton gave me a knowing look and guided the boys out the front door. I pressed a hand to her forehead and found her skin hot and clammy. I made a chamomile compress and placed it on Maria's forehead. We didn't have the herb feverfew, only meadowsweet for a few cups of tea, but it was better than nothing.

Quickly, I prepared the morning meal of gruel and eggs and set the food on the table.

I went to Maria's bedside with a cup of tea and took her hand. "Here, drink this tea."

"Janos, is that you?" she murmured. She opened her eyes and searched my face. She pushed my hand away and wouldn't drink the tea.

"No, it's me, Mira."

"Mira, my head hurts too much, and I'm hot." She rubbed her forehead and pushed off the covers.

"You need to rest and keep warm." I pulled the covers back over her and frowned. Seeing Maria behave in such a manner worried me.

Anton poked his head in through the front door and looked at me. I gave him a slight nod, and he pushed the door all the way open. The boys came inside and sat at the table to eat. Anton walked over to my side.

I whispered to Anton, "She's confused and very hot. She needs the doctor. I'll go fetch him while you stay and watch her and the boys. Try to get her to drink this tea and keep the compress moist."

His brow furrowed with worry. "Please hurry."

I slipped from the cottage and hurried down the road. Dr. Schwarz lived right on the edge of the village.

Zelda, the doctor's wife and my friend, stood as I approached her garden. "Mira, whatever is the matter? Someone sick?" she said in Magyar.

"Yes, my mother-in-law, Maria. She's sick with fever and a headache. Where is Dr. Schwarz? Is he here?" I glanced over at the cottage, hoping to see him through the window.

"No, he left a little while ago to make a call at the count's estate. Come inside and sit. You're out of breath. Wait here until he returns."

We went inside. I was struck with awe every time I visited. Everything looked clean and sparkling. They built the house of stone like the rest of the village buildings, with a wood roof and floor. There were several rooms for only the two of them. Zelda longed for children, but after three miscarriages, they had given up hope of having a family.

We sat at the finely carved wood table.

I fidgeted with my hands. "Should I go to the count's estate?"

"It's a long walk, and you can't just go up to his estate and knock on the front door. It's just not done," she said in a disapproving tone. "Perhaps the other doctor?" She patted my hand with a look of concern.

"Does he treat Slovaks? I thought only your husband did."

"Well," she paused, "that is true. In this case, he might."

"Would he? Maria is delirious. I fear for her. I trust your husband." I stood. "I must go to the estate. I've never been there. Can you tell me the way?"

"I'll show you the route my husband took in case he's already on his way back." Zelda drew a little map and handed it to me.

"Thank you so much." We hugged, and she kissed me on the cheek.

Map in hand, I hurried out the door to make the long walk to the count's estate. I walked as fast as I could, but quickly grew tired. By the time I reached the end of the village's main street, I had slowed considerably. A glance at the map confirmed I needed to turn right. The flat land called the Great Plain stretched out before me in fields of corn and wheat. The count owned all this land. There were virtually no tall shade trees, only bushes and some wildflowers along the road. Not a single cottage in sight. A small breeze blew the corn and wheat stalks, cooling the air for a moment.

Unlike my family and the other villagers, who used hand tools or an ox to plow our tiny plots, the count could afford modern machinery to plant and harvest. He employed laborers, mostly landless Slovaks, a few Slovenians, and Croatians who were even poorer than our families. Some were migrant or seasonal workers, like those who helped Papa with his fields. Papa would give them a percentage of crop sales or food for their labor. The count paid tiny wages, and they worked from sunup to sundown, six or seven days a week, earning barely enough to feed their families.

Judging by the sun's placement in the sky, I had been walking for about an hour when the pain in my belly grew more insistent. I pushed forward and finally spotted a cluster of tall trees in the distance, surrounded by a stone wall. According to the little map, I had reached the count's estate. As I drew closer to the trees, buildings with sloped roofs, wood shingles, and stone walls appeared. I hurried my pace a little more.

A huge flower garden in full bloom created an explosion of color to the right of the large house. Several other smaller buildings sat off to the left side of the house. I reached the wall and walked alongside to the open gateway, then stopped. I peeked around the corner and up the drive. A large, elegant carriage and the doctor's one-horse cart sat at the front door.

Behind them, one of those fancy motorcars sat in the house's shade. I couldn't believe only one family lived here.

The smell of freshly cut grass from the green lawn filled the air. I hesitated to go inside the gate. How would I be greeted? What if they refused to let me see the doctor? I forced myself forward, trying to step lightly on the gravel drive. A woman knelt in the garden working. She looked up, and I cringed. She had to have heard the crunch of my boots. She stood, and I halted.

"Who are you?" she asked in Magyar.

She started toward me, a stern expression on her face, and stopped twenty feet away. She wore a plain dark green skirt and a full-sleeved blouse of the same color, very well made, and of fine cloth. I wondered if she was a servant.

"Please forgive my intrusion. Dr. Schwarz's wife told me I could find him here?" I replied in Magyar. "My mother-in-law is very sick, and I couldn't wait for the doctor to return home, so I came here." I bowed my head and peered at her through my lashes.

"Wait there and don't move." The woman marched to the house and disappeared inside.

Afraid to move, I furtively surveyed the beautiful grounds, trying to stay calm. After a few minutes, the front door opened, and Dr. Schwarz stepped out onto the porch. His long beard waved in the breeze. Though it was a warm summer day, he still wore his black jacket over an embroidered shirt with long pants in the Hungarian fashion.

"Mrs. Lacko." He waved me over.

I rushed to him and spoke swiftly. "Dr. Schwarz. I'm relieved to find you. Your wife told me where you were. I'm sorry that I couldn't wait for you to return home. It's my mother-in-law, Maria." I gulped a quick breath. "She has a high fever, headache, and isn't herself. Can you come to our house right away?"

"There, there, Mrs. Lacko, calm yourself. I'm here checking on a sick house servant. Come wait for me inside, but don't touch anything." He motioned me to follow him inside.

"Oh no, I couldn't." I took a step back. "I will wait out here for you."

"Well, if you insist." He paused and looked at me closely. "Are you all right? You look pale."

"I am fine, doctor. I've been hurrying to get here. I'm just hot and tired."

"Very well. I will be a little longer. I'll send someone out with something cold to drink."

He went back inside, leaving the door open. I peeked into the large entry area. A room off to the right had a long, ornately carved wood table with high-backed upholstered chairs.

A young girl came to the doorway, and I stepped back. Without a word, she handed me a glass of water and shut the door. I saw just enough to know I didn't belong there.

I was grateful for the drink. The cool water refreshed my parched mouth. I drank it all, set the empty glass on the steps, and turned my attention to the yard. My mind spun, and exhaustion stiffened my aching legs.

The woman from the garden emerged from around the side of the house. She looked over at me and shook her head, then resumed her gardening. I didn't care. All that mattered was getting help.

A little time passed before Dr. Schwarz came outside carrying his medical bag. He ushered me to his cart. I had never ridden in a cart and needed his help to climb onto the two-person bench seat. He put his bag in the space behind the seat and pulled at the reins, guiding the chestnut brown horse onto the drive and out the front gate.

While holding on tight to the seat as we jostled about on

the bumpy road, I explained Maria's condition. He listened intently and asked me a few questions. It was well after noon by the time we reached our cottage. The doctor tied his horse to our gate, and we hurried inside.

Much to my surprise, my mother-in-law was sitting up in bed, smiling.

"Dr. Schwarz." Anton extended his hand to the doctor. "Thank you for coming, but it looks like my wife has revived. I had been forcing her to drink the meadowsweet tea Mira made, and it seemed to help."

"Very good. I'll examine her to be sure." Dr. Schwarz went to Maria's bedside while Anton and I stepped to the kitchen out of earshot.

"I don't believe it," I said in a low voice. "I had to walk all the way to the count's estate to find the doctor, and now she is fine?"

"She started coming around not long after you left." He lifted his brows in question. "You went to the estate? Mira, what happened? They didn't throw you out, did they?"

"No, but I feared they might. Thankfully, Dr. Schwarz was still there."

"Thank you, Mira, but you don't look so good. Rest a bit. I'll let you know when the doctor finishes with Maria."

Anton sent Ivan outside to do some chores, then sat quietly to wait for the doctor. I took Little Jan into our room and put him down for a nap. There was too much going on for him to relax, but eventually, he dropped off to sleep.

Finally, a tap sounded at my door. I quietly slipped from the room, and Dr. Schwarz motioned me into the main room to speak to Anton and me.

"She is going to be fine," he said. "She has a small fever and is a bit dehydrated. Get her to drink more fluids."

"That's good to hear, Doctor. Thank you," said Anton.

The doctor handed me a small white envelope with a

string tied around it. "This is aspirin powder for the fever and pain. Dissolve a small spoonful of this powder in a glass of water and give it to her three times a day. I've already given a dose. The next one would be later tonight."

As I took the packet from him, a sharp pain seared through my abdomen. I doubled over, dropping the packet on the floor. The doctor took hold of me, and I fell into his arms. Warm, thick liquid flowed down my inner thighs.

"Mira!" Anton reached out to me.

"I've got her," said the doctor. "Let's get her to the bed so I can examine her."

The two of them helped me into the other room.

"Don't wake Little Jan." I forced out through the pain.

"Try not to speak," said Dr. Schwarz.

Once on the bed, the doctor looked me over. "You are bleeding out. It could be the child." He turned to my father-in-law. "Please bring me clean cloths right away and some hot water."

"What is happening?" My voice sounded as if I were in a deep hole. I thrashed, and hands gripped my shoulders and held me still. "Is the baby coming? It's too soon...too soon." I screamed with each contraction.

Anton and the doctor spoke. I couldn't understand the words. I was in labor, but it didn't feel like when I gave birth to Little Jan. With each contraction, the most intense pain I'd ever had grew sharper. The water broke, and I could feel the baby coming. A moment of clarity hit, and I could see Dr. Schwarz standing over me.

"Push, Mira, push," Dr. Schwarz said.

This was all wrong. Fear ripped through me and I resisted. My vision blurred in another jolt of searing pain.

"Mira," Mama said. Was she real or imagined? Her gentle hands stroked my face, and she kissed my cheek. "Everything will be all right."

Then...blackness.

I awoke to find Mama sitting beside me on the edge of the bed, holding my hand.

"Mamička?" I murmured.

Her eyes glistened with unshed tears. "Thank God you're awake. We were afraid we would lose you, too."

"Me too? The baby?" I looked wildly around. "Where is it? A boy? A girl?"

Tears rolled down her cheeks, and I knew. The baby was gone, slipped out of me, dead, without my being aware. My heart clenched hard.

"You had a little girl. We've already prepared her for the funeral." She took a breath. "We will bury her today. It is summer, and we can't wait."

"Today?" I wanted to scream to God. *Why?* Everything happened so fast.

"Yes, my dear," she said. "We will still hold a vigil. Family will be here, and we will bury her in the church graveyard. You're too weak to do anything. The doctor says you must rest."

I sobbed.

Mama held me tight. "There, there, let it out. That's good for you." She petted my hair, lightly brushing the loose hairs from my face.

At last, my sobs subsided, and Mama wiped my tears.

I spoke in a ragged breath. "I want her named, though she was born early. Please? I was going to call her Karin, after your mother."

She gave me a wan, kind smile and kissed my forehead. "Karin it will be."

THEY PROPPED ME UP IN THE BED IN THE MAIN ROOM during the vigil. Maria laid the tiny bundle in my arms. Barely two pounds, translucent skin, fingers perfect. I touched her lips and whispered her name.

The next morning, the milk came. My breasts ached for my baby. I cried until the tears ran dry, then cried again. Mama came daily to care for me and Maria. She told me of the two babies she had lost.

She patted my hand. "The grief never leaves." Her sadness mirrored my own. "But you will learn to live. You must, for Little Jan and Janos."

In that sorrow, we drew closer than before.

Chapter Six

September 1908

Several weeks after losing Karin, I had a strange dream that was different from the usual silly, nonsensical dreams. This one in particular stayed on my mind. It was clear and detailed, the colors very intense.

In the dream, I stood in an empty room with a little girl of walking age, who sat in the corner. She had curly reddish-brown hair and was dressed all in black. I didn't recognize her, but I felt a deep connection. I wanted to go to her, but I couldn't move. I was allowed only to observe her from a distance. Then I woke up and lay in the early morning quiet and listened to Anton's snoring, until I dropped back into a dreamless sleep.

Maria had returned to her usual daily chores. I, on the other hand, refused to venture anywhere except the garden. Aneta picked up any mail and brought it to me. Her visits were the only thing I looked forward to.

Losing the baby was a bloody and painful ordeal, and I grieved that I would never know baby Karin. The realization that I wouldn't see her grow up, marry, and have children of her own tortured me to my very core. But I had a guilty secret. I was relieved to no longer be pregnant.

I had feared going through pregnancy again. What would my mother-in-law think, or my own mama, if they knew how I felt? Being a wife and mother was expected of women.

The worst part was that I hadn't written to Janos about losing the baby. I didn't know how to tell him. The words wouldn't come.

ONE MORNING, LITTLE JAN AND I SAT ON THE BED IN our room, playing the hand-patting game. I missed a move while lost in thought, and Little Jan broke out in an infectious giggle. I smiled and held my hands up to start again, just as Maria appeared in the doorway.

"Mira, why not visit your mama and Aneta? It's been a couple of weeks now since your mama was here, and you haven't left this place to go anywhere," Maria said.

I looked from Little Jan to her and was startled at how old she looked. She had been keeping her hair well hidden under her headscarf. But today, she wore no scarf and hadn't done up her hair; the gray tresses cascaded down her back. The hair around her face had turned almost white. The tanned lines on her face had deepened. Her hands were weathered from a lifetime of hard work, and I wasn't helping her. Guilt welled up within me.

Little Jan frowned. "Mama, are you leaving?"

I hesitated. I couldn't leave my sweet Little Jan, and though it pained me to think about Karin, I imagined Little Jan playing with his sister. I had longed to have a daughter. Could I go through another pregnancy? I shook my head. It was too soon to consider having another child.

"We could all three go for a visit," Maria urged. "You and Aneta could go to the post together like you used to, yes?"

"Maybe." I smiled with sudden energy and turned to Little Jan. "Will you come with us?"

He nodded, smile beaming and eyes sparkling.

"That is good, very good." Maria put up her hair and tied on her headscarf.

While she rushed around the house finishing up minor tasks, I got the hairbrush and managed to tame his unruly hair. At last, the three of us ventured down the road to my parents' cottage.

"Time to go into the village," Aneta said half an hour later.

I nodded slightly, then gave Little Jan a hug. "We'll be back soon."

He smiled and went toward the door. Who couldn't smile at such a sweet boy? We waved to everyone and headed toward the village.

It was a warm day. The sun shone so bright that I had to shield my eyes. We passed a few neighbors tending their gardens along the way. We waved to them and, because we were in our community, we offered greetings in Slovak.

At the edge of the village, we came upon Dr. Schwarz's house. Zelda rose from where she had been picking dandelions as we approached and put them in the basket on her arm.

"Hello. Mira, Aneta, please come," Zelda said in Magyar, and waved us over to her yard.

"Morning, Zelda," I replied in Magyar, and pointed to her basket. "For soup?"

She chuckled. "Yes, yes, we have plenty of weeds, but they're tasty too."

Aneta stood by, not taking part in the conversation.

I thought it odd, but turned my attention to Zelda when

she said, "I'm glad to see you out and about. You and your mother-in-law are feeling better now?"

"Yes, I'm feeling a little better and actually glad to be out. It's good seeing you, too. Thank you again for your help on... that day."

"It was a very sad day, Mira. Anytime I can help you now, or in the future, please call on me, *ja*?"

"I would love to come by later this week to visit with you, if you like." I wanted to share the dream with her. Zelda had once told me her people believed some dreams held messages.

"Of course, my dear, anytime."

"Thank you. We are on our way to check for mail, but I'll see you later this week."

I gave her a quick hug and kiss on the cheek. She smiled and waved us goodbye.

We continued to the Notary Office. Aneta remained silent, lips pursed and head down.

"Why were you quiet around Zelda?" I asked.

She scowled. "I don't understand why you are friendly with her."

"Why would I not be? She is a very generous and kind woman."

"They're Jews," she muttered.

"Aneta! I'm surprised by you. What difference does it make? Her husband is an excellent doctor. We're lucky to have them living so close and willing to serve the poor. I'm not even sure if we paid him properly for his services. I don't know what I would have done if Dr. Schwarz hadn't been there when I needed him."

"Well," she paused, "that is true, and I'm glad of that. But there have been things said about how the Jews take up the jobs and their influence in businesses and such. What about us? The Slovaks keep struggling, and the Jews are getting more prosperous."

"We weren't raised to be prejudiced. And we're farmers. I don't know where you get these notions."

"I heard it from Tomas's cousin. You remember him? The political one who came to the wedding party? He's well-informed and gets all the news from Budapest. He says over half of the doctors in Budapest are Jewish. It seems like they get more educational opportunities, too."

"Zelda told me they aren't allowed to own land. Her people must find other means to support themselves. I like Zelda and her husband. Her religion matters nothing to me."

"Well, that is your choice," Aneta huffed.

I hesitated, uncertain how to reply. It sounded like Tomas's cousin had poisoned her mind. Today wasn't the time to discuss it, but we *would* later.

There were very few people in the Notary Office besides the office staff. I was relieved to find the Notary absent when we reached the postal counter. His young assistant handed us our letters. We opened our letters while walking back.

"Oh, my!" Aneta exclaimed.

"What is it?" I looked up from my letter.

"Tomas is sending for me." She looked at me, eyes wide.

"Sending for you? You mean to America permanently?" My mouth dropped open.

We both stopped.

"Yes. I knew he was unhappy, but I wasn't expecting this." She eyed me and frowned. "Mira, you look like someone hit you."

A knot formed in my stomach, and I stumbled to one of the rare shade trees on the side of the road and leaned against the trunk. "You won't go, will you?" Tears filled my eyes. "I know it's selfish, but I can't lose you, too." I covered my face with my hands, ashamed of how much I needed her.

She hugged me. "Now, Mira, you'll make me cry. You know I

must follow Tomas. I love him. He's my husband. And I'm a little eager for the adventure. Wouldn't you do the same if Janos sent for you?" She offered a sweet smile and lifted my chin with her hand.

How could she smile when I was hurting so much? What if Janos wanted me to go to America? I shuddered at the possibility. That was not the plan. He was to come back to our life here.

"I'm not an adventurer like you, Aneta." I pulled free of her and resumed walking. I didn't want her to leave, but neither did I want her pity.

She fell into step alongside me, and I kept my eyes straight ahead as I took a handkerchief from the pocket of my skirt and wiped away my tears and blew my runny nose.

"When will you go?"

"He said before Christmas."

"So soon?" My insides constricted, and my shoulders slumped.

She intertwined her fingers with mine, and we took one step at a time in sync, like we did as young girls.

"What did Janos say in his letter?"

"Oh, my goodness, I haven't read all of it yet." I stopped short and looked down at the letter still in my hand. I began to read. My heart jumped into my throat. "He found out about the miscarriage."

"What? How?" She tried to read the letter.

"I should have known she wouldn't let me tell Janos in my time."

"Who?"

"Anna Sterba, Vamos's wife, from our sewing circle. She wrote to her husband about it, and he told Janos." I handed Aneta the letter. "Janos is very upset that I didn't tell him. Now I have to deal with this too." I stomped my foot on the ground, and a small flurry of dust rose in the breeze. "Why is all this happening at once? First, Janos leaves, I lose my baby girl, and now you will desert me. It's too much."

Aneta finished reading the brief letter and handed it back to me. I stuffed it into my pocket.

"Janos didn't sound very upset, Mira. He says he is very sad about the baby and wishes he was here to comfort you. That was very nice of him, yes?"

"Yes, he's a good man, but I could sense his embarrassment at hearing the news from Vamos and not from me. I miss him terribly. St. Mikuláš Day can't get here soon enough."

"And by the way, I am not deserting you." She gave me a gentle shove. "You know we will always be with each other in our hearts."

"I know. It'll be difficult without you. How will I bear it?"

I needed to work through my emotions, my way. I would cry the way Aneta didn't. She saw everything as an opportunity. To me, it seemed like everything was against me. As soon as I reached home, I gathered the words in my mind to write to Janos and explain why I hadn't written sooner about the loss of the baby. Words I wasn't sure I could find.

———

Two days later, I walked to the village to mail the letter to Janos. I arrived at the Notary Office, and Zelda stood at the postal counter collecting her mail.

I tapped her on the shoulder. "Well, imagine finding you here. I was planning to stop by your house on my way back," I said in Magyar.

Zelda turned and grinned. "How wonderful to see you."

We gave each other a hug and kissed each other on the cheeks.

The Notary stood behind the counter in his usual stance, hand on hip, looking down his nose through his glasses. I cringed and waited for some snide remark, but he just grunted with disdain and took the letter from my hand.

"Thank you," I said, and Zelda and I hurried out to the street.

"Come along with me while I make a stop at the butcher, ja?" Zelda offered in German.

She tended to slip in and out of Magyar and German. I followed along, more or less. It was always a pleasure to practice the German Zelda had been teaching me.

We walked slowly down the main street toward the shop. I told her about my dream in a low voice. We stopped at a bench in front of a shop and sat.

"Hm. Well, I think you already know who the little girl was, ja?" She smiled.

"Maybe," I hesitated. "I want to believe it was my Karin. She wasn't a baby in the dream. How could that be?"

Zelda took in a deep breath. "Dreams come in many ways. It is not always clear why. The description of her sounds like the little baby that was taken from you, just older, so you could connect better, maybe. I don't know." She took my hand in hers. "The feeling you had, the deep connection. It is a good thing, not bad, ja?"

"Yes, it was a wonderful feeling, almost a peacefulness." I nodded slowly. "I think Karin is in Heaven and I am not to be sad."

"You believe in Heaven. The dream is telling you not to be sad, and she's in a better place."

"I know you don't believe in Heaven. What would the dream mean to you?"

"I believe in the concept of Heaven, for God dwells there. But the message is for you, Mira, not for me. Remember, dreams are for the dreamer only. Be happy, my dear. You have Little Jan. You have your Janos, though he is not here right now, and your sister and parents, too."

"That's right, you don't know. Aneta is going to America." I stifled a sob, determined not to cry in public.

"My goodness, that is surprising. But you will always have Aneta in your heart."

I knew she was right. I had the love of my family, no matter where they were, and it meant everything to me. Before we parted, Zelda made me promise to tell her about any other dreams I may have that were similar to this.

———

October 1908

THE DAY CAME TOO SOON, WHEN PAPA WOULD MAKE the long walk with Aneta to the train station that went to Port Fiume. Though he offered to go with her to the port, she insisted he let her travel the rest of the way alone.

"Are you sure?" I asked her. "Aren't you nervous about traveling such a distance alone?"

She laughed, practically jumping with glee. "You know me. I'm excited about this adventure. I'll be fine."

We hugged each other tight; I didn't want to let go.

"It's time, Aneta," Papa said, her large carpet bag in his hand.

Mama and I stood at the gate as the two made their way down the road. It felt just like it did when Janos left, and a sob threatened.

Mama put her arm around me. "It is a sad day to see a daughter leave and not know when I will see her again."

"Oh, Mamička. I hope we will." The thought of never seeing Aneta again was just too much. Another hole in my heart, and I didn't know how I would bear it.

Chapter Seven

December 1908

THE HOLY SEASON ARRIVED ON THE FIRST DAY OF the month, and our community grew busy with the usual preparations for the coming festivities. I washed and polished all the furniture and kitchen utensils while my mother-in-law brought in clean straw for the freshly swept floor. She took special care laying the straw to point east to west, a ritual to provide protection and prosperity for our home and family.

In Janos's last letter, written weeks earlier, he told me they would arrive on St. Mikuláš Day, December sixth. We Slovaks adopted the Hungarian custom of St. Mikuláš visiting the village children, giving them chocolate for being good or a birch stick for being bad. Janos sent extra money to buy the chocolate for Little Jan and Ivan.

However, Aneta filled most of my thoughts. With her in America, the holidays wouldn't be the same. I missed her so much.

While Maria worked in the kitchen, I wrapped myself in my thick, boiled wool jacket to keep warm from the cold winter air and went to the garden. I sat on a bench under the plum tree, pulled a letter from Aneta out of my pocket, and tucked a few stray hairs up under my headscarf. The aromas of festive cooking wafted toward me from our neighbors' kitchens. I opened the letter.

> My dearest and beloved sister,
>
> I'm writing to you in a hurry, for we are leaving. Not sure where I will be able to post this letter and hope it reaches you soon. Tomas decided we should move to Colorado where he will work in the coal mines there. They pay very high wages, and Tomas said he could earn a lot more money there than he can here. He didn't like this city. I hope he changes his mind, but you know me, I'll follow Tomas to the ends of the earth.
>
> There's much to share about my voyage on the ship, but I'll write more once we reach Colorado. I don't even know where Colorado is, except that it's in the mountains. I've always dreamed of living in the mountains. I'm very excited.
>
> Tomas said there was no time for me to tell Janos and Denny goodbye. The train leaves today. He left a letter explaining everything. Everything was rushed. He says we had to get there right away since he had a job lined up already.
>
> I hope you are happy for me.
> Your devoted sister,
> Aneta

How odd. Janos mentioned nothing in his letter about them moving. Maybe he mailed the letter before Aneta and Tomas left?

———

Six days later, Anton called us outside. "Come, hurry."

Maria and I pulled Little Jan and Ivan behind us as we hurried outside. I breathed in the St. Mikuláš Day morning air.

Anton pointed at two distant figures approaching. "They are here."

The figures didn't look familiar in their strange clothing, but as they neared, I realized they were Janos and Zdenko. I held my breath, and a nervous flutter rose in my heart. I clutched my jacket while Little Jan and I ran down the road. Zdenko ran toward us. I stopped to greet him, but he continued past us.

I kept my eyes on Janos.

"Papa!" Little Jan shouted. "Papa!" He broke away from me and ran ahead.

Janos scooped him up as I caught up with them.

"My goodness, you're getting too heavy for me." He gave a good-natured laugh and hugged Little Jan close.

I stopped a few feet short, panting. The sight filled me with joy.

When Janos put our son down, Little Jan threw his arms around his legs.

"Now, now, Little Jan, easy." He gently pulled Little Jan's arms from around his legs and looked at me. His eyes searched my face. Was he looking for my happiness?

"Mira," he said, voice low as he stretched out his hand.

I took a step forward, and another...then rushed into his

arms. His strong arms closed around me. Tears spilled down my cheeks, and I shook against his sturdy chest. Little Jan wrapped his arms about our legs. There were no words. Only our hearts spoke to each other.

Later, we all gathered in the big room. Maria sat in the room's corner near a lamp to mend clothes. The rest of us sat on the benches.

"The voyage over was like no other," Zdenko said.

"Tell us more, Zdenko," I said.

"Please, call me Denny," he said, kind but firm. He stood up straight and seemed taller. He carried himself and spoke more maturely than before he'd left.

"Yes, yes, the voyage over was quite an adventure. I was proud of Denny and how he held himself in America." Janos's eyes sparkled like his old self. He patted Denny on the back.

Denny hung his head, somewhat embarrassed, though he gave a small smile.

Janos continued, "On the train, we passed through countryside different from here, mountains, deserts, and many villages. By the time we arrived at Port Fiume, we were exhausted, though we still had to get a passport before we could board. It took almost two days of filling out forms and waiting because there were many of us traveling to America—mostly Slovaks, some Magyars, and Germans. There were more long lines to go through before we could board the ship. Remember the stories we heard from our friends who traveled a few years ago about how horrible the steerage conditions were?"

We all nodded.

"Well, it's called third class now, not steerage, and cleaner than expected, with more privacy. They used to house forty to fifty people in a single room. We bunked with four others in a cabin with a door. The communal rooms where everyone would gather made the air heavy and didn't smell good. Many had the seasickness, but not Denny and me. We tried to spend as much time as we could on the third-class deck. The ocean air was wonderful. Sometimes we went up there even during foul weather."

"Then I got sick," Denny said with a long face. "The doctor came around every day to check on us and said I had a fever. They worried I might be contagious. I was placed in a special room on the ship, and when we arrived in New York, they put me in a hospital on Ellis Island."

"Janos wrote us about it," Maria chimed in from her corner. "We were all very relieved you got well, my dear. Tell us about Ellis Island. Did you see the Statue of Liberty?"

"Yes, it was everything we had been told. She was impressive and quite the sight. I brought you postcards, instead of mailing, so you can frame them. Then there were the hours and hours standing in line. One by one, each person was verified, then examined by doctors. Even though Tomas and I had been examined on the ship because of Denny getting sick, we still had to go through the official examinations. It was tedious." Janos shook his head.

"What was New York like, Janos?" Anton asked.

"We didn't get to see much. I visited Denny each day. They put Tomas and me in a boarding house nearby, and once they released Denny, they provided transportation from the island to New York, where a bus took us to the train station for St. Louis." Janos pulled a pipe and a small pouch of tobacco from his shirt pocket and methodically filled the bowl. "All we saw of New York were very tall buildings and many people on the sidewalks. The streets were crowded with horses, carriages, and motorcars."

He lit the pipe and took a long draw before offering it to his father, who waved his hand and pulled out his own pipe. I hadn't seen my father-in-law smoke since Janos left. It was something they enjoyed together. The pipe smoke filled the room, enveloping us with its comforting aroma.

"What next, Janos?" asked Ivan, eyes wide.

He sat beside Janos on the bench, bumping Denny and causing him to fall to the floor. Denny pulled Ivan down off the bench, and they rolled on the straw-covered floor.

"You boys stop, now! Or you'll get the strap." shouted Anton. "I had forgotten how they can be together." He shot a glance at Maria, who just rolled her eyes.

I cringed at the possibility that the boys might be punished. Whenever that happened, I usually left the room. I kept silent and held Little Jan to make sure he didn't get caught up in their antics. Still, it was a delight to have a full house once again.

"Now, now, Denny, Ivan, that is enough." Janos yanked Ivan off Denny and plopped him down on the bench.

Denny stood up, his hair tousled, and his shirt pulled out of his pants. "That isn't fair. I was sitting there."

"Over here and be still." His father pointed to the space next to him. "Remember, you're the older brother, and we expect more maturity from you, especially now you've been working in the American factory."

Denny reluctantly sat down.

"So," Janos glared at Denny, "the train was a long ride to St. Louis. We couldn't afford a sleeping car, and we slept sitting up. We sat next to other Slovaks who had been there before, and they explained the towns and terrain we traveled through. I can't remember all the names. There were lots of mountains and trees, many bridges over the rivers we crossed."

Once Janos and Denny had finished sharing more of their journey, it was our turn to share news.

"I was surprised to hear that Tomas and Aneta moved to Colorado," I said.

Maria's eyes widened, and Anton frowned. Denny glanced at Janos.

"They left in a hurry, it seems." I faced Janos. "I wonder how they are doing in Colorado."

Janos shrugged, "It was unexpected and sudden." He averted his eyes.

I glanced at Denny, but he was focused on Ivan.

After the meal, and the table had been cleared, Janos took my hand. "Come with me. I want to reacquaint myself with everything. Papa said there have been some improvements with the money we sent."

I followed him outside, and we walked around the side of the cottage toward the henhouse and the barn.

"Here, see, we have many more chickens and a rooster, enough now to eat every week and plenty of eggs. And we planted a new plum tree." I pointed to the tree, and Janos stopped me.

"Never mind that, Mira. I only said I wanted to see the improvement for the benefit of my parents. We need to talk privately."

He led me inside the barn. He sat on a bale of hay and patted the space next to him.

"Jani, you look so serious. What is it?" I sat beside him, took his hand, and held it in my lap.

"It's about Tomas and your sister." He pulled his hand free.

"All right," I said slowly. "In her letter, she said Tomas left you a letter explaining everything about their move. What did it say?"

He jumped up and balled his hands into fists. "Letter, she said? There was no letter."

I flinched. "I don't understand."

"Either she lied to you, or he lied to her. When Tomas returned with Aneta from New York, instead of staying at

Vamos's, who had an extra room for them, they stayed in another apartment building down the street. A few days before Denny and I needed to leave to go to New York, I discovered the money I had hidden in our room was gone."

He raked a hand through his hair. "Thank God we already had our tickets, or I wouldn't be here. I went to confront him, but they had already left. No note or letter. I could have killed him." He paced the barn floor.

I stared in disbelief.

"I knew something wasn't right with him—constantly complaining about this and that, never satisfied, and then sending for Aneta so soon. He couldn't have saved enough money to have sent for her and then travel by train to Colorado. I should have put the money in the bank." He stopped and looked at me. "They are dead to me. They are dead to you, too."

I clutched my throat and choked out a cry. "No, Jani. It can't be true. How are you sure Tomas took the money?"

"He had a key."

I shook my head. "Even if you're right, I don't believe Aneta had any knowledge of Tomas's actions. Her letter says she didn't understand why they had to leave in such a rush. You know how she is. She trusts everyone, and to her, Tomas can do no wrong." I stood and stepped close. Light filtered from the tiny windows. His expression hadn't softened. "Please, can we keep this to ourselves? Let's not ruin *Vianoce*."

"Fine, tell your parents what you want. But you understand me. You are to have nothing to do with your sister or her husband. They are no longer our family."

"But, Jani—" I reached out to him.

He turned and strode out of the barn. I stared, numb. Could it be true? Had Tomas taken our money? Even if he hadn't, Janos believed it. Still, how could he demand that I turn on my sister?

I finally left the barn and caught sight of him walking through the fields, head down and shoulders hunched, fists still clenched. Either Janos had changed, or I was seeing a side of him I didn't know.

———

ŠTEDRÝ VEČER, THE BOUNTIFUL EVE OF CHRISTMAS, arrived. Anton and Janos hung the tree upside down from the rafters in the old tradition. The V-shape represented the Holy Trinity. We all decorated the tree together with tinsel and painted wood ornaments.

At dusk, my parents joined us, and we gathered in the living room. Maria gave each of us a bowl with bread, salt, and dried beans. Like every year, we went outside and slowly walked around the cottage and barn while placing dried beans in the cracks in the walls. Our parents chanted the ancient Slavic incantation to protect our buildings from fire. One day, Janos and I would lead the procession. Last, we gave the bread and salt to the animals and chickens to ensure their health in the coming year.

We returned to the cottage where we enjoyed our first big feast since Aneta's wedding to Tomas, over a year ago. I savored the aroma of the roast duck, a rare treat, along with a potato and cabbage casserole, and kolac, the same pastries we served at the wedding.

We sat around the table, waiting patiently for Anton to start. Anton broke off a piece of the *oplatky* and passed it to Maria. She broke off a piece and passed it to the next person while Anton said the Slovak Christmas Eve prayer.

"On this glorious feast of the birthday of Christ our Lord, I wish you all from God health, happiness, and abundant blessings. May it be yours to enjoy comfort from your children, salvation for your soul, the Kingdom of Heaven after death, and for the family's welfare, may you have whatever you ask of God."

Anton looked to Janos, and they got up, went to the larder, and pulled out a bottle of *slivovitza*. They filled a tiny glass for each of us, except for Ivan and Little Jan, who were too young for such a strong drink. We gave them watered-down plum wine.

We raised our glasses for the traditional toast of health and Merry Christmas.

"*Nazdravye! Veselé Vianoce!*" We shouted and took a sip.

The rest, we tossed onto the straw-covered floor, an ancient symbol of feeding the unknown gods. I always thought it interesting that we still practiced this pagan ritual, given that we had been Christians for hundreds of years.

After dinner, Mama and I cleared the table. The men stayed at the table, and Maria was occupied with Little Jan.

I longed to tell my mother about Aneta and Tomas but dared not with Janos present. He was busy talking with Anton. I would wait until he and Denny returned to America just to be safe.

We finished cleaning, then went back to the table. Janos smiled, and I clasped his hand. I loved him with all my heart, but his anger toward Aneta caused a void between us.

That night, in our bed, the electric passion that had always existed between us flared to life when he touched me. His heat consumed me as he drove into me with a possessiveness I'd never felt from him before. I bit back a cry of pleasure. How could I need his touch when anger filled my heart? I had thought to deny his affections. Instead, we were more drawn to each other with an intensity closer to lust than love, and we clung to each other as if this were our last day together.

At last, spent and sweating in the cold night air, we lay on our backs in the quiet. Once our breathing slowed, he rolled toward me and stroked my face, wet with tears of passion and sadness. His rough fingers traced the outline along my jaw, lips, and neck, then he kissed me lightly on my cheek, turned his back to me, and fell into a deep slumber.

I lay there, desperately wanting sleep to overtake me. My thoughts jumbled together with different conversations I'd had with Aneta, the argument with Janos in the barn, and the passionate lovemaking of that night. Finally, dawn came, and I dragged myself out of bed to begin another day.

Chapter Eight

January 1909

At the end of the month, Janos and Denny returned to America. The days prior had been amicable. Everyone acted normal—because no one knew the truth. But it was time to tell my parents about Tomas and the situation with Aneta. Filled with dread, I prayed my parents would give me the comfort I needed.

Outside, a light dusting of soft snow covered everything as I headed to my parents' cottage. I arrived fifteen minutes later and stopped inside the gate. I gazed at the plum tree, bare of leaves for the winter, and the garden where I would sit reading my favorite books. Even the mud-brick cottage with its faded, white-washed walls made my chest tighten with memories. I imagined myself and Aneta when we were little, running around the tree, laughing, and playing our silly girlish games. We talked of marriage and raising a family like every young Slovak girl. No one talked about all the hard work, the possibility of losing a child, or misunderstandings with husbands. I was twenty-four, and my child was five, but the girl inside me still lived.

I understood why I had been forced to live a life I hadn't chosen, but that didn't change the fact that Janos had abandoned us, and my anger surged.

How I missed Aneta. I needed to talk to her. Tears burned my eyes. Would I ever see her again? I couldn't—wouldn't—cut her off. Janos had chosen to go to America. I chose to write to Aneta.

Mama had just put the kettle on for tea when I entered. I removed my winter jacket and mittens and hung them on wall hooks. We sat at the table with Papa while I shared with them what Janos told me about Tomas and the money.

"Janos doesn't want me to speak to Aneta or Tomas."

"I don't believe it," Mama cried. "How can this be?" She wrung her hands.

"Tomas was always too impulsive, acting without thought," Papa muttered. The vein along his temple pulsed in a rare display of anger. "I understand how Janos feels, but he will calm down and be reasonable soon enough and eventually realize he is being too harsh against Aneta. He is smart and logical. Don't worry, Mira, all will work itself out."

Papa wrapped his arm around me and petted the top of my head like he used to do when I was little. Mama did the same, and the three of us embraced.

"Oh, Papa, Mamička, I can't do what he wants." Tears poured down my cheeks. I wiped them away. "God forgive me, but I will write Aneta." The kettle let out a loud whistle, and I jumped to my feet to make the tea, talking over my shoulder. "Janos didn't tell his parents what happened. He said I could tell you whatever I wanted, but I had to tell you the truth."

"My dear, I'm glad you did. This is very distressing news. I am worried about Aneta. We had no idea Tomas was the kind of person who would do something so deceitful and vile." Mama turned to Papa. "Should we do something?"

Papa shook his head. "It's best we keep the situation to ourselves. There isn't anything we can do, anyway. It's Janos's word against Tomas's. Why stir up trouble? If Janos tells his parents, that's up to him."

"What about Tomas's family? Since Aneta and Tomas left, I've seen little of them." I filled the cups with the tea and took them to the table.

"Neither have we." Mama gave me a sad smile and took the cup I offered her. "Next time we see them, we won't say a thing. We don't have any proof, anyway. Why make accusations? They have no control over Tomas—not that anyone ever did."

"Papa, something to drink?" I asked.

He took the cup and forced a small smile. "I agree with your mama. We keep this in the family."

———

A FEW WEEKS LATER, I RECEIVED A LETTER FROM Aneta, postmarked from Colorado.

February 1909

> *Dearest Mira,*
> *My hope is all the family had a happy Vianoce and your Janos and Denny arrived safely. I was sad to spend the holiday here in America, but Tomas did his best to raise my spirits. The job in the mines isn't what he expected. Each day, he comes home—if I can call our tiny room at the*

boarding house home—exhausted and filthy from the coal dust. The money is a little better than what he made in St. Louis, though not what he imagined either. We are saving to rent a place just for us and the baby. Yes, I am with child! I am excited but wish you were here to help me through my first time. I'm lonely for you, Mamička, Papa, and your Little Jan. He must be growing up fast.

Please write soon with all the news. Though the way Tomas is talking, we might not be here for long. He is too restless and impulsive, but you know that. He has been talking about working in the vineyards of California. I hope we don't move again. I long for stability and a nice home for our family.

Your loving sister,
Aneta

I was happy for her, but I worried about how a child might affect Tomas's changing moods. And they might move again? My disappointment in Tomas not providing stability for my sister and their coming child weighed heavy on my heart. Our husbands' desires had forever changed both our circumstances. I had given much thought to those changed circumstances since Janos left. I didn't feel married.

I looked over at Maria, deep in her own thoughts as she carded wool. Ivan and his father tended to the animals outside. Little Jan had tagged along, aspiring to be like his Uncle Ivan. He didn't ask about his father much. Little Jan clung to Ivan and his dedko for his role models. Anger bubbled up in me again. Janos should be the role model for his son.

I lived the traditional Slovak family life with my husband's family. I had always dreamed of having my own home, and Janos had the same dream. He'd gone to America to make enough money for us to buy land and build a house. Buying land would cost much more than building another house on his parents' land, as other families had done. But every day he was gone, our dream seemed further and further away. I longed for Janos to return home and resume our life. He hadn't said when we would have enough money or when he would come home for good.

Chapter Nine

September 1909

I ENTERED MY PARENTS' COTTAGE WITH MY RECENT letter from Janos. Mama stopped cutting vegetables at the table and gave me a worried look. I held the letter up, gave it a little wave in the air, then dropped onto a seat on the bench opposite her.

"Mira, what's wrong?"

"I just received this letter from Janos. Do you want to read it?"

"No, dear. That is between the two of you," Mama said. "But I would like to know if he still mentions the problem between him and Tomas."

"No. But his letters have changed some. His tone is different. I can feel the distance between us grow. Does that make sense?" I pressed a hand to my heart.

"It makes sense. I feel it from our Aneta, too. Sometimes I think she is keeping something from us." She moved to sit beside me, pulled a letter from her pocket, and put it in my hand. "This came for you yesterday when I picked up our mail."

"From Aneta? How wonderful. Did she send you one, too?"

"She did, in the same envelope, like you told her to do. It was a very nice letter. But she doesn't say much about Tomas or how they are getting along. It worries me. When she first went over, her letters were filled with her energy and excitement of a new life there. Now, she sounds...I don't know, disillusioned?" The corners of her mouth drooped.

"I've thought the same thing. And here, I am keeping something from her, and it's difficult writing like everything is fine to both Aneta and Janos. I hate it."

"There, there, my darling, things will find a way to work themselves out. I continue to pray for a happy outcome for Aneta and you." She stroked my arm. "Remember why Janos is in America? He is working hard to improve all our lives. You know the Slovak saying, 'No reward without effort.'"

"You are right." I scanned Aneta's letter. "It is brief as well." I folded the two letters together and stuffed them in my pocket.

We hugged each other, and I returned to my in-laws' cottage.

———

THE SUMMER HAD BEEN UNUSUALLY DRY AFTER THE harvest, and our rain barrels were low. We planned a trip to the Tisza River to fill the barrels and make a picnic of the chore. River water wasn't as good as rainwater, but it was better than no water. Maria and I prepared food to take with us, and the men loaded the two-wheeled wood cart with the water jugs. Anton pulled the cart since we didn't have a horse or donkey.

"Papa, can I please help pull the cart today?" Ivan asked.

"When we return, the cart will be much heavier, and then we can pull it together."

Ivan smiled and pulled the brim of his hat down over his eyes. He walked alongside his father while Maria, Little Jan, and I followed behind the cart. White fluffy clouds floated lazily against a brilliant blue sky. A soft breeze kept us cool. We waved to a few neighbors along the road and sang Slovak songs as we walked.

Once we reached the river, we found a perfect dry, flat spot under a big shady tree away from the riverbank. Tall shade trees and dense vegetation stood along the river, and yellow and purple irises dotted the ground.

Maria spread out a large quilt over the thick, wild grass and secured the corners with stones. "It's so lovely here, Mira. Why do we not come more often?" she asked.

"We work too hard and worry too much. We need more joy in our lives. I love it here." The wind picked up, and I tightened my headscarf. The rich smell of mud and algae from the river made my nose twitch.

"Yes, we all need more joy." She nodded and placed the baskets of food on the blanket.

I watched Anton, Ivan, and Little Jan working together at the water's edge to fill the jugs. "Little Jan, don't wander off. We'll eat soon," I called out.

"Yes, Mama," he shouted back.

Anton pulled Little Jan over to him. I couldn't hear his words, but he had a stern look. Little Jan turned away and sulked.

"Come, eat now." Maria waved them over.

They loaded the filled jugs back onto the cart and joined us on the quilt. We had salted meats, jars of fruit jam, rye bread, and soft-cooked eggs. We even had a little wine. I leaned back on an elbow and smiled at the boys fussing in the good-natured way they did. I knew they loved each other.

"Little Jan, are you eager to start school next month?" Maria took a bite from a thick slice of bread covered in a layer of soft butter.

"Yes, Baba, and I will be six too!" He grinned and picked up the small ball he brought to play catch with Ivan.

"Not for a couple of months. Soon, though," I corrected.

At twelve, Ivan grew taller every day. He would grow to be as tall as Janos. Anton wanted to pull him out of school to work in the fields because his brothers were gone. That saddened me. Aneta and I were fortunate that our parents allowed us to finish high school. Poor Ivan didn't have the same learning opportunity.

Ivan got up, grabbed the ball from Little Jan, and ran a few yards away. "Here, catch." Ivan tossed the ball.

The ball fell through Little Jan's fingers, bouncing on the grass. He laughed, scooped it up, and threw it at Ivan.

"Silly, you throw funny," Ivan taunted.

"I do not." Little Jan stomped his foot on the ground.

Ivan grabbed the ball again and ran off into the bushes. Little Jan followed.

"Stay close by, you two," I called to them.

Maria and I cleaned up and packed everything in the cart. It was time to head back to our home before it grew dark. I looked around and didn't see Little Jan or Ivan.

"Now, where are they?" I looked at Maria, and she shrugged. "Anton, where are the boys?"

"They were just here." He looked around, then walked down to the water's edge and looked up and down the riverbank. "Jan. Ivan. Come!" He shouted.

No response. He ventured farther down the shore.

Moments later, Ivan burst through the bushes to the left of us. "Papa! Papa! It's Little Jan. Come quick!" He halted beside his father. Water soaked his clothes and hair.

I ran over to Anton and Ivan. "Where is he?" I grabbed Ivan's shoulders.

Ivan looked from his father to me. "I tried to get to him, but the current was too fast."

"The current? He's in the river?" I choked out the words.

Anton and I exchanged a look, then he spun and raced along the shore. I released Ivan and frantically looked across the fast-moving water.

"I'm sorry. Aunt Mira, I was looking for that dumb ball in the bushes. When I found it, Little Jan was already in the water." He sobbed. "I jumped in after him, but—"

Maria reached us. "Ivan, you're soaking wet. What happened?"

He stumbled over his words and repeated his story. She tried to calm him, but the fear on her face mirrored my panic. I turned and ran to the shore where Anton waded into the water. Once neck deep, he swam with the current. I hurried along the shore, scanning the water for my boy.

"Anton, be careful!" Maria shouted behind me.

My heart beat a wild rhythm. I couldn't see Little Jan in the river. Dear God, where could he be? I watched helplessly while the current swept Anton out of sight. Bootfalls crunched on the rocky bank behind me, and I whirled to find two men—Hungarian, judging from their attire—approaching.

"Is there something wrong?" one demanded as they neared.

"Yes! My little boy is out there." I pointed to the river. "He can't swim. My father-in-law went into the river to find him, but we lost sight of him. Please help us."

"Do you see him?" the one asked as they reached me.

I shook my head.

"Where did the boy go in?" he demanded.

"Downstream from here."

They looked at one another, nodded, then took off at a run along the bank.

I hurried after them until I caught sight of them not far from where Anton's head bobbed up and down in the water before he disappeared around a bend. The men raced after him.

"Ivan! Come back here right now!" Maria shouted.

I glanced back to see Ivan running toward me. When he neared, I grabbed for his arm, but it was no use; he sped past. I broke into a run, stumbled, caught myself, and picked up speed.

"Ivan," I shouted. "Come back."

He ignored me.

"Anton! Little Jan!" I shouted.

"Mira, wait for me," Maria called.

I kept running. "Little Jan!" I shouted. "Ivan."

No answer. Tears spilled from my eyes. The sun had dropped low on the horizon, and the sky turned blue gray, streaked with orange and yellow. We had to find Little Jan before darkness fell.

"Mira." Maria caught up and grasped my hand, and I squeezed hers as a moan released from deep within me.

We slumped to the ground, huddled together in silence. The minutes dragged on, and I couldn't see any of the men.

Voices floated toward us. I raised my head from my silent prayers, and Maria let out a gasp. We jumped up as four figures came toward us along the riverbank. One man was carrying something...someone.

"My boy?" I whispered. "No!" I raced toward them.

Anton laid Little Jan on the ground as I reached them. Ivan was crying and tried to cling to Little Jan. His father pulled him away as I sank to my knees beside my son. I hugged his cold body to my breast. He was so still. Hot tears streamed down my face as I rocked him back and forth. I rocked harder to will him back to life.

"He can't be dead." I brushed the wet locks from his face. "God, please, I beg of you, please bring him back to me," I shouted at the sky.

I hugged him close until the sun dipped nearly below the horizon, and I began to shiver.

I jumped when Anton touched my shoulder.

"It's nearly dark. We must take him home," Anton said.

I shook my head and sobbed harder. Anton lowered onto one knee and met my gaze. The sorrow in his eyes mirrored my own. I never realized how much he loved his grandson until that moment. Still soaked, he reached for Little Jan.

"No!" I shrieked and turned away.

When Anton finally wrenched his small body from me, I clutched at Little Jan's clothes. Maria helped me up from the ground and wrapped her shawl around me. She kept her arm around me as we followed Anton, Ivan, and the two Hungarians. Once at the cart, they laid him on the quilt from the picnic, which seemed like eons ago. I trembled. Maria put her arms around me, and her tears fell on my face when she kissed my cheeks. My mind was in a fog. I stumbled through until we reached home, and someone urged me to change my clothes and get into bed. It wasn't until Maria tucked a blanket around me that sleep took over.

———

MAMA ARRIVED THE NEXT MORNING AND SAT ON THE side of my bed. "Please, sweetheart, you need to help us prepare Little Jan." She stroked my cheek.

I turned away, and tears came again. "I can't, I just can't."

"You will regret it later. Come." She took my hand and gently pulled.

I yanked my hand from her. "I can't look at him, if he is really dead."

"This is why you must participate in the ritual. It will help you accept your loss, and you need to know how for when it is time for your papa and me."

"Don't talk about that," I whispered. "I've lost two babies. I can't bear the thought of losing you, too."

Maria came to the doorway. "Is she coming out?"

Mama stood. "Not yet, hopefully later. Mira, I'll come again for you to help with the food preparation. You rest now." She crossed to the door and closed it with a soft click.

WHEN MAMA RETURNED LATER, I FORCED MYSELF out of bed and helped prepare the food for our guests. Then I went to lie on my bed and cried. When the guests arrived to pay their respects, my parents came into my room.

"My darling child, please come back out and be with the rest of the family," Mama pleaded.

"Why?" I shot back. "I lost a son, not them."

They looked at one another.

"Come be with us, Mira. You shouldn't be alone." Papa sat on the edge of the bed and held my hand.

I pulled my hand away and turned my back to them. "Leave me alone." My voice didn't sound like mine. It sounded dead, like my son.

My husband was thousands of miles away, and my only son, my heart, was gone. What remained for me? Little Jan's beautiful face rose in memory, his cheerful voice and giggles, his thick auburn hair, and even his stubbornness. He was much like his father. My stomach twisted.

I needed my husband. He should have been here. Would Little Jan have died if Janos were still with us? I dragged myself up from the bed and went to the tiny table in the room's corner next to Little Jan's bed. My heart thumped. I sat and pulled out a sheet of paper to write a letter to Jani.

> *Dear Jani,*
>
> *It's with the heaviest of hearts I must write to you that our beautiful son drowned in the river two days ago. We were having a picnic, and he and Ivan ran off to play. I told him to stay nearby, but he didn't listen. He went into the river, and before Ivan realized, the current swept Little Jan away. Ivan tried to save him but failed. He isn't to blame.*
>
> *I blame you! For not being here. For deserting your family. Little Jan would still be alive if you had never left. And now I must suffer this grief alone. I don't know how I will ever forgive you.*
>
> *This isn't the life I wanted. We need you here. I need you here. I'm heartbroken, not just for Little Jan, but for our marriage. It doesn't feel real anymore. I don't care about the money. I would rather suffer here, with you, than without you.*
>
> *That is all.*
>
> *Mira*

I handed the letter to Mama when she and Papa left to return home. I avoided looking at Maria and Anton. My letter would hurt Janos deeply, but I didn't care.

———

A few days after Little Jan died, I had another dream about the little girl. Little Jan was there, too, in the garden outside our cottage. The brilliant light intensified the colors of the flowers and the vivid green of the leaves. Little Jan, dressed all in black, stood under the plum tree, looking at the blooms of white flowers with red centers. He walked over to the bench near the tree and sat with a little girl with light reddish-brown curls, who also wore black. I had thought her Karin from the first dream. They started playing the hand-patting game, laughing and smiling, looking very happy. They didn't notice me. I wanted to get closer, but I remained frozen in place. I could only watch. I tried to reach out to them, to call out, but I couldn't speak. Slowly, they faded away.

Suddenly, the dream changed to an unfamiliar place with a wood-fenced, wood-floored enclosure with lots of plants in clay pots. A feeling of joy overcame me when I noticed three children, a girl and two boys, sitting and playing in the corner. I didn't recognize them. The girl looked a year or two older than the two boys, who were about seven or eight years old. She was very pretty with straight dark hair that fell to her shoulders and brown eyes lined with long lashes. Her coloring reminded me of my *Baba*, whom I barely remembered. Mama had told me about her. The girl looked up and stared directly at me with a steady gaze. She perked up like she recognized me, then she gave me a brilliant smile and waved.

Then I woke up.

The room was shrouded in darkness, and it must have been very early in the morning. My heart beat quickly. I lay there thinking about the two dreams and tried to calm myself as soft slivers of light slowly filtered through the shutters. I felt certain the first dream was about Little Jan and Karin together in Heaven. I covered my mouth with my hand and shuddered a sob of joy. I quickly blinked away tears and gave thanks for the small sense of peace. I didn't need to worry about them.

But I needed to talk to Zelda about the second dream.

———

"WHAT AN INTERESTING DREAM," SAID ZELDA, AS she placed a cup of tea for me on her dining room table. "It reminds me of a similar dream my mother told me about when I was young." She tapped her finger on her temple, as though she was thinking back.

"Oh? What did hers mean?" I scooted my chair closer to the table and sipped the hot tea.

Zelda sat across from me, took a sip from her cup, and looked at me intensely. "Her dream was of two children she did not recognize, a boy and a girl. The boy was in black, and the girl was older but dressed in a bright blue dress. My mother learned shortly after the dream that she was pregnant, but the child was born dead."

Fear crept up my spine, but I managed to say, "I am sorry."

"It happens to many of us, just like you. But she got pregnant again within the next year, and it was a girl. She believed it was me, because when I got older, she said I looked very much like the little girl in her dream."

"So, you think the three children in my dream are my future children too?"

"I do, my dear." She reached across the table and patted my hand. "It's a blessing, to be sure."

"Then where was the place? What does it mean?"

"I don't know. These aren't regular dreams. These are dreams of your future. You will find out eventually."

I believed her. However, the idea of having three more children concerned me. I loved the two children I'd lost with all my heart, but my fear of pregnancy sent my heart into a gallop.

Chapter Ten

Late November 1909

I SAT IN THE BIG ROOM OF MY PARENTS' COTTAGE, embroidering to pass the time. My life had transformed. I no longer felt a part of Janos's family. With him in America and Little Jan buried, I had moved back in with my parents. My mother and father-in-law didn't want me to leave, but they understood. My parents needed me, too, and they embraced me back into the household.

Things were different from before I married, however. Aneta was gone. I wrote her a letter about what happened to Little Jan, and she wrote back right away, saying how sad she was for my loss. Her life in Colorado was busy with her new baby boy. They had named him James, an American version of Jakob, after Tomas's father. It seemed strange to me. Where I had lost a son, Aneta gained a son. She hadn't mentioned more about a move to California for months. I assumed Tomas had settled into the coal mining work. I wanted to be happy for her, but grief came easily those days.

There had been no word from Janos since I sent the

terrible letter blaming him for Little Jan's death. Maria told me they heard from him, but she didn't tell me what he'd said. Without a doubt, my last letter had hurt him. I regretted my words but wasn't ready to apologize.

Mama returned from town, her arms full of parcels. I jumped up to help.

"I stopped in at the Notary's office. He was his usual snide self. I wish they would do something about him." She let me help her put the parcels on the table. "Here is a letter for you from Janos." She removed the letter from her pocket and held it out to me.

My breath caught, and I hesitated. Did I want to read it? Would he chastise me for my terrible letter to him?

"Thank you, Mama."

I bundled up against the cold and went to sit on the bench in the garden. I studied the envelope. For a farmer and laborer, Janos had nice handwriting. I remembered watching him write, slow and careful, to make each letter perfect, just like he was at everything: diligent, determined, and hardworking. Tears blurred my vision. I wiped them away with the back of my gloved hand. He was a man. He was doing what he thought best for our family, and I blamed him. Realizing how much I missed him, I tore open the letter.

Dearest Mira,

I needed time to grasp all you had written in your letter. I understand why you feel the way you do. Life has been hard on you for the past two years. I'm sorry about that, for the loss you feel. I feel it too. You know why I came to America. It has not been easy for me.

I won't be going home for Vianoce this year.

*Instead of buying tickets, I will send you the
money. It's the best for now.*

*It broke my heart, losing our Little Jan. Tell
Ivan I don't blame him. Please forgive me.*

I love you.

Janos

I stared at his words. His not coming home for Vianoce was the last thing I had expected. Papa came around the corner of the cottage wearing his sheepskin cape. He nodded to me and continued inside. I followed him in and waited for him to remove his cape and fur hat, then I removed my jacket and gloves and leaned against the door. Mama worked in the kitchen area, preparing the evening supper. Papa washed up and sat in the rocker to read the newspaper Mama had brought him from the village, one of the extra splurges allowed with the money Janos sent us.

"He's not coming home," I whispered.

"What did you say, Mira?" Mama asked, not stopping what she was doing.

"I said"—I cleared my throat—"Janos isn't coming home for the holy season."

Papa looked up from his paper. "Well, I suppose it's his way of coping." His mouth twitched, and he returned his attention to the paper. "Not the best decision, in my opinion."

"It is my fault. I pushed him away." I dropped onto the bench near the doorway.

"What do you mean? How could you possibly push him away?" Mama wiped her hands on her apron, then came over to the bench and sat beside me. She put her arm around me, and I sobbed into her shoulder.

"*Miláčik?* Darling, what happened?"

"I wrote awful things to him, blaming him for Little Jan

because he wasn't here. Anger overcame me, and I wanted to hurt him, like how he hurt me last year about Aneta."

"There, there, don't fret. You were distraught with grief." She held my face in her hands and kissed my cheeks. "It will all work itself out in time."

"How can you be kind to me? I'm a terrible wife, and he isn't coming home. How can it work itself out? Maybe he'll never come home again."

Mama pulled a handkerchief from her skirt pocket and dabbed away my tears.

Papa put down his paper and looked over at us. "These past two years have been very hard on you, Mira. On Janos, too. I agree with your mother. Give it some time. He'll come around. You're his wife. He loves you very much, and he is a responsible, committed man. Trust in that, my daughter."

"You may be right, but I'm very ashamed."

Mama stood and took my hand. "Come."

I stood, and she guided me over to where Papa sat. He got up and gave me a gentle hug.

In a soft voice, she said, "Let's say a prayer of healing for our family, and for Janos and his family."

We held hands and said a few blessings. I said a special prayer to heal my marriage.

Chapter Eleven

February 1910

Vianoce came and went without Janos. I held onto my anger. Despite my guilt over my terrible accusations, I hadn't apologized, and there had been only a couple of perfunctory letters between us. Every Sunday, when we went to church, I visited the graves of Little Jan and his sister Karin. Each week seemed the same until I received surprising news from Janos and Denny.

> *Dear Mira,*
> *I don't know how much you may already know*
> *from my parents, but I wanted to tell you. Denny*
> *is getting married. She's a nice young Slovak girl*
> *he met at St. Lucas Lutheran. Her name is Marta*
> *Nagy. She's eighteen, and her family is from*
> *Budapest. They came over ten years ago. Her*
> *father works in the same factory as Denny and*

me. He's a supervisor and has done well here.

This means Denny will stay in America. I know this will surprise you as it did me. The boy is in love, and I'm happy for him. The wedding will be in April, and they want it American-style. We wish all of you could be here for the ceremony but will send photos. Denny and Marta will live with her parents. Marta works at a sewing factory. That isn't traditional. Our people here are changing, adapting to the American life. I try not to change. Our traditions mean too much to me, but I have learned the language and how to write it a little. It's necessary to protect myself from unjust treatments many here experience.

Other than that, all is the same here.

I miss you.

With Love,

Janos

Denny was getting married? He was only seventeen. I wanted him to be happy. Still, it was difficult to accept because I had lost yet another member of our family.

I looked up at my parents, my expression twisted in a mix of joy and worry.

"What is it?" Papa asked.

"Zdenko...Denny...he's getting married. He's decided to stay in America with his new bride."

Papa gave away no emotion, as if thinking on the news.

"We need to make him a wedding gift. A good, traditional Slovak gift to remind him of home," I said.

"The farm is doing well. We can set some money aside," Papa said.

"Mamička, what if Janos stays, too?" I asked.

"Janos loves you. He would not just leave you for America," she said.

"After everything, I just don't know."

"Janos is a good man, he'll come home, you'll see," Papa said.

I took another look at the letter. My heart leaped to hear Janos missed me, and his *"With Love"* gave me hope we would mend our anger, and he would come home soon. But what if he decided to stay with Denny?

———

THE POSSIBILITY OF JANOS STAYING IN AMERICA haunted me, and I often returned to memories of Little Jan. I needed to get my mind on something else. I hadn't attended the women's sewing circle in some time. The next time was to be at the Sterba's cottage. Anna, Vamos's wife, and her three children lived with Vamos's parents.

Mama, Maria, and I went together. The Sterbas's cottage looked similar to ours, but they had added two small rooms to the main big room, which was a little larger than ours. They decorated it with brightly colored embroidered pillows, wall hangings, and tablecloths. The sweet smell of *cukrík*, a candy made with nuts, filled the air, something I hadn't had in a long time. There were other delicious foods for us to snack on with our tea when we would break from our sewing.

Everyone greeted each other with kisses on the cheeks and brief hugs. I sat next to Mama, and Maria sat on the other side of her. Ten of us women filled the room with chatter. I listened, glad to be doing something normal, and wondered if there would be an announcement.

Some brought their children to play with Anna's children in an adjacent room, and the cheerful laughter made me think of my sweet Little Jan and Karin. Anna's twelve-year-old daughter watched over the other children. Anna and her mother-in-law joined the circle on the other side of the room from us.

We settled and went to work on our embroidery projects. The excited chatter dulled to scattered conversations about the projects. Eventually, Anna cleared her throat to gain our attention. We all quieted and waited for her to speak.

"I have important news to share with you all." She looked around the room, then paused to look at me for a moment. "Vamos is coming home in a couple of months...for good."

My heart fluttered. If Vamos is coming back, would Janos? Cries of congratulations and questions filled the room. Anna's smile appeared forced.

"You must be thrilled, Anna," I said over the excitement.

She nodded, said a few words to the two ladies next to her, then came over and squeezed in beside me on the bench. "I wondered if Janos had written to you about his return," she said in a low voice.

"Why, no, he hasn't. We just received a letter from him that his brother is engaged. He said nothing about Vamos. I was going to mention the engagement today, but your news takes priority."

"How wonderful about Denny! Then he is staying in America?"

"Yes, his bride-to-be lives there with her parents. They have been there quite a while, I believe."

"I understand." She paused and looked up at the ceiling, then looked at me. "Vamos misses the land. He is tired of factory work, and he is coming back. But...I am concerned."

"What is there to be concerned about? Your husband will be home and with you again." I smiled to hide my jealousy.

Anna whispered, "We have become accustomed to the extra money. Without it, we won't be able to buy the things this farm can't produce. Don't misunderstand, I am very happy Vamos is coming home. It has been difficult without him. As it is for you, too, I'm sure, especially with the loss of your Little Jan." She gave my hand a gentle squeeze.

My heart constricted. "Thank you, that is very nice of you. I miss Janos and look forward to seeing him next Vianoce." I couldn't speak of Little Jan, nor could I tell her of my fear that Janos might stay in America. "By the way, Anna, did Vamos ever mention any bad treatment he and other Slovaks experienced there?"

"Oh, that? He's mentioned it. I guess no matter where Slovaks go, we must suffer prejudice." She sighed in resignation.

"I see. That is disappointing." Denny must not be bothered with the treatment if he chose to marry and build a life there. What about Janos?

Anna nodded and returned to her seat to resume her sewing.

First, Denny stays in America, and now Vamos is leaving. How was all this affecting Janos? I couldn't ask him in a letter when—or if—he was returning home. With Little Jan gone, was I enough to bring him back home?

Chapter Twelve

March 1910

THE PLANTING SEASON FOR POTATOES ARRIVED MID-
March, and the corn would be planted in April. For as long as
I could remember, Papa always hired out at least one migrant
worker. Goran had worked for Papa in previous years. Goran
was a striking man with dark, wavy hair and gray eyes. He
came for the planting and, sometimes later in the year, for the
harvest. I had only met him in passing.

Goran arrived early the first morning of work and spent
the day with Papa in the fields. Mama made a special place for
him to sleep in the barn. I was watching out the window when
Papa and Goran approached the courtyard. They slapped their
clothes to loosen the dust from the fields, then washed their
hands in a bucket of water by the door.

Mama greeted them at the door. We all sat down, and Papa
said a short grace. Mama served the soup from the large tureen
in the middle of the table and sat next to me. Goran gave me a
brief look and a nod before grabbing a spoonful of soup.

Papa glanced at him, then me. "Goran, you remember my daughter, Mira? She is living here with us now." Papa gestured toward me while he spooned soup into his mouth with loud slurps.

I looked up and smiled. Butterflies fluttered around in my stomach.

"Yes, I remember. Dobrý deň, Pani Lacko." He smiled, addressing me as a married woman.

"Dobrý deň, Pán Sabol," I responded and returned my attention to my food.

What was the matter with me? Like all the farmers in our community, he was soft spoken with sun-darkened skin but was still somewhat light. Like Janos, he was older than me by several years.

"So formal, you two," said Papa.

"You may call me Goran," Goran said.

"And you may call me Mira," I offered.

Papa chuckled.

"Your husband is still working in America?" he asked.

I kept my head down but could still feel his eyes on me. "Yes," I replied.

I dared not look at him, wondering what my parents were thinking. I peeked at each of them, and they were busy with their meal, seemingly unaware of Goran's staring.

"Is your son visiting with your husband's family now?" he asked.

I dropped my spoon and shot a look at Mama.

She looked up sharply and spoke for me. "Goran, I'm sorry, you don't know...Little Jan was taken by God last September. It was a swimming accident."

That was one way to put it. *Thank you, Mama.*

His face went ashen. "I'm very sorry for your loss. Please forgive my ignorance. I should not ask a lot of questions."

Papa winced with embarrassment. "I'm sorry, Goran. I should have told you."

We sat in awkward silence until the meal was done and the men returned to the fields. Mama and I cleaned up the dishes side by side.

"I should handle these kinds of situations better by now," I said.

"You will, dear. You will. It takes time." She gave my shoulder a gentle squeeze.

THE NEXT MORNING, I WAS FEEDING THE CHICKENS in the courtyard when Goran approached from the barn.

"Dobré ráno, Mira," he said, bright and cheerful.

His voice glided across my skin like warm butter. When he raised his arm to take off his hat, his scent wafted toward me. I found it familiar. The butterflies returned, and I shifted uncomfortably. "Uh...d-dobré ráno, Goran." Why did I stutter like a child? I was completely unnerved.

"I'm sorry about yesterday." He met my eyes squarely. "Did I upset you by my prying?"

"No need to apologize. You didn't know." I went back to tossing crumbs and seeds onto the ground.

"My wife and I lost a child a few years ago. I know how you must feel."

I stopped and side-eyed him. "You did? A boy?"

"A girl. She was only two years old. Sick with fever."

My chest tightened. "I lost a girl last year, stillborn." We gazed at each other with the shared pain of losing a child. But there was something more, an electric charge pulsing in the air between us.

He reached out to me, then withdrew his hand. An ache I hadn't realized existed ran through my body. How I longed for a man's comfort. I shivered.

He frowned. "Are you all right?"

"I'm fine."

He studied me, eyes gentle but insistent. "If you like, I could help with your morning chores tomorrow."

"No," I blurted to halt the *yes* on the tip of my tongue. I winced. The word had come out harsh. I shook my head and added gently, "I will manage."

The light in his eyes dimmed, and he gave a small, formal nod, then turned away. I watched his retreat. Why had I been so rude? I had sent him off as if he were nothing. I was foolish to think his offer was intended as anything but helpful.

I quickly gathered the eggs, then headed for the cottage. At the door, I paused and looked over my shoulder, but of course, Goran was no longer in sight. After all, why would he have lingered?

I went inside. Mama had stopped cutting potatoes on the big table. She gave me an odd look. "What were you talking about with Goran out there? You look flushed."

I put my hands to my warm cheeks. "Am I? It must be from the sun." I crossed to the table and set the eggs beside the bowl with the potatoes. "Oh, he was just apologizing for his questions yesterday. It was nothing," I said, trying to sound casual.

"How nice of him. He is a family man. Lost his farm a few years ago and had to work for others to keep his family fed."

"He mentioned they lost a little girl two years ago," I murmured.

She nodded slowly. "I remember him telling me last year. They have three other children, I believe." Mama finished the potatoes and put them in the soup pot of boiling stock on the stove burner. The steam rose in a small cloud.

"Three children? He didn't say. I guess they are blessed, despite losing the farm."

My voice steadied, yet my mind raced. I had only ever desired Janos, and I thought I had experienced every emotion and passion with him. Why, then, did Goran confuse and intrigue me?

Chapter Thirteen

May 1910

WE HELD A BIG FAMILY GATHERING AT THE LACKO
cottage to celebrate Denny's and Marta's marriage locally.
Family and friends came to congratulate Anton and Maria and
to see the wedding photos Denny sent. Maria did a beautiful
job of preparing everything with the help of her sister Agata.
Her presence eased my guilt over leaving Maria to be with my
family.

I inhaled the divine aroma of the roast duck and kolac
sweets in the cottage. With the additional money Janos and
Denny had sent home to their parents, Maria prepared some
bryndzové halušky, soft potato dumplings with a rich sauce of
sheep's milk cheese, and *kapustnica*, a soup made from sauerkraut and klobasa. Another dessert was the *orechovník*, a delicious, sweet walnut roll. Too much food—but it was a
wedding feast.

The room burst with the blues, reds, and greens of our
community. Everyone dressed in their krojes. Mama and I
wore our festive embroidered dresses. To commemorate the

occasion, we wore new, handmade white headscarves with elaborate, brightly colored embroidery.

Mama made Papa a new wool vest in a lovely rust color with embroidery down the front and the opening lined with tiny metal buttons that went over the wide-cuffed white shirt. He wore his usual boots and black felt hat.

Janos's uncles and families arrived from a neighboring village. We all sat on the benches against the walls, with the big table off to one side covered with Maria's best tablecloth, embroidered in blues and greens. We left the center of the room open for dancing. The clamor of voices lifted my mood, and for the first time in a long while, I relaxed.

I sat with Mama chatting with a neighbor lady who lived near Maria and Anton, when a woman's high-pitched voice called across the room. "Mira!"

Janos's Aunt Agata bustled over to me, a very plump woman with a crooked nose.

Mama and I stood.

"Aunt Agata, it's nice to see you again. It's been since...Aneta's wedding, I think. I hope you have been well." Being pleasant to her was always difficult. But I showed her the respect I was taught to give to my elders.

We gave each other quick kisses on the cheeks. Aside from her prominent nose that she poked into everyone's business, she looked a lot like Maria.

"My dear Mira, we were sorry to hear of your loss. Our hearts go out to you. Little Jan was a darling child." She gave a wan smile and an exaggerated tilt of her head. "We would have liked to have been at the service, but it all happened very fast. We didn't know in time to make it here." Her tone had a sarcastic edge, and she thrust out her lower lip in a pout.

I stiffened.

"Agata, only the immediate family was at the service."

Mama put her arm around me. "There was no time to notify everyone. I'm sure you understand."

Was that condescension in her voice? The desire to laugh forestalled the tears that always came when I thought of Little Jan.

I squared my shoulders and tried to look strong. "Thank you, Aunt. It has been hard without him and Janos. Life goes on, yes?"

"You sound strong. Listen to you." She clasped her hands.

"I think it's time for Anton to say a few words," I blurted.

"Yes, yes, you are right. I'm thrilled to be here today to share in *this* celebration." She waved a hand and returned to where her husband stood across the room.

Mama and I sat back down on the bench. She gave me an understanding smile.

Anton held up one hand to hush everyone while he gripped a letter from Denny in his other hand. "Thanks to all of you for coming today for this joyous occasion. I know we all would have wanted to attend my son Zdenko's wedding. We call him Denny. He has become quite the Slovak-American." He opened the letter. "This letter is from Denny with help from his bride, Marta. Denny was not always the best writer." He chuckled.

Maria looked toward Anton with her head tilted down, her face reddened with embarrassment as he read.

To all our family and friends in our homeland,
We are very happy to share with you our
wedding photos. We wish you could have been here
with us. It was a wonderful wedding at St. Lucas
Lutheran Church, where we met less than a year
ago. Marta's family provided the flowers and food,

prepared by many in her family. They immigrated over ten years ago from outside of Budapest. I'm fortunate to be a part of their family. My brother Janos was my best man, and Marta's sister, Lora, was her maid of honor.

As you can see in the photos, we are very American now, wearing traditional wedding clothes. I'm wearing my new suit in the Western fashion, and Marta's dress is all white lace over silk.

Anton paused, and Maria passed the photos around the room. Many *oohs* and *aahs* drifted up, and I understood why when the photos came to me. I wasn't sure I liked the plain, solid white wedding dress. The Americans must not like colorful clothes.

Mama handed me the next photo, and my breath caught. Janos stood alongside Denny in his American suit, a white rose in his lapel. His hair was parted in the middle with some kind of pomade that greased it down almost flat. I didn't like that, but he still sent my heart into an erratic pattern. How could I hate and love a person at the same time?

Denny also looked very handsome standing next to Marta. The maid of honor, Marta's pretty younger sister, Lora, stood next to Janos. An alien twinge of jealousy caught me off guard. I heard Lora was only fourteen, but seeing my husband photographed with any other girl or woman hit me like a dagger to the heart.

Lora's hair was styled the same as Marta's, very puffy on the top and sides. No headscarves? I guessed they didn't braid hair in America, at least not for weddings. These first photos I had seen of American fashion were odd.

A neighbor beside me was looking at the photos I held, and I realized I had taken too long. I smiled and passed her the photos while Anton continued with the letter.

We even had a flower girl and ring bearer like American weddings have. They were Marta's sister Greta and a cousin. The flowers were large white gladiolas. Marta's bouquet was white roses, and the men wore white roses on the fronts of their jackets.

The wedding ceremony was in the style of an American Lutheran wedding, but we still broke the plate on the floor in the Slovak tradition. It was an excellent day.

We hope you enjoy the photos, and we send you our love.

Sincerely,

Denny and Marta Lacko

Everyone applauded, and the murmur of voices grew louder. One of the male guests began playing a *Gajdy* bagpipe made from goat's skin with the fur on the outside and a pipe that looked like ornately carved cherry wood. Another guest joined in with the fujaras. He was once a shepherd in the Carpathian Mountains, where Papa's family was from. Papa had brought his accordion and played along with some lively country dance music. Everyone clapped to the music, and a few people danced.

Ivan came over to me and made a curt bow. "Aunt Mira, would you dance with me?" He stood very straight with his shoulders squared, looking most mature.

A twinge of guilt washed over me, for I hadn't seen much of him since Little Jan's death. I had told Ivan that Janos and I didn't blame him. I prayed he didn't blame himself.

"Of course I'll dance with you," I said, and we joined the others, stepping lightly to the music and swinging each other around, our elbows hooked until the song came to an end. Ivan escorted me to my chair, where I sat and caught my breath.

Anton came up to me, a letter in hand. "From Janos," he said over the noise. "It was addressed to you, and I didn't open it. If it's something you wish to share, you may read it out loud. Just let me know." He gave me a sympathetic smile.

I thanked him, took the letter, then slipped away to the quiet of the wood bench near the garden. I took a deep breath and opened the letter.

My Dearest Mira,

I hope this letter finds you well. I'm doing well. It was both happy and sad when Denny married. I was happy for him for finding someone to love and to love him. It made me realize how much I miss you and our life together. So much has changed.

I feel I have family here, what with Denny's wife's family. They are very good, wholesome people. Northern Slovaks, but still our people. America is great in many ways. There are many opportunities here.

After Denny moved out, I found another place to live cheaper, since it's only me now. I found a new job at another company and it's a little more money and with the cheaper rent, I will save more money.

I want you to think about coming to America. I know that wasn't our plan. Plans change, life changes. I know it was hard on you that I wasn't with you at Vianoce. It wasn't easy for me either. It made me think clearly about life—our life. I think America is where we need to start over. Let us build a new family here, together.

I love you and need you. Please think about it.

Your Jani

I stared at the words *I think America is where we need to start over*, which cut me to my core.

How could he do this to me?

Chapter Fourteen

August 1910

GORAN WALKED TOWARD ME WITH A BAG SLUNG over his shoulder as I headed to the Notary to post a letter to Aneta. The butterflies in my stomach returned. I'd hardly thought about Goran since our mild flirtation in the spring. My thoughts had been clouded by Janos's decision to stay in America.

I stopped and waited at a portion of the road where there were no cottages nearby. I worried about how things would look with me talking with a man alone.

"Dobrý deň," he called as he neared and waved.

I replied when he was just a few steps away. "Goran. Dobrý deň to you. You are late." I squinted. The hot sun behind him blinded me and shadowed his features.

"I'm sorry about that. Did your father receive my message? There was a family matter that delayed me." He swung the bag from his shoulder and set it on the ground. "You look well."

His eyes looked a lighter shade of gray than I remembered? Why was I thinking about his eyes? "He received your message," I said. "I'm going into town. Papa will be pleased you have arrived. He's in the field finishing the potato harvest."

I started past him, and he put out his hand to stop me. A familiar electric current leaped in the air between us. The flutters in my stomach grew stronger.

"Can I see you later, alone? There's something I would like to discuss," he said in a low voice.

"Uh, a-alone?" I stammered. "I don't know if that would be possible." His gaze unnerved me, and a shiver ran down my back.

"Think about it," he said. "I'll wait in the barn—or somewhere else?"

"Maybe." I hurried past him and didn't look back.

Maybe? What was I thinking? I should have said no. It would be such a risk. So, why was I already devising a way to slip out of the cottage without my parents knowing?

———

AT THE EVENING MEAL, MAMA PLACED BREAD, sheep's milk cheese, and stewed vegetables on the table. I poured hot tea into mugs for all of us and sat next to Mama. Papa made a short grace before we served ourselves.

Papa was having a polite conversation with Goran, while Mama and I discussed sewing projects. Goran's glances burned into me. I focused on my food, Mama, and anywhere but him.

"Mira, you seem tense. Are you feeling all right?" Mama asked.

I started. How had she noticed?

"I'm fine." I smiled. "I'm not tense."

Once everyone's plates were empty, I rose and cleared the table. I made quick work of the dishes and dried my hands on a cloth. "I could use a walk." I purposely did not look at Goran.

"Didn't you have a nice long walk to town today?" Papa asked.

"It was warm then, and the cool night air would be refreshing."

"That sounds like a good idea," Mama said. "We might join you. Papa?"

"Not tonight, my dearest, too tired. You two go on."

I resisted the urge to look at Goran to see if he was disappointed, too, as I picked up my shawl from the bench near the door. Mama and I went outside together. The cool breeze wafted across my face while the sunset cast a soft pinkish light through the clouds.

"Well, silly me," Mama said when we'd taken only half a dozen steps, "It's chillier than I expected, and I'm getting another one of those headaches." She shivered and rubbed her hands over her arms.

"Here." I swung my shawl from my shoulders and draped it across hers.

"Never mind." She shrugged my shawl away. "I don't feel up to a walk. I'm going back in. You go on."

"If you insist." I gave her a quick hug and exhaled. "Don't wait up. I have a lot of thinking to do about...well, you know, moving to America." Lying didn't come easy to me, and I prayed she didn't notice.

"It is a big decision and one you hadn't considered. Take your time, dear."

She turned back to the cottage, and I halted as she opened the door. Goran stood near the table. His eyes shifted to me in the instant before Mama closed the door.

What a wicked woman I was. Despite my inner warnings, something inexplicable drew me to Goran. I crept around to the back of the cottage toward the henhouse, which was visible from the kitchen window. I continued past the barn toward the fields, not wanting to feel trapped in an enclosed space when I talked to him.

The moonlight illuminated the tall corn stalks fluttering in the breeze. I paused at the edge of the cornfield and looked over my shoulder. Goran stood near the barn, watching, waiting. I turned and moved through the stalks until I reached the far end of the cornfield, where there were no cottages beyond.

At last, the gentle rustle of corn leaves told me he was approaching. Keeping my back to him, I pulled on a leaf, feeling unsure about what I was doing.

"Mira," he called in a whisper.

I turned as he stepped into the moonlight, and my knees wobbled. He came closer, and I lifted a hand to stop him.

"You said you wanted to talk. I'm here to listen." My voice sounded steady, but the nervous flutter in my stomach had returned. I pulled my shawl tight around me and waited.

He seemed uncertain, and I thought he had changed his mind.

"I've thought about you every day since I left. Perhaps you have thought of me, too. Even if not every day? I sensed you're interested in me, and not just as a laborer for your father. Yes?"

I nodded, tongue-tied. He stepped closer. I didn't stop him.

He spoke rapidly, gesturing with his hands. "I-I have a wife and children who depend on me. Speaking of my feelings for you is wrong. I can't help it." He swallowed hard. "I'm drawn to you in a way I have never been with any other woman." He dropped his arms back to his sides.

Like him, I spoke quickly, "I've never thought of any man other than my husband. We've been apart now for over two years. I'm lonely, but it might be different for you."

"I feel loneliness too." He paused. "I'm not asking anything of you. Just maybe hope?" He lifted a brow.

I hesitated. "I don't know about hope. This is all strange."

"Where do we go from here?" He eased closer.

I stared at the ground, afraid to meet his eyes. He took another step. I waited. He gently grasped my arms. I looked up, and he grasped my hand. The tremor rippled through my body at the warmth his touch. I went rigid, flooded with mixed emotions of guilt, loneliness, and, to my utter shame, desire.

I closed my eyes and pulled my hand away. "No, Goran. I cannot. I am a wife foremost." My voice cracked.

He stepped back, his jaw tight, and hurt shadowing his face. "I would never dishonor you. But I thought...I thought you needed someone."

"I do." Tears blurred my vision. "But it cannot be now, and I'm not sure it could be you. I'm sorry."

For a heartbeat he said nothing, then he turned and strode into the night. The empty space he left swallowed me whole. My knees felt as if they would buckle beneath me, and I bit my lip with my arms wrapped tight around me to keep from calling him back. The choice was mine, and I had made it. Yet the ache of watching him walk away hollowed me out more than the loneliness I carried before. Was this what I really wanted? I wish I knew.

———

THE DAYS THAT FOLLOWED WERE FILLED WITH silence. I kept to my work and avoided the barn, making lame excuses to Mama so she would milk the cow. But every chore reminded me of him—and every meal with him sitting across from me was torture. At night, loneliness pressed on me hard, and I could barely breathe. And my obsession pushed Janos from my mind at night, sending me into fits of guilt.

Several nights had passed since we talked in the field. I told

myself just once more—to speak, perhaps to thank him properly, to end things cleanly. What harm could come from a few
words between two lonely souls? The thought sounded inno-
cent enough to let me breathe again.

Once my parents fell asleep in their room, I rose from my
bed in the main room, pulled on my boots, laced them
quickly, wrapped my long shawl around me, and crept to the
front door. I glanced toward their room and waited. No movement. Carefully, I slipped outside. Again, I waited, but they
didn't stir and closed the door with the merest click.

I hurried to the barn where Goran slept. I stopped at the
entrance, my heart pounding. The full moon shone through
the small window. I pushed the door open, stepped inside,
then listened for movement.

"Goran?" I whispered.

A shadow shifted where he stirred from his pallet. "Mira?"
His voice was rough with surprise. "Is something wrong?"

I stepped toward him. "No," I said, afraid my trembling
would betray me. "I just needed to see you, to tell you...." To
tell him what? I hadn't considered what I would say.

He rose, the hay rustling under his bare feet. "You
shouldn't be here," he murmured, even as he stood before me.

I looked up into his face as the moonlight cast his features
in shadow. "I know."

His hands found my shoulders, hesitant at first. "Mira..."
he said, his breath shallow. "What do you want of me
tonight?"

"Just hold me. Can you do that? I'm not ready for more,
but I need your presence."

He took my hand and guided me to his pallet. We lay
together with his arms around me, and my tremors stopped
completely.

"Don't let me fall asleep, you feel good." I cuddled closer.
"I must return to the house soon."

He nodded and kissed me gently. His arms pressed me to him.

A couple of hours later, we parted with smiles on our faces, and I hurried back to the cottage and slipped under the covers, thinking only of him.

———

WE MET SEVERAL MORE TIMES, KISSING AND holding hands. Sometimes we lay together and talked about our childhoods and dreams, while he stroked my hair the way Janos used to. When his passion would build up, I would shut down and flee back to the house. I never stayed long, too terrified Papa or Mama would discover me gone.

All too soon, his last night arrived. I decided not to let him leave without finally giving myself fully to him.

He stood outside the door to the barn, as if he knew I would go to him. I reached the barn, and he stepped inside as I fell into his arms, wearing only my nightshift and boots.

"Are you sure, Mira?" he murmured as he snuggled my neck.

I smiled. "Yes, now I'm sure."

He cupped my face with his hands, and when our lips met, passion burst in me. He kissed every part of my face. Slowly, we removed each other's clothes, and he unlaced my boots. I had never been naked with Janos. I always wore my night shift, and he never tried to remove it. I thought that was normal.

With Goran, I allowed him to remove it easily and was surprised to feel no shame or shyness. He pulled me close, and my heart pounded. His touch, light like a feather on my breasts, my neck, and my face, made me shudder.

"You are very beautiful, Mira." He nibbled on my earlobe, then trailed his tongue down my neck to capture the fullness of my breast with his mouth.

I gasped with pleasure. It had been too long. My body trembled at his touch. The intense hunger between us drove us to the height of ecstasy until we lay breathless and spent.

"Goran," I whispered.

"No words." He took my mouth again with his.

Before dawn, I crept out of the barn, the place between my legs sore but deliriously satisfied. I tried desperately not to think of him leaving in a few hours. I returned to the house without a sound and slid under the covers, pretending to sleep, until the sun appeared on the new day.

———

When Goran left, there was no big farewell. We would see him the following spring. After he left, Mama and I went inside and stood side by side, preparing the midday meal.

"You will need to be more discreet next year," she said while scrubbing a pot.

Warmth spread across my cheeks.

Wiping her hands on a towel, she faced me. "You are a grown woman. You have experienced much loss, and I know you're lonely. I just ask you to be careful. We don't want anyone to find out. You would be ruined, and Janos humiliated. It doesn't matter that you are alone and he is in America. Our people have expectations of you to be the ever-faithful wife, no matter how difficult your life, how painful your loss, or how lonely you feel."

"Oh, Mamička." Tears slid down my cheeks. "I'm sorry."

"I understand, but it isn't me you need to worry about. It's our community, family, and your father might not be as forgiving as I." She wiped away my tears with her apron.

"He might not return, and then there would be nothing to worry about," I said in a flippant tone.

"You know he will be back, and you have only a few months to think about what you will do when he does. You must protect yourself from harm."

"What do you mean, Mamička?"

"When was your last cycle?"

"Oh!" My impulsiveness to be with Goran had made me careless. I hadn't considered the potential consequence—how stupid and dangerous.

"There are ways to be protected, such as certain herbs in a tea, or simple withdrawal. If you find yourself safe this time, next time you need to be prepared or stay away from him," she urged gently.

"Do you recall which herbs?" That sounded easiest.

"Only willow was whispered among young mothers when I was your age."

"Did it work?"

"I have no idea."

"I will be good, Mamička, and will not bring scandal into our family."

My cycles weren't always right on time. I worried for days until my time of the month arrived. Relieved, I asked myself if it was worth the risk. I missed Goran already, but I was also filled with guilt when I thought of Janos. What a mess I was making of my life.

Chapter Fifteen

December 1910

I almost didn't recognize Janos when he walked through my parents' cottage door. It had been two years since I'd seen him. He dressed in American-style long pants, shoes, a plain brown vest over a beige shirt, and a narrow-lapel coat under a long wool coat with two large buttons. Instead of the traditional hat, he wore a black cap with a brim.

He removed his hat when he stepped inside. Even his beautiful light auburn curly hair was different, shorter, parted in the middle, and flattened down with pomade that darkened it, like in the photos from Denny's wedding. Lines had appeared at the corners of his eyes. He looked older than thirty-three.

I wondered if he thought I had changed, too.

We embraced, and he gave me a quick kiss on the mouth. The stilted mood did nothing to ease my anxiety, and I remained stiff.

"Dobrý deň," Janos said to my parents.

Papa smiled.

"Dobrý deň, Janos," Mama said.

Before anyone could say anything else, Janos turned to me with a solemn expression, "I want to see our children."

I nodded, and we walked hand in hand through the village to the church graveyard without a word. We stood for a long time in front of our two children's little graves. I gripped his hand with such might that I could feel the blood drain from my fingers. I didn't care.

Papa had made wood plaques topped with crosses for each grave, with the names and dates beautifully carved.

"I will have a stone made while I'm home. They both deserve one." Janos's voice was hoarse with emotion, and he jerked against me.

I turned to him, and my heart lurched. He was sobbing. I had never seen him cry.

We fell into each other's arms and cried together.

Janos grasped my shoulders and held me at arm's length. "Mira, please, tell me everything that happened the day Little Jan died. No one ever told me all the details, and I need to know."

The despair in his eyes nearly brought my tears again. I took his large hand in my small one.

"It was a beautiful day, the weather perfect. The two boys played with each other, laughing and teasing. We had all been in a great mood, enjoying each other's company." I swallowed hard. "When it was time to leave, Little Jan and Ivan were nowhere to be found. We called and called for them. Then Ivan ran toward us, wet and terrified. He explained how Little Jan went too far into the river and was pulled in too fast. Ivan dove in after Little Jan. Such bravery. But he could not reach him. Anton took off running along the riverbank to find our boy. He fought the river current, and Maria and I feared for him. Two Hungarian men ran to help. We lost sight of them at the bend in the river."

I squeezed Janos's hand and forced myself to look into his eyes. "When they brought his little body to me, his life had already washed away. I thought I might lose my mind. My heart shattered, and I was angry. Angry at God." Tears streamed down my cheeks. I would never forget the pain of losing him.

Janos drew a deep breath. "Thank you, my dearest Mira," he said in a soft voice.

A reverence hung in the air, of divine spiritual grace and forgiveness, and I thought Janos could feel it, too. His face relaxed, and he looked at peace.

On December 24th, we all went to the Lacko cottage to celebrate Štedrý večer. I was relaxed and surrounded by family on the eve of Christmas. I thought of Aneta and Tomas, knowing I couldn't mention them in Janos's presence, but I had made my peace with his decision. I wanted to feel happy, and I kept all the negative thoughts at bay.

It was a feast like in the old days. The extra income from Janos helped make everything special. Everyone laughed and filled their plates.

Toward the end of the meal, Mama had barely touched her food. "Aren't you hungry, Mamička?"

"My head is hurting a little, and it makes me nauseated. I'm fine, dear, don't worry." She flashed a bright smile.

Papa and Janos fetched some apples from the larder while Maria, Mama, and I cleaned up the table. Mama worked in silence but seemed to perform her tasks with little struggle. We finished up and sat back at the table with the men.

Ivan placed an apple in front of everyone at the dinner

table as we performed the traditional cutting of the apple. Together, we each cut an apple in half horizontally. Janos's seeds formed a star, symbolizing happiness and good health for the family. I looked around the table, and everyone got the star except Mama. Her pieces weren't face up. She flipped her half over, exposing the cut side. Her seeds formed a cross, meaning problems, illness, or even death for the coming year. A hushed gasp escaped us all as we looked at the cross shape in her apple.

"Here," I said, and handed her another apple from Ivan's remaining bunch in the middle. "Cut another one."

"No, no, I can't do that. It just isn't done." She refused the apple, her face devoid of any fear or emotion. What was she thinking?

I held my breath and tried not to show my fear.

Papa broke the silence. "It is nothing. Do we even remember what happens from year to year?" He gave a nervous laugh.

Oh yes, we remembered, but everyone chimed in with positive words. Mama smiled, but the emotion didn't reach her eyes.

———

Janos and I spent the night in our old bedroom at his parents' cottage. I agreed to stay there while he was visiting. That night, I did something for the first time. Despite the cold, I removed my nightdress and slipped under the covers, warming myself against him.

"Mira, what is this?" he said with surprise. "Why now, after all these years?"

"Because it has been 'all these years.' Our time apart has made me want you more than ever," I said with complete honesty.

He wrapped his big arms around me and gave me a deep,

passionate kiss as if his life depended upon it. I responded in kind, drinking in his unique scent and reveling in his moist skin as I ran my hands over him in places I had never before dared touch. When he touched me in my most secret spot, it was like the first time we had ever been together, exploring each other in wonderment and joy.

"I love you, my dearest Mira," he whispered once our passion had spent.

"I love you, Jani. I wish you would never leave." I was honest, but he tensed slightly.

Without another word, he made love to me again.

Each night we blazed with love and passion. Afterward, when he lay sleeping, one question kept me awake...would I be enough for Janos to stay and forget America?

———

THE DAY BEFORE JANOS WAS TO RETURN TO America, we made a final trip together to the village for supplies. He was providing money to both our parents, and I had wondered how he managed after sending so much to us.

"So, tell me about where you are living. Since Denny moved out, I mean."

"It's of no significance." He tossed off the question with a wave of his hand and kept walking.

"What does that mean? Is it a hovel?" I had heard stories about men who went to America and lived in horrible conditions to send as much money as possible to their families.

"Depends on what you mean by a hovel. There is a bed, and bath down the hall. Meals are served downstairs once a day. It's all I need." He frowned. "Why do you ask?"

"I do not want you sacrificing your comfort in order for both our families do well."

"Isn't that why I work in America?"

"You need to take care of yourself, too."

He didn't respond but muttered unintelligibly. We reached the shop and made our purchases.

Outside the shop, he stopped walking and faced me. "Come to America with me. Come now."

"Now?"

"Yes. Come with me. I'll get a larger place. We can start a new family there. We need another child, Mira."

All my joy and happiness drained away. "Janos...I was planning to ask you to stay here, with me."

I clapped my hand over my mouth and looked around. I hadn't planned to have this conversation in the middle of the street. People were milling about, and some were watching us. I started walking.

"Don't walk away from me," he said under his breath, and caught up with me.

"People are staring," I hissed. "Please, can we not talk about this here?"

He let out a frustrated sigh. We walked in silence all the way to my parents' cottage.

He stopped again in front of the gate. "We will talk now."

Without a word, I pushed past him, opened the gate, and hurried into the cottage. Mama was busy cooking our evening meal. She never seemed to stop working, and lately she always looked tired.

I put my parcels on the table. Janos stormed in and slammed the door. Mama looked up sharply.

"Janos? We don't slam doors in this house. You know better." She waved a finger at him like he was a child.

"Sorry." He turned to glare at me. "Mira, we need to finish our discussion."

"I do not like your tone. You can't tell me what to do after being gone for two years."

"The two of you should go back outside and finish your

discussion," Mama said. "I certainly don't want to hear it. It seems like a private matter." She placed her hands on her hips. She meant business.

I nodded at Janos, and he reluctantly followed me outside and behind the house, out of the sight and earshot of our neighbors.

"You told me you would think about going to America," he blurted.

"Yes, and I am still thinking about it." My voice was unsteady and low.

"You won't go with me tomorrow?" His arms hung stiffly at his sides, one hand flicking at a fingernail, a sign his temper was flaring.

"No, not now. I won't leave my parents. I think there's something wrong with Mama. She hasn't gone to the doctor yet, but until I know she's all right, I won't make any plans."

"Your mother seems fine. You are making this up," he snapped.

Anger shot through me. "I would never use my Mama in that way. You insult me! What must you think of me?"

I pulled my shawl tight around me and considered walking away, if only to stop the argument. The apple incident warned of illness. I had decided to take her to the doctor after the holidays. However, if I were honest, I had other reasons for not wanting to go to America.

"Mira, I only want you with me. I truly believe America is our answer to our future happiness. I'll still send money to both our parents." He put his hand on my arm and slid his fingers down to my hand.

The pressure of his warm fingers was comforting. "I understand what you want," I said. "But moving to America wasn't the plan. You working there was supposed to be to improve our condition here. You changed your mind about our future, and it's not what I want. I'm confused by it all."

"Yes, yes, I know I changed my mind," he said in frustration. "But I'm sure it is the right decision."

I didn't answer right away. He dropped my hand and turned his back on me, exasperated.

"All I know is my parents need me here. This is my home, Janos." I pressed a palm to his back, and he spun around, hurt in his eyes. "Please give me more time," I begged. "I've been very happy these few weeks with you here. The memories will keep me satisfied for some time to come. Let's not ruin it by fighting. That is the last thing I want." I gave him a pleading look and put my arms around him. He grudgingly put his arms around me, and I held him tight until his body relaxed.

The next day, my parents and I watched with teary eyes and aching hearts as Janos trudged down the road alone, away from the village and away from us. He turned and gave me a reluctant wave. I wouldn't see him again until the end of the year. We tried very hard to part on good terms, though that morning he made one last attempt to change my mind. I held firm that this wasn't the time for me to leave.

We wanted the same thing, to be together, but we wanted that in different places.

Chapter Sixteen

March 1911

IN THE WEEKS SINCE VIANOCE, MAMA HAD TAKEN TO her bed to rest more often and had lost weight from loss of appetite. After much resistance, she agreed to see Dr. Schwarz at his cottage.

Despite walking slowly, Mama arrived out of breath and needed help to get to the doctor's examination room at the rear of the house. I waited at the kitchen table with Zelda.

"Don't worry, Mira. My husband will take care of your mama. Has she been this way for very long?" Concern in her voice.

"Since before Vianoce. I noticed she seemed more tired than usual, with frequent headaches, and she chilled more easily. That's not normal for her, and she barely eats. But she would not see the doctor until now."

"Many people are afraid to see the doctor. They don't want bad news. I hope, whatever the cause, she will be better soon." She poured me another cup of tea and placed a small plate of pastries in front of me. "I have news to share with you."

"Oh? What is going on with you these days? It has been ages since our last chat." I took a bite of one of the lemon bars and took a sip of tea.

"Well, I know you won't be happy about this, but...we're moving to America."

I almost choked and dropped the teacup. "Why?" I stared at her.

"Ezra has family in Pennsylvania, and one of his cousins asked him to join the practice. We have no children or family close by. I admit we have missed family, and there are very few of us Jews in this area. We've felt a bit isolated."

"I'm saddened by this news. You have been a good friend to me, and I will m-miss you terribly." The lump in my throat made me stumble on the words. "It seems I have been losing too many people."

"My dear, yes, you have. But you still have your parents, and though Janos is gone most of the time, at least he came for Vianoce. It must have been good, yes?" She patted my hand, her eyes moist.

"Of course, it was good." I swallowed hard. Thinking of Janos only made me sadder, and I changed the topic. "When do you leave?

"Not for a few months. There is much to do, packing, shipping, and such. I will see you before I go and give you our address to stay in touch."

The doctor came out from his examination room, Mama right behind him. Zelda and I stood.

"Mira, I took some blood samples to send off to the hospital in Szeged for testing. It's probably anemia. If it is, I'll prescribe iron salts, but until then, just get plenty of rest. Don't overdo."

Making Mama rest and not work would be difficult.

"Thank you, Dr. Schwarz. How long does it take for the test results?" I asked.

"Two weeks. I have a phone now, they'll call me."

"Zelda told me about your move to America. How exciting."

"America?" Mama said with surprise, turning to the doctor.

"Yes, yes, lots of changes," he said. "We are not leaving right away. It will be a few months. I will be here to tend to you until you are well," he assured Mama.

We said our goodbyes and left.

"How are you feeling?" I asked when we reached their gate.

She caught her breath. "I'm fine, dear. Let us take it slow again." She took one step at a time, holding her side.

"Are you in pain? Did you tell the doctor?"

"It isn't bad. Just a twinge. I told the doctor sometimes I had discomfort up here." She pointed to the stomach area under her breast. "He took note of it. Not to worry. Like he said, he thinks it's anemia." She gave me a wan smile, and we moved on toward home.

———

AFTER SEEING DR. SCHWARZ, SHE DRASTICALLY slowed down. I had no trouble getting her to stay in bed. Some days, she would do little. I was anxious about the test results.

After two weeks, we received a note from Dr. Schwarz to see him about the test results. I wrote a reply that Mama could not walk to see him and asked him to come to our cottage. He came the following day and examined her.

Papa came in from the fields to be there. I had never seen him look that worried. We were all in my parents' room. The doctor stood at her bedside.

"Mr. and Mrs. Vargas, Mira…as I suspected, the tests show Maria is anemic, which is typical in such cases with abnormal white blood cells, and too many," Dr. Schwarz explained.

"What does it mean, doctor?" asked Papa.

"I'm very sorry to tell you this," he paused and swallowed hard, "it's leukemia, blood cancer." The doctor's eyes passed over each of us with a sympathetic look, ending on Mama.

I gasped and rushed to Mama and clutched her hands in mine. "Mamička! No," I cried.

She shushed me, her voice weak. "Mira, quiet now. Let the doctor finish."

"Is there any treatment?" Papa's voice was strangely calm, his eyes red. Had he been crying?

"At the present time, there is not very much we can do. I will provide pain medication to make her more comfortable, but that is about it. You may notice more symptoms, such as fever, chills, sweating, and bruising or bleeding easily. Keep her out of direct drafts and away from sick people. She is susceptible to infections." The doctor opened his bag, withdrew a packet of powder, and handed it to me.

"This is the same medication I prescribed for your mother-in-law when she had the fever."

"I remember." I took the packet from him and stared at it as if it had magical power to heal her.

He turned to Mama, "Mrs. Vargas, when your pain becomes unbearable, send someone for me, and I'll come as soon as possible. I will provide an injection of something stronger, which will help." He turned to Papa. With genuine sincerity, he said, "I wish there swas more I could do. Just take care of her the best you can."

"Doctor?" Mama's voice was low. "Am I dying?"

I choked back a sob and held my breath.

"Yes," Dr. Schwarz said with finality.

"How long?" Tears formed in Papa's eyes.

The doctor exhaled a long breath. "That's difficult to predict. This has been going on for some time, and the disease is far along. It could be months or weeks."

Papa and I gave each other shocked looks. *Weeks?* Tears blurred my vision. I lay my head on Mama's shoulder, and she put her hand on my head and said nothing. Her chest rose and fell with short, quick breaths. She might cry, but she rarely cried in front of others.

After the doctor left, I fluffed the pillows and pulled up the covers. Mama had closed her eyes and looked asleep. Yes, sleep was good. I wanted to sleep for a thousand years and wake up to life like when I was younger and happy.

Papa went into the big room and sat in the rocking chair. I followed, in a trance, to prepare our meal. My stomach ached as if someone had punched me. I thought I might double over when a knock at the door yanked me out of my stupor. Papa and I looked at each other, wondering who it could be. He answered the door since I was busy with the vegetables.

Goran. I was so concerned about Mama, the fact that Goran was to return slipped my mind. Only Mama filled my thoughts. Papa stepped outside and guided him to the garden, where I could see them talking through the window.

"Mira?" Mama called, and I rushed to her room. For the first time, I noticed how sunken her eyes had become, and her face looked ashen. It frightened me.

"Yes, Mama?"

"Is it Goran?"

"He's outside with Papa. That is of no importance now. Can I get you something, some tea?"

She nodded.

I returned to the stove and prepared the tea, then placed the teapot and cup on a tray and set it on the small table beside her bed. She looked still. My heart skipped a beat, and I held my breath.

When she opened her eyes again, I breathed.

———

Several days after Goran arrived, I received a letter from Aneta. I eagerly opened it.

Dearest Mira,

I'm with child again! Due in May. I am tired all the time with this one. Must be all the stairs. We moved to a different building, and it has a separate bedroom. It will be nice to have more room when the baby arrives.

Tomas still grumbles daily about his job. Sometimes, I just tire of hearing it, but I try to be understanding. Working in the mines is hard work and dangerous too. He is not used to it, even after two years. Lately, he has taken to drinking more than usual, I think to deal with all our troubles. He's talking about moving to California again, this time to work in the vineyards, probably because of what happened a few weeks ago.

A tunnel collapsed. I was frightened, something had happened to Tomas, but he was safe. There were several injuries and deaths, too. The families of those who died suffer much. I joined with some other wives who try to help them as we can. There's a priest here, but no Lutheran pastor. He is better than no one to offer spiritual comfort.

On a happier note, enclosed is a photo of little

Jamie, our son. He looks like Tomas already and is just as feisty.

I will post this today and hope you get it soon. Much love to you, Papa, and Mamička, and please don't tell them everything in this letter. I don't want them to worry. I'm fine, really. I don't have anyone here I trust to talk with about these things. I miss you so much, Mira.

Your loving sister, Aneta

Another child? Deep within me, I envied her having two children to love and care for. I looked at the small photo of my nephew, Jamie. She was right. Even at two years old, he looked very much like Tomas. I hoped he grew up to be like someone else. I knew Aneta loved Tomas, but he hadn't impressed me as a husband or brother-in-law. I doubted his ability as a father. The increased drinking concerned me. I worried about my sister.

I hated having to write to Aneta about the seriousness of Mama's sickness. I didn't want her to feel bad for not being here, but there was no avoiding it. She had to be told, and with two children, it would be expensive for her to come home with them. I asked her anyway, hoping for a miracle.

When I wrote to Janos, I asked if he could come home, too, though I knew he would not. He had just been here, and the cost would be too much. How I wanted my family to be with us. I knew Mama wanted them here too.

———

FROM THE COTTAGE WINDOW, I WATCHED GORAN outside the barn. He tipped his hat, and I waved, almost smiling. Exhausted from the extra work and caring for Mama, my emotions had run ragged. I had barely spoken to Goran since he returned, except during meals, but I missed being with him.

That night, after I drank the special willow bark tea, I went to him. I slipped out of the house wearing my nightdress with my shawl wrapped around me and my boots laced up. He stood at the entrance as I fell into his arms. We kissed with a passion that took my breath away. With one strong arm, he held me tight and stroked my hair that tumbled down my back. I shuddered with joy when he swept me up and carried me to his pallet, where we lay in each other's arms. Just being with him in the quiet, his warmth and musky scent comforted me.

He rose to remove his shirt, and I could see him clearly beneath the radiant moonlight coming through the window. How was it that each time we came together, there was a full moon? He lay down beside me, and I nuzzled his fuzzy, dark chest hair and ran my hands along the muscles defined by his hard labor. A familiar sense of safety and comfort overcame me as I cuddled close. I started to speak, but he silenced me with his hungry mouth, devouring my lips.

All my pent-up emotions burst into a shower of intense passion. He pulled my night shift up over my head and drank in my nakedness with his eyes and hands.

He nodded and kissed me gently.

The hours passed too quickly, and the time neared for me to return to the cottage.

"I don't know when we can be together again, but I need you. You being here is giving me something to live for, even if it's only for a short while. Mama's illness is almost too much to bear." I tried to hold back the tears.

"Mira—"

"Wait, let me finish. I need to give everything I can to her.

Yet, I feel I'm being selfish, because I need your strength to help me get through it. Do you understand?"

"Yes, I do." He paused and caressed my face with his fingers. "You can use me for whatever you need, because you are giving me something too. I will tell you one day, but not now. Now is about you and your mother."

I kissed him deeply again and rose, put my nightdress on, and laced up my boots. We walked to the barn entrance, hand in hand. One last kiss, and I ran to the cottage, crept in the door, removed my boots, and slid under the covers. I thanked God for bringing me Goran, my salvation.

A few tears trickled down the side of my face as my last thought was of Janos, wondering how he could be apart from me all this time. If the loneliness was too difficult for me and I found myself in the arms of another man, had he done the same thing? I didn't want to think about it and willed myself to sleep.

Chapter Seventeen

May 1911

MAMA HAD NO FIGHT LEFT. I WATCHED HER WITHER away while I filled my days and evenings caring for her. I helped her with her toilet and bathed her as she did with me when I was a child. She slept so soundly that sometimes I thought she had died until her chest rose and fell, and I relaxed. We expected each day to be the last.

Papa went into his shell and rarely spoke. He spent what time he could with his beloved wife. Dr. Schwarz came regularly to give morphine injections for the pain. Mama agonized while waiting for those injections. Eventually, the doctor gave me a small bottle and showed me how to administer the injections myself.

The days dragged on, one after the other, blurring into constant stress. Zelda came around a few times to check in on Mama and me. I treasured the blessed interludes. We would take walks together, talking about her moving plans and the practice where Dr. Schwarz would work.

On one of my walks with Zelda, we stopped by the Notary and got our post. A letter came from Aneta addressed to Mama, and I was eager to read it to her.

"Mamička," I said as I walked in the door, "a letter came for you from Aneta."

Mama offered a weak smile but didn't turn her head in my direction.

"I will read it to you." I opened the letter, and two photos fell out. I set them aside and began reading.

> Dear Mamička,
> The spring has been mild and delightful, but June is around the corner and the summers are usually quite warm and dry. Jamie is getting big, they really do grow up fast. He's very playful, you'd love him. He has lots of energy, it's hard to keep up! Especially with me big now. I've included some pictures. I wish we could be there and you could see him in person. There is much more I want to say, but I can't find the words. Tell Papa I love him. I love you, too, Mamička.
> Your loving daughter, Aneta

I picked up the photos as I finished reading. Aneta was very large with the coming baby. I wondered why she hadn't mentioned Tomas.

"Isn't that nice of Aneta, Mamička?" I placed the photos in her hands.

She gazed at her daughter and grandchild. Her eyes lit with

joy and pride. It was a rare sight, and my heart filled with a mix of happiness and sadness.

"Aneta is beautiful, yes?" Mama asked, her voice soft and weak. "Little Jamie looks like Tomas."

"Yes, he does. Aneta wanted to come home to be here for you."

"Of course she did, but the cost, and being with child? It would be too much. I will always remember her on the day of her wedding...happy day." Her hand dropped to the covers, and the photos fell to the floor.

I picked them up from the floor and looked up at her. She had fallen asleep. I kissed her forehead. "Sweet dreams, Mamička, I love you with all my heart."

———

Papa sat in the rocking chair, reading the paper by the oil lamp. The creaks of his rocking back and forth were audible from their room, where I sat next to Mama's bed, knitting wool socks. Her breathing pattern changed, and I glanced up. Her eyes were closed. I checked her pulse as the doctor had shown me. Slower than usual. Her breaths came from deep in her chest, with pauses in between. I watched her for a long time, listening to her strange breathing. When the breaks between breaths got longer, I knew the time had come.

The rocking sounds stopped. I went into the big room. Papa had dozed off, and the paper had fallen to his feet.

"Papa?" I touched him lightly on his shoulder. "It's time. Come."

He woke and got up without a word. We went to Mama's bed. I sat on one side, Papa on the other, each of us holding one of her hands. We watched, listened, and waited. It seemed forever until the breaths were fewer and further apart. Then they stopped. Her mouth slacked, and her eyelids stilled. I kissed her on the cheek and glanced over at Papa.

"Do you want time alone with her?"

He nodded, tears running down his cheeks.

I tiptoed from the room and sat in the rocking chair.

"*Rozlúčka*, Mamička," I whispered. "I will miss you and hold your love in my heart for the rest of my life until I see you again in Heaven."

———

WHEN LITTLE JAN DIED, IT IMMOBILIZED ME. MARIA and Mama had prepared his small body for the vigil in the home. But it was Papa and I who prepared my dear mama's body.

We laid her on the big table, which I had covered with an old cloth. I held her worn, callused hands and washed them gently with a wash towel and a bit of soap, moving to her face, neck, and shoulders. I combed her long, gray-streaked hair. In her illness, her wavy and lush hair had become thin and lackluster.

I divided her hair into thirds and began to braid. Right over middle, left over middle, and with each step, a memory of her came to my mind. Her dimpled smile lovingly accepted everything I said or did...right over middle...when she braided my hair on my wedding day, her soothing voice made me calm...left over middle...the day Little Jan was born. She rushed to my side to help Maria during the birthing, her gentle hands smoothed my hair and face with each painful contraction...right over middle and done. I wrapped the braids around her head and pinned them into place.

Papa and I dressed her in her kroje, last worn on Vianoce only months before, and laid her in the plain wood coffin Papa crafted to prepare for that solemn day. No more tears to shed, as I had shed them all for months. All I had left was a heavy heart. When done, we stood side by side and watched her to make sure she was truly gone and no chance of a mistake, a tradition we followed, though we knew there was no mistake.

Papa went into town to send a cable to Aneta to let her know right away. I knew she would feel guilt for not being here, but that couldn't be helped. I missed her more than ever.

Maria helped me prepare the food for the overnight vigil. Our guests would arrive at dusk. We served bryndzové halušky, klobasa, and hot tea with sugar. Many of our guests brought food to share, as was the custom and was greatly appreciated.

Anton and Ivan arrived early to help Papa rearrange the furniture in the big room to accommodate guests. Our neighbors and Mama's many friends from our church came in a steady stream throughout the night. Even Papa's two male cousins from a village west of us came. Everyone loved Mama.

Papa was gracious to everyone, though I could see the loss was taking its toll on him. His face held deep furrows from strain and worry over the previous few months. His hair showed more streaks of gray, and his shoulders hunched from years of manual labor. He looked much older than fifty, and life would never be the same for him.

People retold stories about Mama and the helpful things she had done for them. Those who had grown up with her recounted childhood memories. Papa kept quiet. I couldn't tell if he was listening or reliving his own memories of Mama. When he turned and looked at me, his face brightened with a slow smile. Tears welled in my eyes. He had made peace with Mama's fate.

Dawn light filtered through the windows as the last person left. Papa and I tried to rest. I couldn't sleep, and soon the time came to take the coffin to the church for the service. Anton and a couple of neighbors helped Papa load the coffin into the cart, and they pulled it into town. Maria and Ivan walked with me behind the cart until we reached the church. Papa sat next to me and held my hand during the service. I feared my heart would burst with the ache of loss, but I refused to break down in front of everyone.

The pastor said many kind words about Mama. She was a perfect mother and wife. Some people say there's no such thing, but just ask Papa and Aneta. They would agree. She was perfect. The pastor said special prayers for the dead, and the choir sang hymns.

Afterward, they carried the coffin out to the church graveyard. The pastor spoke the final blessings, and we buried her next to my babies' resting places.

Feelings of abandonment by Janos and Aneta compounded my grief over losing dearest Mamička. A heavy weight rested on my heart. How would I muster on?

Everyone had left except for Anton, Maria, Ivan, and, of course, Papa and me. Ivan offered to pull the cart back to the cottage, and we took our time on the return home. When we arrived, we promised to spend more time together, since our family had gotten smaller.

I sat and wrote a long letter to Aneta about Mama's passing, and Papa added a note at the end. Then I wrote a letter to Janos, explaining why it had been so long since I had last written. I restrained myself from casting more blame on him for not being here. It wouldn't make me feel any better. That lesson I learned.

THE NIGHT OF THE FUNERAL, I HAD ANOTHER strange dream. Mama was in the big room of our cottage, in the rocking chair, moving back and forth with Karin in her lap. They both smiled. Little Jan stood next to them and looked down at Karin. I wanted to wrap my arms around all of them, but, like the other dreams, I couldn't get close to them.

Mama looked up at me and spoke. "Look within yourself to find what makes you happy. I'm here for you, in your dreams. Look to your future, Mira. You can still have the family you always wanted if you make the right decision."

Then I woke up.

Ah, my life's lesson—to find my happiness. I knew she was right. Happiness wasn't what others gave me; it was what I found in myself. Something she had told me often. I guess I didn't listen very well when she was alive. She was still telling me. I also wondered about the decision she mentioned. Did she mean about Janos or Goran? The dream gave me much to ponder. I was comforted thinking Mama was still close by. I couldn't wait to tell Zelda before they moved.

———

THE RAIN SOAKED THROUGH ME, WITH MY BOOTS covered in mud by the time I arrived at the Schwarzes' to say goodbye. I knocked on the door, and Zelda answered almost immediately. She looked me over and stepped aside.

"Mira, dear, come in, come in." She urged me inside.

I stopped to remove my boots, and my stockinged feet squished on her beautiful wood floor.

"I don't want to get your nice furniture wet. I didn't think it would rain before I got here." I stood there, shivering.

"It's fine, do not fret." She ran to grab a coverlet and wrapped it about me before putting a towel on the floor for my feet, then hustled me to the living room.

I sat on one of the straight-back chairs and took off my headscarf. Zelda hung it over the back of another chair to dry. I rubbed my feet till they were almost dry while Zelda prepared tea.

"Looks like you have been busy packing." I looked around the room cluttered with crates.

"Yes, almost done." She carried in a tray with cups and a teapot, set them on the tea table, then sat in the chair next to me. "I am glad you found the time to come before we left, even though this has been such a sad time for you and your papa. I've written down the address where we'll be with family until our belongings arrive. We will stay in touch, ja?"

"Yes, of course, I promise." I sniffed, forcing back tears. It seemed all I did those days was cry.

"You have become my most treasured friend, and I will not forget you." She reached over and we squeezed hands and kissed on the cheeks.

I told her about the dream of Mama, Karin, and Little Jan.

Zelda clasped her hands together with a look of joy. "What a wonderful dream to see them all together." She gave me a serious look. "Her words to you are significant. Heed them, my dear Mira. She is right, your happiness is up to you, and you must make a choice."

"You both are right, as always." I sighed.

We spent the rest of the day talking, laughing, and telling stories until the rain stopped and I was dry. My heart clenched when I hugged Zelda as we bid our final farewells.

Zelda and Dr. Schwarz left at the end of the month, another step toward a loneliness I feared would push me into a deep depression.

———

In June, we received a letter from Aneta. I called Papa in from his work to read it together.

> *Dear Mira and Papa,*
> *My heart is broken Mamička is gone, but glad she is no longer in pain. I don't know how to*

express in words my sadness. I hope she knew I would have been there if it was possible. Please forgive my absence and know you are all in my thoughts every single day.

Mamička will always be in my heart, and I will tell my children about their kind and generous Baba.

Little Katie, actually Kathryn, it's the English name for our blessed Mamička Katarina, arrived in May, a little dear and such a good baby, too. She was born on the same day Mamička died. It will be a mixed blessing day each year, and I can't bear the thought. I promise I will write more later and fill you in on all the news, but in short, we are moving again.

With much love,

Aneta, Jamie, Katie, and Tommy

"That is good news about Aneta's baby girl, yes?" Papa said. "I wonder where they are moving to this time?"

I shook my head and groaned. Although I tried to be happy for Aneta's baby girl, all I could think about was losing Karin and Mama.

Janos wrote back, too, and expressed his sadness about Mama's death and that he looked forward to seeing me at Vianoce. How could I feel the joy of Janos visiting when my heart was filled with sadness and loss?

Chapter Eighteen

July 1911

PAPA HAD COME IN FOR THE MIDDAY MEAL, AND WE sat outside on the bench under the plum tree to eat sandwiches. My heart had a gaping hole after losing Mama. Despite the message she gave me in the dream, the hole needed to be filled with something—or someone.

"Should be a good harvest this year," Papa said. "Goran will be here soon to help."

The guilt from deceiving Papa about Goran weighed on me. I swallowed and cleared my throat. "Papa, there is something I need you to know, and I feel ashamed."

He put up his hand to stop me. "I know...about you and Goran." He took a bite of his sandwich.

I choked. "What? Mama told me not to tell you."

"Your Mama couldn't keep secrets from me, and she made me promise not to let on I knew."

I hung my head, and the searing heat of shame flowed across my face. "She understood somehow and didn't judge me."

"She was all love, yes?" His brow furrowed. "Don't think that I approve of what you are doing. But...the loneliness and separation you feel from Janos, I feel it now, separated from my Katarina. There is an emptiness I've not known before."

"Oh, Papa." I gave him a big hug and cuddled close to him like I did when I was little.

He wiped his mouth and hugged me. "I just wish the busybodies in the church would leave me alone. I think they want me to be looking for another wife. They insist it isn't good for a man to be alone. I barely lost my wife, and I am in mourning. What are they thinking?" He waved a hand in the air as if brushing them off.

"Don't listen to them, Papa. They know there is a one-year mourning period. Maybe they are trying to prepare you for when you are ready, hoping you would pick someone out by then. There are not very many men left here to marry." I gave him a sly look and a playful push to his shoulder. "What about Agata, Janos's aunt?" I teased.

"Agata? You must be joking. I could never be with a pushy, controlling female such as her, especially after such a good, kind, and gentle wife as I had in Katarina. No, there will never be anyone else for me."

"Yes, I know, Papa. Who could ever replace Mama?"

A huge butterfly with wings covered in brown and white spots circled us.

"How odd. See that?"

"They've never been this close to me," Papa said. The butterfly landed on his head, so he kept still. "Or, it could be Katarina checking up on me," he whispered.

"What a lovely thought."

We sat there, side by side, with the butterfly atop Papa's head.

———

When Goran returned in August, things were different. It could have been my depression, but something had changed between us. At first, it felt strange with only Goran, Papa, and me.

Goran was understanding and comforting when I told him about Mama. He was sad he wasn't there for me when she died. Although I needed comfort, and we fell into our old routine of secret meetings in the barn at night, I couldn't be intimate. He didn't press me, and when I asked him to just hold me, he complied without hesitation.

Some days, I went out into the fields with him and Papa. We had a fruitful crop that year, and they needed my help. It was natural, the three of us working, eating, and living together. Even Papa acted as though it was normal. He never chastised me for my nocturnal visits, though I was sure he knew about them.

Though Goran still lived in the barn, a fantasy ran in my head: that Goran was my husband and I cooked and cleaned for him and Papa, as if Janos, Little Jan, and Mama never existed. It helped somehow to deal with the pain and grief. I knew the fantasy had to end eventually, and I would need to face the harsh reality.

The time for Goran to leave came, and we went out into the empty field to walk beneath the full moon. Without the cornstalks to hide inside, we did not hold hands, and we kept a distance between us.

"Goran, will you tell me that *something* you mentioned when you were here in the spring? You don't have to. I was just wondering about it." I bit my lip, worried I shouldn't have asked.

"Yes, I need to tell you, and today is good."

I held my breath and waited.

"It's about my wife." He ran his hand through his hair and looked away from me when he spoke, like he had been rehearsing what words to say. "She had been sick for a long while. My mother had to take care of her and the children while I was gone to find work."

"I'm sorry to hear this. Why could you not tell me?"

"Because you were going through too much. We agreed, remember? No talk of our spouses or children. We needed each other. I was feeling lonely. My wife and I hadn't been intimate for a long time when you and I got together." He shuffled his feet, still avoiding my eyes.

"I understand."

He smiled, then gave me a solemn look. "This last time I went home, she was much better and livelier than she had been in the last couple of years."

"That is good, is it not?"

"Yes, it was, is," he brightened. "So, you see...."

"Goran, are you trying to tell me you and your wife have rekindled your passion? Is that why you haven't pressed me for, you know, what we used to do?"

"Yes. But, also, to tell you, I'm sad."

"How so?"

"Because I love you," he blurted.

My mouth dropped open.

"This thing between us wasn't intended to be about love. Sometimes, or all the time, we can't control who and when we love." He studied me.

"True, we can't control love. I love you too," I said, shocked that the words came out of my mouth. Yet I knew it to be true.

"Hearing you say it makes me happy and still sad."

"Me, too. I think I know where you are going with this. I've been thinking the same thing." I pressed my lips together to hold the words in, but they needed to be said. "We need to end this."

"We do." His eyes glistened with unshed tears.

We embraced and held each other for a long time.

"When you leave tomorrow, you won't return, will you?" I pulled away.

"It's the right thing to do. I will find work elsewhere. Your Papa need not know why."

"He knows about us."

"Oh? How awkward." Goran hung his head.

"I just found out recently. He understands and isn't angry with us."

He sighed. "He is a decent and proud man. It has been an honor to work for him."

"Be sure to tell him that when you go," I urged. "He needs to hear good things right now."

He turned and pulled me with him. "We must go back."

I decided that was the last time I would ever see Goran alone. Letting him go freed me to finally decide about Janos and America. I loved Goran, but my love for Janos was much stronger.

There remained one problem: I couldn't leave my Papa. He still needed me, and I wanted to be there for him. America would have to wait.

Chapter Nineteen

December 1911

I FOUGHT THE CONSTANT DESIRE TO CURL INTO A ball and shut out the world since Mama passed and Goran left. Having Papa there helped. Together, he and I performed the daily chores and shared our memories of Mama over our meals together.

Though my heart wasn't in it, I went through the motions of preparing for the holiday. I kept thinking of how Mama would do it, and she always did it better. Even sweeping the floor, I could hear her voice telling me to sweep toward the door in her gentle, loving way.

I helped Papa hang the tree upside down from the ceiling. We spent the evening decorating it together. Yet another year without Little Jan delighting in the tree and decorations tugged on my heart.

But, this holiday, Papa and I agreed we could feel Mama's presence watching over us, along with baby Karin and Little Jan, just like my dream.

And then there was Janos. It seemed I had lost him and

myself, too, along the way. Through all that, I rediscovered myself, and my love for him, and anxiously awaited his homecoming.

———

Janos couldn't get passage on a ship home for St. Mikuláš Day to exchange presents. He came on Štedrý večer.

I stood on the steps of the front door, awaiting his arrival. The gate creaked open, and I held my breath as he came around the side of the cottage. When he saw me, he broke into the biggest smile. I rushed into his waiting arms, determined to repair the tears and holes in our marriage.

"Miláčik." He wrapped his powerful arms around me and enveloped me in his scent—the scent I had missed.

"Jani, my love." I hadn't spoken those words in such a long time. They were honest and from my heart.

We kissed passionately, not caring if anyone saw us. Papa stood in the doorway, looking pleased. It would be an excellent Vianoce.

Papa invited Janos's parents and Ivan to join us for the evening meal at our cottage. They arrived soon after Janos, and the cottage resounded with cheerful and eager voices. Everyone gathered around the dinner table, except for the one extra place, which was set for those no longer with us, Little Jan and Mama. In Mama's memory, I prepared her favorite after-dinner dish, *lekvar pirohy*.

Papa pulled out his accordion and played Mama's favorite Slovak carol, "Thy Nativity."

We all joined in and sang the lovely tune.

Come, we shepherds whose blest sight
Hath met Love's noon in Nature's night;
Come lift up our loftier song,
And wake the sun that lies too long....

All through the many stanzas, I could almost hear Mama's lovely voice singing with us. It was a blessed evening.

Eventually, Janos's parents and Ivan left, and I finished cleaning up. Papa had already fallen asleep in the single bed in the main room. I took Janos by the hand and led him to the other room, where we reconnected once again with love and intimacy.

————

ON VIANOCE, WE WERE TO OBSERVE HOW WE behaved toward others. How we acted that day, we were to do so all year. I planned to show love to everyone. I had experienced enough sadness and loss to last me a lifetime. I could hardly wait to give Janos the special gift I had made for him.

Papa sat in the rocker, reading his newspaper from the previous day.

"Let's go for a walk," Janos said.

I nodded and grabbed the gift from the room, then met Janos by the door. I pulled him to one of the benches and handed him the wrapped package. "We missed St. Mikuláš Day. This is my gift to you."

"Ah, how nice." He unwrapped the package and removed the dark red scarf I had made with homespun wool. "This is very beautiful, Mira, just like you." He kissed my cheek and let me fold the scarf around his neck.

"You told me how cold it is in St. Louis, you know, the snow?"

"It is perfect." His blue eyes sparkled with pleasure.

Janos wrapped my shawl around my shoulders, and he put on his overcoat, leaving the scarf on, even though it wasn't that cold outside.

We stepped outside. The early-morning rain had dampened the ground. Our next-door neighbors were outside and waved to us. We waved in return and made our way toward the fields.

"Ah, Mira, it's good to be with you again, even for a little while." He breathed in the cool air and patted his chest.

"I've missed you, Jani. I hope you know how happy I am you are here."

"I do, yes. We have had a lot of struggles these past few years. My being in America has put a strain on you. I'm sorry for everything you had to go through without me here. You blame me for much."

"But—" I started.

He pressed a finger on my lips. "It's true, in a way. I left you and Little Jan. I believed it was the right thing to do."

We continued to the backside of the barn, where the fields began, then halted. Janos looked out across the land. "I thought I could make enough money to buy land just for us. But there is no land here to buy." Sadness laced his voice.

"There is this land, my parents'. Papa needs help," I said.

"I know. But there's more, I have changed."

"How have you changed, Janos? Do you not love the land anymore?"

"I do love the land. I do. I want to start again, away from the losses we both suffered in America." He faced me and took my hands.

I knew the question would come and was prepared with an answer.

"Please forgive me for taking a long time to decide, Jani. I can't leave Papa here alone. If you don't want this land, then perhaps he could come with us?"

"Of course, he can come. It would be wonderful!" His expression relaxed. "If he would. Have you talked to him about it?"

"Not yet. I do have one condition." The big issue was yet to be resolved.

"A condition?" He raised a brow.

"It's about my sister, Aneta."

He dropped my hands and looked away.

"Please hear me out, Jani, please. It has been three years since you told me about Tomas and the money. Since that time, I have lost a baby girl, Little Jan, and my Mama. Aside from Papa, Aneta is all I have left of my family."

"I understand," he replied in a soft voice.

I touched his arm. "She is in Colorado—the last I heard. I don't know how far it is from St. Louis."

"It's far," he murmured.

I would never confess that I had never stopped writing to Aneta. "If you allow me to communicate with her in letters, with your blessing, then I will go to America." There, I said it.

There was a long pause before he spoke.

"I understand everything now. Aneta probably had nothing to do with Tomas's plans. I know how she followed him as a good wife should and believed everything he said, even when much of it was nonsense." He took a deep breath and put his arms around me. "Forgive me, Mira," his voice hoarse, "I was wrong to demand you give up your sister."

"Really, Jani?" I cried on his shoulder. "Thank you." The surprise and relief overwhelmed me. I knew how difficult it was for him to apologize, and it touched my heart deeply.

We continued our walk along the fields, and we both showed forgiveness, a noble behavior for Vianoce.

Chapter Twenty

1912

Janos returned to America in January. Someone showed interest in buying the farm, and we arranged everything for the move to America. By March, that person pulled out of the pending deal.

"I must stay now, Mira," Papa told me. "I can't go with you without selling the farm first. And to be honest, I'm not ready to leave behind the life your mama and I built. The deal falling through is a sign the timing is not right."

"I understand, but I can't go without you," I said.

"But you must. Janos is right, there is more opportunity to start fresh there. Start a new family, a new life, away from the pain and memories trapped here. You're too young to spend the rest of your life taking care of me. And Janos needs you. He needs your strength."

"Promise me you'll think about coming when you're ready?" I pleaded.

Papa nodded and smiled.

"Okay, then. We'll go get the tickets tomorrow, after planting is over."

I wrote a letter to Janos, letting him know Papa's decision. I'd have to book the departure in June. I'd have to at least stay through May, the one-year mark after Mama's passing.

———

My Dearest Mira,

I'm sorry to hear that your papa doesn't feel ready to come to America, but I understand it's a big change. He has lived a lot of life there with your mama. It can't be easy to leave. It was hard for you, and you are coming. Maybe he will change his mind.

I'll make sure we have an apartment for when you arrive in June. I've sent some money so you can make a new, American-style outfit to wear on the voyage. There're also some photos from magazines to see what women wear here. It will help you fit in and not stand out when you get to New York City.

I'm very excited to have you here with me. I love you.

Your Jani

I appreciated his understanding about Papa, since he wasn't very close to Papa. His own parents had no interest in emigrating and turned Janos down when he asked. Perhaps Janos was hoping my papa would fill the place of having parents in America. I hoped the same thing.

I made new clothes as Janos requested, a plain white blouse with long sleeves that puffed just a little at the shoulders and a high collar. I thought I would choke whenever I tried it on. I also made a skirt, long to the ankles and very plain. I didn't like the new clothes I made. I planned to take the outfit with me and change into it before I saw Janos.

IN APRIL, DISTURBING NEWS REACHED OUR VILLAGE. I'd just made it to the Notary Office to check the post.

"Nothing today," said the Notary's assistant. "But did you hear the news?" he asked in just above a whisper.

I shook my head.

He leaned forward. "The largest ocean liner ever built, the RMS Titanic, hit an iceberg in the North Atlantic and sank!"

I gasped and widened my eyes in horror.

He continued, "Not sure about how many lives were lost. The facts change daily."

"T-thank you for letting me know," I said, and rushed home.

I was surprised to hear about the ship, but what surprised me most was how frightened I became at the idea of making the voyage across the ocean.

I burst through the door of the cottage and blurted the news to Papa.

"Mira, please calm down." Papa pulled me down beside him on the bench in the big room.

"Oh, Papa, I'm too frightened. There is no way I can go to America now. What will I tell Janos? He will never forgive me."

"Perhaps by the time you leave, you will feel differently," he said. "Or we could change the ticket to a later date."

I slumped. "I don't know if I will ever go."

"You will go. I know it. Maybe the time isn't right."

I leaned into him, and he put his arm around me. My heart was pounding from the anxiety, but the answer was clear to me. I was not going.

In mid-May, I wrote to Janos telling him that the sinking of the Titanic made me too afraid to make the voyage. Papa cashed in the departure tickets, and I put the money in the bank account. I packed everything for the trip in a wood box and stored it away. Three weeks later, I heard back from Janos. The same day, I received a letter from Aneta.

> Mira,
> You have disappointed me very much. I'm trying to understand what you are feeling. Many here have expressed their fears of sea voyages as well because of the Titanic tragedy. But you didn't say when you will come. Are you telling me you will never come? Please tell me this isn't so.
> I await your reply.
> Janos

I crumpled the paper and threw it on the floor. While the sinking of the Titanic terrified me, I feared I was using the incident as an excuse not to leave Papa. What would I tell Janos? I had to write back eventually, but I opened Aneta's letter to take my mind off the decision.

> My dearest sister, Mira,
> I'm sorry it has been so long since my last

letter.

We moved again from the vineyards. Tomas didn't like it. He goes by Tommy now. I keep forgetting. There was much going on with little Jamie and Katie, and then the moving. Enclosed is a photo of them. Aren't they darling? I'm sending my new address. It's hard to believe you are finally coming to America! You will be much closer to me, though now far from St. Louis.

We are in San Francisco, the city. It is very different, with lots of hills and streets that go up and down. Tommy works in a factory doing something mechanical. He tried to explain it, but I don't understand. There is a lot of buildings and new businesses here. I also found work sewing in a clothing factory. The children are being cared for by our neighbor. She is very kind, or I wouldn't be able to leave them each day. The money is good and with both of us working, I think we might do a lot better here.

I'm very unhappy. I had made many friends in Colorado and I miss them. We weren't long at the vineyards and I didn't make any friends. Nothing satisfies Tommy, no matter where we go. I don't know what to do about it. I'm supportive and try to understand. He's drinking even more, and it costs our precious money. I want stability, to stay in one place and make a permanent home.

I'll try to tuck a little money away somehow,

and someday we will see each other again.
Please write as soon as you arrive in America.
With much love,
Aneta

I couldn't believe they had moved again—and Aneta was working in a factory? Too much to take in. And what was going on with Tomas? Or Tommy.

I looked at the photo of my three-year-old nephew and niece, almost a year old. She was right. They were adorable, both wearing white dresses, even Jamie. Katie's dress was much more feminine, with lots of frills and lace. Jamie was sitting next to Katie on an upholstered bench with his arms around her. I wondered why she barely mentioned them.

To make matters worse, I had decided not to go to America. At least not right now. ***

By November, my relationship with Janos had become very strained. I tried to explain to him in my letters what I was feeling. He didn't understand, and often I didn't understand myself. However, I received a letter from Janos a couple of weeks before St. Mikuláš Day that made me face the reality of our situation.

Mira,
I have been very patient with you for months,
trying very hard to understand your fears and
refusal to come to America like we planned. Our
future as husband and wife depends on you being
here. We agreed to start over and begin a new

family in America. I won't change my mind.

I've decided to stay in America permanently, and there is no point in my going home for Vianoce. I want you to come here as soon as possible. I wrote to my parents, too, explaining my decision. I hope they understand. There is no future for me in Hungary. It's time to decide what you want.

If you don't come to America by early next year, I will let you and our marriage go.

Jani

One line in the letter made my blood boil. *We agreed to start over and begin a new family in America.* Yes, I had finally agreed, but I was coerced. I thought if Papa went with me, I could do it, then he changed his mind. I found myself right back where I started, feeling betrayed and manipulated by Janos's decisions being made without me.

Now he threatens a divorce? I never wanted that. I do love Janos, despite our pushes and shoves for control. How do I overcome this? What should I do? He's made it perfectly clear; he's not coming back. A knot formed in the pit of my stomach.

To save my marriage, I realized I was the one who needed to change—not because I was wrong, but because Janos had already decided there would be no other way.

I went outside to search for Papa and found him in the barn feeding the cow and the ox.

"Papa?" I called from the barn doorway.

The hunch in his shoulders had worsened over the last

year, and his hair had turned almost completely gray. He had suffered great losses as well: one of his daughters had left for America, he lost a granddaughter, a grandson, and finally his wife of almost thirty years.

He straightened as much as he could and leaned on his pitchfork as he looked at me. "Is something wrong, my dear?"

I rushed over to him. "Very wrong, yes, this letter came today from Janos." I thrust the letter toward him.

"I'm sorry, Mira, but my reading glasses are in the house, and it's too dark in here."

"Forgive me. I was too anxious to talk to you. Janos...he... he has given me an ultimatum about going to America."

"I see. So, what did you think he would do? You refused to go to America." He sighed.

"I don't know. I guess I hoped he would come home and stay. Now, he says if I don't go to him, our marriage will be over." I dropped onto a bale of hay.

Papa hung up the pitchfork and sat beside me. "There, there, Mira, it isn't the end of your life." He patted my hand. "I know in your heart you love Janos and respect him as your husband, as all Slovak wives must, yes?" He spoke in his usual calm and gentle voice.

"Yes, I do, very much, despite my actions the last couple of years with...well, you know."

"I haven't judged you where others might. You know what you have to do. Be the good and strong woman I know you are and go to America."

The chill in the air deepened, and I had run out of the cottage without my shawl. I shivered, and Papa put his arm around me.

"You are right, but Papa, I simply can't leave you here alone." I clung to him and held in a sob. "That has been the main reason I stay."

"I have been thinking much about this situation the past

few months." He took a deep breath. "As small as this farm is, it's just too much for me, even with help. And when you leave, and I know you will, what is left for me here?"

"What do you mean? Are you saying you are ready to leave this place and go to America with me?" I hiccupped and wiped away my tears with my handkerchief.

"I will sell the farm. Then yes, I will go to America to be with you and Janos."

"I was afraid to ask you again. You told me you couldn't leave and how much you love the farm, because of all your memories here."

"I loved this farm when your mama was alive. Not much anymore," he said with resignation.

"Papa, this makes me very happy!" I gave him a big hug. "There is much to do then. I will write to Janos and tell him what we have decided. How long do you think it will take to sell the farm?"

"I don't know. We will have to see." He gave me a wan smile, stood, and resumed his work.

My fear of the ocean voyage still persisted, but I decided it was the right thing to do. I would find the strength to make the long journey ahead.

Chapter Twenty-One

September 1913

Papa fell ill in January, which delayed his search for a buyer of the farm. He needed me to care for him, and I couldn't leave. After several months, he was well enough to search for a buyer. He convinced me to go ahead to Janos, promising he'd follow. Janos understood.

To prepare for my journey, the Lutheran minister, who was fluent in English, taught his parishioners enough English to board the ships for our voyages to America. Though I spoke three languages—Slovak, Magyar, and Rusyn—I found English very difficult.

I wrote Aneta, letting her know why Tommy really left St. Louis for Colorado and that I was finally coming to America.

The day I was to leave, I bid my farewells to our neighbors, friends, and our minister. The last was Janos's family. Maria, Anton, and Ivan came to our cottage to say goodbye. I was remiss for not spending much time with them since I moved back in with my parents. They were kind when Mama passed away.

Maria pulled me aside from the others, and we went into the bedroom and sat on the bed.

"I need to ask you for your forgiveness." Her thin mouth stretched in a straight line.

"Forgiveness? For what?"

"First, you and I have not always seen eye to eye on things, and maybe I didn't say or do things to show you how important you are to our family. I'm sorry. And...." She looked deep into my eyes and pursed her lips. "The day I got sick, and you rushed off to find Dr. Schwarz...."

"What about it?"

"I feel responsible, mostly for you losing your Karin."

She looked away, but not before tears welled up in her eyes. It was the first time I had ever seen her cry.

"No, Maria, you weren't—"

"Please,"—she looked up sharply—"let me say this. You sacrificed your baby for me. If you hadn't cared about my welfare, Karin might be with us today. I'm sorry for not thanking you for what you did. I've regretted it ever since." She hung her head.

I stared, stunned. "There is nothing to forgive. It was my fault for ignoring the signs that something was wrong. I convinced myself it was nothing."

She looked me in the eyes. "I know you didn't blame me for losing Karin, but you blamed Janos for losing Little Jan."

I flinched. "I was wrong to blame Janos for Little Jan, and we forgave each other." I shifted my weight on the bed and touched her hand, an act I didn't think I could have done before.

"You are a good daughter, Mira, and a good wife."

With a twinge of guilt, I smiled, and we embraced.

"We are all right now?" she asked, her voice brighter.

"Of course, Maria."

We went back into the big room where Anton, Papa, and Ivan had been chatting.

"Anton, I don't think I ever thanked you properly for trying to save Little Jan from the river that day," I said.

He blinked. "Little Jan was my only grandchild, my dear. There is nothing more you need ever say." He swallowed hard, choking back a sob.

I gave him a hug, and he patted my shoulder. They were never a demonstrative family. All the hugs and tears were quite unusual.

Ivan came over to me. He had grown into a nice young man who, at sixteen, was as tall as Janos.

"Aunt Mira, I will miss you very much, and if you would allow me, I would like to write to you and Janos from time to time." He shuffled his feet but held my gaze.

"I would love to have you write to me. Please do and tell me what is happening in your life. I promise to write back." The surprising gesture touched me.

Ivan gave me a big hug, and we kissed each other's cheeks.

"We'll help here as much as I can. He is family, he will not be here alone," Anton promised.

Papa didn't say anything, but I knew Papa would let them. He would need a lot of help with me gone, and knowing that made me feel a little better about leaving him behind.

On their way out, Maria and I promised to write as often as possible, and we bid our goodbyes.

"Rozlúčka!" We shouted.

———

PAPA TRAVELED WITH ME ON THE LONG WALK TO THE train depot and by train to Port Fiume. I appreciated him by my side. He eased my fear somewhat. The locomotive and all the cars mesmerized us. Papa smiled and pointed out things in wonder. We rode in the third-class car full of people from many cultures.

Papa pointed out a young Slovak family, and we found seats across from them. They had two little children; one sat on each parent's lap.

"Dobrý deň," I said.

The woman smiled and adjusted the child in her lap.

"Dobrý deň," the man said.

"Where are you heading?" I asked, excited and nervous.

"America, of course. Pennsylvania."

The child on the man's lap grew fussy, and he refocused on his children. I looked out the window, marveling at the landscapes we passed.

The stench in the car was unbearable from the many bodies, dirty diapers, and the food people brought. However, before long, we grew accustomed to it.

We brought food, too, and I was hungry. The long walk from our cottage to the train station had tired us both. Papa had already fallen asleep. I opened some bread wrapped in paper and ate a little before I fell asleep.

We woke up several times because the train made stops. New people boarded, and only a few got off, which made it even more crowded.

As we traveled through the mountains, the beautiful scenery enraptured me. I had never been out of our small village.

Papa awoke and looked out the window. "This reminds me of when I was a boy. You remember my stories."

"Yes, Papa. From when you migrated with your parents from the Carpathian Mountains."

"My parents took work along the way. Of course, we were relieved to settle at our home. We'd been traveling since I was a boy, and by the time we arrived, I was nearly a man."

"Why did they leave the mountains? Was it really because of our religion?"

He nodded. "I believe so. Lutherans were a minority and still are. The Catholics persecuted them."

"And they were Slovaks too. I never understood that type of prejudice. What was it like living in the mountains?"

"I don't remember living there, only moving around from place to place. But my parents talked about the beauty of their homeland."

"It's interesting you mention those mountains today, since the name of my ship is the Carpathia. Another sign I am doing the right thing, you think?"

Papa yawned, his eyelids drooped, and I let him be. I continued to gaze out the window as the sun inched its way down the horizon and darkness fell.

After traveling throughout the night, we arrived at Port Fiume two days before the ship's departure. They directed us at the train depot to take the electric tramway and find a hotel close to the embarkation center.

Janos had sent us instructions on where to go and what I needed to do, but the city confused me. We knew no Italian and couldn't read the signs. We stood outside the station looking around, uncertain which way to go. The family who had sat across from us on the train walked up to us.

"I've made this trip before, I can help," the man said, holding one of his children.

I looked to Papa. He nodded, and the man explained where we needed to go to Papa.

"Ďakujem," Papa said.

The man shifted his weight and nodded, then turned and headed off with his wife, who carried his other child.

Papa and I made our way to the tram. Luckily, we found two seats together on the full tram. Those left standing held onto poles in the aisle. We stared wide-eyed out the window while the tram moved along the tracks and through the busy city. Tall buildings four and five stories high, the tallest I'd ever seen, towered over us. Just as Janos had told us about New York, Fiume was noisy, and people crowded the sidewalks and streets alongside horses, carriages, and motorcars. Were all big cities like this?

We found a cheap hotel and slept most of the day. The tiny hotel room had two small single beds, a washstand, and indoor toilets down the hall. I couldn't help staring at the indoor plumbing. I touched everything. It was all new to me, and my first time in a hotel.

We spent the next day getting the paperwork needed to board the ship. Eventually, the time came for me to leave Papa and say goodbye. We stood outside the embarkation center, holding hands. I didn't want to let go.

"*Šťastnú cestu*, Mira," Papa said.

"*Čoskoro sa uvidíme*, Papa." My voice caught, and my eyes teared up. I held them back, not wanting tears to be the last thing Papa remembered of me.

He nodded, his eyes also filling with tears. At last, I had to let go, and I entered the building with my heavy bag in hand. I turned and waved to him one last time. I thought my heart would break in two.

Chapter Twenty-Two

RMS Carpathia, Bound for New York

TEN DAYS LATER, I GAZED OVER THE RAILING AND watched the water gush and hurl against the hull of the steamship. Pinks and oranges streaked across the horizon beneath the dark clouds overhead. The sunset over the ocean transfixed me, but I shivered in the icy wind on the upper deck and clutched my wool jacket around me with my mittened hands. I wore the American-style outfit I had made. When I had boarded the ship, it became painfully clear why Janos had been concerned about me fitting in. The other ladies' clothing was more stylish and westernized than my shabby peasant attire.

The style of clothes I made was similar, but certainly not as beautiful as what some other ladies wore. Their clothes were in unfamiliar fabrics, like sheer silks covered in beads and pearls, and shiny satins worn in the evening. Even in the daytime, they wore beautiful dresses or skirts with smartly tailored jackets. I chose a thin wool fabric, a dark gray for the skirt, and our homespun white linen for the simple blouse. However, Janos was right. I was less conspicuous and fit in.

My fear of the ship sinking had vanished. I enjoyed the ocean voyage. Funny how our minds and hearts can get mixed up and confused.

Had it really been five and a half years since Janos first left for America, and two years since we were last together? It was difficult to believe, yet I was anxious about living with him again. Would Janos and I be happy? I prayed we would. Yet a part of me wondered if I made the right choice. Both of us had changed.

And there was Papa, alone on the farm. I already missed him terribly.

Only a few others milled about on the second-class deck. I'd overheard one of them talking about the ship and how it had been built to transport Hungarian immigrants from Port Fiume to New York. It relieved me that none of the others on the deck were visibly seasick, but the stench from people throwing up in barrels on deck the first few days nearly made me sick. Even walking along the inside passageways, the smell permeated the cabin air. Fortunately, I loved the roll of the ocean beneath my feet.

A man's loud voice boomed in English from behind. I turned. I spoke and understood enough to answer the required questions needed to board the ship.

I replied in Magyar, "Sorry, sir, I speak very little English."

The uniformed man responded in Magyar. "We are going into a storm. Everyone must leave the promenade deck and go inside." He spoke loud enough for others to hear.

I nodded and followed the other passengers inside.

The storm rocked the large ship as I ran my hand along the walls to steady myself. I reached my cabin, which I shared with a Slovak woman, Tatiana, and her twin daughters, Sonja and Ema. The cabin comprised of four bunks, with a porcelain bowl sink on a wooden stand in between, and two tiny end tables next to each bunk. There were two extra chairs, one a rocker, and a colorful hook rug on the floor between the beds.

"Ah, Mira, there you are. We worried about where you had gone. It's almost time for the dinner bell," Tatiana said in a deep, rich voice. She pulled at her long, dark red sateen skirt, smoothing a few unavoidable wrinkles as she sat in the rocker.

"Just on the promenade deck, watching the ocean. There's a storm, and they ordered everyone below deck." I removed my jacket and hung it on the hook behind the door.

"Ah, yes, the ship is rolling a great deal. Well, come sit over here with my girls."

I squeezed in on the edge of one of the lower bunks next to the fourteen-year-old identical twins working on an embroidery project. I wouldn't have been able to tell them apart if not for the different colors of their modern dresses. They both had dark blond hair and vivid green eyes, quite striking in appearance. Sonja had been born first. She told me the first time we met to make sure I knew she was more important. Ema had been born a full ten minutes later. She was less affected by the priorities, Sonja told me, and kept to herself, letting her older sister take all the attention.

Tatiana and her daughters were from New York City. They were returning after a long visit with family in a Slovak village outside of Budapest. Tatiana's family, like most Slovaks in the North, had assimilated into Hungarian culture, losing their language and traditions. They spoke only Magyar and English.

When we met that first day in our cabin, she had said, "Oh my dear, after my first voyage across the ocean, I promised myself never to travel third class or steerage again. It was simply awful." She went on to tell me every detail of her adventure. She could be long-winded. "It took us years to save enough money for the three of us to travel round-trip in second class; this makes me happy." She ended her story with a loud sigh.

I liked Tatiana. She was very different from any other woman I knew. She was outspoken, dramatic, and seemed knowledgeable about the world.

We watched the girls sew, the ship rocking back and forth, until Tatiana broke the silence.

"Lots of seasick people, but this is much better than the voyage that took my first husband," she said matter-of-factly.

I looked at her. "Oh? I'm sorry to hear of the loss."

Tatiana waved her broad hands vigorously in the air. "The conditions on the ship were terrible, and he contracted meningitis. Died before ever reaching New York. It was months before I received any word." She clucked her tongue.

"How terrible for you." A shudder went through me thinking about what it would have been like if Janos had died going to America, and I thanked God he hadn't.

"Yes, yes. They buried his body at sea. No one to mourn his death with a proper funeral." She looked into a small hand mirror and adjusted her hair, done in the modern puffy style like many of the other ladies on board the ship. She handed the mirror to me with a smile.

"Thank you." I took the mirror, wishing I had not left mine behind, and eyed my braids wrapped across my head as usual. I had stopped wearing my headscarf since Tatiana didn't wear one. "But how did you manage?" I asked. "Were you alone in your village, or did you have any family there?"

"My goodness, no, I was still living with my parents outside Budapest. We visited them on this trip. They are very old now, and this was probably the last time I will ever see them. Others of my family moved to America years before. Eventually, I was able to get enough money to make the voyage alone and connect with family in New York. Within the first year, I had married again and had these two lovely girls." She sighed. "Life has a way of working out, no?"

As if on cue, the dinner bell rang.

"It is time. Shall we all go together?" I asked.

The storm still raged, and we clung to the rails along the wall of the narrow passageway.

Tatiana said, "The dining saloon isn't much different from first-class."

"I've not seen it," I said. "We aren't allowed."

"I know. Someone told me."

We pushed through the doors and into the large dining area. The dark wood-paneled walls gleamed with polish. Elegant columns stood throughout the large room, furnished with round tables covered with white starched linen.

Even after ten days, I still gaped in awe at the finery of the beautiful room. I settled in the dining chairs upholstered in rich brocade and deep seat cushions. They were so plush I never wanted to get up. I carefully touched the silver table service, the fine gold-rimmed China with the Carpathia insignia in the center, and the fancy folded napkins at each place setting.

At my first meal in the dining saloon, I was awkward and hesitated to touch anything. I had stared at all the various utensils, not knowing which to use. Tatiana slyly pointed to what I needed, and no one noticed. I dreamed of having a table setting just like it one day, only with a colorful embroidered tablecloth.

The food took some getting used to, being more British style, since the ship was from England. Thick, sliced beef and the ever-present mashed peas, which I disliked. At the morning meal, they called 'breakfast', they served black pudding, a pork sausage made with blood. Bland, not spicy like Slovak klobasa. But I enjoyed the crumpets and biscuits, which were not much different from our Slovak dumplings and pastries.

Three full meals every day was more food than I'd ever eaten. I worried my new clothes would no longer fit by the time we reached New York. But I ate anyway, reveling in the luxury.

ON THE LAST NIGHT OF OUR VOYAGE, EVERYONE AT dinner was full of talk about the next day when the ship would pull into New York Harbor. I was more eager than ever and thought about finally being reunited with my Jani.

Chapter Twenty-Three

October 3rd, 1913, New York City

THE DAY THE SHIP REACHED NEW YORK CITY, I learned second-class passengers didn't go through Ellis Island, as Janos and Denny did. We were to be examined by visiting doctors on board the ship. The doctor was very respectful, for which I was grateful, and I passed through the inspection without issue. Some people still had to go through Ellis Island for further examinations. I was sorry for them and hoped it wasn't anyone I met. I didn't want to get sick on my first day in America.

After the examinations, Tatiana, her daughters, and I made our way out on the decks, along with many others, to watch as the ship edged its way through what was called the Narrows. The voices filled the air over the sound of the steam engines, so loud that I put my hands over my ears.

"Look," said Tatiana, standing next to me. Her girls pressed against the barrier in front of her. She pointed across the rails. "See? There is Manhattan Island. Lots of people with lots of money live there."

There were too many buildings scrunched together; I couldn't imagine living there. The voices stopped, and only the sound of the ship hummed. I looked around at the others on the deck. People were pointing. Hushed whispers and *oohs* and *aahs* peppered throughout the crowd.

The imposing Statue of Liberty came into view. Even from a distance, she towered taller and larger than I ever imagined. Tears welled up in my eyes, and a lump formed in my throat. The reality of what lay ahead was right in front of me. A whole new world, new fears, new challenges, and new experiences.

When the ship docked in Manhattan, I disembarked with the other first and second-class passengers down the gangplank. I could see the third-class passengers below, herded like cattle across the pier to a waiting area, where they would be ferried to Ellis Island. I was even more grateful to Janos for making it possible for me to avoid that process. Aneta traveled alone and in third class. It must have been awful, yet she never mentioned it in her letters.

In the chaos of disembarking, I lost track of Tatiana and her girls. The crowd was impatient and pushed me aside until I could not see them. I scanned the faces, hoping to find them.

"Mira! Over here!" Tatiana's voice carried over the noisy walkway. She waved to me.

I pushed through the people to reach them. "Thank you for not letting me get lost!"

"I wouldn't forget you, my dear. We go through customs first, remember me telling you?"

"Yes, I remember." I breathed a sigh of relief.

The lines were lengthy, and we stood for hours. There must have been several hundred people, and not just from the Carpathia. Other ships had come into the port.

Would Janos be waiting for me in the reception center? My stomach somersaulted with anxiety at seeing him after so long apart.

"I'm hungry," Sonja said.

Ema nodded in agreement. "Me too."

"Good idea." Tatiana turned to me, excited. "I'll get something for you, too, if you stay and hold our spots."

"Yes, of course," I smiled.

I stayed in line while they went to a place in the embarkation center called a cafeteria, where they could get pre-prepared food. The line moved a bit, but it would be a while until we reached the customs counters. Finally, they returned with sandwiches wrapped in waxed paper and bottles of *something*.

"We are back," Tatiana said. "Here you go." She thrust a bottle at me.

"What is this?" I peered at the dark-colored liquid in a green glass bottle.

"Coca-Cola. You have much to learn about America. Your first cola." She chuckled.

The girls watched me and giggled.

I took a sip and almost choked. "What is that, bubbles?"

"It is called soda. It is fun to drink, yes?"

We all laughed. I drank more and got used to the refreshing bubbles right away. The line moved again, and we finally reached the customs booths in the enormous hall. Tatiana and her girls went to one booth. A uniformed man waved me to another.

I gave the man my papers and waited. He asked me a few questions in English, then spoke a few words in Magyar, stamped my papers, and waved me on through.

The crowd pushed me forward into another huge room filled with people of different cultures. Many languages crossed over each other: English, Magyar, Italian, and German, too. Long wooden pews faced each other in rows that filled the hall. It must have been the reception area Janos described. I looked around for Tatiana. Where was Tatiana? I couldn't believe I had lost her again.

Then I looked all over for Janos but didn't see him. I eventually caught sight of Tatiana and the girls.

"Tatiana!" I waved.

She looked up, smiled, and waved. A man walked up to her and embraced her, and she wrapped her arms around him. The girls huddled in with them.

I stood looking at their family all together. I thought of Little Jan, and my heart sank. I remembered the dreams, and as much as I hated to be pregnant, I looked forward to having more children one day.

Tatiana motioned for me to join them.

"Mira, this is my husband," she said as I approached.

He smiled and shook my hand.

"I'm sorry, but we must leave you before your husband arrives. Hopefully, he will come for you soon," she said with sincerity. We gave each other a kiss on the cheeks and a brief embrace.

"Thank you for everything. I will always remember your kindness, Tatiana," I said.

"*Jó utat*," she said, and I replied the same in Magyar.

I hoped we would meet again, though I doubted it since I would be almost a thousand miles away in St. Louis.

Feeling conscientious, exhausted, and alone, I looked around for a place to sit. I found an empty seat next to a couple I thought were speaking German.

I listened for a moment, then said, "*Guten Tag.*"

"Ja, Guten Tag," replied the woman, and I was immensely glad for the bit of German Zelda had taught me.

The woman studied me closely. "*Haben Sie aus Deutschland angekommen?*"

"*Nein, Austria-Hungary*." I wasn't sure if I had an accent. Zelda had said there was a hint of my Slovak tongue.

"*Sprechen Sie Englisch?*" she asked.

"Little English."

"Ja, me little English." She chuckled. "You speak Deutsch well."

"*Danke*, uh, thank you. I wait husband."

"Ah, yes." She pulled on the man's sleeve next to her. "My husband," she said proudly. "You live here?"

"*Nein*, go St. Louis, Missouri."

They both raised their eyebrows.

"Long time to get there." She patted my hand.

"Mira!" A familiar male voice called.

I jumped to my feet and looked around. Janos strode through the crowd, a hat in his hands, his face in a broad smile. I rushed toward him. I threw my arms around him and kissed him, not caring what others thought. He held me in his strong arms and kissed me back.

"Jani, my love," I whispered into his neck, not wanting to let go.

Part II

AMERICA

Chapter Twenty-Four

October 1913, New York City

Janos treated me to a decent hotel for one night. It was nicer than the one Papa and I stayed at in Fiume. That evening, we ate in the hotel dining room. I wished I had something nicer to wear after traveling for ten days. I did my best to spot-clean the blouse and skirt and smooth out as many wrinkles as possible.

Janos impressed me with how he carried himself, speaking English to the man who showed us our table in a quiet corner. If I hadn't traveled second class and learned how to eat and act from Tatiana, I would not have been relaxed. A waiter arrived, speaking only English.

Janos pointed to the menu and asked, "Would you like the roasted chicken or the pork dinner?"

"The chicken." I figured roasted chicken wouldn't be much different from how we roasted them.

He smiled and turned to the waiter, then said in English, "My wife will have the chicken, and I will have the pork chops. And...we will have some red wine, too."

"A bottle or by the glass?" the waiter said.

"By the glass is fine." Janos winked at me, like I was supposed to understand.

I frowned. "What?"

"You will see."

When the glasses of wine were set on the table, my eyes popped. I whispered, "Janos, can we afford this?"

He waved his hand. "Do not worry, my little Mira. This is a once-in-a-lifetime experience, as they say here."

I had never seen him like that. He was a different person in New York. Had he changed that much? I wondered how he would be when we got to St. Louis.

THE NEXT MORNING, WE STEPPED OUT OF THE HOTEL onto the crowded sidewalk, and the chilled air made me shiver.

"Are you warm enough?" Janos said.

"I'm glad I have my wool jacket," I said, wishing it were longer than its waist length to cover the thin wool skirt, and I wished I'd worn my own, still rolled up in my travel bag. Frustrated by my lack of knowledge about American clothing, I would later see if my Slovak skirts would fit under the narrow skirt. I hadn't thought of that while on the ship. "I will need to make more clothes when we get to St. Louis."

Janos nodded, probably assuming I knew what I needed. How I wished I had asked Tatiana for advice. As we strolled along, my eyes were on the women and the long, straight silhouette of their outerwear, just like the ladies on board. No form or style to them, I thought. No embroidery either. I pushed my worries about my attire out of my mind and enjoyed the new experiences.

When I started to slip my arm through Janos's, he took my hand instead. We hadn't held hands while walking in a very long time. I smiled broadly.

"Where are we going today?" I asked.

"To Central Park. A very famous place, I've been told. This will be my first time, too. There is a lake, and perhaps we might feed the ducks." Janos sounded excited, and his enthusiasm influenced my mood.

Automobiles and streetcars filled the roads with people walking in the midst of them. It was frightening, and I pressed close to Janos as we crossed. He was attentive and protective of me, just like when we were first married.

When we reached the park, he guided me around cyclists and the people crowding the park paths. At a large bandstand, we stopped to listen to some lively music. No seats were available. We stood and listened along with dozens of others. After a while, we moved on and stood on the bow bridge, overlooking the lake, where several row boats with passengers passed beneath us. I was mesmerized by the beautiful tall pines surrounding the area.

"This is a magical place, Jani," I said. "It's no wonder why so many New Yorkers come here. Thank you for bringing me here."

He released my hand, wrapped his arm around my shoulders, and gently squeezed. "It is truly beautiful, yes."

I hated having to leave, but we needed to retrieve our baggage from the hotel and get to Grand Central Station in time to board the four o'clock train. The last two days with Jani were treasured, wonderful times.

Janos had learned the American ways well, and I marveled at how comfortable he was. I hoped to be that comfortable one day.

———

Janos had bought tickets on the Southwestern Limited, with stops in Buffalo and Cleveland, arriving in St. Louis in only twenty-six hours. Still, that was a long time to sit up since we didn't have a sleeper.

We quickly found our seats on the train and settled in. The seats faced a couple sitting across from us. They had a boy and a girl, around ten and eleven years old, who slept curled up in their seats.

"Hello," Janos said to the woman.

"No English," she said. "*Vy govorite po-russki*? Russian?"

I shook my head. "*Hovoríte po slovensky?*"

The woman stared blankly at Janos and me, then smiled apologetically. We gave up and only smiled at each other from time to time. By the time the train left the station, and we were out of the city, the sun was setting, and soon it was too dark to see much out the window.

I slept through the night, leaning against Janos's shoulder until the sun streamed through the misted window and woke me. I raised myself, gazing at the hills, mountains, fields, and towns speeding by.

"Oh, look!" I tapped on Janos's shoulder and pointed outside. Rolling green hills met the snow on the distant mountaintops.

"Yes, yes, Mira, I have seen them many times." Janos yawned and pulled his cap lower over his glazed eyes. "It's too early. Go back to sleep."

I had slept enough—the unfamiliar sights and sounds excited me. Yet a fear grew deep inside and formed a knot in my stomach as we got closer to our destination. I worried that I didn't speak much English. Would I make any friends? Janos had previously said not to worry, for there would be plenty of people in our neighborhood who didn't speak English, and he had reminded me that his brother Denny had family there. My mind spun with too many thoughts, and I feared it might burst.

Eventually, other passengers woke up and moved around.

The acrid odors were worse than the train to Fiume. The different languages clashed, and the English was harsh to my ears.

The Russian woman woke her children with a gentle shake of their shoulders. The girl frowned and mumbled while she stretched her arms out wide, accidentally knocking her brother's head. He woke up yelling at her, and the two fussed and shoved each other. The mother admonished them. The commotion woke the father, who reached over and slapped the boy on the back of the head.

I cringed. Seeing a parent strike a child bothered me. But it worked, and the children settled down.

Janos slept through the ruckus. I pulled out the food we purchased before boarding the train in New York, some cheese and sausages wrapped in paper. The sausage wasn't like the fresh sausage on our farm, but it satisfied my hunger.

The smell of the food wafted in the air, and my husband stirred. He stretched a bit and pushed up his hat, revealing his handsome face. He peered at me through his thick dark lashes, with those lovely aqua-blue eyes that captured my heart the first time we had met.

"Ah, Mira, I am hungry." He held out his hand, into which I placed a hunk of cheese and a long link of the sausage. "I'm glad those two children quieted down," he said in Slovak with a taut voice.

I gave him a sharp look. "I thought you were asleep."

"Who can sleep with all that racket? I'm glad their papa took care of it. The mama is too soft on them." He took a big mouthful of the sausage and cheese.

Mouth agape, I stared at him through narrowed eyes. He didn't even notice. Anton had been tough on the three boys. Little Jan was well-behaved and didn't cause any trouble, and I didn't see what kind of disciplinarian Janos would be. He wanted to start another family. There was no guarantee our future children would be as well-behaved as Little Jan. I couldn't help but wonder what kind of father Janos would become if we had boys like his brothers. I shuddered. Maybe I didn't want to rush into getting pregnant.

We ate in silence. We had spent nearly three days alone together. In our ten years of marriage, not only had we lived apart for over five of those years, but we had never spent even one day alone together. When we first married, we lived with his parents and two brothers. The men worked from sunup to sundown while I spent the days with my mother-in-law doing the domestic chores. We spent the evenings with the family, until we were alone in our bed, and we rarely talked then. Now, here we were, just the two of us.

The decision to leave my homeland and move to America had been difficult. I loved Janos, without a doubt. But which man did I love? The one I married ten years ago? Or the one sitting next to me? Did I understand what was ahead of me?

Janos stood. "I'm heading to the washroom," he said.

I wrapped the rest of the cheese and sausage and put them in my large bag. I gazed out the window as the landscape sped past.

———

On Sunday, the train pulled into St. Louis around six o'clock p.m., and we deboarded to seek transportation. The city also had electric trolley cars throughout the city, similar in size to the ones in New York—which we hadn't ridden—and twice as large as the one my Papa and I rode in Port Fiume.

Attendants stood at both ends of the trolley to collect our payment. Janos and I traveled to the Soulard District, where our apartment was located. We waited at the designated locations for the streetcar to stop so we could board. Some streets were lined with telephone poles, motor cars, and horse-drawn carriages.

Janos tried to explain all the places we passed, but the trolley's rattle and the buzz of conversation around us were too loud. There were tall buildings for banks and businesses, a cathedral with tall spires, and beautiful green parks with trees and playgrounds for children. With all the brick and concrete buildings and the paved streets, I longed for the open fields and my garden. I had seen several large cities since leaving my village, and now I decided I didn't like them. They were loud, smelly, and filled with too many people.

"You must see Denny's new apartment and meet his wife, but it's too late today."

Relieved, I smiled and gave a slight nod in agreement. I was exhausted. All I wanted to do was fall into bed.

"We will visit them next week for breakfast," Janos said. "Then we could join them for church at the Slovak Evangelical Lutheran Synod, the same church where Denny and Marta were married, though they changed the name just this year. It's nearby their apartment."

We changed trolley cars twice, then got off and walked another block. We halted in front of our building, a red brick walk-up with half a dozen steps leading to the front entrance. Many similar buildings lined the street.

"That is a tall apartment building," I said.

"Four stories, we're on the fourth," Janos said.

I shivered from the cold wind and stared up at the red brick building. Four flights of stairs? My feet would be in agony by the time we reached our apartment.

"What are you standing there for?" Janos frowned. He pulled me up the steps into a small entry area with a narrow stairway in the center and doors on either side. The air had the comforting and familiar smell of cabbage and spicy sausage.

I almost didn't make it up to the fourth floor, even with Janos carrying both bags. I clung to the rail and pulled myself up the last step. He laughed at me. I scowled, which he ignored. There had been more stairs during my journey than I had ever climbed in my entire life. The unused muscles in my legs cried out for rest.

Each floor had four apartments, two on each side of the stairwell. Janos stopped at a door on the right of the stairwell and dropped our bags. He retrieved a ring of keys from his front pants pocket and unlocked the door.

"You must lock the doors here?" I said in surprise.

"This is the city. You can't trust everyone like we did in our community, where everyone knows each other." He pushed open the door, picked up the bags, and entered. I waited until he turned on some lights. "Are you coming in?" he said in an irritated tone.

I stepped inside our new home. It was tiny, but clean. Light shone from wall-mounted lamps, much like the gas-powered lamps in the hotels where we stayed. The sitting area near the window overlooked the street. I was glad we had a front-facing apartment. Janos had furnished it with the basics, a small sofa, a rocking chair in the living area, and in the tiny kitchen, a table and four chairs.

"Come, come, Mira, I am tired and need to sleep. I must go to work in the morning." Janos took our bags into the bedroom and dropped them on the floor. I followed and sat on the side of the bed.

"The bed is nice. The furniture, too," I said.

"We will get more later. It is a start." He waved me out of the bedroom. "Here, this is the bathroom."

He opened the door to a sink and bathtub; only the sink had faucets for running water. Then he went to another door next to the bathroom. "This is the toilet. It flushes, like the one at the hotel."

"No outhouse?"

"No. It is nice, yes?" He smiled.

I gave him a hug, and he wrapped his arms around me. "It will take time, but I will adjust."

We quickly washed up. I removed my clothes down to my shift, and we went to bed. Completely exhausted, I cuddled against him, and we both fell asleep right away.

It was strange, waking up to find Janos already gone to catch the trolley to go to work. He left me a long note explaining how to get to the market for food, meat, and other small items.

I went to my travel bag, retrieved the packet of willow bark for tea, and put it in the dresser under some clothes. I had worried that the time with Janos in New York would result in my becoming with child. I wasn't ready to bear more children yet. Since it seemed to work when I had been with Goran, I would continue to drink it. This morning, though, my monthly started, and I breathed easier.

When he came home from work, he showed me how to use the pot-bellied stove so I could prepare meals.

"Marta will help you with everything else that women need to know. I called them from the phone at a small shop across the street. Denny has a telephone. They will expect us on Sunday morning for breakfast and then church. Sound good?" He patted me on my shoulder.

"That sounds good, Jani."

———

JANOS KNOCKED ON THE DOOR TO DENNY'S apartment on the third floor the following Sunday, and Denny opened the door. He looked very grown up, just like in the wedding photos he had sent, dressed in his American clothes, hair parted in the middle and slicked down.

"Janos." Denny smiled and hugged him. He stepped back, looked at me, and paused. "Mira, it's been too long."

We hugged and kissed each other on the cheeks, and Janos and I entered the apartment.

A woman walked up to Denny's side, and he beamed. "Mira, meet my wife, Marta." He extended his hands as if presenting her and giggled, a nervous habit he clearly hadn't outgrown.

Marta looked just like her photo, pleasant looking with dark hair and brown eyes, a firm square jaw. To my surprise, she was plump with child. I threw a look at Janos, exasperated that he hadn't told me. She wore a loose-fitting, oversized blouse tucked into a full skirt cinched above her protruding belly.

"Mira, *vitajte*," Marta said, and we hugged and kissed each other's cheeks, as though we had known each other for years. She showed me to the small sofa in the living area. The small sofa bounced a little when I collapsed into its softness, but it was a welcome reprieve.

She sat beside me. "I'm very happy to meet you at last."

I nodded and looked at Denny and Janos, already deep in conversation at the table.

"This is a very nice apartment." I looked around the small but clean space. It was similar to our apartment. I returned my gaze to her. "And congratulations on the baby, Marta. When are you due?"

"In January. I can't wait. That is why we moved here, because of the baby. Denny wanted our own place. We were thinking I couldn't have children. It's been three years since we were married. You know how it is expected to have children right away."

"Yes, our son was born within our first year married." I smiled despite the tightness in my chest.

"I'm sorry I never knew your Little Jan."

"Thank you. We hope to start a family here, though."

"I wish you many healthy children, Mira. But some days I wonder, it is difficult to go up and down those stairs being this big." She patted her round belly. "And I will get bigger too, I'm told."

"I'm not used to stairs either." I was glad to hear I wasn't the only one.

After a delicious morning meal that Marta said was Americanized Slovak recipes, we strolled together down the wide sidewalk, Marta alongside me and Janos and Denny behind us. We passed more apartment buildings and closed businesses. The occasional tree growing from small patches of dirt, surrounded by pavement, provided shade, and there were other couples and a few children out. Fumes billowed out of the backs of passing automobiles, and I coughed.

"You will get used to it in time," Marta said.

I doubted her, yet she didn't look bothered.

Up ahead, the three-story church building sat on South Ninth Street. As Janos had explained earlier, thirty-six Slovak families formed the church in 1905 to support immigrants. The congregation had grown considerably, and they were planning to buy a larger parish and building next year.

"Denny and I met there, and that's where we got married," Marta pointed at the building.

I nodded and smiled.

We entered the church behind a large crowd to find the foyer full of Slovak parishioners. They looked familiar and different at the same time. Because I knew we were going to a Slovak church, I wore my headscarf. I was relieved I did because although everyone wore American-style clothing, the married women wore scarves covering their hair. The young girls did not, however, and wore their hair either in a long braid down their backs or loose and flowing with colorful ribbons tied across their heads.

Janos introduced me to some of his friends. Denny introduced me to Marta's parents and two younger sisters. Though everyone spoke either Slovak or Magyar, I felt overwhelmed and said little.

It was strange hearing everyone address my husband as John instead of Janos. He had told me in a letter that he went by John at work, but I didn't realize he, like Denny, was using the Americanized name everywhere. They had also changed their last name from Lacko to Lacks. Many Slovaks were following suit in the effort to fit in. Janos thought it easier, too, so he was using Lacks. Why hadn't he explained things better? I wasn't sure if he was forgetful, assuming I knew things, or just inconsiderate. How could he not have known how uncomfortable not knowing these things could be for me?

A woman appeared to be watching Janos. She stood alone in the corner of the narthex.

"Who is that?" I asked Janos.

"Just someone else from the church," he said.

Her eyes followed his every move. Her expression reminded me of my sadness when I watched Goran leave the farm for the last time. My hand flew to my throat, and I glanced at Janos. He was laughing and talking with Denny and another man. I looked back at the woman. She was gone. I looked all around the room, but she was not there. Had there been something between them? Did I want to know? The hot burn of jealousy scalded my insides.

I recalled my own affair. I knew how much it would hurt Janos if I told him about Goran. I couldn't be mad if Janos had found comfort elsewhere, but the idea of being face-to-face with her? That would devastate me. Some things should be kept secret.

Marta spoke, pulling me back into the bustle of conversation. I forced myself not to think about the other woman—at least, not that day.

Chapter Twenty-Five

November 1913

Signore Donati, the Italian owner of the closest meat market to our building, peered over the counter and down his hooked nose at me. "What can I get you?" he asked again in English, his bushy eyebrows scrunched together. The tapping of his shoe was discernible even above the noise from people crowded into his shop. A line formed behind me, increasing my anxiety.

I stumbled over the English words. "If please want four klobasa?"

"Klobasa? We don't have that kind of sausage here. Will dry salami do?" he said, his voice laden with disdain.

He reminded me of the notary in our village.

"Um, yes. Good. Thank you." I wasn't sure what dry salami was. I didn't want to walk the extra blocks to the Polish deli where their food was similar to Slovak food. "Uh, one chicken...please?" I found it strange to buy a chicken already plucked and drawn, instead of going out to the chicken coop to pick one, kill it, pluck it, and prepare it for our meal.

I rarely left our apartment, especially while Janos was at work. He would leave very early in the morning and take the trolley to the bridge, walk across to the factory in East St. Louis, and return when the sun was setting. I would have waited for Janos, but I'd been inside for too long and needed fresh air.

Signore Donati pushed two paper-wrapped packages across the counter and shouted out a dollar amount. I fumbled in my small purse for some money, not sure of the currency.

The disgruntled people behind me voiced their impatience. My slowness only increased my embarrassment. Someone spoke Slovak in my ear. I turned and looked up at a tall woman with a broad face and high cheekbones. Her dark hair peeked out from a modern short-brimmed hat, and she wore a long, wool coat with wide lapels and large buttons.

"May I help you pay for your purchase?" She gave me a warm smile that reminded me of Mama. Everyone was reminding me of someone from home.

"Ďakujem," I said in Slovak, and released a sigh of relief. I put some coins in my hand and showed her.

She counted out an amount and gave it to the man behind the counter, thanking him in English. When she turned, she put my two packages in the basket on my arm.

"Here you go. My name is Ivana, but I go by Ivy."

"Miraslav, but I go by Mira. Forgive me. I am slow to understand English, and it is nice to speak Slovak."

"I was the same way when I arrived several years ago, and I still don't speak much English—just enough to buy things I need. Do you live nearby?"

I nodded.

"Wait for me to get my order, and we can leave together, yes?"

I nodded again and moved out of the way. I listened to the

voices around me. Some spoke Italian, some spoke Rusyn or German, but mostly English. The deli was a small shop with no place to sit, but it was freezing outside, so I pressed myself up against the window to allow more people in. This was not a good time to go to the meat market. I made a mental note to go later in the morning or walk the extra distance to the other market.

Ivy got her order, and we left the shop.

"I live on this street, the left side about halfway down," Ivy said.

"I do too, same side. We must be neighbors," I said.

"How wonderful." She smiled.

We walked together down the sidewalk.

"When did you move here?" Ivy asked.

"October."

"Alone? Or are you married too?"

"Yes, I am married. My husband was already living here. He met me in New York," I said, my voice cheerier than just minutes before in the meat market.

"Of course, of course. My husband came first, too. Then I came. We have lived here for eight years now and have two children. I try to learn English, but I rely on my husband to speak it for me, and I stay close to home, where there are those who speak languages I understand, like Slovak and Magyar. I understand Rusyn, too, though few Rusyns live around here."

"I speak Rusyn. Too bad there aren't many here."

"Your husband speaks English, yes? Is he not teaching you?"

"He tries." Janos's impatience with me proved more detrimental to learning than helpful. "I don't know why English is more difficult for me to learn than Magyar or even German. It just is," I lamented.

"You speak German?"

"Very little. The doctor's wife was teaching me, until they moved." My heart tugged. I missed my dear friend Zelda.

"Good. Many Germans live in this district, mostly down that street." She pointed to a street as we passed. "And down that street," she waved her hand in the other direction, "are the Czechs, and two streets over, are the Hungarians. Each street seems to attract a different culture."

"Where do the Slovaks live?"

"Like in the old country, we live all over. Some on our street, some elsewhere. Most Lutheran Slovaks live near the Slovak Lutheran Church. The Catholic Slovaks live closest to the Slovak Catholic Church. My husband is Lutheran, I am Catholic. We live on this street. It is easier."

She didn't bother to explain. I understood. Mixed religion marriages had become more frequent.

"My brother-in-law and his wife live next to the Slovak Lutheran Church. Too far for me to walk alone." Janos hadn't explained why he'd chosen an apartment on this street instead of one close to his brother.

"You need a longer winter coat than your traditional jacket. Do you sew?" Ivy eyed my skirt. It bunched a little because I had one of my old skirts underneath, but it was warmer than without.

"By hand, yes," I said.

"Good, but I have a Singer," she said with pride. "I can show you how and help you dress more warmly and in the American style. I'm guessing you don't know about the Soulard Farmer's Market?"

"A farmers' market?"

"Oh yes, it is well-known and very large. People come to it from all over the city. They have the best fresh produce, cheese, and preserved fruits. It's wonderful."

"How kind of you, Ivy. I am glad to have met you."

"Me, too. You will come to my sewing circle? I will introduce you to my friends in the neighborhood." She smiled and hooked her arm through mine as if we were old friends.

For the first time since arriving in America, I was optimistic.

———

EVEN WEEKS LATER, I WAS STILL GETTING USED TO the new environment. We had two sinks with running water, one in the tiny kitchen and the other in the bathroom. I watched in awe as the water filled the sink.

"No, no, Mira, you are wasting the water!" Janos shouted and turned off the faucet. "Water costs money."

"I'm sorry. I-I didn't know," I stammered.

Janos's impatience with me stood out. Everything was strange and new, and trying to learn from him made me feel stupid.

For the bathtub, we heated water on the pot-bellied stove in the living room and filled it. We no longer had to carry water in from outside, as we had on our farm. I liked that change. I used the tub to wash our clothes and bedding, and I sat in it to hand bathe. We didn't want to waste the water by filling it up.

However, I missed smelling the fresh country air when collecting eggs and working in the garden. Janos said someday we would find a place to have a garden, but in the meantime, I would need to make do.

Marta explained that the pot-bellied stove was common in older city apartments like theirs and ours. Newer buildings had central heat, but the rents were much higher. They provided much warmth during the freezing winter, and we used the flat surface on top for cooking. I could put two or three small pans or a cast-iron skillet on the top. For baking, I used a Dutch oven on the stovetop. It wasn't the same as baking bread in our brick oven on the farm, but it was better than nothing. There was much to learn. Sometimes I made mistakes or burned food. I got better over time, though. Marta was an enormous help.

Ivy said they had an icebox, like the one at Marta's and Denny's, with a cupboard with a block of ice on the top shelf and food on the lower shelf. I asked Janos why we didn't have one. He said we had to buy one, but we couldn't afford it yet. I longed to own one, then I wouldn't have to go to the market as frequently. Each week Janos got paid, I set aside a small amount just for the icebox.

Another new and amazing discovery was the mail. No more walking miles into town to see if letters had arrived. The mail came to a little box downstairs on the first floor, and I needed a key to open it each time. I often went down those four flights of stairs to check for mail, only to realize I had forgotten the key, but it was still better than walking to the notary.

My late Mamička taught me how to stretch a tiny amount of cash to cover the things the farm didn't produce. Janos agreed to turn over his paychecks to me to run the household and send money to our families. There was much to learn about living in a large city and the cost of living, all on top of buying food that we used to grow on our farm.

———

AN UNEXPECTED SHIPMENT CAME FROM PAPA. I opened the box to find on top Mama's beautiful, blue-flowered ceramic dishes. Tears welled up and blurred my vision when I pulled out three bowls broken in half. I set them aside in hopes of mending them. Two cups and saucers had only minor chips, but the remaining plates were shattered into unrecognizable pieces. Piece by piece, I pulled the ceramic shards from the box and piled them on the table. Not one of the scalloped-edged plates survived intact.

I slumped into the chair at the table. "Papa," I cried. Memories of Mama serving her special meals flooded my mind. Gently, I wrapped the broken pieces in the box's wrapping paper and tied it with some string.

There were other items in the box wrapped in paper. Embroidered scarves, table covers, and wall hangings were all undamaged. With a sigh of relief, I laid them all out on the table to decide what to place where.

There were more tears as I thought of all the times Mama, Aneta, and I would work on our embroidery together in our cottage, happy just to be together. I brushed the tears aside and got busy putting two of the wall hangings over the sofa. They needed to be hung on a small rod, but I wanted to hang them right away. I created little loops of thread at each corner at the top and hung them from nails hammered into the wall.

Next, I spread the large table cover over the small dining table. I didn't care that it was too big and almost touched the floor. I was happy to see the fabric again, with its intricate scrollwork, blue and red flowers intertwined with leaves, and edging in a geometric pattern. The smaller squares with red cross-stitched Slovak ladies all along the edge were placed on the two little tables next to the sofa and the rocker.

I stood back and admired the room. Finally, our little place looked like a Slovak home. I removed more pieces of embroidered fabric cut from cuffs and necklines of old shirts and blouses. At the very bottom of the box was my kroje, my best clothing. The white linen blouse, embroidered vest, and full skirt still looked nice. I hadn't brought them with me because Janos said I wouldn't need them right away, if at all. I wrapped them again in the paper and stored them in the bottom drawer of the dresser in our bedroom.

I retrieved some paper and a pen to write Papa.

Dearest Papa,

Thank you for sending the package of Mamič-ka's dishes, tablecloths, and decorations, and my kroje. It was very thoughtful of you, and they make me feel more at home here. I am still settling in, getting to know people, and learning how things are done in America.

Janos started a new job as a pipe fitter for a manufacturing company across the river in East St. Louis, which is actually part of the State of Illinois. He tried to explain to me exactly what he does, but I'm afraid it is not clear to me. When you come, he can tell you. He travels far by streetcar to the bridge and walks across the river. The new job pays higher wages, because he can speak and read a little English. He is very ambitious and wants more for us. He is learning to read and write English better to make more money. I am very proud of him.

I miss you and think of you every day. We are looking forward to you coming to be with us soon.

Your Mira

I couldn't tell Papa about the broken dishes, because I didn't want him to feel bad. And I didn't dare tell him of my struggle to adjust to living here, or the changes I had seen in Janos. I hoped things would all get better over time, and once Papa was living with us, I knew I could be happy. I just needed to hold out until then.

Chapter Twenty-Six

December 1913

Vianoce was different in America. Marta and Denny had already been celebrating the gift-giving tradition on Vianoce, December twenty-fifth, instead of our traditional St. Mikuláš Day on the sixth. Janos and I decided to do the same.

"We should get a Christmas tree," Janos said.

"Yes! Can we afford one from a sidewalk vendor?" I said, excited to get out of the house with Janos.

"I think so. Let me check." He pulled his wallet from his trouser pocket and sorted through it. "Yes. Let us go now."

Snow had left a light dusting on everything, and it looked pretty. Janos pulled on his cap, and I snuggled against him in my new winter coat, which my friend Ivy had made possible. The coat fell to my ankles in thick, light gray wool, with wide lapels and big buttons, like Ivy's. I had also made a warmer blouse, to which I added the same color embroidery to the cuffs and collar, and made a thicker wool skirt from my old skirts re-tailored to fit under the narrow style. I was a lot warmer. Janos wore his heavy winter coat over his everyday pants and shirt. We looked like an ordinary American married couple.

Once we had selected and paid for the perfect tree, Janos dragged it behind us to our building and up the four floors. He tried hanging it from the ceiling but couldn't find a secure spot, so we used the wooden stand that came with the tree and set it on the floor. It looked strange to me, but that was the American way.

On Christmas Eve, we went to the Nagys', Marta's parents' duplex. We took the trolley as close as possible and walked the rest of the way. Janos carried a basket of Slovak treats in one arm, and I held tight to his other arm while we trudged along the sidewalk. His work boots handled the ice and snow well as he guided me around the slippery patches. I gazed at the gray sky and shivered in the cold winter air as I huddled against him.

Janos knocked when we arrived, and after a short delay, Denny opened the door, his face tense and lined with worry.

"What is it?" Janos demanded.

"Marta is in labor already. The baby is coming." He waved his arms around, gesturing toward the inside, visibly nervous, then pulled us both inside.

"Isn't it too early?" I said.

"They're all in Lora's bedroom, second door on the right." He pointed the way.

I moved through the house, admiring the Slovak wall hangings, pillows, table covers, and a hook rug on the wood floor. The decorations emanated the culture of our people and warmed me to my soul.

Paul Nagy, Denny's father-in-law, gave me a brief nod. He sat calmly in an upholstered chair in the living room, smoking his pipe. I suppose having had three children, he was well familiar with the situation.

I continued to the room. Marta lay in Lora's bed. Lora and her other sister, Greta, stood nearby. Hana, their mother, gathered things she would need if the midwife didn't arrive in time.

"Can I help with anything?" I asked Hana.

Hana nodded. "We have everything under control in here. However, it would be helpful if you could get the food out for the men. I'm sure they're very hungry. Greta will help you." She motioned to Greta to take me out of the room.

I nodded, grateful to be of use, and followed the young girl. Their kitchen had plenty of counter space, a gas stove with burners, and an oven. From the kitchen window, I could see the backyard and a snow-covered vegetable garden, and a twinge of envy passed through me.

Greta, the youngest sister and just eight years old, was a pleasant girl with a bright, cheerful demeanor. She had the same strong jawline and dark brown hair as Marta, which she wore in a single long braid down her back. With the patience of a more mature girl, Greta showed me how to light the burner on the gas range and set the oven temperature. A large pan of water simmered on the stove, which I assumed was for the birthing.

Janos placed the basket we brought on the counter. Greta retrieved the pastries and put them on a plate, along with some other sweets Hana had made.

Marta's moans and groans carried throughout the house. "The contractions are coming closer together," Hana shouted.

Greta and I gave each other a knowing look. "Have you seen a baby being born?" I asked.

"Once, last year with my cousin."

There was a knock on the door. Paul got up from his chair and answered it.

"Dobrý deň," said a woman's voice, "I'm the midwife. I am late."

"Send her in now," shouted Hana from the bedroom.

The woman hurried inside and down the hall.

When the water was hot enough, I took it into the bedroom. Marta's face was red from the strain and pain, and her damp hair stuck to her head in mats. The midwife examined Marta's progress. I set the pan of water on a table in the corner. They definitely did not need me—it was crowded enough.

Greta peeked in from the doorway.

"Greta, not now." Lora waved her out.

I pulled Greta away, and we returned to the kitchen.

We placed the food on the dining table, and the men followed the aromas of cabbage rolls and chicken casserole into the alcove. I thought the baby would come soon after the midwife arrived, but several hours passed. Marta's moans had turned to screams.

Denny paced the room. "Why is it taking so long? Is Marta all right?" He bellowed and pulled at his suspenders.

"Denny, calm down. This takes time." Janos pulled out his pipe and tried to look calm. "I'm sure she's fine. I remember when you were born, our mama was in labor for almost a whole day."

Denny looked alarmed. "A whole day?" His shoulders slumped, and he sat next to Janos.

At two in the morning, the screams subsided, and a burst of infant cries came from the bedroom.

Lora emerged from the hallway into the living room. "It's a boy, and he's perfect."

We all heaved enormous sighs of relief and smiled and laughed with joy.

"*Blahoželanie*," said Janos and Paul, and slapped Denny on the back.

I congratulated him, too, and gave Denny a big hug.

"Ďakujem," he said, then ran to the bedroom.

The women wouldn't let him in until they cleaned everything and had Marta changed into a fresh nightgown.

The midwife came into the living room, her bag in hand. "Everything is normal. Hana has it from here," she said, and left.

Eventually, Hana allowed Janos and me to see the tiny baby boy. I was very honored to be a part of their family. Janos put his arm around my shoulder and gave me a knowing look and a wink. I knew what he was thinking. He wanted more children.

In time, Jani. In time.

They named the baby Anthony after Denny and Janos's father, Anton, and had already nicknamed him Tony. Very American. His name would not be final until the christening, which they hoped to have as soon as possible.

———

THE WEEK AFTER *VIANOCE*, A LETTER ARRIVED FROM Zelda, which my Papa had forwarded. That meant it had crossed the ocean twice! It was a wonderful gift, and I tore it open as fast as possible to read the elegant script of Zelda's hand.

Dear Mira,

I hope this letter finds you well. I was very happy when your last letter said you would move to America to be with your dear Janos, especially since we will move to St. Louis too. How small the world is, yes? Ezra has accepted a position at a hospital there. We should arrive sometime in March. I will write to you as soon as we get settled.

I have missed you terribly and look forward to seeing you soon. We will catch up on all our news when I see you.
    Your friend,
    Zelda

The thought of seeing Zelda filled me with such happiness. It was almost unbelievable that she was moving to St. Louis. Blessings came in the most wondrous ways.

Chapter Twenty-Seven

March 1914

I ran up the four flights of stairs to our apartment with barely a break on the landings. My hands shook so much that I couldn't fit the key into the lock when Janos opened the door.

"You are home early," I said, surprised, rushing inside. "I went across the street to the little store for butter and didn't see you come home. I just checked the mailbox on my way up. Look!" I waved the letter in the air. "A letter from Papa!"

"Good, good, read it out loud." He shut and locked the door.

We both settled in our chairs, Janos in his rocker, me in an upholstered armchair he had found at a used furniture store. He had good taste in furnishings.

I opened the letter.

My little Mira,
Hope you and Janos are well.

Good news. I think I found a buyer for the farm! Our neighbors to the south of us are inter-ested if we can come to an agreement. They want me to accept payments. It may be the only way, since no one else has shown interest. It will take some time before I can leave. There is much to do. I will write as soon as we complete the agreement with the farm.

It is lonely here without you, but plenty to do to keep my mind busy.

Your Papa

"Isn't that wonderful, Jani?"

"I am glad to hear it." His voice sounded disinterested as he tapped the pipe on the edge of the side table. The old, burned tobacco fell onto an old newspaper on the floor. He filled the bowl with fresh tobacco, pushing it down with his thumb.

"We need to think about where we will put him. We need to get a bed for him to sleep on and put it in the corner there?" I twirled a few stray hairs around a finger, a new habit I had developed since I no longer wore the headscarf, leaving my hair exposed but still in braids wrapped across my head.

"Let us worry about that when the time comes. Once we know when he will arrive, we can get a bed." He put the pipe in his mouth, lit it with a match, and took a long draw. He blew the smoke in a steady stream into the air.

"Well, if that is what you think is best." Disappointed, I opened the front window to clear the air of the pipe smoke. Sometimes it bothered me, though that day I wasn't sure which bothered me more—the smoke or Janos.

———

THE STREETCAR SQUEALED DOWN THE TRACKS toward the stop where I waited, surrounded by a crowd of people. Someone pushed hard on my back, and I almost fell into the street, but I grabbed the handle on the side of the streetcar as it stopped. All the seats were taken by the time I boarded. I looked around, frustrated that I was forced to stand and hold on to the pole in the center of the aisle. At the next stop, a man got up from his seat to get off, and I quickly slid into his place.

I couldn't contain myself when Zelda's invitation to visit their home in St. Louis arrived. Three years had passed since I'd seen her. Had she changed much? Had I?

They lived northwest of us, close to Forest Park, and my very first trip alone on a streetcar to visit someone filled me with trepidation. Would I miss my stop or get lost? I watched out the window for the landmarks Janos told me about. The streetcar jolted, and I held my breath for a moment, worried something was wrong, but the car continued.

The neighborhoods became more and more elegant. The streets widened, and the buildings grew taller. Men dressed in finer suits, and the ladies wore elaborate hats, so large they had to hold on to them to keep the wind from blowing them away. Their jackets and coats were more fitted. I was glad my simple styles were hidden under the long winter coat.

The streetcar stopped again, my stop. I hurried out of the car and onto the sidewalk, not sure which way to go. I spotted a newsstand nearby and thought the man working there would be able to help me with directions. I walked toward the stand and passed an alleyway where several young boys, around eleven or twelve years old, clustered together smoking cigarettes. It surprised me to see young boys smoking. There were stacks of newspapers around them. They were newsboys that sold newspapers on the street corners. Their voices clamored over each other, and they looked like they were having fun. I smiled.

The man at the newsstand was busy helping a customer, and I waited. When he finished, he turned to me.

"You need a paper or magazine?" he said in a low, husky voice.

"I need help, please? Uh, where is—" I pointed to the numbers on the piece of paper with Zelda's address.

"Oh, that's the Shaw Neighborhood. It's down that way, two blocks on the right." He pointed in the direction for me to go.

I smiled. "Thank you," I said, and turned to follow several people crossing the street at the corner. Many of the businesses had red-and-white striped awnings that stretched out over the sidewalks, their wares prominently displayed in their store windows. One was a produce market offering bright, shiny red apples with a little sign that said, *"Shipped from Washington State."* My mouth watered, and my stomach grumbled. I should have eaten something before leaving the apartment. Knowing Zelda, there would be delightful snacks for me upon my arrival. I kept walking.

I soon left the retail buildings behind, and two-story, standalone brick houses lined the street, though some were duplexes like the Nagys'. They all had small yards in front. Some had flower gardens bursting with color. At one house, I stopped to look at the flowers along the sidewalk with primroses in a profusion of reds and purples. I leaned over to smell the honeysuckle and noticed someone peering from the front window. The young woman frowned at me and motioned me to keep going.

Embarrassed, I continued my walk down the street, hunting for numbers that matched what was on my note. Then there it was—I stopped short and gasped.

The elegant home stood two stories high, made of red brick. Brightly colored flowers covered the sloped incline and were flanked by two sets of steps leading up to the house level. Full white columns stood at the entrance to the front porch. Over the large front window was a half-circle of stained glass, with white half-columns attached on either side of the wall.

I clutched the railing, which gave me courage as I made my way up to the porch and front door. An engraved metal plaque next to the door read "Pull for Bell." I pulled the cord. Chimes rang, and there was movement through the door's etched glass inset. The door opened.

"Mira! *Meine Lieben*," Zelda wrapped her arms around me and kissed both my cheeks. She smelled of lavender and vanilla cookies. How I had missed the sound of her voice.

"Zelda! You will crush me," I replied to her in German, and laughed.

"Come in, come in, please." She took my hand and drew me into the house.

The home was even more beautiful inside. I gaped at the foyer. In the center stood a large round table covered with an intricate lace tablecloth. A tall crystal vase sat in the middle and was filled with purple and white irises and yellow daffodils. Rich, dark wood paneling shone with a high polish, reminding me of the dining room on the Carpathia. I followed her into the living room.

"Let me take your coat, and please have a seat." She pointed to the sofa under the stained-glass window. The window looked pretty from the inside, with light filtering through the colors of the floral design.

I handed her my coat, and she disappeared into another room. I sat and took in the room. I recognized some things from the house in our village, but many were new.

Zelda reappeared with a tray and placed it on the low table in front of me. It held her favorite porcelain teapot, cups, and saucers decorated with tiny purple flowers and green leaves. As I expected, she had a plate of little sandwiches and an assortment of cookies next to a teapot. My mouth watered.

"Your home is very beautiful, Zelda. You and the doctor have done well since coming to America. You are blessed."

"I do feel blessed and, yes, we have been very fortunate indeed. Are you comfortable conversing in German, or would you prefer Magyar?"

"My German is rusty."

Zelda nodded and switched to Magyar. "You must be famished." She sat next to me and promptly poured a cup of hot tea from the teapot. "How long did it take you to get here?"

I took the teacup she handed me and sipped the hot brew. "Hm, thank you." The tea warmed me. "About an hour, what with walking to the closest streetcar stop, then a transfer to get several blocks from you." I took a small bite of a finger sandwich from the plate. Although I was famished, I didn't want to look like I hadn't eaten in days. "I wasn't sure how to get here. Janos looked it up. He knows the city."

Zelda eyed me up and down. "You look good, Mira. Very American."

I laughed. "I don't care for the American fashions, though I like what you're wearing. It is a nice color on you."

Zelda smiled and smoothed the skirt of her lavender dress that perfectly matched her dishes. It had a high neckline and long sleeves, edged with dainty lace and pearly buttons down the front. She'd gotten plumper since I last saw her, as well.

"Are you happy to be in America, Mira?" Zelda's brows crinkled.

I couldn't hide my feelings from her. "I–I, well...happiness has not come easy for me these past several years. Many bad things have happened." Tears welled up in my eyes, and I looked away.

"I know you have had so much loss." Zelda pulled a fine linen handkerchief from her pocket and pressed it into my hand. "I hated leaving you right after your Mama passed, but you are finally reunited with your beloved Janos. That must be good, yes?"

I dabbed the corner of my eye with the handkerchief and sniffed. "It is good, though Janos has changed." I hesitated, not wanting to divulge too much. "I miss my Papa. He is selling the farm and coming to America as soon as he can. I think then I will be very happy."

"There it is," Zelda exclaimed, "your beautiful smile. That is wonderful news about your Papa. He is a special man."

I relaxed, thinking about Papa. "Tell me all the news of the doctor and why you moved to St. Louis. Weren't you happy in Philadelphia?"

"Well," she began and took a deep breath, "it is all very exciting. My Ezra was offered a position at the new Barnes-Jewish Hospital being built near Forest Park. Have you been there yet?"

I shook my head. "How wonderful for him."

"Yes." Zelda picked up one of the crescent-shaped vanilla cookies and bit off the corner. "But"—she swallowed—"the" hospital isn't completed yet. In the interim, he is teaching at the university that will merge with the hospital."

Before she finished the cookie, she picked up another.

"How very impressive." I ate another little sandwich and poured myself more tea.

"Yes, and my position as his wife requires more social activities," she replied. "I'm involved in many of the local Jewish women's charities, especially since the hospital caters to the poorer communities, which brings me to something I want to discuss with you. Or ask you, I should say."

I nodded encouragement.

"I hope this does not offend you, because you are a very special friend to me." Zelda paused and bit her lip.

I paused in lifting the teacup to my lips. "How could you possibly offend me?"

"Well, I simply cannot keep this house up the way I should, what with all the other activities I am in and will be involved in soon. I am hoping you might be interested in working for us?" She gave me an expectant look and waited.

My mouth dropped open. "Work. For you?" I stammered. "What would I do?"

"Well, different things, depending on what needs to be done. I would show you, of course, anything you weren't familiar with. Cleaning, maybe ironing, and helping in the garden."

"You have a garden, too?" I jumped up, almost spilling my tea. "Where is it? Is it a vegetable garden?" I looked out the windows.

Zelda gave a hearty laugh. "Mira, you are such a delight. Yes, it is a small vegetable garden, but I would like it to be bigger. I know how much you loved working in your garden. Come, sit down. I'll show you later."

I lowered myself back onto the sofa and set the teacup on its saucer on the table. "Sorry, I got excited. I miss my garden. We have no place for one."

"So, does that mean you want to work for me?"

"I want to, yes. I have been frustrated not having enough to do with my time. This would be the perfect answer. I need to talk to Janos about it. I'm not sure how he will take it."

"I agree. You must discuss it with him and get back to me. Do you think he will disapprove?"

I looked down, afraid I had said too much. "He wants very much for us to start a new family."

"Well, of course he does. I understand. You talk to Janos

and then call me. We have a telephone. Do you have one nearby your apartment, or in your building?"

"You have a telephone here? There is a telephone across the street from us, at a little store."

Working would give us extra money for when Janos and I have another child. He would agree to that, right? Why was I worried about what Janos would say? My stomach turned.

"All right." Zelda wrote her telephone number on a piece of paper and gave it to me. "You call me and let me know if the answer is yes. Then we can make a schedule."

———

THE REST OF THAT DAY, I WAITED AT HOME, EAGER to talk to Janos about working for Zelda. I kept busy cleaning and cooking his favorite meal, *Kuracia Polievku*. The aroma of the chicken, parsley root, carrots, and rosemary filled the apartment. I stared at the small clock in the living room as if that would speed up the time for Janos to come home.

At last, he opened the door and heaved a huge sigh. His shoulders slumped, and he winced when he removed his jacket and hung it on the hook by the door.

"Dobrý večer, my Mira," he said, the same way he did each day.

"Dobrý večer, Jani. Are you all right?"

He rubbed his right shoulder, rotating it around a few times. "It's my shoulder. It will be fine with some rest."

"After dinner, I will make a hot compress for your shoulder. That will help."

"Ah, you are good to me, Mira." He gave me a quick peck on the cheek, then strode to the bathroom to clean up.

Janos was thirty-five, but working as a laborer had taken a toll on him. He had said it was his plan to move into another position that would be easier and pay more money. That took time, though he had been with the company for over five years.

I finished placing the dishes and meal on the table and was pleased that nothing was burned or undercooked. I hadn't yet mastered cooking on the pot-bellied stove, and I wanted everything to be perfect to put him in a good mood.

Janos sat and said his usual short grace for our meal, and I filled a large bowl with the soup from the tureen and set it ceremoniously in front of him.

"Hm, looks delicious, Mira, you know I love this." He smiled. "So, tell me, how was your visit with Zelda? Did you have any trouble finding her house?" He leaned forward with genuine interest and took a big spoonful of the soup.

"Your directions were perfect. I got there just fine, and it was wonderful to see Zelda. Her home is large and beautiful. They are doing well here. Dr. Schwarz is teaching at the university, and when the new hospital is built in Forest Park, he will work there." I tried to keep my voice steady, but I was proud of my friend and hopeful about the opportunity.

"Good for them." He pulled a hunk of bread from the round dark rye loaf, dipped it in his soup, and slurped up the dripping juices.

"She is very busy with many social and charity activities. It takes up a lot of her time. She needs someone to help her." I peered at him, held my spoon over the bowl of soup, then took a deep breath. "She asked me to work for her."

Janos froze, looking at me in surprise. "Work for her? Why would you want to do that? I know you see her as a friend, but they are Jews."

"Jani, I am surprised at you. You sound like Aneta. Where is this prejudice coming from?"

"It's not prejudice, just facts. They are German, we are Slovak, they are Jewish, we are Lutheran. Facts." He said this with an off-handed tone, like it was nothing significant. He continued eating.

I chose my next words with care. "Yes, you are right. We are all different. I do not think differences are a reason to segregate ourselves." I watched him for a response.

"That is you, Mira, not me."

"Are you saying that I can't work for the doctor and my friend?"

"I don't know. What kind of work would you do?" His expression curious.

Still, I didn't want to upset him and be refused. A different Janos had come to light since I moved to America. I wondered whether his years in America had changed him.

"Well," I said, with caution, "some cleaning, laundry, and help in the garden. You know how I miss my garden. It would be wonderful." I clasped my hands together and looked at him.

"I don't want you to work. I work enough for the both of us. You should be raising our family." His sharp tone startled me.

"Jani, I can't control when I have children." I lied. "Either they come, or they do not."

He could never know I had been drinking the willow tea to keep from getting pregnant. Janos couldn't understand. I had drunk it when I was with Goran, and it was partly helpful —that and him withdrawing at the right time. But Janos would never agree to delay children. Guilt heated my cheeks, and I ducked my head and took a bite of my food. Not getting pregnant was the one thing I felt like I had some control over. I lived in an unfamiliar world, and reconnecting with Zelda would be a lifeline.

He sighed. "This I know to be true, and I am sad you are not yet with child." He stopped eating and gave me a sad, but understanding, look.

I relaxed a little.

"Until the blessed event comes, I could be productive and earn additional money for when we do have another child. Papa will be moving in sometime this year, and we need a larger place." I took another breath, watching him for any signs of more resistance. "Marta worked before Tony was born, and even her mother worked. My friend Ivy works...and the money would be good, yes?" I worried my voice sounded desperate.

He continued to eat but looked thoughtful. I waited.

"I don't know. Let me think about it," he said finally.

I didn't know how long he meant to think on it, but I didn't ask and went about clearing the dishes, then cleaning and straightening up the apartment. Janos sat in his favorite chair and read the Slovak newspaper.

Later that night, after he turned off the gas lamp on the wall and we were in bed, he finally spoke. We rarely talked in bed, and his voice startled me.

"I don't want you spending all your time at the Schwarzes'. Tell Zelda yes, but only a few days a week."

"You say yes? It is yes?" I exclaimed, not believing my ears, and turned toward him in the bed.

"Yes, yes, Mira. It is all right. But like I said, just a few days. The extra money will be helpful. I had never thought of you working for anyone. I want to provide for you here in America like I couldn't do in Hungary."

"I understand, Jani, I do, and you are doing a wonderful job providing for me. I am not busy enough like I am used to. This work will be good for me, and working in the garden will make me happier."

"Did she tell you how much she will pay you?"

"Yes, the standard rate for house help."

"Good."

"Also, she offered to help me learn English."

"You don't need to speak English with Zelda. She already taught you German, and she also speaks Magyar." He paused. "But if you really want to learn English, I'm glad she will do it. I'm sorry I wasn't very good at it. I have no patience. And besides, I don't need English at home. We will speak Slovak." He kissed me on the lips and rolled over and fell right to sleep.

What a surprise that he acknowledged his failure in teaching me English and his impatience. Jani rarely said he was sorry. That was a positive change in him.

Knowing I would work for Zelda and have her friendship again meant a great deal. Renewed hope filled me and brought me the closest to happiness since I had come to St. Louis.

However, the way Janos had acted when I told him about the job offer and what he said about the Schwarzes disturbed me. How could he not realize his prejudice? How could I not have seen this in him? We hadn't mixed with many others in our village. We kept close to our Slovak family and friends and those we knew at church, who were all Slovaks. In school, we had Slovaks, Magyars, and other minorities like Slovenes and Rusyns. They never bothered me. In fact, most of them became my friends.

I couldn't recall my parents saying anything against other people, except maybe the Magyars. That was because of how they treated all non-Hungarians in the empire. It was the treatment, not about specific Magyars.

At any rate, I was going to work for Zelda, and that's all I wanted. I didn't want to think about the changes in Janos. He was my husband and good to me. That's what mattered.

Chapter Twenty-Eight

May 1914

I HATED BEING ALONE IN OUR APARTMENT. WHEN I lived in Hungary, family members were never far away, and I never felt alone. Janos didn't understand. He had forgotten or didn't want to remember.

It was easy for him to go to work and speak English with others. I felt certain it had been difficult for him when he first moved to America, but he wouldn't talk to me about that time. Whenever I brought it up, he would brush it off as not important. He expected me to get through it the same way he did, and that was that.

I stood in front of Ivy's door, having just knocked, and thought how lovely it was that she invited me to her sewing circle. My friendship with Ivy had become very important to me.

Ivy answered the door and offered a warm smile. "Mira! I'm glad you came today."

"Thank you for inviting me," I said.

She ushered me inside, where several ladies had already arrived when I got there.

"This is my friend, Mira, from Hungary. She speaks Slovak, Magyar, Rusyn, and a little German," Ivy said to everyone in Slovak in a bragging tone.

I blushed at her flattering introduction. "Dobrý deň," I said. "Does anyone speak English?" I asked. "I want to learn to speak it better."

Most of the ladies shook their heads. That was disappointing.

"I only speak a tiny bit of English. My name is Alica." She spoke in Czech, which was close enough to Slovak that we could mostly understand each other.

"Hello, Alica," I said.

She smiled, showing a few missing teeth, and sat next to me while we worked on a small embroidery project. The group reminded me of the sewing circles back home. All the ladies wore American-style dresses but wore traditional headscarves, even Ivy. I found it amusing that I had been trying to fit into American ways, and I was the only one with my hair uncovered.

They all told similar stories. They kept close to the neighborhood and didn't think they needed to learn English.

"What do you do while your husband is at work, Mira?" Alica asked.

"I work for a German doctor and his wife, mostly housework and gardening," I said.

A lady sitting across from me responded, "You're lucky. Most of the women who work have to work in factories. Tedious work."

I knew my opportunity to work with Zelda was fortunate, but I didn't realize how bad it was for the other working women. I was very lucky to work by choice and not because I had to. I was grateful for Janos and his ambition.

The lady sitting on the other side of me spoke, "Dobrý deň, Mira, I am Nela. Do you have children?"

"No, we don't right now."

"You will start a family soon?"

"We hope to, eventually." Between the two little graves in Hungary and my secret remedy, I was uncomfortable when the topic of children came up.

Everyone shared stories about family connections and where we were from, but most did not want to talk about their lives before America. Some may have come from extremely poor conditions.

My family had a tiny farm, but it was more than most. Many Slovaks had nothing of their own and traveled from town to town to find work, as Goran did. Some lived in hovels, or they burdened families who had permanent homes.

My thoughts lingered on home and the conditions of other Slovaks while the other ladies moved on.

"I feel stupid around my children," Nela said. "They go to school and know how to read and write in English, and I can't even read or write in Slovak to write letters to my family in Austria."

"Me too," said Alica. "I would love to send letters to my family. I just received a letter from a cousin who can write Czech. Would you read it to me, Mira?"

"I can try, and I'd be happy to write letters to your families, Nela."

"That is very generous of you." Nela's face lit up, and her eyes twinkled.

"I'd love if you could help me, too," one woman said.

"Yes, me as well," said another. "I'm sure someone can read them the letters when they arrive."

I smiled and nodded. "I'm sure as well." Joy filled me. I remembered the excitement of getting letters from Aneta and

Janos back home and how happy it made me to hear from them after their long journey to America.

I looked around the room at these different and yet similar women, who were smiling and chatting while working on their projects. When I first arrived in St. Louis, I was insecure and shy, afraid of fitting in. Now I was making friends and adjusting to this country.

———

Janos and I agreed to put my earnings into a savings account for emergencies and when we had our first American child. Working for Zelda brought me great satisfaction. I needed to be productive. My mood improved having a place to go and someone to talk to during the day.

People in Zelda's neighborhood spoke only English. Sometimes I needed to speak English on the streetcar or at the market near Zelda's house. I struggled to learn the language, even with Zelda as my teacher. We agreed to only speak English while I was at her home. She said it would strengthen her own ability to speak the language.

"Book on brown table," I said in English, pointing to the book on the table in her kitchen.

Zelda frowned, "No, Mira, *the* book is on *a* brown table. You make the same mistake in German, like when you forget the masculine and feminine *der* and *den* before the nouns. English has only one form of the article—*the*. You see?"

"Yes, yes, I forget to say *the* and *a*." I pounded my fists on my lap. "Slovak does not have ar-ti-cles." I emphasized that stupid word. "I hate English!"

"You will learn with practice. It will take time."

"When I forget, people laugh. They know I am Slovak and will call me *hunky*."

"I have heard this term. Do people really call you that?"

"Janos says people call him hunky at work. I don't want to be hunky. Like in Hungary, when Magyars looked down on Slovaks."

"Ja, I understand, we Jews have been called 'off-white.' It is very upsetting."

"I didn't know that. Yes, Janos told me we must become *White* to fit in. I do not understand. We are already White."

"Unfortunately, in America, there is a social expectation of being White, much like Hungary wanted us to be Magyar. It's a shame you are feeling the effects of this. We will work hard to improve your English, ja?"

Why couldn't I learn faster? I didn't like speaking English, but I also didn't like being different. I thought we had left all of that in Hungary.

———

ZELDA HAD BEEN TEACHING ME TO COOK NEW DISHES in their style, and I enjoyed learning new recipes. I spent a lot of time in her kitchen and became familiar with her fancy kitchen appliances, especially her refrigerator. Zelda was surprised we didn't have one and understood the cost, and I explained to her that we were saving up for one. One day, when I arrived at work, a delivery truck had parked in front of the house.

"There you are, Mira." Zelda rushed toward me. "Just in time, too. Look." She dragged me to the kitchen. "What do you think?"

An enormous refrigerator, twice the size of the one Marta and Hana had, replaced the one Zelda already had. The new one had two compartments on top for large blocks of ice, and below was a double-sided compartment, with three shelves on each side for food and beverages. My eyes nearly popped out of my head.

"It's wonderful, Zelda. Why did you buy a new one, though? The other one seemed to be fine."

"We needed something bigger to accommodate the entertaining we will be doing."

"I see. What will you do with the old one?"

"Ah, that is an excellent question. And I have just the answer. We want you and Janos to have it. Ja?" Her smile stretched from ear to ear.

"My goodness. How generous." I hugged Zelda and kissed her on the cheek. "You are so wonderful to me. Thank you."

"Now don't you worry about the transport either. Ezra said he would have it delivered to your apartment. You just let us know when."

"I'm not sure what Janos will say, though."

"I know how proud Janos is. You just tell him this is a gift from the doctor and me, ja?"

After dinner that night, Janos and I were sitting quietly in the living room. Only one gas lamp on the wall provided light in the combined kitchen, dining, and living area. Janos used a kerosene lamp for his reading. The flame flickered, shedding additional soft light. The rocker made its usual creaking while Janos rocked back and forth. His pipe hung from his mouth while he read the Slovak newspaper.

I told him about the gift from the Schwarzes. "Remember how we were talking about Zelda's kitchen and all the appliances?" I asked.

Janos didn't stop reading or rocking. He just grunted.

"They are giving us a refrigerator for our kitchen," I said, hesitant but still very excited.

"They want to *give* us a refrigerator?" Janos looked stunned and stopped the rocker.

"They bought a new, larger one and want to give us their old one, which is in excellent condition. Dr. Schwarz said he would have it delivered whenever we are ready." I beamed, feeling happy until I saw his brow furrow.

"I don't think we can accept this charity."

"It isn't charity, it is a gift."

"Same thing. We must pay for it, somehow, or refuse the gift, as they call it."

"Janos, please, if we refuse, they will feel insulted."

"Tell them we must pay them something. It is the only way I will accept."

"Yes, Janos, I will tell them."

Janos returned to reading his paper, and I shook my head. Sometimes, Janos's pride could be such a hindrance.

When I told Zelda what Janos wanted, she understood.

"Janos needed to feel he was providing," she said. I think she understood him better than I.

They agreed to accept a small payment and take it out in installments from my weekly pay. They repaid the amount that was withheld for the refrigerator to me in vegetables. Janos never complained about that.

―――――

Working in Zelda's garden quelled the yearning for my former home in Hungary. The warmth of the earth between my fingers brought back fond memories of working alongside my parents. Digging up the fresh vegetables and being outside in the fresh air invigorated me.

Eventually, I was also preparing their dinner meals on Mondays, Wednesdays, and Thursdays. Friday was their holy day, the Shabbat, and they didn't need me.

Mama died in May, and for the last three years, I suffered through losing her. But May was also the month I had married Janos, and that happy memory got buried each year with the sadness I felt about Mama.

I wanted this May to be different. I prepared a special supper for Janos of Jewish-style schnitzel and potato latkes. I smiled all day and hummed my favorite Slovak tune while shopping for the ingredients I needed to go with the potatoes Zelda had given me.

Our kitchen area was tiny, one counter with a wood top, a few drawers, and the sink. I set out everything that was needed. First, I pounded the veal cutlet very thin with a meat mallet Zelda had loaned me. I dipped the cutlet into the egg wash and dredged it in the flour.

Preparing and cooking food was awkward because the pot-bellied stove was in the living area. I had to carry the food from one end of the room to the other. On my walk to the stove, I tripped over the rug, spilling everything onto the floor. I let out a frustrated cry and dropped to the floor to mop it all up and start over.

Exhausted and with my apron covered in flour, egg, and splatters of fat, I finished cooking, and the aromas of fried foods filled the apartment. I opened the living room window to vent some of the smoke from the frying.

I glanced in the mirror. "Oh dear," I said. Tufts of white flour covered my hair. I rushed to clean myself up and put a fresh apron over my simple button-down dress that Ivy helped me make.

The table looked lovely with my Mama's embroidered tablecloth that I used for Sunday dinner. Though it wasn't Sunday, we would be celebrating our anniversary. I couldn't remember the last time we had been together to celebrate our wedding. Would Janos remember?

I finished just as he came in the door.

He sniffed the air. "What is that smell?"

"A special dinner for you, Jani. Go wash, and I will put the food on the table."

He gave me a small peck on my cheek and sneaked a curious look over my shoulder. I shooed him away.

"Yes, yes, I am going." He headed toward the bathroom.

I arranged the schnitzel in the center of a large ceramic platter and covered it with gravy. I placed the potato latkes around the sides and sprinkled chopped fresh parsley over everything. Pleased at how it looked, I set the platter in the middle of the table and sat. Janos took his seat and squinted at the food, then said grace.

"What is it?" He wrinkled his nose.

"Jewish-style schnitzel and German potato latkes." I dished out a large helping on his plate. I served myself and waited for him to start.

Janos stuck his fork into the schnitzel and cut a piece with his knife. He took a whiff and turned it all around, dipped it into the gravy, and took a tentative bite.

"Hm...tastes like something my mama made, but the coating is a little different. Thinner, I think." He looked pleased.

I sighed with relief. "I think what your mama made was similar. I remember that. This is the traditional Jewish style. The veal is pounded thinner. Your mama made it with chicken, and the coating was much thicker. You like?"

"It is good, and the little...what did you call them?"

"Latkes."

"Yes, they are fine. Zelda taught you to make this?" His eyebrows raised, making his eyes sparkle beneath his thick lashes.

"You know I cook for them on some days. Yes, they eat this and other Jewish foods, but I wasn't sure you would like them."

"Maybe, maybe not. I don't know. How are your English lessons coming?"

I thought he didn't care. "They are going well. I get frustrated, though."

"English is difficult. I struggled too. It will come."

Another surprise. So, I ventured forth.

"Do you know what month this is?"

"It is May, so?"

"We got married eleven years ago this month."

He stopped eating and put down his knife and fork on the plate. "Oh, Mira. I forgot a very important thing." He ran his hand across his chin and pursed his lips. "I missed a lot of Mays, didn't I?"

A lump formed in my throat. We both reached across the table and clasped hands.

My voice was hoarse with emotion. "Let's make this the first anniversary of our new life together in America, yes?"

He lifted my hands to his lips and kissed them. "Yes. Let us do that."

For the first time since moving to St. Louis, Janos and I were close like we used to be.

Later that night, we made love with the same passion and tenderness as our first time—exploring each other's bodies, brimming with love and hope.

Chapter Twenty-Nine

June 1914

I EXPECTED PAPA TO ARRIVE IN AUGUST. WITH THE extra money I made and Papa's income from the sale of the farm, Janos got us on a waitlist for a two-bedroom apartment in our building.

I had written to Aneta in San Francisco about Papa. She replied that she would come for a visit but didn't know when. I was thinking about how we would fit everyone in our apartment if we didn't get the two-bedroom when someone knocked on the door.

I answered the door, and my mouth dropped open. My sister and her two small children stood in the hallway. "Aneta?"

She had changed from the pretty, vivacious Aneta I last saw six years ago in Hungary. Instead, a plumper, tired version stared back at me with a deep sadness in her eyes. An extra layer of face powder attempted to cover a bruise on her face.

She rushed into my arms with the children holding tight to her skirt. I almost fell over.

"Come in, all of you. Sit, sit," I said in Slovak and pointed to the living room, but the children wouldn't let go of her.

Aneta shuffled her feet and dragged the children inside. She pried her boy's fingers from her skirt and pointed him toward the love seat. She picked up the little girl, sat next to the boy, then put the girl in her lap. I could see fear in their eyes. Aneta had tears running down her face.

"Mira, how I've missed you."

I sat in Janos's rocker. "It is wonderful to see you, but why didn't you tell me you were coming?"

"I—I just decided I needed to see Papa and you, and, well...." She glanced at her two children, then gave me a *we'll talk about it later* look.

I understood and nodded. I turned my attention to her son. "Who is this handsome little boy?"

"Jamie, say hello to your Auntie Mira." She nudged the almost-five-year-old, topped with a tousled mass of dark curly hair. He avoided looking at me and hung his head.

"And this little angel,"—Aneta turned the little girl around to face me—"is Katie, who just turned three. Doesn't she look like Mamička?"

"She does, with the dimples too! You are a beautiful little girl, Katie." I gave her the biggest smile I could.

She smiled back.

"Will you let me hold you?"

She nodded, and Aneta handed her over.

I bounced Katie in my lap. What would Janos say when he got home? He didn't like big surprises. I would need to borrow some bedding and pillows for the floor.

Aneta helped me with dinner while the two children napped in the bedroom. We laughed and talked just like when we were young.

I finished preparing the *Oravska pochutka* and put it in the Dutch oven as the aroma of the sausage and sauerkraut filled the room. A church member from northern Hungary had shared the recipe with me. Though it's Slovak, I'd never had it at home.

I took a deep breath and leaned into Aneta. "Please tell me what has happened?" I whispered, not to wake the children.

She cried and plopped down on one of the dining chairs.

"Please forgive me for showing up like this. Really, I am sorry,"—she sniffed—"but everything just came at me all at once, and I snapped."

I wiped my hands on my apron and sat next to her. "You know you can tell me anything and I will not judge," I said, my voice calm.

"I told Tommy I wanted to see you and Papa. He said no. No explanation, just no."

"Why? Did you not have the money to travel?"

"I had been saving my own money from the job at the factory."

"And he still wouldn't let you?"

"No. Instead, he wanted all the money I had saved. I refused. He got very angry."

"He hit you, didn't he?" I traced a finger along the bruise barely hidden by the makeup on her cheek.

She pushed my hand down and turned her face away from me. "No. Well, just that one time. It wasn't just that. It was all the moving around...his drinking. That's where most of our money was spent and why I had to work."

"Aneta, dear, why didn't you tell me?" I clasped her hands and gently squeezed.

"I couldn't admit that I had made a terrible mistake. Not that I could have changed anything. I hoped and prayed things would get better and that he would settle down and be happy."

"Has he been violent with the children, too?" I held my breath, fearing the worst.

"No, oh, no, not that. Though he would shout and throw things when he was drunk. He would threaten." She shrugged. "Who knows, one day he might have—if we stayed." Her expression twisted into an intense fear, and it startled me.

I wrapped my arms around her and hugged her tight. "My dearest."

"I took all the money I had been saving and paid for the train tickets to get us to St. Louis. We took the trolley from the train station and then walked the rest of the way. We are all very tired."

"Of course you are. You poor dear. You are here now, and we will figure it out. It's wonderful to be together again."

"I hope Janos doesn't mind me being here."

Just then, the door opened, and in came Janos. Aneta and I froze. Janos took off his cap and hung it on a hook by the door. He turned around and looked at us sitting at the table.

"Dobrý deň," he said. He looked at me, and then Aneta, eyes wide.

"Dobrý deň, Janos," Aneta said, with a forced smile. "Have I changed that much?"

"Don't you recognize her? It's Aneta." I put my arm around Aneta's shoulder and squeezed.

"Ah, sure, sure, Aneta. Mira mentioned you wanted to come for a visit. I didn't know it would be today."

"I hope it is not an imposition," Aneta said.

"Not at all. Mira has missed you."

"Mama?" Jamie stood in the bedroom doorway, rubbing his eyes. Katie stood close behind.

Janos gawked at the children. Aneta jumped up, ushered the children into the living room, then seated them on the sofa.

"Janos, dear, why don't you go wash, and I will have your supper on the table right away." My voice was surprisingly steady, since my insides had turned upside down. I wasn't sure how he would react.

Without a word, he went into the bathroom. I followed him and shut the door behind us.

"Mira," he said in a hushed whisper, "what is this?"

"I didn't know she was coming. It was a complete surprise. This isn't just a visit. She needs our help. She and Tommy are separated."

"Ah, I see. Finally, she realized what a louse he is."

"Can you please be nice to her? She is in awful shape, and the children are confused."

"I know how much she means to you. This isn't a problem. We will help. She and her children are your family, and that makes them mine." His expression softened, and he kissed me on the cheek. "I'm hungry."

Janos said grace. After a moment, Aneta cleared her throat and faced Janos. "I would like to apologize for the terrible thing Tommy did when we left here all those years ago. I had no knowledge of his deceit." Her eyes pleaded.

At first, Janos looked surprised. "I know you didn't have a part in it. Let us say...it is a bridge over the water gone. Yes?"

"Yes, that is good. Thank you." Aneta glanced at me with a broad smile.

After dinner, Janos dragged over two dining chairs, and we all squeezed into the living room. Katie sat in my lap again. Jamie clung to Aneta, and Janos read his newspaper while smoking his pipe.

"You've told me very little in your letters. What is it like living in San Francisco?" I combed my fingers through Katie's soft curls.

"It is a beautiful place. Everything is green, like here in Missouri, but I miss the ocean beaches." Aneta's eyes sparkled like her old self. "We would take a picnic lunch with us and play in the water."

"That sounds wonderful." I tried to imagine the ocean beach but couldn't. "Was there a Slovak community where you lived?"

"I met no Slovaks near where we lived. It forced me to learn English faster, though. While Tommy was...uh," she looked down at Jamie, "at work, I needed to speak English everywhere."

"Really? I wish you had told me, Aneta."

"I didn't want you to feel sorry for me. I learned some English in Colorado. There were more Slovaks there. I didn't need the English as much, and I even made a couple of friends." Tears filled her eyes.

"It must have been difficult moving." I patted her knee. The room was tiny, and our knees almost touched.

She smiled gratefully. "It was very difficult, but we managed, somehow."

"We go to a Slovak Lutheran Church here every Sunday. The congregation has grown a great deal, and they had to move to a larger building. You will like it. The people are nice and friendly, like home."

"I look forward to going with you and Janos." Aneta gave me a wan smile.

Jamie said, in English, "Mama, I'm thirsty, and can I have another cookie?"

Janos frowned. "Why is he speaking English when we are all speaking Slovak?"

Aneta looked at me sharply, then back at Janos. "I've been teaching him English. It's required for acceptance into kindergarten this fall."

I was speechless. It hadn't occurred to me that the children speaking English would upset Janos.

"That is fine, but I want everyone to speak only Slovak in my home. It is my rule. Right, Mira?"

"This is true, Aneta. I forgot to mention it."

"But Janos, how am I to teach my children English if they are not allowed to speak it here?"

"I'm sure you will find a way. Mira has." Janos pulled up his newspaper and resumed reading.

"I understand, Janos, and thank you again for letting us stay here." Aneta rolled her eyes and gave me a questioning look.

I mouthed, *"later."* As long as we kept the children from speaking English when Janos was home, what we did when he wasn't home wouldn't matter. Janos could be so stubborn and irrational at times. I hoped that once we had children of our own, he would be more understanding.

Luckily, Jamie lay his head on Aneta's lap and fell fast asleep. Katie squirmed and wriggled out of my lap and stepped over to Janos. I jumped up and stepped toward her, but she grabbed the paper and yanked hard before I could stop her.

"What is this?" He snatched the paper from the little girl's grasp. But when he looked down at her, his eyes softened.

"De-De," she said and looked up at him. She was trying to say dedko, even though Janos was not her grandfather.

"Well, it's little Katie." Janos gave her a big smile.

Katie held her arms up to Janos. He picked her up and set her on his lap. She laughed and smiled as Janos bounced her up and down on his knee, rocking back and forth.

Aneta looked just as surprised as I. We nodded at each other. Though he didn't always make sense, he loved little children.

———

When Aneta showed up, I had worried about how we would all manage. But as soon as our family and friends found out, their overwhelming generosity laid my concerns to rest. Before I knew it, we had two single mattresses, extra pillows, and bedding. My heart swelled. Their generosity reminded me of our community back home, where everyone came together to help.

Janos didn't complain. He mentioned they were really all for Aneta and her children, and he was glad he didn't need to spend any extra money. I held my tongue and considered myself fortunate.

When I told Zelda about Aneta's arrival, she was happy for me and gave me extra food, a few bars of soap, and towels—too much to carry on the trolley. Zelda insisted I wait until the doctor came home, and then they could drive me to my apartment in their motorcar.

When we arrived home, they came up to see the apartment for the first time. To my surprise, Janos was very polite and thanked them for the help. Aneta was gracious, too. I guessed she had let go of her animosity toward Jews since we were all in this new country together.

Our luck continued when, a couple of weeks later, a two-bedroom apartment on the first floor became available. The living room and kitchen were about the same size, but the extra bedroom made all the difference.

Aneta had already found work at a sewing shop, similar to what Marta used to do, just a few streets over. Aneta worked long hours during the week and half days on Saturday. Her income covered part of the rent and food for the three of them. A woman in the building next door took in the children on the days I worked. On my days off, I cared for the children.

We knew we would need to make more changes when Papa arrived, but things were working out.

Chapter Thirty

July 11, 1914

After working in Zelda's garden, I arrived at our building, drenched in sweat. I removed the straw hat I wore to shield my eyes and face while in the sun. I stopped at the mailbox and found one letter addressed to Aneta with a California postmark. The letter had to be from Tomas.

I continued to the apartment, unlocked the door, and stepped in. Aneta entered shortly after me with Jamie and Katie in tow.

"Whew!" Aneta wiped her brow. "I didn't know it got this hot here."

"Neither did I." I set down my bag and fanned my face. "Zelda's thermometer reached one hundred and two degrees before I left her house today. Her neighbor told us it was a record high. Janos never told me the summers were hot like our village. We didn't get the high humidity we have here. It's a good thing we moved to this first floor. I heard the fourth floor is stifling."

"I hate to say it, but I'm missing the lovely California

coastal weather," Aneta laughed, and ushered her children into the living area.

"Mama, *som smädný*." Jamie was thirsty.

"Suny," Katie said, trying to imitate her brother.

Aneta and I often spoke English to each other to help me, and hopefully Jamie, learn. We spoke Slovak to the children in front of Janos. We needed to make more of an effort to teach Jamie before school started.

Katie's speech hadn't progressed much for a three-year-old. Little Jan had been further along by age three. Aneta didn't show any concern, but I wanted to talk to Dr. Schwarz about it.

"Here you are." I handed each of them a tin cup of water, and I put the letter in Aneta's hand.

"For me?" She turned it over to look for a return address. Her face fell as she sat on the sofa. The children climbed up next to her. "Easy, don't spill the water." She collected the cups and put them on the end table.

"Are you going to read it?" I sat in the rocker across from her and retrieved my knitting from the basket on the floor.

"I don't know if I'm ready." The letter wrinkled in her tight grip.

"Go into the other room. I'll watch the little ones."

"No, just sit here with me while I read it. All right?"

I waited.

She opened the letter, her hands shaking. Her face cringed as her eyes moved across the paper. "Well, that was short." Aneta folded the letter, put it in the envelope, and sighed. "He doesn't understand why I left. He wants me to return right away because he needs me." She rolled her eyes.

"That's all he said?"

"He also said he can't live without me. Well,"—she put the letter on the table—"I can't live *with* him."

"Who, Mama?" asked Jamie.

Aneta flinched. "Uh, well, my darling, we will be staying here with Auntie Mira and Uncle John."

It looked like they were staying indefinitely, which was fine with me.

"We aren't going home?" He pulled at Aneta's dress.

"Not right now. We need to live here. Your dedko will come here soon. Don't you want to meet him?" She put Katie in her lap, and Jamie hugged her arm.

"I miss Papa," Jamie said. The corners of his mouth drooped.

"Yes, Papa," Katie said.

Aneta stifled a sob with her hand.

"You know you can stay here as long as you want." I smiled but worried she might go back to Tommy out of obligation.

"Thank you." Aneta held tight to her children.

Later, after the children were in bed and Janos had gone into our bedroom, Aneta and I sat at the dining table drinking tea.

"Mira, believe me, I'm done with Tommy. I feel it is best for the children. I don't want them growing up in that environment. Though I am very sorry, the children won't have a father."

"What will you tell people? I mean, will you get a divorce?"

"I'm not ready to make that kind of decision. I'll just tell people we are staying here until Papa comes, and we can all be together. That's all anyone needs to know, right?"

"That sounds like a reasonable story."

———

EARLY SUNDAY MORNING, I WOKE UP FEELING ILL. I rushed to the toilet, hoping not to wake anyone, but my retching awakened Janos and Aneta. They stood outside the door when I came out.

Janos reached out to me. "Mira, you are never sick," he said, voice heavy with concern.

"I'm fine, Jani, go back to sleep. It's too early for you. This is your day off." I nudged him toward the bedroom. He shrugged and returned to bed. I shut the bedroom door behind him and turned to Aneta. She raised an eyebrow and patted her abdomen.

"No," I said in a hushed voice. "At least, I don't think so." There had been a lot happening in the recent month, and I hadn't noticed missing my monthly a second time.

She gave me a quick hug and whispered in my ear. "Congratulations, Janos will be thrilled." She chuckled and went back to bed.

I stood there in disbelief. Another child? I counted backward in my head. It must have happened the night of our anniversary dinner in May. Janos and I had been swept up with sudden passion, and I forgot to drink the willow tea. It seemed too soon after coming to America, but Janos would be happy. I still dreaded giving birth. My chest tightened. I had lost two children. Could I handle another loss?

How could I go through another pregnancy? I would, of course. I could never attempt to end a pregnancy. As much as I feared what might happen, I feared the wrath of God more.

I slipped back under the covers and cuddled up to Janos, who was still awake. He rolled over to wrap me in his arms, and we snuggled close.

"I think I'm with child," I whispered.

"I suspected as much but wanted you to tell me. This makes me very happy, Mira." He gave me a big squeeze and a kiss.

"And I want you to be happy." My mind whirled, for I wasn't sure if I would be happy about it too.

———

As with all good news, there must be the bad.

On July 28, exactly one month after the Archduke of Austria had been assassinated in Sarajevo, Austria-Hungary declared war on Serbia. Our Slovak community and the world reeled with the shock. Within six days, Germany declared war on Russia and France; Britain declared war on Germany; and Austria-Hungary declared war on Russia.

I worried about our relatives overseas, like Papa, Janos's parents, and seventeen-year-old Ivan. They could draft him into service. Aneta and I received a major blow when Austria-Hungary closed the borders and banned emigration from the empire. Papa couldn't come to America.

We cried in each other's arms. We had no way of knowing if Papa would be safe. We scanned the newspapers every day for any information about the fighting.

Everything happened quickly. The mobilization of the war was in full force in Europe, and we were anxious for news about our families, especially Ivan. Somehow, letters trickled out of the Empire, and we finally heard from Maria and Anton.

> Dear Janos,
> We hope this letter finds its way to you. Your father and I are safe. There has been no fighting in our area. But they've taken Ivan to ⟨Censured⟩. He had just turned seventeen. There was nothing we could do, even though he is our last son with us. We are very worried about him. He promised he would write to let us know where they sent him, and he said he would write to you and Mira as

well. ‹Censured› He has been such a good worker on the farm. Most of the Slovak boys his age and older are gone already.

Not much else to share. We miss you and hope all is well with you.

Your loving parents,
Mama and Papa

The censors read civilian letters and blocked out information they didn't want shared, but it was clear that Ivan was in the Austro-Hungarian Army. He could have been sent anywhere in the empire where combat raged.

"This is my fault!" Janos bellowed after reading the letter. "I should have convinced him to come here, but he wouldn't leave our parents."

I recoiled. I hadn't seen Janos this angry since he told me about Tomas stealing from him.

He looked at me. "I'm sorry, I shouldn't have said that. You had your reasons, and Ivan had his."

"You couldn't have known this would happen." I rested my hand on his shoulder, but he pulled away and paced the room.

"Why? I do not understand this war. It makes no sense, this struggle for power. Ivan won't do well in the army. He is too soft and kind."

I was upset and worried too, but I sat quietly and watched Janos until he found his calm. He was right about Ivan, a sensitive, quiet boy content to blend into the background of the family. Janos and Denny were the adventurers. Ivan never asked to leave his parents and join his brothers, like other boys in our village. Ivan did as he was told. Perhaps he would do all right in the army. From what I understood, it was better to be a follower. We prayed every day for his safety.

Several days later, a letter from Papa arrived. Aneta and I read it together.

> *My Dearest Daughters,*
>
> *It is with my deepest sorrow that I am unable to travel to be with you in America. ‹Censored› The and I have no idea when. I have settled the arrangements with our neighbors to take over the land and will go live with my cousins in the village west of us. You remember them? From Aneta's wedding and your Mama's funeral? They have room for me since their sons are gone, too. I will be fine. Please write to me at their address once you get this letter. I don't know how long the mail takes these days.*
>
> *Sending you all of my love and hoping you both are safe. I am happy the two of you are together, but I do not understand why Aneta is living in St. Louis. Please write to explain for how long. Send me more pictures of the little ones. I wish I could be there to watch them grow up.*
>
> *Your loving Papa*

I remembered the cousins. It was a comfort to know he still had family to help him.

Chapter Thirty-One

November 1914

I pulled the skirt over my head, then hooked the waistband just above my swollen belly, under which the few buttons on my blouse were left undone. My oversized winter coat pulled a little in front when fastened, and I hoped it would still fit come January, or I would have to move the buttons over. My back and swollen feet ached, yet I continued to go to Zelda's house three days a week. Soon, I would need to make larger clothes to fit better or visit the second-hand store a few streets over in search of something suitable.

I thrived on the work, especially in the garden. The root vegetables, like carrots, radishes, turnips, and Zelda's favorite Jerusalem artichokes, kept well in the ground and could be harvested throughout the winter. The ground hadn't frozen yet. Zelda helped me cover the crops with a deep layer of leaves. I heaved myself up from the ground.

"Let me help you, Mira." Zelda stretched out her hands.

"No, no, I'm fine." I brushed her hands away. "If I can't

get up and down, I might have to admit this work is too much for me."

"You can be almost as stubborn as Janos. Remember what Ezra said, to not overdo. He wants your baby to be well."

"I want that, too." I smiled.

"Mira, let me look at you." Doctor Schwarz's firm voice echoed through the yard.

Zelda and I turned in surprise.

"Ezra, dear, we weren't expecting you home this early." Zelda walked to her husband and kissed his cheek.

"Guten tag, *Herr Doktor.*" I followed them inside, shaking the dirt from my apron and wiping my hands.

We used the kitchen for the checkups since the doctor no longer had patients in his home. He didn't charge us for the checkups. I think he felt responsible for the miscarriage and could have prevented it somehow.

"Everything looks fine," he said after the examination. "Do not overdo and rest more. I want you to stop working in the seventh month, December."

"If I can't manage the travel, then I will stop in December, but if it's okay, I would like to stay until the New Year, if possible."

He looked at Zelda, who smiled. "Okay, Mira, that is fine."

———

IN NOVEMBER, THE AMERICANS CELEBRATED A VERY important holiday—Thanksgiving.

Janos, Aneta, and I decided we had much to be thankful for and would celebrate Thanksgiving as well. We invited Denny's family and the Nagys to our apartment. Twelve people crammed into our tiny space. Everyone pitched in with the food, and we borrowed an extra table and chairs from a neighbor and moved the furniture around to accommodate.

We even cooked a small turkey that fit in the Dutch oven. Marta and her family brought prepared food. And we had to have our special Slovak dishes, of course. Delicious aromas of roasted turkey, cabbage rolls, and bryndzové halušky filled the air.

With everyone squeezed in elbow-to-elbow at the tables, our family waited for Janos to say the grace.

He stood, his face somber, and raised his hands. "Lord God, Heavenly Father, bless us and these Thy gifts, which we take from Thy bountiful goodness, through Jesus Christ, our Lord. Amen."

"Amen," we said in unison.

"Now," Janos continued, "because this is a day of thanks, I would like for each of you to share what you are most thankful for on this day. I will begin...." He cleared his throat. "I am most thankful to have the love of this family and all of you to be here today." He nodded to Denny sitting next to him.

"Well, I am thankful for my wife, Marta, and our son, Tony, and to be sharing this bounty in our lives," Denny spoke with clarity and turned to Marta.

"I am thankful for my caring and thoughtful husband, our beautiful son, and to have my parents and sisters with us today." She smiled and turned to Lora.

"Uh, I am thankful for all this food and my family."

Greta spoke up next, "I am thankful for everyone." She giggled and turned to her father, Paul.

He said, "This is a most wonderful day to be here, and I am thankful for the blessings we have received since coming to America, my family, and our newest family members." He looked at me, Aneta, then her two children.

Aneta stood. "I am most humbly thankful for all of you who have welcomed me and my children into your family, and to my sister and her husband for giving me a home." She looked around the table at everyone, and their appreciative faces beamed at her in response. Aneta sat and looked at me.

"When I first arrived in St. Louis, I didn't expect the love and acceptance I would find here. I am thankful to the Nagys, Denny and Marta, my dear Janos, and that my sister and her children are making their home here. It is wonderful," I choked and held back tears of joy.

It truly was a day of Thanksgiving.

December 1914

SCHOOL WAS OUT FOR THE WEEK OF VIANOCE, OR Christmas. Zelda gave me the week off to be with the family while they celebrated Hanukkah.

Janos brought home a small tree that just fit in the living room corner. Aneta and I decorated the tree with felt ornaments and colorful ribbons.

We pooled our money together, so Aneta's two children, and Denny's and Marta's little Tony would have small gifts. Aneta and I shopped for toys for each of them. In the old country, it was rare for us to have gifts, like the year Janos had sent extra money home to buy Little Jan some chocolate.

DENNY, MARTA, AND TONY CAME TO OUR apartment on Christmas Day.

After the midday meal, we gathered around the tree while Janos pretended to be *St. Mikuláš*, or 'Santa Claus' in America. He wore a red shirt I made special for the occasion.

"Here you are, little Katie." Janos held out a baby doll with a painted porcelain face and a pink and white cotton dress.

Katie ran to him, and he placed the gift in her hands.

"Da-kem," she said, not quite pronouncing 'thank you' in Slovak correctly. She ran back to Aneta, showing off her new toy.

"And, for Jamie...." Janos picked up a bright red toy train engine from beneath the tree.

"Oh, boy," Jamie said in English, and took the train engine. He turned it over and over in his hands.

Janos frowned but picked up the next gift for baby Tony.

"Here you go, Tony." Janos handed the stuffed bear to Tony, who sat in Marta's lap.

Tony hugged the soft toy close, and we all oohed and aahed. While the children were happily busy with their gifts, I gave tiny glasses to all the adults. Denny brought out a bottle of slivovitza and poured the clear liquor into the glasses.

Holding up our glasses, we toasted to our health, "Nazdravye!"

We sang songs and remembered the past happy Vianoces.

AFTER DENNY AND MARTA LEFT AND WE PUT THE children to bed, Janos sat in his rocking chair and smoked his pipe while Aneta sat at the table.

"I asked Dr. Schwarz about Katie's difficulty with her speech," I told Aneta while I prepared cups of tea for the three of us.

"What are you talking about?"

"Well, you know how she seems to struggle with certain words and hasn't really progressed as quickly as most children."

I took a cup to Janos, but he refused the offered tea. I placed two cups on the table for Aneta and me and sat across from her.

"And you talked to the doctor before discussing this with me?" she snapped.

I looked at her in surprise. "Yes, because I am closer to them, I thought—"

"You thought?"

Janos looked over at Aneta, his brow raised. "Is there a problem?"

"Are you upset with me?" I asked.

"Mira, you know how much I appreciate everything you do for the children while I am working. But I am still their mother."

My stomach turned. "I didn't realize it would upset you this much. I was trying to help."

"That is how you are, and that's wonderful, but I just wish you had told me first." Her voice softened. "Well, what did the doctor tell you?"

I hesitated, then said, "He talked with a speech therapist at the hospital and told me that until she starts to learn English, there wasn't much the therapist could do if all she is speaking in Slovak."

"So, what does that mean?" She frowned.

I first looked over at Janos to see if he was listening. He was reading his newspaper, deep in thought.

I lowered my voice. "Katie will turn four next year and must know English before entering kindergarten after she turns five. Once she is speaking some, we can send her to the speech therapist for an evaluation."

"I see. Well, thank you for getting that information for me. I shouldn't have gotten that upset." She gave me a strained smile and sipped her tea. "How will we pay for the therapist?"

"That's good news. The hospital has a special program to assist low-income families, and Dr. Schwarz will get you into that program. It's free."

"That would be wonderful." Aneta relaxed back into her chair.

It pained me to know I had upset her, especially about the children. "Aneta, you know I love Katie and Jamie as if they were my own. I meant well."

"I know, Mira. Just in the future, let's talk about them together before you do anything?"

I reached across the table. Aneta took my hand and smiled. It would be fine.

Janos rattled his newspaper, frowning. "I just don't understand this."

"Understand what, dear?"

"Another lynching of a negro in Georgia. Very sad."

"Another? Why have I not heard of this?" I got up and stood at the rocking chair, then peered at the newspaper in his hands.

He pointed to the article. "They are mentioned in this Slovak newspaper. I'm not sure why. It is upsetting this sort of thing goes on here in America." Janos shook his head in dismay. "The land of the free. For some people, I guess."

Chapter Thirty-Two

January 1915

ON MY LAST DAY WORKING AT ZELDA'S, THE SIZE OF my belly made it difficult to get into the trolley. It hadn't snowed in several days. There was no ice on the sidewalks, and that made it easier to get around. Ivy had explained that because we ate better in America, the babies grew bigger in our bellies. I didn't know about that, but I didn't remember being this large with Little Jan.

Zelda was waiting for me at the door when I arrived. "Mira, welcome."

"*Guten Morgen,*" I said.

Zelda smiled, "Today, we will work inside, I think. I'll need help preparing food for next week, since you'll not be here and the new girl doesn't start for another week or so."

I nodded, followed her inside, and removed my coat. I wore a large blouse that Marta loaned me over a skirt designed for a pregnant woman, which I found at the second-hand store. We worked side by side in the kitchen, preparing the food.

When lunchtime arrived, Zelda said, "Let's have lunch together in the dining room, ja?"

I chuckled at her mix of English and German.

She carried a tray with the teapot, cups, saucers, and bowls of soup to the table. I hobbled in with the plates of sandwiches and dropped into the chair.

"Whew. I can't believe I can sweat in the winter." I wiped my brow.

"It won't be the same without you here, Mira." Zelda frowned.

"I know. But I have to be honest with you. I am worried."

"Worried? About the baby?" She patted my hand.

"Well, you know how I feel about birthing. But no, it's...." I wasn't sure if Zelda would understand.

"What is it? You have me worried now."

"Don't be, it's just me. I've gotten used to working outside the home, traveling through the city. I've been feeling, well... independent. Though I know I'm not. I'm married, and with a child on the way very soon. And that is what's bothering me." I sighed.

Zelda took a bite of her sandwich. "Hm, yes, I think I understand what you mean. I feel it, though I am married. I don't have children but am busy with all these social activities and charities, which make me feel important. That's what you mean, ja?"

"You do understand. But that will change when the baby comes. I won't be able to work outside the home. Janos and Aneta will be working, and they want me to stay home and take care of all three children. Jamie is in kindergarten now, and I haven't figured out how I will get him to school and home, what with the baby too." My stomach rumbled with hunger for both me and the growing baby inside. I dove into the hot soup, waiting for Zelda's response.

"Ah, I wasn't sure about that, but yes, I see now. With you

home with your baby, Aneta doesn't want to leave Katie with the neighbor anymore."

"It makes sense not paying for childcare. With me not working, it sort of evens out. But...." I slouched in defeat. "I feel I'm the only one making the sacrifice. Am I a terrible person, Zelda?"

"No, no, dear. You aren't a terrible person. Life comes with its challenges." She took a sip of tea and looked at me. "In a year, after the baby is walking, and both Aneta's children are in school, you could come back and bring the baby with you?"

"I don't know, Zelda. We will cross that bridge, as the Americans say, when the time comes. Maybe. No matter what, I never want to lose your friendship. You promise we will stay in touch?"

"Always. You will be in my heart."

"With three children to care for, I doubt I will be able to come visit you, except maybe on Aneta's day off."

"Now you stop fretting over the future. We will find time to spend together. You can count on that. Ja?"

We ate the rest of our lunch in silence while watching a little bird on the ledge of the window.

A twinge in my belly jolted me. The twinge deepened.

Zelda frowned. "Are you all right, dear?"

"I think the baby is coming. It's too early...again?" Tears stung my eyes.

"Don't think that, Mira, everything will be fine. I'll call Ezra," Zelda rushed to the phone and made the call. She came back moments later. "He said to bring you in, now."

Zelda allowed me to lean on her as she ushered me out of the house and into the motorcar. She rushed us to the hospital. I thanked God that the labor started while I was with Zelda. My fear of losing the baby escalated with each contraction. Memories of my miscarriage flooded back, and my heart pounded.

Zelda parked the motorcar at the entrance to the Barnes Hospital, where Dr. Schwarz was waiting at the curb with two nurses.

"Hello, Mira, do not worry." His voice was steady and calm. He turned to one of the nurses, "Take her into an examination room."

"It's early, just like my last one," I said through clenched teeth.

"No, Mira, you are much further along, only a few weeks from your due date. You will be fine," he assured me.

A nurse sat me in a wheelchair and took me to the examination room, where I lay on the table while Dr. Schwarz examined me. He gave me a solemn look.

"The baby appears to be in a breech position with his feet down instead of up. If we can't turn it around, we will perform a cesarean."

"What does that mean?" I demanded.

"We would operate and remove the baby. But do not fear. We do this here in the hospital. Be calm." He patted my arm and left the room.

After a few moments, the nurses took me to the maternity ward and put me in a hospital gown. Zelda stayed close.

"Please, get a message to Janos at his work and let him know I'm here," I said.

"I will reach your dear Janos and have him come here as soon as possible."

I nodded thanks and closed my eyes. Surgery to have a baby? I didn't like the sound of that. I prayed Janos would make it to the hospital right away.

Zelda held my hand. "I will be here with you until Janos comes, ja?"

Janos arrived a couple of hours later, and Zelda sprang to her feet and took his hand. "I'm glad you made it."

"Thank you for bringing her in." He turned to me. "Mira, my darling, I am here." He came to the side of my bed and took my hand. "How are you?"

"I'll give you some privacy," Zelda said. She pulled the curtains around the bed and left.

"Janos, did you speak to the doctor?"

"No, is there something wrong? It's a little early, but—"

"The baby, it's...I'm worried. Dr. Schwarz says the baby is upside down, the wrong way." The next contraction came, and I cried out. The pain seared through me.

"It will be all right. The doctor will make sure of it. Yes?"

"I can't lose this one, Jani. I just can't." I moaned again and held onto my belly.

"Don't think of that, Mira. Think positive." Worry lines formed across his broad forehead.

Dr. Schwarz came in. "Hello, Janos. I'm glad you came," Dr. Schwarz said in English. "Mira, I am here to examine you again to see if the baby has turned any. Janos, can you give us a few minutes? Please go to the waiting area down the hall."

"Yes, yes, Doctor. Mira, I will be nearby. Do not worry." He patted my hand and left the curtained area.

There were two other women in the ward with me, and though I couldn't see them, I could hear their moans and the nurses' footsteps around their beds. Dr. Schwarz was very gentle with me, but it still hurt while he pushed and prodded my belly.

"Good news, Mira. The baby is turning," he exclaimed. "It looks like we won't need to perform the cesarean after all."

"That's won–der–ful," I gasped, as the next contraction hit.

"I will speak to Janos and let him back in for a few moments," Dr. Schwarz said.

The labor pains were coming closer together when Janos finally returned.

"It is good news." Janos beamed. "The doctor told me no surgery." He kissed my cheek. His strong, gentle hands stroked my hair, smoothing the stray strands. "I'll be waiting for you. I love you, my dearest, Mira."

"Yes," I gasped.

The nurse ushered Janos out, and the doctor returned.

"The baby has turned into the correct position." Dr. Schwarz said.

A nurse had just prepared a syringe when the doctor stopped her. "I'll do the administering myself today. Mrs. Lacks is a personal friend." He turned to me and held up the needle. "This is called Twilight Sleep, an injection of medication that will render you asleep. You won't have to feel the pain of childbirth." He smiled and gave me the injection.

"No pain?" I did, however, feel the injection. It didn't take long before I drifted to sleep.

WHEN I AWOKE, I WAS ALONE, WITH NO MEMORY OF the delivery. They had pulled the curtains closed around my bed. I feared the baby was dead.

"*Kde je moje dieťa?!*" I asked. Where was my child?

A nurse slipped through the curtain with a small bundle. My fears vanished as soon as she placed my baby in my arms.

"It's a girl," she said, "and she is perfect."

I gazed in wonder at my baby's wrinkled red face and a full head of dark hair. When Janos arrived, he sat on the edge of the bed, staring at the baby and me, his eyes wide and smiling.

"Isn't she beautiful?" I couldn't take my eyes off her.

"Beautiful, like her mama." He looked at me with tears of happiness. "What will we name her?"

"I was thinking about Mary, after your mama, Maria."

"That is a fine American name, Mary."

"Do you want to hold her?" I held the little bundle out to him.

Janos tentatively tucked our daughter close to his chest. He smiled down at our first Slovak-American child. "Hello, little Mary," said the proud papa.

———

"Sweet child," I cooed. Almost two months old, Mary lay on the changing blanket atop our bed, clapping her little hands while I changed her diaper. "Do you know where we are going today?"

Mary gurgled.

"We are taking you to church for you to be baptized and show you off to everyone. Mama is proud of you." I tickled her tummy, and she let out the most joyous giggle.

"Are you ready?" Janos poked his head into the room just as I finished dressing Mary.

"We are. What about Aneta?"

"They're waiting downstairs." Janos was in a pleasant mood.

Janos, Aneta, and I took Jamie and Katie to the Sunday School class, with much resistance from Jamie.

"I want to sit with you, I'm old enough," Jamie said.

"A few more years, still," Aneta said.

Jamie stomped into the class with much indignation. I held back a giggle. Even though he should not have behaved that way, he was adorable.

The three of us adults, Mary snug in my arms, settled in a pew near the front for the christening. When Marta and

Denny arrived, I scooted over for Marta to sit next to me. Denny sat next to Janos.

"Where is Tony?" I asked Marta.

"We took him to the nursery school. You know how loud he can be."

I nodded in understanding. Tony could holler something fierce.

A woman, with what looked like a one-year-old baby, entered from the side aisle and sat at the end of the pew behind us. She was the same woman I had thought looked sadly at Janos the first time we attended church.

"Who is that?" I asked Marta.

"Haven't you met Rozalia?"

I shook my head.

"She's a widow who used to work with me at the sewing factory. She recently returned from a long stay with family in New York City."

"I do recall seeing her once before when I first moved here. We weren't formally introduced. Was she widowed recently?" I turned to look at Janos to see if he was listening, but he was chatting quietly with Denny.

"Her husband died a few years ago," Marta said. "Around the time I married Denny. The child, Peter, is an orphan. I think one of Rozalia's cousins. She brought him back with her from New York."

Marta and Denny had married in 1910, the same year I became involved with Goran. That Vianoce Janos had come home, and we fought about his wanting to stay in America permanently. I pushed him away. Had I pushed him into Rozalia's arms? Even though I had no proof of anything between Rozalia and my husband, guilt flooded through me.

The music started, and everyone quieted. I turned to sneak a peek at Rozalia. She was looking right at me, then averted her eyes.

The church service and my daughter's christening soon replaced thoughts of the mysterious Rozalia.

———

April 1915

MARY WAS AN EASY BABY TO CARE FOR. SHE SLEPT when we slept and took naps when I put her down. She fussed when she was hungry, which was often.

I didn't leave the house except for church on Sundays and visits with Denny and Marta. Ivy volunteered to take Jamie to school when she took her daughter, Ava, since both were in kindergarten together.

Aneta did the grocery shopping. Janos, well, he played with Mary when at home. I didn't remember Janos doing much when Little Jan was a baby. Since I had become the primary caretaker of all the children, my life had become very different from when I was a young mother in Hungary. I had no mother-in-law here to assume that role. I was happy to have Mary all to myself.

ANETA BREEZED IN FROM HER HALF-DAY SHIFT AT the sewing factory one Saturday, her arms full of groceries. Her shoulders hunched forward as she put the bag on the table. I was breastfeeding Mary on the sofa when Aneta turned to look at me with red and swollen eyes. I started to say something, then motioned for her to sit next to me.

As soon as she sat, she blurted, "I'm divorcing Tommy."

"Oh, Aneta." I wanted to reach out to her but didn't want to disturb Mary.

"I can no longer tell people Tommy is moving here. It's been too long." She rubbed her face, then pulled a handkerchief from her pocket and blew her nose. "I hate the thought of being the only one in our family to get a divorce."

"This can't be easy for you. I wish there was something I could do." My heart bled for Aneta.

"You and Janos have done too much already. It's Tommy. He hasn't sent me a cent since I left him last year, not even to help the children. He is despicable." She slumped against the back of the sofa, stretched out her legs, and kicked off her shoes.

"That is irresponsible of him. He's shown you his true self, and you are better off without him," I said in a hushed voice, not wanting the children napping in Aneta's room to hear.

"How did you manage it, Mira, being apart all those years? I always wondered." Aneta tilted her head, gazing with tired, red eyes.

"It was a difficult time, as I wrote to you. When we had been apart for almost two years the first time, I questioned my love for Janos." I hesitated, then thought telling her about Goran might help. "I–I was involved with someone." I turned my eyes away.

Aneta spoke with a calm that surprised me. "You know, Mama made an odd comment in one of her letters. I don't think she even realized what she wrote. But it made me wonder about that laborer you mentioned in one of your letters. Was it him?"

"It was Goran, yes." My cheeks heated. "What did Mamička write in her letter?"

"It was something about how she was glad he was there, because you had been working hard taking care of her and the household chores. That you needed the diversion, or something like that. It wasn't direct; it was more in passing."

"I see. I believed Goran served a purpose. He helped me get through that difficult time with Mama. I felt such desolation and separation from Janos. I still find it hard to believe I did those things." Mary fidgeted in my lap, and I adjusted her. "I grew to love him, though my heart always belonged to Janos. Does that make sense?"

Aneta put her hand on my arm and looked me in the eyes. "It makes perfect sense. I was living with Tommy but was feeling lonely and dejected, especially when he would go on his drinking binges, leaving me alone sometimes for two or three days."

I gasped. "Aneta, I had no idea. Things were far worse than I imagined."

"I couldn't tell you, or anyone. I was ashamed for him, and us." She let out a sob, the tears started to trickle down her cheeks, and she blotted them with the hanky. Her words tumbled out. "There were times when there wasn't enough money to buy milk for the children, or sometimes, less than that. And it wasn't because he didn't make enough money; it was because he had spent his paycheck before ever making it home. He would go to the pubs after his shift and buy drinks for all his friends. You know how he liked to be the center of attention."

"At the expense of his family? My dearest." Tears welled in my eyes. "I am glad you left him and came to me."

"Me too."

We talked until Janos came home, and then Aneta hurried to prepare dinner. She tried to hide her tear-stained face. Janos looked at me questioningly, his hands raised.

I just shook my head and mouthed, *later.*

Chapter Thirty-Three

Spring 1916

AFTER CHURCH, THE SIX OF US TOOK A TROLLEY TO the Nagys' duplex for a cookout in their backyard. Hana had a nice vegetable garden with flowers, too. Blooms of bright reds, purples, and yellows created a striking background for our little party. The flowers were reminiscent of our Slovak community colors in Hungary.

The long blades of grass swayed in the gentle breeze where the children played together as Greta watched over them. Tony, two and a half, jabbered something to Katie, his little arms waving. She nodded and stared at him as if she understood. Maybe she did. I had trouble understanding other people's children while they were learning to talk. I could understand Little Jan when he was at that age. It must have something to do with the parental connection.

Jamie, almost seven, tried to get the others involved with a simple game of ball toss. Their giggling and laughter floated in the air like music.

Mary, at fifteen months, waddled around my chair, her

little hand holding mine for stability. Her shiny hair glistened in the sun, still as dark as it was at birth. Her eyes had turned to a milk chocolate brown. She was chubby and healthy and my heart of hearts.

Having Mary reminded me how much I loved being a mother, and my fear of pregnancy faded. The dreams I had in Hungary about three children came to mind. There had been no similar dreams since, but the girl in the dreams was the oldest, and that came true with Mary. I looked forward to having more.

Lora was the center of attention, having just turned twenty and newly engaged. Her wedding was on the tongues of the women who clustered together to discuss the reception.

Marta glanced over at Tony. "Greta, make sure Tony doesn't fall and hurt himself."

"Yes, Marta, I'm watching," Greta answered politely, but rolled her eyes when Marta turned away.

I bit back a laugh.

"Now, Lora, I have some great ideas for the reception," Hana said.

"I want my wedding to be different from Marta's, though hers was lovely." Lora looked at Marta and smiled.

Lora had been born in Hungary; she was only seven when Hana and Paul immigrated. She looked very American with her dark auburn hair parted in the middle and tied at the nape with a blue ribbon. The ends of the long tail had been curled with a curling wand. She loved clothes and wore the latest fashion. Gone were the long, narrow hems that were difficult to walk in. Lora's skirt had pleats all around, a high waist, and a hem that reached just above the ankles.

I wanted a skirt like it, but I hadn't lost all the pregnancy weight. I worried it would stay with me. The high waist wouldn't look good on me.

"Lora, I would like to help with your wedding, too," I said.

"How nice of you, Auntie Mira."

Hana scooted her chair closer to Lora. "You will be married in our church, of course. You know how nice the reception hall is."

"Yes, Mama. I found a picture of the most beautiful wedding dress. Let me show you." Lora jumped from her seat and hurried into the house. She returned a moment later with a copy of *McCall's Women's Fashion Magazine*. "Here." She held the magazine out to her mother and pointed to the illustration of an elaborate white wedding dress.

I dragged Mary with me to see the magazine, too. Marta and I crowded next to Lora and Hana. I motioned to Aneta to join us, but she declined with a shake of her head.

"It is lovely, Lora." Marta eyed the page.

"It is," I agreed.

"Let me read the description." Lora read it out loud in English, "*Pure white all-silk Crepe Meteor. The body is white silk chiffon over Brussels net. The chiffon is concealed by a full graceful bertha of silk embroidered net. The short sleeves of chiffon are edged with a fringe pearl and crystal beading.*"

Hana looked confused and said in Slovak, "Lora, dear, you know I don't understand all of that English."

I knew Hana spoke mostly Slovak and little English, but it was good that they allowed their children to speak English at home. I wished Janos would be more flexible in this.

"Sorry, Mama," Lora repeated the description in Slovak.

"It says here it costs twenty dollars, and the veil is extra. That much?" Marta frowned.

"I know, but can't we make it?" Lora looked around at us.

Aneta, sitting away from the others, had been uncharacteristically silent. I pulled up a chair next to her and lifted Mary onto my lap.

"You are very solemn. Is everything all right?" I touched her hand.

"I'm sorry, Mira, it's just all this talk about a wedding...and I just received my final divorce decree." She let out a short, sarcastic laugh.

"You did? When?"

"The other day, while you were out with Mary. Ironic, isn't it?"

"I suppose so. You are sad, though it's what you wanted, yes?"

"It was...is. I thought he would fight me on it. But he didn't."

"What are you two whispering about over there? We need your input here." Marta walked toward us.

"Nothing," Aneta forced a smile, shaded her eyes from the sun, and looked up at Marta. "Mira and I can help."

"Yes, we have a sewing machine now," I bragged. I felt bad bragging when Marta and Denny didn't make as much money as Janos. But I was proud of our enrichment in America.

"That's right. I envy you," Marta said.

"Let me see that picture in the magazine." Aneta rose and followed Marta over to Lora.

Aneta looked closely at the page. "I think I can do the fringe of beads on the sleeve. I helped make a wedding dress once, where I work. It might not look exactly like the picture, though."

"Aneta, how wonderful." Lora clasped her hands together and jumped up and down with a giggle. "Mama, what do you think?"

"I think we can do this for you, yes." Hana smiled sweetly at Lora.

The men's voices escalated, and we turned to them.

"It's right here in the newspaper," said Janos. His voice demanded their attention. "It was just reprinted from the

Jednota from last year. Let me read the '*Declaration of Our Slovak Identity.*'" He cleared his throat.

> *"No. We are Slovaks.*
> *The Magyars say that we are Magyars.*
> *And the Czechs that we are Czechs.*
> *But we are Slovak!*
> *And may God grant that we remain Slovaks.*
> *We say so nevertheless clearly.*
> *Why is it our brother Czechs do not understand us?*

"See what I mean?" Janos slammed the paper down.

"That's good, but why are you reading *Jednota*?" Paul asked. "That's a Catholic Slovak newspaper."

"I read a lot of things, Paul." Janos gave him an exasperated look. "The point is, all Slovaks feel the same way, Catholic or Protestant."

Denny stood. "I remember something published just this past February. I can't remember where, though...it went something like, '*we are not Germans, not Magyars,*' but rather '*thoroughly, purely Slovaks.*' And then, I think it was something about '*the deaf-mute-blind idiocy*' of Americans who couldn't tell the difference."

"That's it exactly. It's the same thing being *White*. Even if we are White, we are treated as though we are not," Janos said.

"I agree," said Marek, Lora's groom, a tall man with dark hair and heavy brows.

The other men chimed in agreement, nodding.

"After all these years, why are we still being misunderstood that we are our own people?" Paul's eyes flared.

"All right, all right." Hana carried a tray of tall glasses of iced tea to them. "I think you men need some refreshment to cool down this heated discussion."

"This is important, Hana." Paul took a glass from the tray.

"Yes, it is. I agree, but what can we do to change their way of thinking?" she asked Paul.

"Ah, that is the question." Janos reached over and took a glass from her tray and drew a long drink of the tea. "That is very refreshing, Hana. Ďakujem." Janos looked over at me and winked.

I smiled back. I knew better than to get in the middle of one of Janos's debates.

"Tony, come back here," Lora called out as Tony ran straight to his papa and grabbed his legs.

"Papa, play with me." He looked up at Denny with a questioning gaze.

Denny sighed. "Give me a few minutes. Go over to your mama, and I'll be there soon."

Tony slumped his shoulders and dragged his feet as he toddled to Marta's waiting arms.

"You have a fine son, Denny." Janos gave Denny a pat on his back.

I admired my husband in his casual pants and a cotton button-up shirt. A warm rush rose to my face, and my pulse raced. He still excited me after nearly thirteen years of marriage. I looked forward to later that night.

Chapter Thirty-Four

September 1916

Janos was handsome in his first new suit in years for Lora's wedding. His soft, wavy hair was free of that awful pomade, and the red and gold highlights shone in the sunlight as we strolled toward the church with Mary in the stroller.

"Wait up for us," Aneta called out from behind with Jamie and Katie in tow. "Sorry we are slow. Jamie's shoelace broke."

Janos stooped to tie the broken laces and relaced the shoe. "There you are, Jamie. You look fine today in your new shoes."

"Thanks, Uncle John." Jamie, short for his age, craned his neck to look at Janos.

"Mira, you look lovely in your new dress. Lavender is a splendid color on you." Aneta eyed me up and down.

I turned to the side, making a pose like the fashion model in the catalogs. We laughed.

We walked into the church together. The ushers, brothers of Lora's groom, Marek, greeted us at the door. I took Mary out of her stroller, and Janos pushed it against the wall. One usher led us down the aisle to the bride's side to be seated. They had tied white fabric bows at the ends of the first two rows for the immediate family.

"This must be how an American wedding is," I whispered in Janos's ear as we sat.

He shrugged.

Mary was quiet. I counted my blessings and hoped she would stay that way. She was usually well-behaved if there were no loud or sudden noises. The other usher led Aneta and her children to the row behind us. The pews filled fast; most people were members of the church congregation, and those I didn't know seemed to be friends and family of the groom. Organ music flowed through the room while the ushers brought Hana down the aisle and to the front row.

The mother and grandfather of the groom were next to be seated. Marek's mother was a widow and had immigrated with her father and son in 1905. Lora had told me how they struggled when they first arrived.

Everyone turned to look behind us, and I turned too. Marta, the matron of honor, came in and passed by in a pale green dress with a wide sash at the waist and a layered handkerchief hem. She carried a small bouquet of white flowers.

Shortly after, Greta, the flower girl, made her way down the aisle in a white dress with butterfly sleeves trimmed in lace and pale green ribbon. She carried a basket filled with flower petals and sprinkled them on the floor while she took slow steps, smiling at us when she passed. The organist paused the music. People stood. Janos and I stood too, and we turned around.

Marta had told me the processional was from a famous opera. The organ blared loud trumpet-like sounds announcing the bride. Mary was startled and fussed. I worried she would cry.

After a few moments, Lora stood waiting with her papa,

Paul, next to her. She was radiant in the beautiful wedding dress we helped make. It looked better than the illustration. The white silk and cotton blend shimmered in the light that came through the church windows. The veil did not cover her face but ended at her brow, and a wide lace headband was wrapped around her head. The back of the veil draped across her shoulders and down to the floor, trailing a few feet behind her. She held the largest bouquet I had ever seen, made of white and yellow roses trimmed with long white satin ribbons. It was glorious.

I blinked away tears. Mary calmed down, her eyes following along with everyone else's as Lora walked past our pew, headed toward Marek and the altar. He was a striking man with dark hair and heavy brows, dressed in a crisp, tailored black suit. I could feel the love emanating from them, and it brought back the memories of my wedding and the love that Janos and I had for each other, then and now.

Janos gave me a look and a wink—he was remembering our wedding too.

When the ceremony ended, the organ started again with a loud recessional. Mary wailed almost as loud as the organ.

We followed the crowd into the hall next to the church for the reception and waited in the long line to congratulate the couple and meet the wedding party.

"Oh, look, Janos." I pointed. "There is a photographer. Could we get our photo taken with Mary?"

"Good idea. But let's find a table after we go through the line, then get the photos."

We found our seats, and I saw a couple carrying the new portable cameras with flash were taking snapshots during the reception.

I found Hana and asked, "Who are those people with the cameras? Is it possible to get copies of their photos?"

"They are Marek's family, I'm sure they would be happy to share copies," she said. "I'll ask them for you."

"Thank you very much." I beamed and put a portable camera at the top of my wish list. Just as I turned, I saw *them*. I couldn't believe it. *Rozalia and Peter!* "Is that another relative?" I asked Hana.

"She is a friend of the family, someone Marta worked with. Let me introduce you."

"Oh no, that's fine. I better get back to Janos, he's hungry and waiting on me."

Hana nodded, and I returned to our table. I tried to ignore Rozalia's presence. I needed to control myself, though every time I saw that woman, I got upset.

Janos was indeed hungry. He stood as soon as I reached him.

"You two go, I'll watch Mary," Aneta offered.

Janos dragged me over to the line of people waiting to fill their plates with Slovak food at the buffet tables. The aroma of my favorite stuffed cabbage filled with spicy sausage didn't have its usual effect of comfort. In fact, the smell nauseated me, and I held my stomach, almost doubling over.

"Are you all right?" Janos reached out to steady me.

"No." I left him standing there while I rushed to the ladies' room. I vomited what little food I had eaten that morning.

I groaned. There was only one reason I would react this violently to food; I was pregnant again. I did a quick calculation and concluded the baby would be due in March. I refreshed myself, then returned to our table and sat next to Aneta. Though I felt a little better, I couldn't stand in the food line. Janos looked over at me and pointed questioningly to a second plate. I nodded, and he started to fix me one. Jamie ran over to him and pulled on the bottom of Janos's suit coat.

Janos looked down, smiled, and patted Jamie on the head. My heart swelled.

"I don't want to be here," Aneta said.

"What is the matter now?" I said, irritated that she hadn't noticed Jamie no longer sat next to her. "I've been expecting you to say something about Katie's speech therapy sessions. It's generous of Zelda to be driving her along with me and the other children each week to the hospital. Have you even thanked her yet?"

For a second, a glimmer of guilt passed across her eyes. "I will." She spoke in a whisper, "But haven't you noticed? People are talking about me and whispering things."

"What are you talking about? Who? What things?"

"Someone must have found out about my divorce and is spreading tales."

"Aneta, you are imagining things. I haven't noticed anything."

"Well, it's true," she snapped. "I first noticed it last Sunday when we were here. I can't take it. I don't want to come to this church anymore." She wrapped her arms around herself.

"You can't mean that." I looked over at Janos. He juggled two plates of food while Jamie circled him like a hungry animal. Janos looked like a circus clown. "Aneta, can we talk about this later? Do you think you can handle getting Mary some food when you go up? I'm not feeling well and need to sit here for a bit with Mary."

Aneta frowned.

I couldn't believe how selfish she behaved. She was consumed with her imaginings that she didn't even ask if I was all right. When Janos reached the table with Jamie, Aneta looked surprised but didn't say a word. She grasped Jamie and Katie's hands and took them to the food table.

I was exasperated. It was a wedding, and Aneta was upset

about nothing. However, I looked around the room to see if anyone was pointing or looking at her, just in case, but noticed nothing unusual.

———

LATER THAT NIGHT, WHEN JANOS AND I WERE preparing for bed, I asked him. "Have you heard anything said at the church about Aneta being divorced?"

He gave me a startled look, then shrugged. "I heard something, not bad, just wondering why. You know people talk."

I sighed and collapsed into the bed, then pulled the covers over me. "I know, but it is upsetting to Aneta. She doesn't want to go to church anymore. She's convinced people are saying things about her. Should we change churches, too?" I gave him a sideways glance. I would miss our new friends, but I wouldn't have minded not running into Rozalia either.

"That is ridiculous," Janos huffed. "All our family goes there, and friends. She will get over it. Give her time."

"She will stop, she says."

"Then let her leave. I like Aneta. I do. And as much as I support her in divorcing that bum, Tommy, divorce is not that accepted. It is what it is." He turned out the lamp's flame and rolled over. "It was a good day. I am happy for Lora and Marek, aren't you?" He asked over his shoulder.

"I am." Lying there in the dark, I waited for my eyes to adjust. "I meant to tell you earlier, but I'm pregnant again," I blurted.

Janos turned the light back on and faced me, a broad, radiant smile on his face. "Is that why you ran to the restroom at the church?"

"Yes, I figured it out. This time the morning sickness came later."

"This makes me very happy." He gave me one of his big wet kisses on the mouth, wrapped his arms around me, and we snuggled until he fell asleep.

I lay awake, my mind spinning with thoughts of Aneta... and Rozalia.

Chapter Thirty-Five

February 1917

THE GREAT WAR HAD BEEN RAGING IN EUROPE AND
Japan for two and a half years. Letters came through from
Maria and Papa, sometimes out of order. It had been months
since we had received a letter from either Maria or Ivan. When
I pulled the letter from Janos's parents from our mailbox, it
was all I could do not to tear the letter open. But I waited
impatiently until Janos came home and listened carefully as he
read the letter out loud.

> *Dear Janos,*
> *We have received no letters from Ivan for*
> *some time and are not sure if any have made their*
> *way to you. If you have heard anything, please let*
> *us know, because we received a telegram from the*
> *Austro-Hungarian Army that Ivan was missing in*
> *action.*

They said it didn't mean he is dead, but most likely he is. It also means they may not find his body for confirmation of his death. We are beside ourselves with grief. When we get any further information, we will be sure to let you know. We sent a letter to Denny too.

We are glad you, Mira, and Mary are safe.

We send all our love,

Mama and Papa

Janos shook with rage and hurt. I tried to comfort him, but losing Ivan cut me to the core, and my heart ached along with his. Denny showed up later that day to speak to Janos.

I sat aside and allowed the two brothers to cry and grieve over the loss of their younger brother. He would have been nineteen.

"I thought I was angry at the empire when they drafted Ivan into their army, but what I feel now is ten times that!" Denny slammed his hand down on the table.

"I feel the same, my brother." Janos's eyes flared with hatred.

"I've decided to make my commitment to this country permanent," Denny stated.

"You mean citizenship?" Janos asked.

He nodded. "I submitted my Declaration of Intent for naturalization." Denny straightened.

"Oh, Denny, that is wonderful," I interjected, proud of him for making such a commitment. He and Janos had talked about it at great length.

Janos sat pondering for a few moments, then gave Denny a solemn look. "I, too, will apply for this naturalization."

The brothers hugged, united in their anger, grief, and

commitment to America. But for one reason or another, Janos didn't apply right away. I wondered why, but whenever I brought up the subject, he said he would do it later.

Two weeks after Janos received the letter from Maria, a letter arrived from Ivan, dated months earlier. My chest tightened while Janos and I read it together, knowing he was probably dead. Much of the brief letter was blacked out by the censors, and what we could read had been written in Ivan's awkward hand. Anton had pulled him out of school at age twelve to help on the farm, and the boy had never practiced his writing. I burst into tears, and Janos held me close as we both mourned the loss of such a dear boy.

———

April 1917

Life consisted of joys and sorrows. Losing Ivan made it difficult to be happy about my second baby. With Aneta's children in school, I had only Mary with me during the day. But Janos was adamant about avoiding any mishaps with the pregnancy. I agreed to stay close to home and not overdo it during the last months. Aneta was a blessing, doing most of the shopping and household duties.

The birth occurred on the first of April at home with the help of Marta's midwife and Aneta and Marta assisting. Janos and Denny waited with the children. Despite the long hours of labor, our son was born with no problems. I was relieved and grateful.

"You did well, my Mira." Janos held our new son in his arms with his proud papa face. "Our first Slovak-American son."

"We will call him Stephen, after my father Stefan, yes?" I looked at Janos for approval.

"Absolutely." He glanced down at the tiny baby, whose eyes were fixed on him.

"Stephen, my son."

On the sixth of April, the US declared war on Germany. Janos read in the paper that German submarines sank seven US merchant ships. It wasn't until the next time Zelda came by to pick up Katie for her speech therapy sessions that I fully understood what the war meant to civilians.

I held the door open for Zelda. "You're early today," I said.

"Let's sit and talk before we leave." Zelda took a seat on the small sofa, and I sat next to her.

"What is it? You look worried," I said.

"Have you heard about us German-born, who haven't become US citizens?"

"I don't usually read the paper, and Janos hasn't said anything to me." I wondered if he had and thought it unimportant, even though it applied to my friends.

"Non-citizen Germans must register as an *alien enemy*." Her eyes grew wide.

"Alien enemy? What does that mean?" I frowned.

"It's because the US will be warring against Germany. They don't trust anyone in this country who isn't a citizen. It doesn't seem to matter that Ezra is a respected doctor devoted to the health of all Americans and immigrants." She looked close to tears.

I put my hand on hers. "That's terrible."

"I don't know why Ezra didn't apply for naturalization, especially after the war started. He is an optimist and believed the US would stay out of the war. He will be required to carry the registration card with him at all times, and is at risk of being arrested and interned, possibly to the North Carolina internment camp."

"Oh dear." My breath caught. "This is very distressing news. Does that include you, too?"

"Right now, it is only men. We hope it will not be extended to women. They are prohibiting us from traveling or even moving to a new house. Not that we want to move. It's the restrictions they've put on us that is upsetting and frightening." She squeezed my hand.

"This is a terrible thing happening to the doctor." I wondered what this would mean for us Hungarian-born non-citizens. The US would be at war with them. It was too scary to think about, and I focused on Zelda.

"I just wanted you to know that for now, we are fine. Ezra still works at the hospital. But we feel the suspicion from people who wonder where our loyalties lie."

We hugged each other, then I collected Katie from Aneta's bedroom, and we left.

Later that night, I told Janos everything Zelda had shared with me. "Have you read about it in the newspaper?"

"Yes, but it didn't occur to me that it would include the doctor. I assumed he had become a citizen because of his important work. But this now affects us, too."

My heart skipped a beat. "How do you mean?"

"By association. The government might accuse us of conspiring with Germans. At this time, I think it is best you do not visit her."

I nodded, defeated and worried about my friend. As much as I hated the thought that might happen, I saw truth in his fears.

"Zelda takes Katie to the hospital for her weekly speech therapy sessions. She had been picking up me and the children."

"It's best Zelda no longer come to our residence, at least while we are at war with Germany. If Aneta wants Katie to continue the speech therapy, either you or Aneta would need to take Katie. I am sorry, but we must think of our family's safety. I don't blame the Schwarzes. They are good people." Janos spoke gently, and not harshly like I expected.

"I'll talk to Aneta," I said, not wanting to make another decision without her.

In the end, the decision was made to stop the speech therapy sessions, especially since the therapist said Katie had improved as much as she could, anyway.

I urged Janos to submit his Declaration of Intent for naturalization soon. He scoffed and said that we weren't Germans; we were Slovaks. I still worried.

Chapter Thirty-Six

May 1917

WHEN DENNY ANNOUNCED HE HAD ENLISTED IN THE US Army, Janos almost blew up at him. If Denny had waited for the government draft, he could have taken the financial hardship clause and wouldn't have had to go at all.

Denny explained he was determined to avenge Ivan's death. Both he and Janos had felt helpless when Ivan had been forced to fight on the wrong side of the war. After Denny left, Janos told me he feared he might lose another brother.

Our lives seemed engulfed by a dark and dreadful cloud. The war we endured was not only country against country, but race against race. And it happened right in our own city.

For years, Slovak newspapers printed harmful ideas about the differences between White and Black people, suggesting that Black people were inferior to White people. The paper emphasized how Slovaks struggled to be seen as *White*, even though we were White.

I had heard about the severe mistreatment of Negroes in America. I never thought my people would be caught up in this debate. The Slovak newspapers regularly printed news about the lynching across the country. Gratefully, we hadn't seen lynchings where we lived. Until May 28, 1917.

I PACED THE SMALL LIVING SPACE, HOLDING Stephen. "Where is he? He's never been *this* late."

"I'm sure he's fine," Aneta said, but worry lines furrowed her brow.

"Go on to bed, I've got more to do still. I can wait up." I offered a weak smile.

She gave me a half-hearted smile in return and went to her room. I nursed Stephen, then checked on Mary, who was fast asleep. I laid Stephen in the crib in our bedroom. As soon as I set him down, the front door opened. I hurried to the living room to greet my Jani.

Face ashen, Janos looked like he had seen the devil himself. "It was terrible." He dropped onto the sofa and stared at the floor. "There were thousands of men marching through the streets. White men attacked the Negroes on the street. They burned buildings, too."

"Where were you when this happened?" My heart raced.

"I was at my work when we heard the noises. Most of us stayed inside, not wanting to get involved. I wasn't sure how I would get out of there. But several of us snuck out the back way of our building and escaped from the rioting. Once we were across the bridge, I took the trolley."

"Why is this happening?" I sat next to him. The fear in his eyes made my insides tremble.

Janos slumped against the back of the sofa and dragged a hand through his thick waves. "They say it started from all the strikes at ore and steel companies. They brought in Negroes from the southern states to fill the jobs until the strike was over. I heard that not all the strikers got their jobs back. Some Negroes stayed on, and that angered the strikers, I guess."

"Why did they strike? Your company did not strike."

"No, we didn't strike, but some of us wanted to. Everyone wants more money and better working conditions. Our company isn't as bad as the ore and steel companies. I feel terrible for those poor Negroes on the streets...the violence against them. It reminded me of the Černová Massacre several years ago. You remember, Mira?"

"Yes, I remember. That was all for nothing, too."

"I could have been one of them today."

"Janos, what do you mean?"

"Slovaks have struggled. I have struggled, and there had been much in our Slovak newspapers against the Negro and other minorities."

"But you weren't involved, right?" I wasn't sure what he was trying to tell me.

"No, not today. But I am angry at the injustices. The violence is wrong. No one deserves to be treated this way."

"I'm glad to hear you say that. I think it is wrong, too."

He held me close, and I wrapped my arms around his large body. We stayed that way for some time.

"You can't go back tomorrow," I whispered.

"Our boss told us to stay home for the next couple of days until the unrest cools down."

The next day, articles about the riots filled the papers. The government had called the National Guard in to suppress the violence. We also learned that the rioters burned parts of the city and shot Negroes who were trying to escape the burning buildings. Some were even hanged. What a tragedy. I was afraid to leave our apartment, and I worried about Janos traveling to East St. Louis for work.

Several days passed, and Janos had returned to work. His company was fortunate not to have suffered any damage, and their work resumed unhindered. However, he told me the general mood in the industrial area was solemn among his coworkers. A major cleanup was underway from the fires and vandalism.

What Janos experienced during that period changed him. I think he recognized everyone was just trying to get by in America, and these prejudices and violence against one another weren't the answer.

———

June 1917

DENNY SHOWED UP AT OUR DOOR ONE SATURDAY afternoon, wearing the US Army uniform.

"Already?" Janos's mouth hung agape.

"Oh, Denny," I whispered, for I had settled Stephen down for a nap. Aneta and the other children had gone out for a walk.

"Yep, I'm being sent to France tomorrow." Denny looked down at the floor. "Do you understand now?"

"I try, my brother. Please, just keep safe. Are you in the regiments?"

Denny shook his head. "No, they have me on the supply station. I won't see much action. I'm disappointed, though."

"But you will be safer, yes?" I interjected while putting a kettle on the stove for tea as the two men sat on the sofa.

"That isn't why I enlisted. I want to kill those bastards!" His eyes flared with hatred, and he pumped his fist in the air.

I jumped at his outburst, almost dropping a teacup as I set up a tray.

Janos patted his back. "Yes, I understand that anger. I feel the rage, too."

"At least I can do something," Denny said. "Because I

enlisted, I will become a naturalized citizen earlier than planned, and Marta will automatically become a citizen. With Tony born here, my family will all be US Citizens." He straightened with pride.

"That's wonderful, Denny." I looked at Janos. "See, you need to get your application in soon. Things are changing."

"Yes, yes, Mira, I will take care of it. Denny's leaving is much more important right now. He and I have never been apart for such a long time." Janos's shoulders slumped. "We have never been apart for more than a few weeks when I would go to Hungary to visit."

"You have always been by my side." Denny clapped his hand on Janos's back.

"And you have been by my side as well, my brother. Life will not be the same without you here."

Denny forced a smile.

We sat in silence for a bit when the kettle started to whistle. I got up and poured the hot water into the cups, and the tea bags floated to the top.

"Remember when we first arrived in St. Louis, and we were trying to find Vamos's Uncle's house?" Denny asked.

I held the tray out to them as they each took a saucer and a cup of tea. "Well, I want to hear. You have told me little about your first time here." I set the tray on the small table, then sat in the rocker, looking intently at them.

"I remember. It was quite an adventure, wasn't it?" Janos chuckled. "Neither of us spoke much English, and we were asking everyone for help. I think that one Italian gave us the wrong directions on purpose. He was pointing down one street and holding up three fingers."

Denny laughed. "It's funny now, but we weren't laughing at the time. We thought he meant three blocks in that direction and make a right, not three houses."

Janos turned to me. "We walked around the same block

probably three times before we realized what we were doing. It was nighttime, too. We were exhausted."

"How did you find his house?" I sipped my tea.

Denny laughed again. "Well, had gone back to where we had started, and realized we were too busy trying to follow the man's directions, we had passed the Sterba house three times."

"What?" I laughed.

"We forgot to look at the house numbers." Janos rolled his eyes.

We had a good laugh, but the laughter died out, and the mood grew somber in the silence that followed. Stephen fussed in his crib, and I went to him and brought him out.

Denny kissed Stephen's forehead. "I will miss the children."

Janos put his arm around Denny. "What will Marta and Tony do?"

"They moved back in with her parents this week, and we put the furniture in storage."

"Already?" I asked, a little hurt that we didn't know. I guessed that Marta had her parents to help.

The door opened, and Aneta entered with Jamie, Katie, and Mary. "We're back from our walk." She ushered the children in and then looked at Denny. "Oh, Denny, look at you in your uniform. You look very sharp." She winked.

"Dobrý deň, Aneta. Yes, I'm shipping out tomorrow." Denny stood at attention.

"I didn't know. Well, luck to you. We will be praying for your safety." She gave Denny a hug and a kiss on his cheek. "Come, children, say farewell to your Uncle Denny."

"Where are you going, Uncle Denny?" Jamie asked.

"I'm going to France," he answered.

"Why?" Katie asked.

"I'm doing important work for our government," he said

and smiled. "I'll be back as soon as I can to tell you all about my adventure." Denny gave us a hopeful look.

It was time.

"My brother." Janos choked on the words, and the two of them embraced. Janos's shoulders shook with sobs.

My heart was wrenching, too.

"I will come back, I promise you." Denny's voice sounded confident. "We will not let this war take another one of us."

Denny leaned over Stephen and kissed my cheek.

I said, "I will pray for you every day and write as often as possible. Write to us when you can. We will be here when you return."

———

July 1917

I PUT STEPHEN IN THE STROLLER AND DRAGGED Mary, Katie, and Jamie along with me to the park for fresh air and some exercise, despite their resistance. The children wandered all over the sidewalks, forcing other pedestrians to avoid them. They ignored my pleas to keep close.

"If you mind yourselves and come along nicely, we will get ice cream at the park."

Jamie and Katie immediately stopped. They each took one of Mary's hands and kept close to me.

I stopped at Ivy's building and buzzed her apartment to ask her to join us, but when I got no answer, we continued to the park. When we arrived, Ivy was there with her children, Ava and Nick, near the playground.

"Ivy," I shouted.

She turned, gave me a big smile, and waved me over. "Come sit here with me."

I pushed the stroller in front of the bench and sat. Mary and Jamie ran out to play with Ava. Katie held back.

"Don't you want to play with Nick?" I asked.

"I will, but can I stay with you first?" Katie toyed with the blanket in Stephen's carriage.

"Of course you can." I picked up Stephen and set him in my lap.

Ivy gave me a questioning look, then turned to Katie. "Nick hasn't been teasing you, has he?"

Katie looked up. "No, h-he's been nice."

Nick waved his arms from the merry-go-round and shouted. "Hey, Katie. Wanna ride?"

Without a word, Katie ran toward Nick and climbed onto the merry-go-round. Nick pushed while running to get the wheel turning fast, then jumped on it next to Katie. Her face lit up with laughter. Mary, Jamie, and Ava joined them. Ivy and I laughed, too.

"I wonder what that was all about?" I asked.

"I guess she needed an invitation. Children can be unpredictable," Ivy said. "I'm glad her speech has improved so much. I can barely tell she ever had an issue."

It warmed my heart to see Aneta's daughter happy.

"Yes, she's been doing well in school since the speech therapy sessions started last year."

"You were very fortunate that your friend Dr. Schwarz set all that up."

"The Schwarzes have been very good to me and my family. The sessions ended a couple months ago. I guess I hadn't mentioned that." I didn't want to explain that it had to do with the Schwarzes being named alien enemies, and Ivy didn't press for more information. She just nodded.

Stephen squirmed and reached for my breast. Carefully, I situated my clothing to nurse and covered him with a lightweight coverlet for a little privacy.

"I've missed working. My plan was to go back to work once Mary got older, and then Stephen came along, and now the war."

"You never know what life will give you." Ivy waved to her daughter. "Be careful not to fall, Ava," She turned back to me. "She can be a little uncoordinated. I have to watch her. By the way, did you hear that Alica's son was drafted?"

"No, I hadn't heard." I sighed. "There have been too many taken to war. We've been waiting for letters from Denny. You remember they shipped him to France, but we have no way of knowing if he is still there."

"Yes, I remember. He is in our prayers, too."

The children had moved to the sandbox when a woman arrived at the park with a little boy with reddish hair. A strange feeling overcame me. He reminded me of Little Jan. I couldn't take my eyes off him. The woman's headscarf covered her face from the side, and I couldn't make her out.

She turned and looked right at me. My heart sank. Rozalia. I hadn't seen her since Lora's wedding reception. She sent the boy, whom I realized was Peter, out to play with the other children.

"Ivy, do you know that woman and child over there?"

Ivy looked to where I pointed. "Not much. I've chatted with her only briefly. I think her name is Roza. She's a widow, and that is her cousin's child, Peter."

"Do they live close by? I thought she looked familiar. From the church."

Ivy thought for a moment. "I think she moved to the neighborhood not long ago and lives on the north side of the park. I'll introduce you."

"No, no, that's unnecessary. I only wanted to know who the other child was playing with our children."

My stomach tensed. Did she live close by? Did she know where we lived? I couldn't help thinking Janos knew about

Peter and that he had been visiting them in secret. But when would he have time? He was either at work or at home. I hated myself for assuming the boy was Janos's son. I had no proof. I was driving myself crazy and needed to put it out of my mind.

I waved the children over, and they came running.

"Don't forget, you promised us ice cream," Jamie said.

"Yes, ice cream," Mary chimed in.

I smiled. "It's time for us to go home," I told Ivy.

"You didn't stay very long." Ivy sounded disappointed.

"We will stay longer next time."

We said our goodbyes to Ivy and her children.

We bought our ice cream and headed home. The children chatted about their ice cream, but my thoughts were on Rozalia and Peter.

———

December 1917

"Do not yell at me, Mira," Janos said as he walked through the front door after work a week later. "But you were right."

"I was right about what? And please talk quietly. Stephen is asleep." I peeked into the bedroom to make sure he hadn't awakened.

"I waited too long to apply for citizenship. It doesn't matter my brother is in the US Army fighting the war against Germany. I must register as an alien enemies and carry the registration card with me at all times, or I could be arrested. My supervisor announced it at work. We have many non-naturalized employees from the Austro-Hungarian Empire."

"I won't yell at you," I said, but my heart thundered. "But now we are all at risk."

Janos hung his head. "I am too stubborn. I couldn't believe this would happen, despite all the warnings."

"Did they say anything about whether Slovaks would be interned?"

"Only that mostly Germans were at risk. Paul and I will go down and register as alien enemies together."

"Paul? Marta's father? I thought they were citizens. They've lived here almost fifteen years."

"I thought the same. Where are the children?"

"Aneta took them with her to buy groceries and give me a little break."

Janos nodded and headed to clean up. I sat on the sofa and tried to calm my thoughts. The war affected all of us in many ways. And now, I would live in constant fear that Janos would be taken from us.

―――

April 1918

ALL FEMALES OVER THE AGE OF FOURTEEN FROM THE Austro-Hungarian Empire were forced to register as alien enemies. This new development made me even angrier at Janos for not taking care of his citizenship.

Aneta patted my arm. "I understand how you feel, but now we can go together. Tommy didn't become a citizen, and with us now divorced, I must register too."

I put an arm around Aneta and squeezed. "You're right. I'm sorry for thinking only of myself."

We gathered the children and walked down to our local post office, where we were to register. My stomach knotted as we entered the building, and I realized this was the same humiliation Zelda and the doctor must have faced when they had been forced to register. To my surprise, many other women from our neighborhood already stood in line. The room remained eerily quiet. No one wanted to draw any attention to themselves. The country we had chosen to make our home was telling us they didn't trust us, maybe we weren't good enough.

Marta was the only woman in our family who didn't have to register. Denny became a citizen when he joined the Army, which granted her automatic citizenship.

I thanked God that our children were citizens because they were born here. At least this treatment wouldn't be imposed on them.

Chapter Thirty-Seven

October 1918

As if the world war and being labeled as an alien enemy weren't enough, a new threat appeared and ruthlessly ravaged the planet—the Spanish Flu. A devastating illness that people claimed was worse than the Black Death. By October, the newspapers had released information about the global sickness, and the death tolls had reached all-time highs.

St. Louis was under quarantine, and the schools and other public places were closed. The children were all at home. The fear of contamination and passing the disease to others led everyone to wear masks when in public.

"Don't forget this." Aneta held out the white cotton fabric mask to me as I was preparing to leave for the Donati Meat Market.

"Thank you. When will this end?" I took the mask and tied it around my face.

"Who knows? Please be careful out there and don't touch anyone." Her brow creased in deep concern.

The street was strangely quiet. The few people out wore masks. No one spoke, keeping to themselves. A Red Cross truck sat parked in front of a building a few doors down. Nurses and volunteers wore masks and spoke in low voices. As I passed, two men carried a stretcher from the building with a person covered with a blanket from head to toe. Another death. I held my breath and shuddered. Too close.

The news reports said people between the ages of twenty and forty were the most at risk, as were those under five and over sixty-five. I kept Stephen and Mary in the apartment all the time, but when the schools closed, we kept Katie and Jamie home too.

A note from Dr. Schwarz said Zelda had contracted the flu earlier that year but recovered. There were many others not as fortunate. I worried about Papa in Hungary and whether the dreaded disease had reached his village. There had been no letters for months. Rumors stated that the war was nearing the end, and we all hoped to see Denny home soon.

I reached the market. Only one other customer waited at the counter with her face covered.

"Where is Signore Donati?" I asked in English after I gave my order to the woman behind the counter.

"Haven't you heard? Signore Donati's wife died from the flu this week." She shook her head and tsked.

"I'm very sorry for his loss. I had not heard."

Signora Donati was in her late thirties, much younger than Signore Donati. I didn't know her well, only from doing business with her in the market, but I was sad for him.

"I will send him a note of condolence."

The woman gave me a wan smile as she pushed my package across the counter. I paid her and left. Janos would be home soon. Each day, I worried he might catch the sickness traveling on the crowded trolley to work.

On my way back to the apartment, a man wearing a mask was posting flyers on walls, doors, and the posts of the streetlights.

When he passed me, he shoved a flyer in my hand. "Read this," he said, and hurried away.

I could read enough English to understand what it said along the top of the sheet:

INFLUENZA EPIDEMIC — ADVICE TO SUFFERERS — COURSE OF TREATMENT.

Janos came home pale and covered in sweat. He took off his mask and dropped onto the nearest chair with his hands on his stomach.

"Mira, I am hot and sick to my stomach."

"Oh, no. You must go to the bedroom right away."

He rose as if every part of his body ached. I gave him a gentle push and whispered to him, afraid the children might hear.

"I think you might have the flu." I handed him the flyer.

He read it and looked at me with alarm.

"You need to stay away from the children. I will be the only one to care for you. If I can get the children to the Nagys', I will, if no one at their house is sick. This disease comes fast and hard."

I dragged Stephen's crib into the front room next to Mary's mattress.

Without a word, Janos lay on the bed.

I pulled a blanket over him and tucked in the sides. "I'll stoke the stove to get more heat in here and will call Zelda for any advice."

He barely acknowledged my words, closed his eyes, and shuddered.

Aneta stood outside the door. "What should we do with the children? Are they at risk if Janos has it?" The lines between her brows creased into deep lines of worry.

"Yes, you need to keep the children in your room all the time now. Can you do that?"

"Yes, yes, Mira. Whatever is needed."

"I'm going to call Zelda for any information she can give me. By the way, I heard that Signore Donati's wife died this week. Isn't that sad?"

Aneta blinked. "From the flu? Oh no! My heart goes out to poor Dino."

That was curious. I never knew his first name. With no time to waste, I put my mask on, grabbed a piece of paper with the Nagys' phone number on it, and hurried across the street to the little store to use the pay phone in the back. Three people stood in line waiting to use the phone, yet the first person at the phone wasn't using it.

"Is there something wrong with the phone?" I said to the woman in front of me.

She turned to me. "Too many phone operators are out sick, and the phone lines are difficult to get through. She is waiting to try again."

"I had no idea. I don't use the phone much." I struggled to control my impatience and waited a long time while two more people came in behind me.

Finally, my turn came, and my hands shook when I picked up the receiver. I inserted a nickel, hoping an operator would answer. It rang and rang until someone answered.

"Number, please," the operator said.

Relieved, I gave the operator Zelda's number, and she answered right away.

"Zelda? This is Mira."

"Meine Liebe, I'm glad you got through, what with many

operators sick. Is everything all right there?" Her voice came through the receiver fuzzy.

"It's Janos. He's sick with a fever and very weak. He is in bed. I'm afraid. May I speak to the doctor?"

"Ezra is not here right now. People call day and night, wanting to know what to do. Ezra has left instructions for me to share with everyone. He says to be sure to keep Janos away from anyone else, particularly your baby. You need to reduce the fever—try cinnamon powder in milk and cold compresses on his face. Don't allow him to sneeze on you, and wear a mask or kerchief tied about your face while you are caring for him. Do you understand?"

"Yes, yes, understood." My voice broke. "Zelda, I can't lose Janos, I just can't. I am terribly afraid he will die." I kept my voice low. There was no privacy, even though the people waiting behind me tried to keep at a distance in the small space.

"I know, Mira, dear. I pray he will recover. I understand your fears. Ezra is at the hospital day and night, even sleeping there. It is at capacity with patients sick with the flu. I worry about him catching the sickness, too."

"I will pray for the doctor, Zelda. Thank you."

"If the fever doesn't come down in a few days, call me if you can."

"I promise, my dear friend."

I flicked the receiver lever a few times, inserted another nickel, and, luckily, an operator answered. I looked at the paper in my hand with the Nagys' number and spoke the number into the mouthpiece.

"Hello," Hana answered.

"Hana, it's Mira."

"Is something wrong?" she asked. "You never call."

"It's Janos, he's sick. I need a place for the children. Can they—"

"Marta and Paul are sick too. We are doing everything we can to keep Tony from getting sick. I'm sorry, Mira. Janos is in our prayers, but we cannot risk your children as well."

"I understand. Marta and Paul are in my prayers. I'll try to call again in a few days to check on you all."

"Bless you," Hanna said and hung up.

BY THE TIME I RETURNED TO THE APARTMENT, JANOS was writhing in pain and could barely lift his head. I mixed the cinnamon and milk and helped him drink it. After, I chipped some ice into a bowl of water and made a compress, which I placed on his forehead.

Helplessness overcame me, and I prayed to God to let Janos get through the sickness. Janos coughed, and I stroked his brow with the cool cloth. His body shook from the chills. I layered another blanket over him, tucking it in around him tightly.

"Don't leave me, my Jani," I whispered. "Please stay with me. I need you."

Hours later, he opened his eyes, distant and vacant from the fever.

I leaned in close. "Janos? Can you hear me?"

"Mira...Mira...." His voice was ragged and faint. His eyes closed again, and his head rolled from side to side.

"I'm here, my dearest." I refreshed the compress and put it back on his brow. He opened his eyes but didn't seem to recognize me.

"Mama?" he whispered.

"It's me, Mira," I whispered. My heart raced at the thought of losing him.

All church services were suspended due to the quarantine. On Sunday, I gathered Aneta and the children with me in the living room, and we held a private service of our own. We said prayers for Janos, Marta, and the rest of our family and friends to keep safe from the disease.

Days passed while I sat vigil by Janos's bedside until his fever finally broke.

"Mira," Janos whispered, his voice weak.

I jolted from my stupor, having nearly fallen asleep. "Janos? I'm here, *moja láska*." I got up from my chair, sat on the side of the bed, and took his hand in mine. "Janos."

He blinked as if he was trying to focus. "Mira, I'm thirsty."

"Yes, here you are." I took his glass from the side table and held it to his lips until he drank the whole thing. "You will be fine now. You are through the worst of it. How do you feel?"

He looked at me and smiled. "Happy you are here with me, moja láska, my love."

He closed his eyes again. I watched his chest rise and fall while holding my breath. The day my Mamička passed away, her breathing slowed down until it stopped. I feared he was doing the same thing. But his breathing became stronger with time, and later he was able to sit up in bed to eat. It encouraged us that he would survive since the sickness hadn't settled into his lungs.

Zelda had said to get him out into the sunlight. That sun exposure quickened the recovery time. When he could stand, Aneta and I helped him out to the front steps of the building when the sun shone, and he improved greatly. Still, almost an entire month passed before Janos was strong enough to return to work.

THE WAR ENDED ON NOVEMBER 11, 1918. ON December 1, a part of southern Hungary became part of the new Yugoslavian state. We waited anxiously to hear when Denny would return home.

As the war had ended, Janos was eligible to submit his Declaration of Intent to become a naturalized citizen. Once he was well, I practically pushed him out the door with the form, telling him to march down to the government office to submit it. We would then have to wait at least three years to submit his final papers to petition for his citizenship. I could hardly wait.

Although it was cause for celebration, we were still living under the flu quarantine. It was a wonder that the rest of us hadn't caught the flu from Janos. Such a strange disease that seemed to pick and choose its hosts.

After Christmas, the city lifted the quarantine, and schools and businesses reopened. St. Louis reported fewer deaths than other, larger cities because of the imposed quarantine. We were lucky in that, if you called anything lucky when many perished. Marta and Paul recovered, but Paul's parents died in Hungary.

I was saddened to learn my friend Ivy's husband died from the flu. She moved with her two children to live with family on the other side of the Slovak Catholic Church, too far away to visit frequently. We promised to stay in touch by writing.

Janos was much better, and when the church services resumed, we all went to give thanks. One by one, the pastor called out the names of all the parishioners who had perished. There were more than we had suspected, and a hushed quiet hung over the sanctuary until he recited the last name.

And then, when we stood to leave, I couldn't believe my eyes, for there they were, Rozalia and Peter, several rows behind us. I knew they would appear from time to time, but I could not control how seeing them affected me.

I pointed out the little boy to Janos. "That's little Peter, the boy with the reddish hair. Marta told me about him." I watched Janos for any telling expression.

He raised his eyebrows slightly, "I heard she took in a cousin's child. That was good of her."

Certainly, no signs of guilt or curiosity. I decided to put an end to my fear and forget about them. I focused on Janos's recovery and being happy. He and our children were alive and healthy.

Chapter Thirty-Eight

January 1918

At the first of the month, Janos received a letter from his old friend Vamos.

"Humph, I haven't heard from Vamos in many years. This must be something important." Janos took the letter and sat in his rocker. He opened the drawer in the small end table, pulled out his new pair of reading glasses, and put them on.

I smiled. He looked very intelligent in them. I turned up the gas lamp on the wall to brighten the room.

> *Dear Janos,*
>
> *We thought you might be interested to know of the changes in our village. There was an uproar among the villagers in celebration of the fall of the Hapsburgs, but also in wanting big changes in how our village was being managed. One day a crowd of angry villagers and farmers marched up to the*

Village Notary's office. They pounded on his door, but he had locked it and closed down his operations. People shouted out all the things he had done to them and that he was no longer welcome there. The Notary was gone within days of that outburst.

Everyone here is much happier, but the town and leadership are disorganized, since we are no longer part of Hungary. The borders have changed and our village is now part of Yugoslavia. Our Slovak community will remain as it has always been, despite the changes up north with the formation of Czechoslovakia. Only a few who still have family there are planning to move. We expect the remaining Magyars to move north and more Serbians to settle nearby.

We hope you are all doing well and wish to keep in touch. You can write to us as well

Your old friend,

Vamos Sterba

"Well now," Janos folded the letter. "Isn't that interesting?"

"The Notary was a spiteful and disrespectful man," I said. "Every day I collected our mail, I dreaded seeing him. He always made me feel inferior."

"Yes, as long as he lived there, he was so. He will not be missed."

———

September 1919

NINE MONTHS AFTER JANOS HAD FULLY RECOVERED from the flu, I gave birth to our third child, another boy. We followed the tradition of naming another child the same as one who had died, and called him Johnny, after Little Jan.

A few days after the birth, I had another strange dream. Similar to another dream, when I lived in Hungary, there was a planked deck surrounded by a wood fence with flowers in clay pots. In the other dream, the pots didn't have flowers, but in the new dream, there were dark pink azaleas and white peonies.

A young woman entered with a child in her arms, followed by two young men. The woman looked like an older version of Mary. She sat in a rocking chair. The young men stood behind her. They all looked like they were posing for a photo, with fixed smiles, while looking straight at me, as if I were the camera. Another figure lurked in the shadows, a young man about the same age or a little older than Mary. Who was he? Why was he in the dream?

Then I woke up.

For weeks after, I thought about the dream and the boy in the shadows, wondering who he could be. Another child I was to bear? Or was he Rozalia's son Peter, who reminded me of Little Jan? I wanted to be wrong, for I had put Peter out of my mind. Why now?

I needed to talk to Zelda.

———

I BUSIED MYSELF PREPARING TEA AND COOKIES AND picked up around the apartment in preparation for Zelda's visit. Two years had passed since they had been declared alien enemies, and we had agreed not to see each other until it became safe again. Germans, in particular, were more likely to be interned but, thankfully, the city needed doctors, especially during the flu pandemic, and that offered him a great deal of protection.

I watched out the front window while rocking Johnny's cradle, periodically making sure he was still asleep. When her Zelda's car pulled up in front of our building, I put the baby in his crib and rushed outside to greet her.

"Zelda!" I threw my arms around her.

"Mira! *Meine Liebe*." She kissed my cheeks.

"Come, come." I pulled her up the steps and into our apartment. "Shhh. Johnny is asleep. Please sit down." I urged her down onto the sofa. "I have tea."

She looked into the cradle next to the sofa and whispered, "That would be wonderful, my dear."

I poured a cup of tea on the tiny table and offered her the plate of cookies as I sat next to her.

"Thank you. He looks peaceful. Where are the other children and Aneta?"

"They will be along soon. Aneta took them out for a walk to give you and I a little quiet time together. The children can be quite rambunctious at times."

"I can't wait to see them."

"You haven't seen Stephen since he was born. He's two now and very vocal. It's a lot like the dreams I used to have back in Hungary. It's all coming true."

"Have you had any dreams since?"

"Just one, shortly after Johnny was born," I said.

"Now," Zelda leaned in, "you must tell me about this new dream you had."

I told her all about my grown children, and Mary holding a small child, and of the young man in the shadows.

"My, my Mira, you have the most intriguing dreams." She put her finger to her mouth and tapped, thinking.

"Well?"

"Can you describe the young man at all?"

"Like I told you, he was shadowy, but...and I have this feeling, or it's because I think I know already...he looked a bit like Janos."

Zelda crossed her arms. "What haven't you told me, Mira?"

I gave her a blank look, not sure what to say.

"Your dreams like this have been about your children or your mama. Why would a young Janos be in the dream, and why should he be in shadows?"

"I was hoping you would get one of your epiphanies and figure it out without me telling you all my crazy thoughts."

"Why crazy? I know you, Mira. Just tell me what you think this is about."

So, I told her about Rozalia and about Peter and how he reminded me of Little Jan.

She frowned. "What? Are you not furious with Janos?"

"I don't have any right to be angry at Janos." I dropped by gaze to my folded hands in my lap.

Zelda gasped. "Why would you say something like that? If your suspicions are true, then you have every right to be angry."

"Because he isn't the only one." Shame heated my face.

"Oh. I see." Zelda's voice turned soft and gentle. "Did that happen in Hungary?"

I finally looked at her, afraid to see her disdain. But there was none, only her understanding. "Why are you not disgusted?"

"Because I love you, Mira. There is no need to explain your actions. Whatever happened back then was back then. You came to America to be with your husband. You must have realized your place was with him, ja?" She covered my hands with her hand. Their warmth comforted me.

"Yes. I did. But this thing with Janos. There is a child, and the woman keeps showing up. Is there a message here? Am I supposed to do something?"

"This is just my opinion, and I could be wrong...." Zelda took a deep breath. "Because the child is in the shadows, I think he will stay hidden, so to speak, for a while."

"That would be good." I leaned closer.

Zelda continued, "And his age in the dream might indicate when he will become more important."

"Yes, Mary was a woman. She is only four right now, so...."

"Many years will pass before that situation comes to anything, if at all. He may stay in the shadows." Zelda patted my knee.

"That makes me feel more at ease. I just don't want anything to disrupt my family. Not right now, not ever."

Johnny let out a cry.

"He's hungry." I laughed and lifted him out of the cradle.

Aneta arrived with the rest of the children, and thoughts of the dream, Rozalia, and her boy, faded from my mind...for a while.

Chapter Thirty-Nine

October 1919

THE LEAVES TURNED BRIGHT YELLOWS, ORANGES, and reds of fall. The air was cool and refreshing, free from the summer heat and humidity. The family had gathered for another fine Sunday afternoon at the Nagys' to celebrate Denny's return from Europe, and also Lora's pregnancy. The Army had kept him in Europe longer to help coordinate the return of casualties.

We all surrounded Denny with congratulations on his homecoming, and his usual shy side showed.

"I'm very glad to be home. Thank you." He shrugged and hung his head to hide his smile. "And I'm done with the Army."

"Tell us about it, Papa," Tony asked.

Denny patted Tony's head. "Not right now. Too many stories. Another time?" His eyes clouded.

Tony stuck his lower lip out and shuffled his feet. "Yes, Papa." The little five-year-old ran to Marta, and she whispered something to him, and he perked up.

Janos hugged his brother. "Very relieved you are home and healthy."

Janos and Denny moved over to talk privately. Soon, the food was ready, and drinks were poured.

The children ran around playing and laughing. I was nursing Johnny in the shade, out of the way of the others, when Aneta came over and sat beside me.

"What is it this time?" I gave her a sideways glance. "You have that look on your face that tells me you have a secret, and you can't wait to tell me."

Aneta sat up very straight with her hands clasped in her lap. "You know me too well, Mira. I have something to tell you before I tell anyone else." She leaned close and whispered, "I'm getting married again."

I jolted and jarred Johnny from his latch. He cried.

"What? How could I not know you have been seeing someone?" I readjusted Johnny, and he quieted right away.

"I have been seeing someone for some time now."

"Why didn't you tell me?"

"I didn't want anyone to know because, well, I didn't know how you would take it, or anyone else, for that matter. And...I wasn't sure if it meant anything in the beginning."

"Who is it?" I said in a hushed voice.

"Dino Donati."

I blinked. "Our butcher? He's much older than you."

"He's only four years older than Janos," she said.

"He is? I had always thought Signore Donati was much older."

"At first, I thought he was being, you know, friendly. We talked a lot whenever I was at his market. I always thought of him as a nice and funny man, and I knew he was lonely after his wife died. When he asked me to take walks and have coffee with him...it just sort of blossomed." Aneta leaned forward, elbows on her knees, chin in her hands, wearing a dreamy smile.

"But why keep it a secret from me?"

"I don't know. To avoid comments about the age difference, partly, and the fact he's Italian and Catholic." She sighed.

I rolled my eyes. "You know I don't care about any of that. If he makes you happy, that's all I care about. When will you be married?"

"Soon. I wanted to tell you and the family first. We'll set a date in the next month or so for a civil ceremony, since it is the second marriage for both of us, and our religious differences."

"It seems very sudden." I shifted Johnny. My arms ached from holding him.

"Perhaps, but we've known him five years. We aren't strangers. He wants to take care of me and my children. I won't have to work anymore. His sons are both grown and married. He is a very sweet man."

"Do you love him, Aneta?" I searched her face for the signs I had seen when she was in love with Tommy. She looked different.

"I do. It's different from what I felt for Tommy. A lot has happened to me, and I've grown up. This time, it feels mature and caring." She leaned back and swept her hair off her shoulders.

I nodded slowly. "I can see it in your face. You look almost peaceful."

"Exactly. I feel like I've found my home. Don't misunderstand, I have been at home with you and Janos. But with Dino, I feel on earth, not up in the clouds like I did with Tommy. He was a dreamer. Dino is a realist. Does that make sense?"

"It makes complete sense. I'm thrilled for you."

"And, because Dino is a naturalized citizen, I become a citizen when I marry him. Isn't that wonderful?" She jumped up and gave me a hug, careful not to hurt Johnny, and I kissed her cheek.

Everyone around me was becoming US citizens except Janos and me. It didn't make sense. Johnny finished, and I pulled myself together. "Let's tell everyone."

Once the initial shock passed, everyone was happy for Aneta and wanted to help with a reception. It was a small affair, just family, right before Vianoce.

Janos scowled with his usual disgruntled expression when something irritated him. But by the time the wedding day came, he had grown accustomed to it and was polite to Dino.

———

January 1920

THE APARTMENT FELT STRANGE AND MUCH LARGER after Aneta and her two children moved out. A big, gaping hole existed in the space we had all shared. We put Mary and Stephen in Aneta's old room. Baby Johnny still slept in the room with Janos and me. It felt luxurious to have much more space—until we visited Aneta and Dino's new place.

Aneta and the children had moved into Dino's two-bedroom apartment on the second floor of his meat market building. A few months later, they moved to the Carondelet District to the west of us, to a lovely two-story townhouse with trees and a backyard on a quiet Italian block. They had four bedrooms. Jamie and Katie had their own rooms. Dino sold the market near us and went into business with a cousin who owned a much larger delicatessen closer to their home.

Aneta had a kind and generous husband and a beautiful home. She deserved it. I suspected she hadn't told me every-thing about her life with Tommy. It must have been terrible if she didn't want me to know. Aneta had her pride and didn't want my pity.

Aneta meant well, and she wanted to share her happiness and prosperity. She showered me and my children with gifts. Janos did not always approve.

Aneta had gotten me a dress, and when Janos found out, he demanded I return it.

"What are you saying? I must return this dress to Aneta? It is a gift. Am I not allowed to receive gifts from my sister?" I stared at Janos in disbelief.

"It is not your birthday, or Vianoce. Why must she show off her affluence with gifts to you and our children? Does she think I cannot take care of my family?" He glowered, hands balled into fists.

I folded the dress and placed it back in the box. "She doesn't think that at all. She's just sharing her good fortune. I will not insult her by returning the dress." I stamped my foot and faced him.

"Fine. Just don't wear it around me." He stormed out of the apartment onto the front steps.

I put the box on the top shelf of the closet and joined him outside. "Janos, my dearest, Aneta gives gifts as her way of thanking us for taking her and the children in when they needed help all those years. She knows you would never accept gifts given to you, so she gives to me and our children. It has nothing to do with your ability to provide for our family. Do you not see that?"

His shoulders relaxed, and he hung his head. "When you put it that way, yes, I understand." He looked at me. "You can keep the dress. It is very pretty."

Janos's self-doubt and defensiveness could be frustrating. Thank God, I loved him. That helped keep me calm. And the fact that he usually saw things my way in the end helped.

When Aneta and I worried about not being able to spend

time together, Dino surprised her with a car. It was eight years old, but large enough for all four of them to ride together. Dino taught Aneta how to drive.

One spring day, when Janos was at Denny's, Aneta came by to take the children and me for a drive. When we stepped out to the curb, some of our neighbors ogled the four-door car with no windows. I waved and smiled, proud of my prosperous sister. I sat in the front seat with Johnny in my lap and Mary between Aneta and me, with the boys and Katie in the back. The only other car I had ever ridden in was Zelda's.

After we settled, Aneta put the Ford Model T into gear and headed down the road, with the top up and only a glass shield in front to protect us from the wind. The power of the wind whipping in the car from the sides exhilarated me. The children cried out at the sights and pointed to various buildings and people as we passed by.

"This is wonderful, Aneta!" I laughed and giggled like a young girl.

"I just had to show off the new car and my driving skills. It took a while to learn, and then I needed a driver's license." Aneta shifted the gears and pressed on the accelerator.

"Slow down, Aneta. You have always been more daring than me."

Aneta laughed and kept going.

———

January 1923

MORE THAN FOUR YEARS HAD PASSED SINCE JANOS submitted his Declaration of Intent to become naturalized.

He stared at me like I had two heads. "What is it now, Mira?"

"It's time, Janos. We are the only ones in our family who

aren't citizens. Why are you–how do they say it–dragging [your] feet?"

"Oh, that."

"You need to file your final papers. Just because they give you up to seven years doesn't mean you should wait."

Janos twiddled his thumbs in his lap. I waited. Five minutes passed, and I turned to walk out of the room.

"It's done," he said.

"What is done?"

"I finished the process."

"When?"

"I submitted the papers last week." He winked and laughed.

I wanted to hit him on the arm for teasing me and keeping it a secret.

Months later, Janos received his certificate, which included me. We had a special celebration dinner with the whole extended family. We were Slovak Americans, and I was proud.

Chapter Forty

Fall 1925

Sometimes I wondered how we all managed to get through the war years, riots, pandemic, and all the losses. Yet life had settled down, and I watched my children grow and become interesting and beautiful individuals.

I had reached forty, and my reflection in the mirror had changed quite a bit. Silver and gray streaked my darkened brown hair. I cringed at the sagging skin and bags under my eyes. Janos said he didn't notice. I didn't believe him.

He continued to impose his stringent rule of no English at home, but when he wasn't home, we spoke English. Sometimes the children would slip and say something in English in front of Janos, and he would tense. He said it was one way to hold on to our Slovak culture.

I knew others in our neighborhood who also only spoke Slovak or Czech at home. They said it made them feel connected to their roots, their culture, even though we had all become American citizens. I guessed that was how it was with

Janos. It was true that we were growing further and further away from our Slovak traditions. Keeping the language alive was one area he could control.

That year, when the school reports cards arrived in the mail, I wanted to open them before Janos came home, but I knew better. He wanted to open the important mail.

Mary and Stephen were doing homework at the dining table after dinner. Johnny was drawing pictures with crayons on the living area floor. I motioned to Janos to join me in our bedroom and shut the door.

"What is all this secrecy, Mira?"

"I think the school report cards arrived today and thought we could look at them together in private."

He raised his brows as I handed the envelopes to him. He said nothing, opened them one at a time, read slowly, then handed each to me.

The first was Mary's. As expected, straight A's, perfect attendance, and her habits and attitudes were all commendable or satisfactory.

Stephen's report was mostly average, with a couple of below-average scores on spelling and arithmetic. His learning had been slow going. His teachers said he was improving and passed him through.

The last one was Johnny's, and for a first grader, he was below average in everything. I had worried about him, since I could get him to speak only simplistic English.

Janos scowled. "Why is Johnny doing poorly in school? He's not stupid."

I heaved a sigh. "I've been telling you it is his English. He won't try very hard to learn. He says he doesn't want to."

Janos's face reddened. "This is unacceptable. To not want to." He jumped up from the bed.

"Wait, please." I tried to stop him, but he pulled away and strode from the bedroom.

"Johnny, come here," he ordered.

Mary and Stephen froze.

Johnny stood slowly and took baby steps toward Janos. His gaze fixed on the floor. "Yes, Papa."

"Your report card is terrible. What do you have to say for yourself?"

"Sorry, Papa. I can't learn the English. I'm not good at it. The teachers try, but they don't speak Slovak."

"I didn't have anyone to teach me English when I came to this country. I only spoke Slovak and a handful of words." Janos had told this story many times over the years to anyone who would listen. "But I paid attention and learned to speak, write, and read English."

What he didn't understand was that he already knew how to read and write in Slovak, and that helped him to learn English. Our poor children didn't have that benefit.

"Yes, Papa. I know. I'm sorry." Tears trickled down my beloved son's cheeks.

"When I didn't do what I was told as a boy, you know what my Papa did, don't you?" Janos unbuckled his belt and pulled it from around his waist in one quick motion.

My stomach clenched. I had been praying the boys would never do anything to prompt Janos to punish them the way he had been punished growing up.

I covered his hand with mine. "Please, Janos, can we talk about this?"

He turned in surprise. "What are you doing? It is my job to discipline the children. To teach my boys respect. They need to toughen up to be men."

I gently pulled him into the bedroom and closed the door.

"Please forgive me, my love. I can't let you punish our children for no good reason. They are good boys, good children. They are, right?"

Janos frowned. "They are good boys. Yes, but—"

"My father never beat me or Aneta, and you know how outspoken she was."

"Your father didn't have boys."

"I watched your father beat your brothers for years for the slightest mistake. I swore that would never happen to my children."

"You never said anything to me about your feelings."

"You weren't there for most of the time."

He flinched.

"Up till now, our children have done nothing bad. Do you really think it would help him learn? Why not offer him a treat when he succeeds? That's what my friend Ivy does with her children."

He sat on the bed and slumped. "Does it work?"

"Sometimes. No one is perfect. They just don't get the reward."

"I will think about it. But I still don't want them speaking English when I'm home. You try to work with him more."

I hugged Janos and kissed his cheek. "Thank you for listening and being open to trying something different."

He shook his head. "I don't know if it will make a difference. How do you make someone want something they don't want?"

We returned to the living area. Johnny stood in the same spot where we left him. He had stopped crying, and Mary and Stephen had gone back to their homework.

Janos patted Johnny on the top of his head. "Try better, little Johnny?"

"Yes, Papa. I promise. I will try harder." Johnny smiled and ran back to his drawings.

I sat on the couch in hopes Janos would join me, but he picked up his pipe and matches and left the apartment. Through our first-floor window, I watched him on the front steps of our building. He struck a match, which flared to life, but he seemed to forget it and stared out into the night. My heart ached. Janos meant to teach our son strength, but I knew him well enough to know he feared being weak and afraid that Johnny would grow up to be such a man. The match burned his fingers. He dropped it and turned back toward the door. I drew my gaze to our children. Janos had as much to learn as our children did in some ways, and he, like them, was good.

A few weeks later, Janos came home to tell me he was changing jobs.

"Are you sure this is a good idea to leave a place you've worked at for many years? What about your plan to be promoted?" I pursed my lips.

"This is part of my plan. It's a better job with the car foundry. They pay better wages because they're unionized. My supervisor told me with my good record at my present job, and my fine handwriting, I could be looking at a promotion in a year or so." His voice was energetic and his face full of hope.

"I hope you are right."

"I am happy about it. Be happy for me. For us." His eyes twinkled.

I smiled, "I'm happy." But I still worried.

———

September 1927

THE CHILDREN WERE GROWING, AND THE TINY apartment became cramped once again. Janos had been working at the car foundry for nearly two years with no promotion in sight. The extra money from the job change did help with groceries and new clothes for everyone. I still made dresses for Mary and me, but the boys' pants were still a challenge. Stephen had grown taller overnight, it seemed, and his pants with the deep hems could no longer be lengthened.

Janos came home with a mischievous expression but said nothing.

We all sat around the table for dinner when I broached the subject. "Jani," dear, I will need new fabric to make pants for Stephen. He has outgrown the one pair for school."

"Sure, sure. It is no problem." He reached into his pants pocket and retrieved a two-dollar bill. "Here, get whatever you can with this." He tilted his head to the side and winked.

Why did he wink at me? "This much? Are you sure? We still need groceries this week."

"Use your grocery fund as usual. That is extra. By the by, I think it is time we find a larger place."

My mouth dropped open. "You do? How will we afford it?"

"I was promoted to Team Lead with a substantial raise in pay. I told you it was a good idea to work at the car foundry." He pulled on his suspenders and puffed out his chest.

"Janos, how wonderful!" I got up from the table, ran around to his side, and gave him a big kiss on the cheek.

"We are going to move?" Mary said, wide-eyed. "Where to?"

"Move?" Stephen stopped eating, his fork halfway to his mouth.

"Why?" asked Johnny.

"This is great news, my children. We will all go look at it this weekend." Janos got up, moved into the living room, and began his smoking routine.

"You found a place already? When did you find the time?" I began clearing the table.

"Someone I work with told me about it yesterday. I wasn't

sure until I found out I got the raise today. It is a sign. Mary, turn on the radio and find the music, yes?"

"Okay," she said in English.

"O-kay?" He scowled.

"Sorry, Papa," she replied in Slovak. "My classmates say it all the time."

"I say it, too, sometimes," Janos shrugged.

I laughed.

WITHIN THE MONTH, WE MOVED INTO A WONDERFUL three-bedroom, two-story quadraplex. Each story had two units. There was a large bedroom for Janos and me, and two smaller ones for the children. We put Mary in her own room. She had become quite independent and needed to be separated from her brothers, since she would be twelve soon. We bought bunk beds for the two boys, which allowed for a small dresser and a tiny desk in the third room.

The kitchen had a gas range and oven, and running hot and cold faucets in the sink. The bathroom was fully furnished with a tub, a sink with hot and cold faucets, and a toilet, all in the same room. Finally, we had a normal American home.

In the basement was our first wringer-washing machine, plus a little room for food storage, just like the larder on our farm in the old country.

Janos had a telephone installed. We still didn't need a car —we could walk since everything was nearby. Janos preferred traveling to work by trolley, and the new bus system covered routes the trolleys didn't.

In the back of the building was a small yard just big enough for a vegetable garden. I was in Heaven. Aneta and I shopped for some pots to put flowers on the enclosed deck. Once completed, the wooden deck looked exactly like the dream I had been having for years about the children. Funny how things work out.

Sometimes I thought about the dream with the boy in the background, but it had been years since I had seen Rozalia and Peter. Marta had told me they had moved away, and I was relieved. However, occasionally they would come to mind, and I still wondered...was Peter Janos's son?

Chapter Forty-One

May 1932

MARY CAME HOME FROM HIGH SCHOOL WAVING THE letter in the air and jumping up and down. "I got a scholarship to college for next year." She could barely contain herself.

"That's great news. Is it for the nursing school in Illinois?" Being a nurse was all Mary had talked about in high school. I beamed.

"Yes! The counselor gave me the letter today and explained what the scholarship means."

We could barely contain our excitement as we waited for Janos to come home from work. He was tired, as usual, and didn't give us a single look when he passed by us in the living room.

Mary glanced at me. "Maybe we tell him at dinner."

I nodded in agreement. We cooked the meal and set the table in record time.

The boys were already in their seats at the table when Janos took his place at the head and said grace. Stephen and

Johnny dove in, scooping up large spoonfuls of the chicken and cabbage casserole and shoveling it in their mouths.

"Where are your manners?" I admonished.

"Sorry, Mama," they said in unison.

"Exactly," said Janos, not looking up from his plate.

"Papa," Mary leaned forward in her chair, her lips pressed together.

"Hmmm...?" he responded.

I gave Mary an encouraging smile.

"I have some very exciting news to share from the school."

"The school?" He stopped eating and looked from Mary to me.

"Yes, she got a letter today. Mary, show him." I motioned to her to give him the letter.

Mary hesitated, then pulled the letter from the envelope on her lap and handed it to him.

Janos squinted at the paper. "What does this mean, a scholarship?"

"It means they will help pay for the tuition to the nursing school."

"Nursing school? What nursing school?" His eyes darkened, and he slammed the letter down on the table.

Mary flinched but continued. "Well, the one that is giving me the scholarship, in Illinois, across the river."

"They pay this tuition, you say? Is that all it will cost to go to this college?"

Mary tensed, and I jumped in.

"There is a dormitory on campus where she will stay. There is a cost for that, but Mary will work to pay for that beforehand. Won't you, Mary?" I turned to her.

"Of course. I already know a couple of places to work after school, even now, and by the time—"

"Stop!" Janos shouted.

The boys stopped eating and looked up at him. Mary's face fell, and I knew what was coming.

Janos's brows knitted together. "You finish high school, then get married. That is tradition. Not this...school thing. You've had enough school. Now let me finish my meal."

"But Papa." Mary's eyes shimmered with tears.

I put my hand on her arm to let her know to say no more. She looked at me beseechingly. I shook my head. She pulled away and ran into her bedroom and slammed the door shut.

"Mary! I didn't say you could leave the table, and we don't slam doors in this house," Janos sputtered.

"She is upset and disappointed. The scholarship is an important accomplishment." I struggled to keep my tone even.

I realized Janos didn't understand, but I refused to believe he didn't care.

Stephen finished eating and stood. He gave Janos a defiant look. "Papa, I think it's great that Mary was offered the scholarship. She's the smartest of all three of us, and I think she deserves the chance to do something special." He didn't wait for a response but walked away from the table and into his room.

Johnny followed behind, looking very surprised by Stephen's display of support for Mary, and shot his papa a glance.

"Why are my children defying me?" Janos's expression darkened. He opened his mouth to speak, but I raised my hand, and he stopped short.

"Jani, dear, why are you so angry? Are you not proud of your children?"

He fidgeted with his food and took the last bite.

"Yes, of course I am proud of them. It's just...." He pushed away from the table. The vein along his temple pulsed. "I don't know." He stood and wavered, reaching for the table for support.

"Are you all right, dear? You look flushed."

"I am fine."

"You don't look fine." I reached out to him.

"Yes, yes, just a little dizzy. I must have stood up too fast." He pushed past me and sat in his rocker to smoke his pipe just as he always did every night after dinner.

I cleared the table. Before I carried the last of the dirty dishes to the kitchen, I made one last effort. "Would you just think about the scholarship before making a final decision?"

"I will think on it."

But the look on Janos's face told me he didn't want to think about it at all. How I wondered what went on in that stubborn head of his.

Weeks passed, and Janos said nothing about the scholarship. I didn't mention it either. We had plenty of time to accept the scholarship. I waited.

———

September 1932

THE PHONE RANG AND RANG, AND I RAN FROM THE backyard to answer it, almost out of breath. "Hello?"

"Mrs. Lacks?" a man asked.

"Yes," I said.

"I work with your husband, John. He collapsed at work, and he has been taken to the closest hospital."

My heart dropped.

"Mrs. Lacks, are you still there?"

"Is-is he all right?" I asked.

"I don't have any other details regarding your husband, but here's the name and address of the hospital."

I wrote the information on the notepad we kept by the phone. I wasn't familiar with the hospital.

My body shook with a terrifying fear. I called Aneta. She dropped everything to drive me to Johnny's K-8 school, and the high school for Mary and Stephen to take the children out and then to the hospital.

Every minute that passed felt like an eternity until we arrived. We rushed inside the emergency entrance, and I asked the front desk nurse about Janos. She pointed me to a doctor having a conversation with another nurse. I rushed to him.

"Excuse me. Where is Janos? I mean, John Lacks? Is he okay?"

The doctor gave me a solemn look, "Are you his wife?"

"Yes, I am. His work called and said he collapsed. Is he all right? Can I see him?"

The expression in the doctor's face grew more solemn, "I'm sorry." He glanced at the children, at Aneta, then back to me. "He had a heart attack and passed away just as the ambulance arrived."

"No! It can't be!" I screamed. My legs buckled, and Stephen held me up with his strong arms—just like Janos's.

Aneta touched my arm. "Mira, my dear. I'm so sorry."

"No, Mama," Mary said.

The doctor walked away, and the nurse led us to the cubicle where Janos lay. Mary sobbed, Stephen bravely held on, and tears streamed down Johnny's face. I must have been in shock, for no tears came. My body shook, and my stomach clenched. It was too unreal. I felt as if I were in a tunnel. The voices around me sounded hollow and echoed as if far away.

Aneta stood back as I gathered my children by the bed. Mary stayed with me on one side, holding my hand so tight it lost feeling, and the boys stood on the other side. It reminded me of when Mama died, Papa and I on opposite sides of the bed.

"Kiss him farewell, my children," I said in a strangled voice.

Each of them kissed their Papa on the cheek, said goodbye in Slovak, then Aneta guided them out of the way as I edged closer.

"Mama?" Mary touched my shoulder, and I jumped. "Should we leave you alone?"

"Go to the waiting room with your Aunt Aneta. I just need a moment." I waved them on.

I gazed at the face of my husband, my love, my angst, my trials, and my passion. He was fifty-three, too young to die from a heart attack. I stroked his deeply lined face, dark spots across his forehead from years in the sun. His thick, wavy hair had streaks of gray, and the reddishness had paled. His beautiful aqua-blue eyes were closed forever.

I reached my hand to the lump in my throat.

I picked up his limp hand and held it to my cheek. "How could you leave me, my love, after everything we've been through? We have our family now, the one you wanted. We need you," I sobbed. "How will I go on without you?"

Pulling from my depths, I found the strength to lean over and kiss his unmoving lips.

Voices echoed, and I listened without hearing the doctors and nurses explain what needed to be done. I signed papers, not caring what they were for, and when I called Denny from the hospital, the conversation was a blur.

The drive back to our apartment was painfully silent.

"Mira, is there anything I can get you?" Aneta asked.

"No, I need to be alone." My voice quivered.

Aneta nodded and went into the kitchen to help Mary prepare dinner. The boys were in the living room, both quiet and moved as if in slow motion. One of them turned on the radio. The sounds of lively jazz drifted ironically through the apartment.

I stumbled into our bedroom and stood there until the tears came, wretched and uncontrolled. I dropped onto the bed, the bed where I would sleep alone for the rest of my life. My shoulders shook, and my stomach churned with a sick fear. What future did I have without my Jani?

We held the funeral at the Slovak Lutheran Church, and an incredible number of people attended. I was surprised that, despite being such a hard man to live with, many people loved and admired Janos. Members of the congregation, coworkers, and Denny's family filled the church. It touched my heart when our children took to the pulpit, one by one, and shared loving and funny stories—memories I had forgotten amid my struggles with Janos.

When Denny spoke, he broke down, barely able to continue. "Ďakujem, Janos," he choked out. "Your strength will never be forgotten."

Shortly after Janos's funeral, I told Mary to accept the scholarship.

The days and months that followed pained me beyond expression. I remembered the years in Hungary I had lived without him, and how the loneliness and grief drove me to do things I later regretted. This time was different. Our three children, Aneta's family, and Denny's family surrounded me. I was not alone.

———

1933

"Mama!" Mary whined.

My beloved eighteen-year-old daughter stood in the middle of her bedroom, hands on her hips, her dark hair disheveled, and a frown on her lovely face.

My daughter was a product of America, born here and given all the privileges we could afford, no matter how small. It was much more than I ever had. She had no idea what it was like to be poor. I was glad of that, and it was one reason Janos and I never talked about our life in the old country. We had to change our very existence to survive.

"I'm here, Mary. No need to shout. What is it?" I responded in English. She had insisted on speaking only English for the past year to prepare for college.

"Where is my new blue sweater? I wanted to wear it on my first day." Mary's lower lip protruded in a pout.

"It's drying in the basement with the rest of your laundry you haven't packed."

"Oh shoot, okay, thanks." She ran past me and down the stairs.

I was overjoyed and giddy from the excitement. How wonderful to be able to go to college. Back when I was eighteen and about to be married, being a wife and mother was all I wanted in life. I didn't think of anything beyond our cottage and tiny farm, for it was all I knew. How naive I was then.

Chapter Forty-Two

March 1937

WHEN MARY LIVED IN THE COLLEGE DORMITORY, I rented out her room for temporary boarders and did small sewing jobs for friends of Zelda's. Stephen had dropped out of high school to work in a factory. He wanted to earn a wage and help financially.

When Mary graduated from the two-year nursing school, she found a position at a hospital too far from home to commute. She shared an apartment with two other nurses. I wanted her back home.

She had rolled her eyes. "Oh Mama, I've been living in a dormitory for two years away from you. What's the difference?"

I worried about her all the time, but times had changed, and women living alone or renting with others was common. Mary had a good head on her shoulders. I had to trust her judgment.

Stephen turned eighteen the year Mary graduated. He rushed down to the Navy recruitment center and enlisted. His enlistment didn't surprise me—he had been warning me about it for the past two years.

The big surprise came from Johnny. The teachers held him back in eighth grade until he passed English, and then he turned sixteen. School wasn't for him. He found a job at the same foundry where his father had worked, and it paid good money. Both boys were as stubborn as their father, and I didn't have the strength to fight them. With Mary self-sufficient and Stephen sending me money each month, Johnny's income meant I no longer needed to take in boarders. It was just Johnny and me.

———

"WE'RE HERE. HAPPY EASTER, EVERYONE!" MARY called in English. Her lilting voice floated from the living room to me in the kitchen, and my heart leaped for joy.

It had been some time since all of us were together for a Sunday dinner. I had prepared a special meal with all the Slovak dishes my children loved.

"We?" I hurried from the kitchen to find Mary arm in arm with a tall man with pale blue eyes, horn-rimmed glasses, and curly, bright red hair. "Hello." I smiled.

"Mama, this is Greg Pearse." Mary squeezed Greg's arm and gave me an expectant look. Her brown eyes sparkled as she flipped back her dark brown shoulder-length hair and bounced with excitement. I could hardly believe she was twenty-two.

Greg extended a hand. "Glad to meet you, Mrs. Lacks."

I shook his hand. He had a strong grip. Mary gave me a big hug. I touched her soft hair and kissed her on the cheek. She smelled of honeysuckle, the cologne I had given her last Christmas.

I pulled back and met her gaze. "We expected you at

church this morning, Mary. Promise me you will come to visit more often."

"Yes, Mama. I'm sorry. The long shift at the hospital keeps me busy and, uh, well, and then there's Greg. I went to church with him. He's Methodist."

"I see."

Stephen and Johnny came in from the kitchen, and everyone talked at once. Mary gave each of her brothers little bags of chocolate, something she had done ever since she started working part-time in high school.

"How long are you home, Stevie?" Mary asked.

"Just a couple weeks, then back to Hawaii and out to sea again. I want to save some leave for the holidays," Stephen said.

Mary gave Greg an odd look. Did I see something different there? A glow? Was it love?

Mary had dated a few young men since working as a nurse, but none of them had gotten past the second date with her. Mary pulled Greg over to the loveseat to sit next to her.

"We met at the hospital." Mary beamed at Greg. "Greg works in the laboratory as a technician."

Johnny ran into the kitchen to grab some beers for everyone except me. I had never developed a liking for it. He handed me a Coke.

Stephen started asking Greg questions about his family, his work, and even his friends.

"Okay, everyone," Mary cut in, "I have an announcement."

Stephen, Johnny, and I gave her our attention. I held my breath.

She stuck her left hand out in front of her. How did I miss the glint on her hand earlier? "We're engaged." A small but lovely box-set diamond ring embraced her ring finger.

"What?" I dropped into the nearest empty chair.

The boys crowded around Mary, hugging her and shaking Greg's hand.

"Mama?" Mary jumped to her feet and hurried over to me. "Are you okay?"

"Yes, my dear. I'm just very surprised. This is unexpected. I mean, we didn't even know you were serious about anyone. It's been all about your work when we talk on the phone."

"I know, Mama. I was afraid to, you know, jinx it."

"Jinx? What is that?"

"It's just a phrase. We met a few months ago, and, well, we fell in love. We want to get married as soon as possible. I'm very happy, Mama."

"I can see that. Let me look at your ring up close." She extended her hand. "It's very beautiful, Mary. If you are happy, I am happy." I kissed her cheeks and hugged her with all my might. "My little Mary, all grown up and about to be married. Too soon. I wish...."

"What do you wish, Mama?" She knelt beside my chair and held my hands in hers.

"The many things that will never happen. Like you meeting your grandparents, or your father walking you down the aisle." Tears filled my eyes.

"Don't cry, Mama. I have you and my brothers, my uncles, aunts, and cousins. It will be a wonderful wedding."

"When's the wedding?" Johnny asked.

"Yeah, I hope I can get leave," Stephen said.

"Greg?" Mary sat next to him again. "What do you think?"

My sons took seats, leaning in toward Mary and Greg. Johnny tapped his foot impatiently. Stephen tried to appear calm, but I recognized the excitement in his eyes.

Greg kissed Mary's cheek. "You mentioned six months. Is that still enough time?" he asked.

"It is for me. What do you think, Mama? Late October?"

All I could do was nod as tears of happiness flowed.

After dinner, we talked about the wedding. Mary and Greg left first, and my sons left for a couple of beers. I had just finished cleaning up the kitchen when the phone rang.

I wiped my hands on the dish towel, then picked up the receiver. "Hello?"

"Is this Mrs. Lacks?" a man's voice said.

"It is. Who's calling?"

"My name is Peter. You may have known my mother, Rozalia."

My hand shook as all my fears rushed back to me.

Chapter Forty-Three

April 1937

When I received the call from Peter, I pretended I didn't know who he was. It had been a long time since I thought about him and his mother. Peter wanted to visit me, and a knot formed in my stomach. Still, I agreed to meet him. With Janos gone, what threat could Peter be?

"Dobrý deň, Mrs. Lacks," Peter said.

"Dobrý deň. Please sit down. May I get you something?"

"Oh no, nothing. I know this must be awkward for you."

I sat on the sofa across from him and would have known him anywhere. He had a little of Janos's large forehead, hooded lids, and the same blue eyes. His reddish hair had darkened. He looked more like Janos than my own two sons, which irritated me.

"I know who you are."

He raised his eyebrows and leaned forward. "You do?"

"Looking at you now, a grown man, I can hardly ignore the fact. You look like him—your father."

"Really?" He looked down at the side table next to him at

the photo of Janos I had recently framed and picked it up. "May I have a copy of this, or any extra photos you might have?"

"Not that one, but of course, I'll look for one for you."

"You know, my mother said she wasn't sure you knew anything about me." He placed the photo on the table and leaned against the sofa back.

"There were signs. Whenever I would see your mother, I thought she always looked sad or a little guilty."

"I see."

"How long have you known?" My jaw clenched, my hands clasped tightly, failing at any attempt to be as calm and relaxed as he was.

Peter heaved a heavy sigh, and the corners of his mouth drooped. "Not that long, actually. My mother passed away eight months ago because of an extended illness."

"I'm sad to hear that, truly. Losing your parents is a terrible thing." I thought of Mamička and her illness.

"She told me about a year ago, when she knew she didn't have much time left. I was angry, of course, but I loved her, and she was dying. I forgave her for not telling me sooner."

"I'm sure that was a very difficult time for you." My shoulders slumped, and I was ashamed of myself, for he couldn't have had it very easy. I felt sorry for him.

"It was, yes, thank you." Peter swallowed hard. "My mother didn't tell Janos she had a child with him. She never wanted to cause any problems for you or him, and that's why we moved away. She felt a lot of shame for the affair and said she couldn't bear seeing you and Janos with your family...and obviously happy."

He looked around my house. "She tried to give me a decent life. She worked hard, but we never had much. Janos was able to provide well for you and your children."

"Life for us wasn't always that way. Janos worked hard for

us, too." I tensed despite my sympathy for him. If he only knew.

"I'm sure. Anyway...she told me to do what I wished with the information. After she died, I decided to come here." He gave a nervous laugh. "I admit I spied on you and your family a little."

"You did? I wasn't aware, but I certainly understand your curiosity." I meant it, even though I was uncomfortable hearing about his mother and him. "Peter, Janos is gone now, five years. I'm sorry you never knew him."

"I only found out about Janos when I came to St. Louis a few months ago. We lived in Kansas City. I was disappointed, and also sorry for you and your children's loss."

"Do you live here now?"

"Yes. I work at a commercial bakery."

"Ah, my nephew works at one too. So, what do you want from me?" I leaned forward.

"Oh, that...the reason I am here." He cleared his throat. "I would like to get to know my sister and brothers." He waited for my response.

"I think that is a fine idea. However, I will need some time to talk to the family. They will need to adjust to this information. I'm sure you understand."

"Thank you, Mrs. Lacks. I completely understand. Let me know if and when. I realize it will come as a shock to your children, and there may be some resistance, but I am a patient man."

He gave me his phone number and address and left. I must have sat there for hours just thinking about the whole story. All those years, I blamed Rozalia, not even trying to understand what she must have been going through. I worried only about myself, my family, and our happiness. There she was with a child to raise on her own, and so ashamed of her choices that she left town. Well, I felt I owed Peter to at least help him have some family. I hoped my children would be more open-minded than I had been.

———

First, I called Aneta and told her about my meeting with Peter. She wanted to meet Peter and said she would tell Jamie and Katie for me. That went well.

When I called Zelda, she gave me all the love and understanding she had always provided, offering advice on how I should break the news to my children, which I dreaded. But before that, I needed to see Denny.

After church, Denny, Marta, and I had lunch at their place. They still lived in the same apartment building but had moved into a two-bedroom. We finished eating and moved to the sitting area, where I broached the subject.

"Denny, did you know Janos was involved with another woman before I came to St. Louis?"

"Who told you that? It's a damn lie," Denny snapped.

I jerked back. Denny had never spoken that way to me. "So, you really didn't know?"

"He would have told me. I just don't believe it."

Marta sat next to him and spoke in a gentle tone. "Denny, I'm afraid that what Mira is telling you is true."

It was my turn to be shocked. "You knew?"

Marta hung her head. "I couldn't tell you, Mira. Please forgive me. Rozalia didn't want Janos to know, and I promised I would keep her secret. It was very difficult to lie to you every time you asked me about her when she would show up."

Denny pulled back from Marta, his eyes flared. "Janos had an affair with your friend Rozalia? Why couldn't you tell me? I'm your husband."

"And Janos was your brother. How could I tell you? *He* should have told you. When Rozalia returned with that baby, I thought for sure you and Janos would have asked me. But neither of you did. So, I kept my mouth shut." Marta folded her arms in front of her and looked at the floor.

"What?" Denny stood and paced the tiny room. "That child–that child was Janos's?"

"That is why I brought this up," I said. "Peter contacted me. Rozalia told Peter the truth only a year ago because she was very sick. She died eight months ago."

"Dear Lord." Marta gasped, a hand shot to her throat. "How did she die?"

"Peter only said it was a long illness. I'm sorry to be the one to tell you."

"After she moved away, I only heard from her at Christmas. She didn't respond to my last letter." Tears welled in Marta's eyes. "Now I know why."

Denny kept pacing. "My own brother kept such a secret like this from me? And my wife kept the secret, too? I feel so betrayed."

"Janos never knew about the child, Denny," I said. "I'm sorry you had to find out this way."

Marta dried her tears and looked at me. "What else did Peter tell you?"

"He is all alone and has no family. He moved here a few months ago and is working in St. Louis. He wants to meet Mary, Stephen, and Johnny and hopes to have a relationship with them."

"You are being very accepting, Mira. I don't think I can do it." Denny sat in a chair away from Marta.

"When I saw Peter as a child, he reminded me of Little Jan. Although I had no proof, I couldn't shake the feeling."

"I never noticed," Denny said. "But now that you mention it, I guess he did. Rozalia brought him here a couple of times."

"Several times," Marta said. "I thought surely you would notice, but you never said anything."

"I can't believe you brought them here, knowing everything." Denny's eyes flashed with anger, but his voice had softened.

This was a side of Denny I'd never seen before. He practically worshipped Janos as a boy, and they were close when they journeyed here together. I didn't know what else to say to ease his pain.

"Please don't mention Peter to my children until I've talked to them. I wanted to tell you first, Denny. It will be up to each of them if they want a relationship with their half-brother. I hope they will, and you as his uncle."

Denny frowned. "I doubt it."

"Maybe in time," Marta said. "This is a shock to you, and I am very sorry for my part in it. I hope you will forgive me." She dabbed more tears from her eyes.

Denny didn't respond.

"I know it's not my place, but I hope the two of you won't let what Janos did in the past come between you. Be happy. I'll go now, before it gets dark," I said.

Denny still didn't reply. I would need to check in with Marta regularly. I worried this news would cause problems between them.

That evening, I told Johnny. He handled the news like a mature young man. He felt bad for Peter and said he would be glad to meet him. He knew it wasn't Peter's fault. Johnny loved his father but knew he was imperfect. He told me once, after Janos passed, that he had been angry at his father for a long time. His temper and strict rules against English caused Johnny a lot of stress in school.

Stephen was out at sea, and I thought it best not to write it in a letter. I would have to wait until he reached a port where he could make a ship-to-shore call.

———

Two weeks passed, and Mary was eager to discuss her wedding ideas. She arrived with magazines, notebooks, and even some fabric swatches. I wasn't sure whether to tell her about Peter up front or wait. I didn't have to decide.

Mary set everything on the dining table and turned to me with a defiant look. "I won't meet this Peter. I refuse!"

"Who told you? I was planning to tell you about it today."

"Johnny, of course. He can't keep anything to himself." She plopped down on a chair.

"Oh, honey, I'm sorry this upsets you. Can you tell me why?"

"How could you even meet with him? Isn't accepting Peter the same as condoning what Papa did?"

"No. At least not in my mind. It's not Peter's fault. He didn't even know the truth about his parentage until a year ago. Have pity on him."

"Pity? I don't know, Mama. This whole situation is shocking, and I'm unsure what I feel. Did you know about the affair?"

"I only suspected your papa may have had a relationship with Rozalia after I arrived in St. Louis. A couple of years later, when I saw Peter as a little boy, he looked a lot like our first son, who died in Hungary."

"I don't understand you. You knew? How could you stay with him?"

"Because I felt to blame. I didn't come to America until years after he asked me to."

"Really? You never talked about your life in the old country—especially about your first child." She rose and poured two glasses of lemonade at the sideboard.

"Thank you, dear." I took the offered glass and sipped, feeling a little nervous. "It is always hard to speak about Little Jan, and today is not the day to do so. Another time, yes?"

"Okay. Another time. So, how could it be your fault Papa had an affair?"

"When your Uncle Denny got married and stayed here permanently in 1910, Janos asked me to move here and start a new life. I couldn't leave my parents."

Mary fidgeted with the fabric swatches and pulled one aside.

"Now that's a lovely fabric, Mary." I stroked the shiny satin.

"It's my favorite so far. But why didn't you want to be with Papa? Didn't you miss him?"

I wasn't sure whether I would tell Mary about Goran. She was having trouble enough understanding her father's actions, let alone mine.

"I loved your Papa deeply. I didn't want him to leave us, and I was angry about it for a long time. All I wanted was for him to return to our home in Hungary. I was lonely and figured he must have been lonely, too." I paused. "It was that same year after Denny's wedding that Janos met Rozalia. If I had come here, that relationship would not have happened."

"Wow, Mama, that's awful. But no matter what you did or didn't do, Papa was responsible for his actions, not you."

"That's easy to say." I half-laughed. "Anyway, your Papa is gone now, and Rozalia too. No point staying angry. I spent too much time worrying that Peter would ruin my family. When Rozalia moved away, I was relieved. Now I feel bad for the young man."

Mary gulped down her lemonade. "Gosh, I was thirsty. All this talking." She chuckled.

I patted her hand. "Do you think you will meet Peter?"

"I will think about it. No promises. Too much on my mind with the wedding, work, and finding time with Greg."

"Meeting him is up to you, my dear. I'm not pressuring you, just informing you."

"Anyway, Greg's family wants to throw us an engagement party. They live near that neighborhood where your friend Zelda lives. We need to prepare an invitation list for them. Will you help me with it?"

"That's very nice of them. Greg's parents are well-off?"

"Yes, and they wanted me to ask you something. You know, it's the custom here that the bride's family pays for the wedding."

I nodded, tensing at the thought of the cost.

"They want a big wedding for us and offered to pay for everything. How do you feel about that?" She looked at me through her eyelashes, just like I used to do when I was young and shy.

"Do you want a big wedding?"

"I never imagined we would be able to. I hadn't really thought much about it until I got engaged. To be honest, I would love a big, fancy wedding, as long as you aren't offended."

"It's fine with me. I don't have money for a big wedding, and if they want to do it for you and Greg, that's wonderful." I squeezed her hand, and Mary jumped up and hugged me tight.

"Thanks, Mama. You're the best. There is plenty you can do to help in other ways, like making my wedding dress. I brought magazines of bridal fashions and even a pattern. I heard how you helped make Aunt Lora's dress years ago."

"Your Aunt Aneta helped much more than I. Let's ask her if she would like to help."

"Great idea." Mary was glowing again.

"So, why don't you show me what all you brought today?"

With the Peter issue dealt with for now, we spent a wonderful afternoon talking about her wedding and making plans.

April 1937

THE PEARCES' ENGAGEMENT PARTY WAS A LAVISH affair held at their home. They invited all our family, including the Nagys, Ivy, Zelda, and Dr. Schwarz, and, of course, Mary and Greg's friends. The Pearce family must have known the rest of St. Louis, it seemed. The spacious, beautifully furnished two-story home was much larger than Zelda's and was packed with people inside and out.

Mary didn't invite Peter, though. She wasn't ready to include him in her life.

"Mama, you look beautiful." Mary rushed to greet me when I arrived with Johnny, who drove. "Love your new dress. It's right in style." She hugged me, and we kissed each other's cheeks.

"Thank you, dear. Aneta helped me with it. It's too bad Stephen couldn't make it. He's out to sea but is trying to get leave for your wedding."

"He dropped me a postcard to tell me. He's so sweet." Mary took Johnny and me through the house and introduced us to her soon-to-be in-laws.

A woman dressed in an elegant burgundy satin dress that reached the floor held out her hand, draped with a sparkling bracelet. I wondered if it was diamonds. "Mrs. Lacks, it's wonderful to finally meet you. My son has said very nice things about you and your family," Mrs. Pearce said. A broad smile lit her lovely face. Her hair was styled in the current fashion. She looked too young to have a son Greg's age.

"That's nice to hear. You have a beautiful home," I said. "It's a pleasure to meet you and your husband."

Mr. Pearce, in a tuxedo, extended his hand as well. "We are delighted to have Mary a part of our family."

We exchanged more pleasantries, and Mary introduced Johnny. He was more nervous than I. Then the Pearces moved on to greet more guests.

Mary seemed to fit right in with the party, dressed in a similar style satin dress that came to her knees. A server came by with glasses of something bubbly. Mary took two and handed one to me.

I shook my head.

"Just a couple of sips. It's champagne. We won't be having alcohol at the reception, since it will be held at the church."

"Well, all right." I took a sip. "It's not what I expected, like wine with bubbles."

Mary laughed. "That's exactly what it is, Mama." She turned to Johnny. "What about you?"

"Do they have any beer?" he said.

"I'm not sure, there is an open bar in the corner of the living room. You can ask. I'm glad you came, and you look very smart in your new suit."

He gave a sheepish grin and wandered over to the bar.

The rest of the evening was a flurry of meeting new people. When my friend Ivy arrived, I relaxed. I wasn't used to being surrounded by so many people I didn't know, not since the first time I had gone to the Slovak church with Janos. My heart tugged when I thought of how much he would have enjoyed this party.

Chapter Forty-Four

October 1937

THE WEDDING CAME, AND I WAS JUST A LITTLE nervous about how Denny and Mary would handle having Peter at the reception. Even though Mary had included Peter on the invitation list for the reception, he wasn't invited to the ceremony. I hoped for the best. Stephen got leave for the wedding and was very curious about his new brother.

They held the wedding at the Methodist Church in the Shaw District. I was seated in the front row as the mother of the bride, with Aneta, Dino, Denny, and Marta. Tony, Stephen, Johnny, Katie, and Jamie sat behind us. Mary made my dress herself, wanting it to be extra special. By far the nicest dress I'd ever worn, it reached the floor, with a beaded belt and three-quarter sleeves, all in a soft blue sateen—fashionable yet matronly, just as I had wished.

After her maid of honor, Katie, reached the altar, my pride swelled as Mary walked down the aisle in her beautiful princess-seamed, white satin gown and short train, while smiling at everyone.

I had suggested she ask one of her brothers to give her away, but she said no. She wanted to walk down the aisle alone, but when the minister would ask who gives her away, she wanted me to stand and say so. I agreed.

Large standing vases with all kinds of white flowers flanked the altar. Mary carried a bouquet of white roses surrounded by pink ones, laced with long ribbons.

The service wasn't all that different from the Lutheran service and didn't last very long. Once the ceremony concluded, we made our way to the reception in the social hall. Katie and I stood on one side of Mary, and her new husband, Greg, stood on the other, with his best man and parents. The invitation list was for over three hundred people, more than attended the engagement party, and everyone must have come. Peter waited near the end of the receiving line.

When Peter reached Mary, I introduced them. "Mary, this is Peter, your brother."

Peter extended his hand. "Congratulations, Mary. It's a pleasure to meet you." He gave a nervous smile.

Mary shook his hand. "Peter, thank you for coming. You know, I would have recognized you anywhere. You look a lot like Papa. And this is my husband, Greg. We'll talk later, okay?"

"I look forward to getting to know you. And again, congratulations to the both of you," he said, glancing at Greg. "It's a lovely wedding."

I was pleased by Mary's friendliness with Peter. He beamed as he continued through the line.

When Katie and I finished receiving guests, we found Aneta and the rest of the family seated at a round table up front. Stephen sat on one side of me, and Johnny on the other. The floral centerpiece was huge. I could barely see the other side of the table. A raised dais at one end of the hall seated the wedding party. Mary had told me I would be sat with her, but

I asked to be with our family. She understood. Mary caught my eye and gave a tiny wave.

Peter wandered around on the other side of the hall, looking awkward and uncertain. I went over to him.

"Come on, Peter, sit with us. We made sure to save you a spot," I said.

He smiled and nodded. I guided him to our table. He took the empty seat between Johnny and Jamie, and the three of them struck up a conversation right away. Jamie had graduated from high school and gone to work for Dino as an assistant manager.

Katie brought her guest around the table. "Auntie Mira, I couldn't wait any longer to introduce you to Jack McIntyre. We're engaged."

"Congratulations." I hugged her and shook Jack's hand. My hand hurt from shaking three hundred hands. "When did this happen?"

"Just last night," she giggled, holding tight onto Jack's arm.

"Aha, I wondered how your mama kept this from me." I looked at Aneta, and she smiled.

Denny, Marta, and Tony, who had brought a date, sat at the table next to ours. Tony got up, greeted Peter, and introduced his date. She seemed very nice. Denny shook his head when I looked over at him. He wasn't ready yet. Oh well. I hoped he would eventually.

The best man tapped on the crystal water glass, and everyone quieted down for the speeches by him and the father of the groom. I was too shy to make a speech, but Johnny had offered to do it in my place. He did a fine job.

The cutting of the cake and dancing on an enormous parquet floor followed dinner. The American tradition that the bride has the first dance with her father made my stomach twist. Johnny and Stephen had it all planned out, and both of them danced with Mary. Then the others joined in.

Dino pulled Aneta out to the dance floor and surprised everyone by "cutting the rug" with the quickstep. I didn't know Aneta could dance like that. Wasn't she one for surprises? My good friend Ivy danced with her son, Nick. We smiled and waved to each other.

Johnny gave Stephen a shove. "You should dance with Mama."

Stephen held up his hands. "Oh no, not me. I don't dance a step. You dance with Mama. You're the man of the house now."

"I was planning to. Come on, Mama, dance with me." Johnny stood and held out his hand.

I shook my head. "I don't dance like that."

"Papa told me you danced."

"When did he tell you that?"

"I don't remember. Something came up about Aunt Aneta's first wedding in the old country. He mentioned how you loved to dance."

"Slovak traditional dance, yes. But not like what Aneta and Dino are dancing." I blushed at the thought of Janos talking about that night.

Johnny took my hand and led me out to the crowded dance floor. The music slowed to a waltz. "How about this, nice and slow? Just follow me."

"This is familiar. Where did you learn to dance?"

"Around." He winked.

I followed his lead, and we glided along the floor, bumping into couples. I laughed. Johnny looked older than his eighteen years, and I wondered sometimes how he spent his weekends out with friends. A few tears slipped from the corner of one eye as I danced with my handsome son. Janos would have enjoyed this day for his daughter. I missed him terribly.

Chapter Forty-Five

Summer 1942

"Where do you want this?" Mary held a large platter of bryndzové pirohy with cheese dip. Her eyes danced with excitement.

I directed her to the big table that Stephen and Johnny had dragged out to the deck for the party. I had covered it with my best tablecloth, the one Mamička had embroidered many years ago.

"Smells delicious, Mary," I said.

"I finally learned how to make them the way you do."

Greg gave her a quick squeeze around her waist. "I'll get the baby out of your hair, okay? Hello, Ma." He stooped to kiss me on my cheek. Such a tall man, I had to crane my neck to look up at him.

"Please, give her to me." I reached into the stroller and lifted thirteen-month-old Mira into my arms. "Such a sweet baby she is." I smoothed her tufts of bright red hair. She took after her father.

Baby Mira gurgled and giggled when I tickled her tummy.

"We're here, we're here!" Aneta made her usual grand entrance, decked out in the latest fashion: bright red lipstick, big, bold white beads around her neck, and a black-and-white polka dot dress. Right beside her, Dino grinned, defying his early seventies. He sported a button-down, short-sleeved shirt, tucked into crisp linen slacks, and fancy spats. Aneta's exuberant energy certainly kept him on his toes.

"Aren't you going to change?" She looked at my house dress with a frown. "Let me help you find something." Aneta took baby Mira from my arms, kissed her head, and handed her to Greg with a quick hello. She dragged me into my bedroom.

"Aneta, please, I still have much to do."

"Let the rest of them do some work. You always do everything." Aneta opened the old wood closet. "Not much to choose from." She rummaged through my other house dresses and found a nicer dress I kept for church and special events. "Here. This will just have to do."

"You know I don't spend money on fancy clothes." I took the dress and changed out of my everyday print shirtwaist into the simple dark navy shirtwaist. It was the only style that fit my body. In my late fifties and after several children, I had plumped out very round.

"Let me fix your hair." Aneta reached for me.

I pulled away. "No, no. It's fine the way I like it."

"It's old-fashioned, still, the braids wrapped around your head." Aneta pushed her lower lip out into a pout. "Well, at least you are in your dress and look more presentable."

"Thank you for your help." I took a look in the mirror and frowned. I had changed a lot since leaving Hungary, and not just in my looks. I kept the traditional braids as my one connection to my old life.

We returned to the party and found Denny and Marta talking with Peter. It warmed my heart to see them together after all Denny's resistance. I had grown very fond of Peter, and he had fit into our family quite nicely.

Aneta ushered me to two chairs and insisted I stay there while the rest of them finished setting up. Feeling exhausted, I agreed and fell into one of the matching aqua-colored metal patio chairs Aneta had given me last Christmas. I watched our children and their children, thinking how this would probably be the last time we could all be together or with this kind of feast.

The war had changed everything. Food rationing had started in May with sugar. We didn't know what would be affected or when. Most of the men in my family were at least twenty-eight as of 1941, and safe from the draft, but anything could change during a war.

"Mama, are you listening?" Stephen looked down at me in his Navy uniform.

We were blessed he could be here on leave, but he would return soon. He had been stationed in Hawaii for years. Miraculously, he had survived the bombing of Pearl Harbor, for he was off base that day.

"Yes, dear, I'm listening. What is it?"

Johnny popped his head out the back door of the house. "Mama, Tony's here. He's in the kitchen getting some drinks ready. You want something?"

"Not right now, dear."

Jamie rushed over to Aneta, who sat next to me, "Mama, I'm here!" He hugged her tight and kissed her on both cheeks. "You look beautiful as ever."

"Jamie." Tears filled Aneta's eyes.

Jamie wanted to enlist after Pearl Harbor but hadn't yet.

Johnny had just received his draft letter. I was devastated that my youngest, only twenty-two, who lived with me and supported me, would be taken away. Of course, Johnny was excited, not knowing what war was like. He emerged from the kitchen and stood next to Stephen.

"Hey, Stephen," Johnny said. "Did you hear? I got my draft letter. Isn't it great?"

Stephen gave him a somber look. "All depends on where you're stationed."

I didn't want to hear any more and was relieved when the two moved to the corner of the patio to talk. Katie arrived late with her husband, Jack, and their three-year-old daughter, Lizzie. Jack came from an Irish Protestant family, and they had married soon after Mary's wedding. Katie worked for the phone company, and Jack was an insurance salesman. They lived in one of the new tract homes built in the 1930s.

Aneta leaned close and whispered, "I'm glad Jack can't enlist. He would if he could."

"I can't believe we are going through another world war. Johnny is excited about being drafted. I tried reminding him about his uncle who died in WWI, but he said something about it being different because Uncle Ivan was on the wrong side. I was aghast."

"That's terrible," Aneta said. "He hadn't even been born yet; I guess he doesn't have the connection. I will pray for his safe return to you." She patted my hand.

Zelda came too. Ezra had passed a few years before, and we were closer than ever.

Tony came out to greet me. "Dobrý deň, Auntie Mira."

He bent to kiss me on the cheeks. What a fine man he had turned out to be. He had the same large Lacko forehead and blue eyes. Tony had graduated from high school and worked at the commercial bakery that introduced pre-sliced packaged bread, the very same place Peter worked. Tony became a manager and recently got engaged to his girlfriend of five years.

"Congratulations on your engagement," I said.

Tony smiled. "Sorry, she couldn't be here. Family reasons, you know how it is."

Everyone ate, drank, laughed, and enjoyed being together.

Peter looked fine, and even more like Janos. His hair was the same light auburn waves, and he kept it soft and long. He gave me a big hug, and I kissed him on the cheek. He was family now.

He whispered in my ear, "I've enlisted." My shock must have shown, for he added, "Thank you for everything the past five years. Who knows what the future will bring, but this family means the world to me."

"Peter, you didn't have to enlist."

"I know, but it's the right thing to do." He sought out Tony. They were very close now, especially being coworkers.

I wandered around the party until I found Zelda out in the garden behind the deck.

"There you are." I moved toward her. "Why are you way out here?"

Zelda took my hand and kissed me on the cheek. "My dear, this is *your* family. I'm just grateful to see it all play out well. And...I always enjoy your garden."

"It is wonderful, isn't it? Everyone together, even Denny." I sighed.

"It took him a while, but he came around. He felt left out of that aspect of his brother's life, ja?"

"I guess. I'm so happy you are here."

"I am too." She smiled, and we hooked our arms together and took a short walk.

What a wonderful day.

Epilogue

Aneta 1965

THE NURSE'S FOOTSTEPS ON THE LINOLEUM FLOOR roused me from my light nap as I sat in the chair next to the bed. The nurse checked my sister Mira's vitals and asked if I would like a cot brought in. I nodded, mouthed a *thank you*, and gave a forced smile.

I squinted at the tiny dial on my wristwatch, barely readable in the soft light coming from the open door of the hospital room. It was two in the morning. Johnny had called me two days ago. I packed a bag as fast as possible, and Jamie rushed me to the airport in the middle of the night to catch the next flight out of Chicago.

Mira's children and grandchildren made a steady stream of visits from the time I arrived at the hospital until Mary left for her night shift as a nurse in the pediatric ward here. They all still lived in the St. Louis area, keeping close to their dear mama. Johnny had never married and stayed at home, eventually caring for her until this hospital stay. I was expecting him to return in the morning, and Mary would join as well once her shift was over. I heard Mira's old friend Ivy had come by to visit before I arrived, and I was sorry I missed her.

Watching Mira sleep, my mind drifted back to the last big gathering in 1942, when the war was on all of our minds. Much had happened since then. Peter was sent to Germany and killed near the end of the war. It shocked everyone, and we grieved the years lost not knowing him.

My Jamie enlisted at the end of that year. He was discharged just before the war ended, having earned the Purple Heart for being injured in the line of duty. The injury caused a limp, but he got a job with US Steel and moved to Chicago with his new wife, a nurse he met at the VA hospital. It broke my heart to be separated from him.

When Katie's husband Jack was offered a regional manager position in the Chicago area, she left to follow him. Their daughter attended college southwest of there.

But the biggest blow came when my beloved Dino died in 1950. He was seventy-five and my true love. I will mourn him till the day I die and join him in Heaven.

Zelda, our friend from Hungary, whom I had come to appreciate, passed away last year at eighty-four.

As much as I loved Mira, it was more than I could bear to be separated from my children. Much to Mira's dismay—and she certainly made me feel guilty about it—I moved to Chicago to be close to my children. I knew Mira understood —she would have done the same.

Mira and I kept in touch. I would fly to St. Louis, or she would fly to Chicago. It just wasn't enough. I missed her.

I looked over at my sweet, loving sister, lying so still. She had gone in and out of consciousness, not recognizing that I, or anyone else, was there. Suddenly, she stirred, opening her eyes.

"Aneta?"

"Yes, yes, my dearest Mira," I pulled my tired old body out of the chair to sit on the edge of her bed.

"How long have you been here?" Her voice was weak from effort.

"Johnny called me two days ago, and I flew in as soon as I could."

"That was very sweet of him and you. I—"

"Hush, no need to talk. It's very late. Go back to sleep. Johnny will be here in the morning."

"No—not yet, I—I just want to tell you something." She took a ragged breath.

Her voice was faint, so I leaned closer. "Yes, dear, what is it?"

"Ďakujem...ďakujem." She thanked me in Slovak. We rarely spoke it anymore except with each other.

"*Prosím,* you are most welcome, but for what?"

"For being my sister." She inhaled another raspy breath. "My best friend...and for always being there."

I kissed her on the cheek, my tears wetting her face. I wiped them away gently with my hand. At eighty, she looked pale, her cheeks sunken into her round face. She still wore her white hair in long braids that now lay along her shoulders. Mira smiled, and I thought my heart would burst.

"Ďakujem, Mira. You remember that day I showed up on your doorstep with my children...." I clutched her hand in mine. "I couldn't tell you everything then. Well, not even now...but you literally saved my life, and I thank you from the bottom of my heart for taking me in and letting me share your life."

Mira's eyes closed, and I waited for them to open again, but they never did.

Author's Note

I am a second-generation Slovak-American on my father's side. I began a genealogy project on my Slovak paternal grandparents in 2018. Writing a novel wasn't on my mind.

My late father told me his parents came to the US in 1913. They were born in southern Hungary, which was part of the Austro-Hungarian Empire at the time.

After a few months of researching ship manifests from Hungary to America, I made a surprising discovery. Yes, my grandmother came over in December 1913, but my grandfather was already here. He came over in April 1907, over five years earlier.

My dad knew very little about his parents' life in the "old country," as they called it. In his home, no one talked about their life before America, something I learned was very common among poor immigrants from that time. I can only assume they didn't want to remember it. My grandfather also didn't allow English to be spoken in the home.

I couldn't get those years my grandparents spent apart out of my mind. Why did my grandmother stay in Hungary for such a long time before coming over? My research revealed several types of immigrants. Husbands and sons came to America to earn money, which they sent home to their families. Some returned during the Christmas holiday for a month, then returned to America to continue working. Many returned home for good. Others saved up money to send for their wives and children to come to America. There was no one I could ask why my grandmother didn't join my grandfather in America, since those who might have known had passed on. I knew they had other children in Hungary, but none survived. They started a new family here.

The five years remained a mystery until one day, the idea for this book came to me. Through this fictional tale, I answered my questions while developing a robust family of characters to fill the void. My grandfather died in 1942, before I was born. I remember meeting my grandmother once, in St. Louis. I was five and have few memories of that meeting. She died when I was eight.

Beneath A Radiant Moon is a work of fiction. Mira and Janos are characters I created from many sources, both real and imagined. Basic information from my research helped with the world-building process, such as the birth, marriage, and immigration dates of my grandparents, and the places where they were born, lived, and immigrated to in America. St. Louis, Missouri, is where my father and his siblings were born and raised. The same for Janos and Mira. It helped me to connect with the characters, making them real, as if they were my own grandparents.

Through intensive research online, maps, Google Earth, and documents and books written about Slovaks during the early 1900s, Hungary came alive for me. I read documented interviews with immigrant Slovaks who shared their stories of journeying to America from Europe, pre- and post-WWI, which are available on the Statue of Liberty–Ellis Island Foundation, Inc. website.

And through the genealogy DNA test, I connected with relatives I never knew from my grandmother's brother, who came over the same year as my grandfather. They added some information from their side of the family to throw into the pot.

For the novel, I studied the Slovak traditions and the language, not to speak or read Slovak, but to understand how they spoke to each other. I included select Slovak words, greetings, foods, and holidays to give the story the flavor of the Slovak culture and traditions. As a disclaimer, please forgive any errors I may have made regarding the traditions. I chose those from long ago, not what is done currently.

Brief History of Slovaks in Hungary

The Magyarization of Slovaks was an official policy of forced assimilation in Hungary. The government made Magyar (Hungarian) the official language and outlawed all other languages in 1866. It closed schools and adopted other measures to abolish ethnic cultures in Hungary.

Slovaks were the largest minority population in Hungary. Whatever their motives to immigrate, between 1880 and the mid-1920s probably 450,000 to 500,000 Slovaks moved permanently to the United States.

My genealogy research is ongoing. I am still searching for relatives of my paternal grandfather. If you have the surname Jonas on your family tree, are of Slovak heritage, and have had or have family in the surrounding area of Janosik, Serbia, (which was part of Hungary pre-WWI) we might be related. Please contact me through my website, https://www.pljonas books.com/

Trademark Acknowledgments

Cunard Line
Coca-Cola
Singer
McCall's Women's Fashion Magazine
Jednota Newspaper
Ford

9 781953 100702